LOVELY NOTHINGS

THE SOMEDAY SERIES
BOOK 1

DAISY DELANEY

DAISY DELANEY

AUTHOR'S NOTE

This book contains sensitive content that may be upsetting to some readers. This book was written from personal experiences and is in no way representative of individual experiences. **Skip ahead if you don't want to know anything before diving in.**

This book contains sensitive content, including but not limited to: suicide, emotional abuse, verbal abuse, domestic violence, alcohol and drug use, parental death, murder, eating disorders, pregnancy loss, cancer, stalking, cheating, pregnancy, multiple partners, explicit sexual situations (consensual and nonconsensual), age gap, choking, depression, mental illness, infertility, and gun violence.

Your mental health matters, and if you proceed, I hope you enjoy this book.

Daisy

For my mother,
You deserved more.

For anyone who has ever been hurt by hands you trusted,
it was never your fault.

1

———

M y thighs burn as I run beneath the solemn orchestra of stars in the night sky. The suspended moon low in the sky casts an eerie shadow across the empty fields as I focus on the white line in front of me.

Howling winds carry the scent of fresh-cut grass and distant rain. My heart pounds like a frantic drummer keeping time with the rhythm of my feet colliding against the rough, weather-worn asphalt of the highway.

The town's only overpass looms ahead, and as I scale the grassy embankment, my strained muscles scream in protest. *I can't stop.* There's a surprise rush of adrenaline as I peer over the rail at the deserted road beneath, its emptiness mirroring the hollowness in my chest.

This is it.

Seymour is a small community, and residents will be commuting soon, so someone I know will find me, and I feel bad about that. They don't know I'm unwell and have been for some time, so my death will shock them.

A few will say they saw it coming, but they'll be liars because people haven't seen anything I didn't want them to.

Dragging my leg over the cement barrier, the rough texture scrapes the back of my thighs, and my heart races when I look down. *Don't look down.*

It's quiet up here, and the blood pumping in my ears is the only sound challenging the silence. With a deep breath, I rise on shaky legs on the narrow overhang.

One misstep means game over.

But isn't that what I want?

No big send off. No scandal.

A death as unremarkable as my life.

2

Last night was another failed promise to myself and another example of unfulfilled resolve.

As I looked over the town, my heart echoed the damning truth as a bitter reminder of the desperation that drove me there; I'm trapped in a life I don't want, but too much of a coward to jump into freedom or finality.

My husband's right.

I'm useless.

I can't even die right.

Thanks to the yapping Chihuahua next door, I'm awake too early to him barking at nothing. Not the wind. Not trash flying around the trailer park. Not even a stray cat. Absolutely nothing.

On the couch, I roll to my side and curse the four-pound terror. I tug the blanket over my head to hide from the sun, and a rumble echoes in the distance, reminding me there's a storm coming.

It'd be nice if that dog didn't bark all day since I work nights at the only bar in this shithole town.

"For the love of all things holy, please shut up." I pad down the short hallway of the trailer, closing the bedroom door and adjusting the padlock hanging on the brass hasp outside.

After a scalding shower, I put on cut-off denim shorts, a black tank top, and Converse sneakers. I make sure my shirt covers the marks on my back and spend another ten minutes covering a purple bruise around my eye.

How much of my life has been spent hiding what he does to me? Days? Weeks?

I pep talk myself on the way to the other end of the trailer to face the aftermath of last night.

It's probably not as bad as you think.

The kitchen's as dire as I imagined: a shattered plate on the floor, a flipped chair, and a pot of spaghetti dumped on the ground.

I flip the chair upright, toss the plate in the trash, and scrape the noodles into the pot. Thanks to the hideous rust-colored linoleum we've never gotten around to replacing, marinara sauce stains won't be noticeable.

I scrub the dried blood from the corner of the counter and toss the towel in the trash on top of my blood-stained T-shirt from last night.

Water fills the pot as I lean against the sink and eye the roses on the counter. Wesley must've dropped them off while I slept this morning before he left town. The flowers are full, brilliant pink, and gorgeous by most standards.

There's nothing about them to dislike, yet I loathe them. Every thorn exposes a broken promise, and each petal serves as an apology I don't want.

A hollowness overtakes my chest, and I can't breathe without a sharp, stabbing pain behind my ribcage. Rushing out the back door, I pull air into my lungs and pace the cluttered porch, staring at the blackened sky.

This would be so much easier if I could cry. But the grief festers inside me and feasts on my sorrow, growing day by day.

There's a black cloud of despair tethered to my neck, blocking any happiness trying to break through and strangling me with every breath I take. I'm rotting in a hole that's getting deeper the more I try to claw my way out.

Suffocating. Defeating. Consuming.

Once back inside, I pop two generic ibuprofen tablets to help with the general soreness running rampant through my body, grab my messenger bag from the back of the kitchen chair, and slide the roses into the trashcan at the end of the counter.

Stepping outside, I take in the dark clouds churning on the western horizon, and a deceptive breeze moves my hair as I walk across the patchy grass that's supposed to be a yard. The gentle wind is nice, but make no mistake, something nasty is coming behind it.

Trevor, the tiny toothless terror, barks as I check the mailbox and flip through the stack of mail, mostly late notices and debt collections. I tuck the mail under my arm and squat in front of the chain link fence that's for show because he could push through it if he wanted.

"Hush. You see me do this almost every day."

The tan dog tilts its apple-shaped head, considers my plea for peace, and resumes his incessant barking. No wonder he only weighs four pounds. Who knows how many calories he burns yapping his head off all day.

"Look, Triple T, we've got to come to an understanding. I need sleep, so I'm begging you to ease up on the barking." His little body vibrates, and the barking resumes.

Thunder rumbles through the sky as I walk to work, warning me to pick up the pace if I want to make it there dry.

THE FLICKERING NEON sign of Austin's Bar casts long shadows over the pothole-ridden parking lot. The red brick building, weather-beaten like the souls seeking solace within its walls, stands against fading daylight. The inside holds gouged wooden floors, neon signs, and pool tables with peeling felt in the corners.

Stale beer, cigarette smoke, and cheap perfume fill the building, and a jukebox sits in the back playing "Two Doors Down" by Dwight Yoakam while a white haze hangs over the room from decades of smoking.

It's depressing as fuck, and it's no wonder no one comes here.

The front door opens, flooding the dark room with the evening sun as Elliot Austin walks across the bar, puffing his cheeks and plucking at the blue button-up shirt that matches his eyes.

A couple years older than me, he's the reluctant co-owner of Austin's after stepping in to help his brother Jeff when their father passed away. He's a great example of life not going as planned. One day, he's in college at the University of Texas, and the next, he's running a business that sees fifty people come through the doors on a busy week.

"Why's it already this hot? It's only the beginning of June." He pushes his hand through the wavy brown hair just shy of touching his shoulders.

"Two words—Texas and summer." I tie my black apron around my waist.

Within minutes of powering on the television behind the bar, the local news replays the news conference about the missing woman from the town over. The husband stands with her family surrounding him and pleads for her safe return.

"Do you think the husband had something to do with it?" He slides onto an empty stool.

"It's always the husband." Stretching on my tiptoes, I turn the television off because this place is sad enough already.

As the night stretches on, Gin and Tonic Lottie tips me with double coupons from the grocery store, plows through drinks, and throws coupon stacks down like she's at a blackjack table with no regard for tomorrow. Raunchy Richard nurses the same beer for over an hour and tells jokes, reminding us how he got his nickname.

A few minutes before eleven, the sheriff, Brad Harrington, walks in with a relaxed, almost lazy gait. He offers a quick nod to Elliot as he crosses the room.

Low lighting highlights the beginning of the crow's feet creasing at the corners of his green eyes. Ten years older than me at thirty-five, he's mentally living his third or fourth life already. He keeps his chestnut hair cut close, emphasizing the faint peppering of grey on his temples.

I don't understand how he's single. He's a handsome guy with a decent career in a struggling town where handsome guys and decent jobs are rare.

"I'm not causing any trouble," Lottie slurs as Brad crosses the room. "Am I, Katie?"

"No, ma'am, you're not." I wipe a table down.

"Don't you think you're too old to be at the bar every night?" Brad sits on a stool, leaving several between them. "I have to stop what I'm doing to drive you home at least three nights a week. You know that's taxpayers' dollars, right?"

"I'm a taxpayer." She flicks her cigarette in the amber ashtray. "Just getting my money's worth."

I'm not sure if she notices his subtle eye roll, but I do. "Finish your drink, and I'm taking you home."

"Will that be the protecting or serving, sheriff?" Every puff accentuates creases on her upper lip brought on by decades of the habit.

"Both." He stands and gives me the same annoyed expression I've seen him use when dealing with unruly teenagers.

He leans his hip against the pool table and sets a random ball in motion with his hand. He lowers his head, raising his eyes to meet mine in a way no one else notices. "Want a ride tonight?"

"Don't you have anything better to do than chauffeur women home all night?" I sling the white bar towel over my shoulder and rest my hands on my hips.

He has one of the best smiles I've ever seen and uses it against me every chance he can. "No, not really."

I pick a piece of lint from his shoulder. "I should be done by one."

He pushes off the table. "I'll be waiting out back."

The heavy wooden door flies open as Brad waits by the door for Lottie, and chaos wrapped in denim and lace stands on the other side.

"Howdy, sheriff," Allison Chambers says as she struts past him, wearing skin-tight jeans and a red halter top showing off chiseled abs and brand-new boobs.

"There's my Katie!" She throws her arms around my neck and rocks me side-to-side. "I missed you so freaking much!"

"How were the parents?" I wave to Brad as he escorts Lottie outside.

She tousles her natural blonde waves and pulls me by the hand to the backroom. "Boring as always."

"I can't. Brad's giving me a lift after work."

"He's not your husband, father, or boss. What does it matter?" She pushes through the saloon doors.

"He's the sheriff."

"You should make him your daddy." She winks.

"Does Wesley just not exist anymore?" I shake my head. "And don't ever use that word when you're referring to Brad."

"The hot sheriff is more fun to talk about than the asshole you're married to."

I don't defend Wesley because he is an asshole.

The night air is a welcomed reprieve as I follow her outside. "You're going to get me in trouble." I lean my shoulder into the brick wall.

"But it'll be so much fun." She winks as she pulls a joint out of her bra.

We pass the joint between us several times. "What are you wearing to the party?" She rests her head against the wall and stares at the sky.

"Most likely clothes."

She rolls her head to the side and shoots daggers at me with her bright blue eyes. "Don't be a smartass."

"Don't get your hopes up because I won't be able to come if Wesley's home."

Groaning, she redirects her attention to the stars. "Screw him."

Allison hates Wesley without knowing the reasons she should. Her disdain for him is borderline irrational considering she's never met him.

If I were going to tell anyone the truth, it'd be her.

But her boyfriend is my boss, and I can't because she'd blow up on Wesley. Then he'd come down on Elliot until he had no choice but to fire me. Bartending at Austin's isn't what dreams are made of, but it's my only connection to a world beyond Wesley.

"I don't understand why you're still with someone who treats you like shit." She shakes her head. "I'd drop his ass so fast."

"Speaking of dropping stuff, how about we drop this subject?"

"Fine." She pushes off the wall. "Roofy him if you have to,

but I need you at the party because I don't fit in here any more than you do."

"Gee, thanks."

"You know what I mean. Us outsiders have to stick together, or they'll eat us alive."

Footsteps from the side of the building startle us, and Jeff Austin emerges from the shadows.

In his mid-fifties, he and Elliot are often mistaken for father and son instead of brothers because he was a senior in high school when his parents adopted Elliot.

A bit rough around the edges, Jeff's a man's man. He likes his whiskey neat, his music sad, and his money foldable, walking away any time Elliot tries to explain cryptocurrency to him.

He's been married to the same woman for over thirty years, never had children, and owns the only bar and motel in Seymour. Socializing isn't his thing, so he stays behind the scenes and lets Elliot deal with the people part of the businesses.

"What did I tell you about smoking that crap out here?" Jeff stops in front of Allison with his hands on his hips. "I don't know how you find the worst-smelling shit, but you have a knack for it, don't you?"

"Sorry."

She's not sorry.

If there's life after death, I'll miss Allison the most.

What will it be like not to exist? Is there a consciousness that survives physical death? Would that be what people consider a soul? Or will I simply cease to be?

When my mom died, that's what it felt like.

One minute she was there, and the next, she wasn't.

She'd be disappointed if she knew what I was planning.

AFTER A DAY OF TRIPLE-DIGIT TEMPERATURES, the parking lot sends waves of heat upwards, and the air tastes like dust as I drudge across it.

Brad stands by his Tahoe, a playful challenge in his eyes as he pushes away in a display of mock impatience.

"Starting to wonder if you were standing me up." He opens the passenger door.

"Why would I do that?" I climb into the passenger seat and drag the seatbelt across my chest.

I turn the vent, and the rush of cold air makes me nauseous as I lean forward until my face is inches from the crisp air drying my eyes out. It's better than sweating my ass off. Not that I couldn't stand to sweat some of it off because Wesley says I've let myself go and the twenty pounds I've gained this year say maybe he's right.

"You okay?" He asks.

"Do I not look okay?"

"You always look great, but you seem like you've had a lot on your mind the past few weeks." He checks traffic before pulling onto the highway.

"Nothing more than usual." I turn my head the slightest bit because I'm not ready to give up the air conditioner. "I'm fine."

I lean back and use the headrest to hold my hair up as we pull into the trailer park. Wesley prefers it long and in its natural wavy state despite me begging him to let me cut it.

"Get inside before your husband comes looking for you. Hold on." He crooks his finger to lure me closer. "There's something on your..." He pinches the back of my arm. "Smile. I promise it doesn't hurt."

"You're such an ass sometimes." I swat at his hand and walk to the driver's side. "He left this morning." I fold my arms over the cool metal of his window. "But ass or not, thanks for the ride."

He flicks his eyes toward my trailer. "When's he coming home?"

"Not sure. Maybe this weekend."

"I've got a lot going on this week, but let me know when he leaves out again."

"I always do, don't I?" I smile.

"Do you think we should skip a few weeks? People are starting to talk."

"People have been talking for a while." I slap the side of the door, step back, and wave as the window rolls up.

I'm rummaging through my messenger bag when he whistles and waves me back over.

"I almost forgot." He pulls a small plastic bag from the center console and passes it to me. "Picked up something for you in Dallas last weekend."

"You spoil me." I pull out a can of pepper spray shaped like a unicorn. "No one will attack me because they'll be too busy laughing. It doesn't even look like a weapon." Examining it closer, the spray shoots out of the unicorn's mouth. *Wow*.

"That's the point. Promise you'll keep it on you? Can't be too careful, especially since you walk alone at odd hours."

"Still no news about that woman from Vera?"

"It's like she vanished into thin air," he says.

I hold the unicorn up. "It'll live in my bag."

He points to it. "You can put someone's eye out because the horn doubles as a weapon if you position it between your fingers."

"Of course it does." I hug him through the window.

He inhales and leans back. "Your hair smells like marijuana."

"It's medicinal."

"That's what they all say."

"I'm sorry." I poke my bottom lip out, hoping he'll forgive me. He has high expectations of me for whatever reason, and I don't like letting him down.

"Don't apologize to me. Apologize to the brain cells you're killing."

I wave him off and enter the trailer, where the stale stench of copper hangs inside. I turn the window unit on to circulate the air, plop down on the couch, and stare at the ceiling.

Brad will be called when someone finds me, and I regret that has to happen. However, he's professional enough to compartmentalize, and he'll be fine.

As the temperature drops, I take off my shoes and curl up with a blanket and pillow. I close my eyes and focus on the air conditioner's hum, and the low, steady rattle calms my mind.

Wesley's parents will be mortified when the details of my death get out, especially his mother, Mary.

Wesley won't care, but Mary Reese won't be able to show her face publicly for weeks, possibly months, because of the shame and embarrassment. The humiliation my death will bring upon their family name will be too much for her.

That alone makes me smile and gives me something to live for...at least temporarily.

3

The bell over the door dings when Wesley pulls it open, laughter and clattering silverware greeting us, accompanied by the sound of sizzling grease from the grill.

The aroma of caramelized onions weaves through the air, a sweet disguise over the stale scent of unchanged fryer oil. The cool air is a sanctuary from the sweltering Texas heat.

Donna, the unfriendliest server I've ever met, leads us to a booth in the back where the late afternoon sun blasts the window, making the old blue vinyl painful to sit on when wearing shorts, which I am. She drops two laminated menus on the table and leaves.

I study the sticky menu, flipping it front to back like there'll be something I've never seen before.

"What are you getting?" I ask Wesley, and it's easy to remember why I fell so hard for him.

Blonde hair, blue eyes, and broad shoulders.

I didn't just fall in love with him; I became consumed by him and would've done anything he asked because there were no boundaries. I wanted what he wanted and needed what he needed. I gave up who I was to be part of his world because I'd just buried mine.

Sometimes, I pretend he's still the guy I fell in love with because I miss him. There are occasional glimpses of the old Wesley, but I have to work hard to recall what he was like before we became who we are now.

When things are good with him, they're so fucking good. But when things are bad, I'm reminded I'll have to die to be free from him.

'Til death do us part.

"Probably the chicken fried steak. You?" He doesn't raise his attention from his phone.

"Just a coffee."

"You should eat something," he says.

I slide the menu to the side of the table. "Okay."

Donna returns, and I go along when he orders two of everything because it's easier than protesting.

My thighs stick to the vinyl when I shift as I push the pile of mashed potatoes around on my plate. My stomach growls, but I knew from the moment I opened my eyes this morning I wouldn't eat unless he made me.

"What time do you have to be at work tomorrow?" He shovels greasy meat in his mouth.

"Six."

"Be careful walking home at night. Have you heard about the woman from Vera?"

"It's been all over the news." I move the macaroni and cheese around, switching it up so it isn't obvious I'm not eating.

"Did you hear they found her body?" He asks.

"No, I didn't."

"We should get Elliot to drive you to work until they catch whoever did it."

"I'm careful." I sip my water. "Brad gave me a can of pepper spray and he gives me rides when he can."

"I don't know what I'd do if something happened to you. You don't understand how much I love you and the thought of you being hurt, or worse..." His voice trembles and makes me sick to my stomach.

"Are you coming home next weekend?" I ask, hoping it's enough to stop him from regurgitating that bullshit.

He glances up as his ex-girlfriend, Mia, passes our booth, but his eyes return to me.

My gaze lingers on her longer than his because I still compare myself to her. She's tall and thin with board-straight jet-black hair cut into a sharp bob above her shoulders. Wesley has a type, and she's it.

I am not.

"Not sure." He waves Donna over for a refill. "Might pick up an extra load if they let me have the hours." He reaches across the table and holds my hand. "We're getting there. If we keep plugging away, we'll be able to buy a house in the next few years." Donna rolls her eyes before walking away.

I smile because it's what I'm supposed to do.

He rubs my finger where a wedding band should be and leans over the table. "Did you think I forgot what today is?" He lowers his voice. "How could I? That day was just as bad for me."

"I don't want to talk about it." I try to pull my hand back, but he tightens his grip. His touch makes me want to crawl out of my skin to get away.

"We don't have to talk about it." He pulls a small jewelry box from his jeans. "I knew today would be hard, so I got something to give you a good memory." He opens the red velvet box and pushes it toward me with pride. "Maybe these can replace the bad one."

Inside, there's a pair of beautiful emerald earrings in a rose gold setting nestled in a velvet cushion.

"They're real." He beams.

I lift the box and examine them. They look real—not that I'm a gemstone expert or anything. "I can't keep these, Wesley. They're gorgeous, but we can't afford them."

"Don't worry about that."

"You didn't borrow money from your parents again, did you?"

He stares at me with the same glacial blue eyes I spent hours gazing into during our whirlwind romance in Jackson three years ago. He says fate assigned that route through Tennessee so he could meet me, and there was a time I agreed.

"If you must know, Elliot owed me some cash and offered these instead. They were his mom's, and Jeff will be pissed if he finds out, so you can't wear them to work."

"Wesl-"

"Can you just say thank you?"

"Thank you." I close the box and slip it inside my messenger bag.

He picks his phone up from the table and swipes the screen. "I want us to be happy again." He types. "Like we used to be. Remember that?"

I zone out, staring at the pie case.

Cheesecake was the first and only craving I experienced, so I gave in that night. In fact, I ate two slices: one with cherries and one topped with strawberries. The tangy cream cheese was still on my tongue when blood flooded my mouth, and I haven't been able to eat it since.

He catches me looking at the desserts and snaps his fingers to get Donna's attention.

"Let me get two slices of cheesecake," he says.

"I can't ea-"

"Strawberry or cherry?" Donna asks.

"One of each." He winks at me and smiles from the corner of his mouth.

My eyes swell with tears I can't let fall because we're in

public, so I stare out the window and focus on the trees swaying in the distance.

The sun takes its time sinking below the sparse tree line, leaving the sky stained with streaks of orange and pink as a reminder it was there.

Donna drops the cheesecake off, and Wesley slides the piece with cherries in front of me with a big grin. "Cherry is your favorite, right?"

Nodding, I stare at the plate. Today's a fitting day to be reminded of the taste of grief, to chew my sorrow and swallow the misery.

I eat the cheesecake and choke back tears with every bite. It's working. Cramps radiate throughout my stomach, as they did that night and the following three days.

After I finish the dessert, I excuse myself to use the bathroom. It's outdated like the rest of the diner, but it reeks of bleach, so I assume it's clean. Kneeling over the toilet on the cold tile, I shove my finger down my throat for the first time since I was a teenager.

I tried to tell him I didn't want the fucking cheesecake.

4

The wind whistles through the steel girders of the overpass as I dangle my legs over the edge, the rough concrete scraping the back of my thighs.

Seymour sprawls beneath me, a patchwork of lights flickering in and out of existence as a thunderstorm broods on the horizon.

The moon doesn't dare show its face tonight, and the stars cower behind storm clouds like they saw what Wesley did when he came home drunk earlier.

A light breeze tousles my hair, the movement painful when it tugs my bleeding scalp as it whispers secrets in my ear. Lightning streaks across the blackened sky, illuminating the town.

Storms are common this time of year, or so I've been told. This is only my third and last summer here.

When I was a kid, my dad told me if I was lucky, I'd find someone to love me when I grew up. I wasn't pretty, at least not like the other girls in the neighborhood.

Mom scolded him for nagging me about how much food I piled on my plate. She used to say he was "going to give the kid a complex" if he kept drawing attention to those things. He laughed her warning off and did his best to make me like the other girls.

There was a list of acceptable foods, which he measured on the scale before dinner every night, counting each calorie mom ate as well. I thought she went along with it to be supportive; the whole misery loves company thing.

In reality, it had more to do with the younger woman dad went on so many business trips with.

Mom said no matter how pretty I was, there'd be someone prettier. No matter how thin I was, someone would be thinner. If I was a good wife, another woman could be a great wife.

For her, love was a battlefield, and she endured every day in the trenches, fighting to keep her man because every woman was her enemy.

I wanted to make him proud, so I never deviated from his plan.

I never snuck to the kitchen when everyone slept for more food because his meager portions left me entertaining chewing my arm off to make the hunger pains cease.

My desire to make him happy worked because I dropped thirty pounds that summer, and when I started high school, boys noticed me for the first time. Dad was adamant the weight had been hiding my beauty, but I think the newfound attention had more to do with my breasts doubling during the summer of starvation.

That's what life was like before he left us.

When I think of my childhood, it's divided into two categories: before the divorce and after the divorce.

After the split, my mother became lost in her depression. She gave him everything, and what did she get? The privilege of dying in her sleep on a second-hand recliner in a roach-infested one-bedroom apartment after the cancer took her will to live.

But until the end, she refused to admit my dad had been the real cancer in her life.

He was right about one thing, though.

I felt lucky when Wesley walked into the diner and chose me. He could've picked anyone to be his wife, but he chose me, and it never occurred to me that I didn't have to choose him. I had no idea that was the beginning of a new separation in my life.

Before Wesley and after Wesley.

The only thing that scares me more than jumping off this overpass is ending up like my mother, dying alone in my piss and wondering what I did wrong.

The train comes through town at three every morning. Three has always been my lucky number, so I'll jump at three on my third year here.

I dangle my legs over the edge and lean forward. No one will notice the other injuries because the impact will be traumatic, and Wesley will get away with what he's done forever.

The train horn blares in the distance and my heart races.

It's almost time.

Headlights appear around the east bend, and I freeze. Should I just jump? This is the only thing I've had control over in a long time, and I want to do it on my terms.

I lower myself down and swing one leg back over for stability as the vehicle approaches.

I'll do it when they pass because I don't want to rush it.

The truck rolls to a stop on the shoulder, and metal grinds as the door swings open. The driver remains a featureless outline thanks to the blinding headlights behind him.

"Are you alright?" A male voice calls out over the rattle of the engine.

"Everything's okay," I say.

With that simple declaration, he gets back in and slams the creaky door.

I expect him to carry on to his destination, but the engine falls silent, and the headlights go dark. The squeaky door wails as he steps out again, slamming it once more. The truck's old, so he should be kinder to it if he expects it to get any older.

He approaches with caution, but why wouldn't he? I'm sitting on the side of an overpass at three in the morning with blood all over my shirt and a bleeding head wound for the second time in a week.

As he gets closer, I can make out more of his appearance; his shoulder-length, wavy, sable hair matches his beard, but his black cowboy hat makes it hard to see his eyes. He's wearing jeans, and a dark T-shirt hangs off his slender, tall frame.

"I'm fine. You didn't have to stop."

"I believe you." His voice has the subtle Texas twang all the locals have. My lack of it has always been the giveaway I'm not one of them. "I've been on the road for a while. Mind if I join you for a minute?"

"It's a free country."

He pulls a cigarette from above his ear and places it between his lips, dipping his head to light it. A breeze catches the smoke, sending it my way.

"Is that weed?" I ask.

He takes a quick draw from it and holds the smoke in his lungs, thrusting the joint toward me and urging me to take it with a nod.

I take a long drag and cough as my lungs ignite. I can't relinquish the joint back to him fast enough. "Wow, that's stout."

He leans his back against the concrete and faces south while I observe the sleeping town of Seymour to the north.

"So, why are you sitting on an overpass at three in the morning?" His eyes flick to the blood on my shirt, but he doesn't ask about it.

"Waiting on a strange man to stop and offer me drugs."

"What a small world." He puffs from the joint again. "I was

driving and hoping I'd find a beautiful woman on an overpass waiting for a strange man to offer her drugs. Suppose it's meant to be, huh?" The corner of his mouth turns up like he's fighting a smile and losing.

"Do you smoke pot with strangers often?"

He shrugs. "Depends."

"On what?"

"If I have any." He turns around and presses his stomach against the concrete, peering over the edge to the road below. "That's a long way down."

"Yeah."

"You could fall if you're not careful."

"I might."

"You're not scared?" He places the joint between his lips and hoists himself onto the barrier beside me.

"What are you doing?" I shriek.

He dangles his legs over the side and wraps his fingers around the edge of the concrete. "Turns out when you stop running from death, it forgets about you."

"Please get down."

The train roars through town, its horn echoing from the tracks behind the trailer park.

"Look, I don't know you, and you don't know me, so get in your truck and keep driving and I'll..." My throat tightens. "I'll finish what I was doing."

"What were you doing?"

"Don't make me say it."

"Well, if that's what you were about to do, maybe you can help me with something on my bucket list. What do you have to lose if you aren't planning to see the next sunrise?" He slides off the concrete barrier and stands with both feet planted on the highway in front of me. "What do you say?"

"How can I agree if I don't know what I'm agreeing to?"

He steps closer and stops short of touching me, but I can

see his features now. He's handsome, but his brown eyes look tired.

"Well, I've always had this fantasy of kissing a stranger. You'll never know my name if you do what you're planning when I leave, and if I skip the papers for a week, I'll never know yours."

I hold my breath as he lifts the black cowboy hat off his head. *Fuck me, he's really handsome.* Would kissing him be the worst last thing I do on earth?

He's careful as he places the hat on my head like he's nervous he'll startle me if he moves too fast.

"What do you say?" He uses his index finger to tip the hat back and doesn't allow me to hide behind it like he did.

He reeks of whiskey, and an electric jolt scans up and down my spine as he leans in, wrapping his arms around my waist. I close my eyes because why the hell not? But the asshole doesn't kiss me. Instead, he yanks me off the barrier, and we fall to the ground, asphalt digging into my shoulder blades because he's on top of me.

"What are you doing?" I pound my fist against his chest and try to get out from under him.

"Saving your life." He sits back on his heels, and I can't move because he's pinning me down. "No matter what you're going through, this won't fix it." His chest rises and falls like he's wrestling an alligator.

And I'm the alligator.

"Let me go!" I slam my closed fists against the tops of his thighs. "Now!"

He leans forward and holds my wrists together with one hand, forcing them above my head with an ease that pisses me off. I squirm and balloon my chest out, but it's pointless. He has total control over me, like every other man in my life.

"Two options will get you off this ground. Hospital or police department. You pick."

The missing woman floods my thoughts. Why did I let this guy get close enough to grab me? What if he's the one who grabbed her? For all I know, he could be. I watch true crime shows so I should know better. That joint could've been laced with something. I would've totally fallen for the free puppy in the white van when I was a kid if the opportunity had presented itself.

"I'm not going anywhere with you."

"Well, I'm not leaving you here so you can hurl yourself over that barrier."

"What if you're planning to do worse to me?"

"I'm trying to save your life, not fucking take it."

"How do I know?" Locking my eyes with his, I search for any glimmer of panic that I've figured him out.

The next thing I know, I'm on my feet, and he's pulling me to his truck by my arm. I scream and tear at his exposed forearm because I've watched so many forensic shows I know I need to get his DNA under my nails.

"Would you stop fucking scratching me?" He yanks the door open.

"Stop trying to kidnap me, and I'll stop scratching you." I put my foot on the edge of the floorboard and refuse to go inside.

"Jesus fucking Christ!" He pushes a cell phone into my hands. "By all means, call the police so they can come pick you up." He still hasn't let go of my arm. "You can be their problem instead of mine."

"Unlock it." I hold the phone out.

He taps the screen several times. "There."

We're wedged between the seat and door, and I bet he can hear my heart slamming against my ribcage.

"So, you're not a rapist or murderer?" I keep my fingers on the screen to prevent it from locking again.

"Why do you care? You're afraid I may not value your life, but you don't even value it, so what would it matter?"

"I'm no expert, but I don't think you should say stuff like that to someone like me."

"Why? Are you going to jump off a bridge because I hurt your feelings?"

"Wow, asshole much?" I roll my eyes.

This situation is dangerous, and he could have ill intent planned, but I believe him. At least if he does away with me, I won't have one final sin tallied against me when I get to wherever I'm going, if such a place exists.

"Do you live around here?" He asks.

I nod.

He sucks his lower lip between his teeth and clamps down so hard the skin turns white. "I'll drive you home."

"No." I blurt out. "Just take me into town, and I'll walk the rest of the way."

"You expect me to believe you? How do I know you won't come right back here?"

"It's a long way back, and I'm tired," I say.

His nostrils flare as he stares at me. "Fine. Get in."

Clutching the phone in my lap during the ride, I'm ready to call for help at the slightest whiff of trouble.

But there's no whiff of anything. No danger. No small talk. No anything. Only an uncomfortable silence between two strangers as I direct him to pull into the diner's parking lot because it's near the trailer park, and I don't want this guy to know where I live.

After stepping out of the truck, I feel safe enough to give up the security of the phone, laying it on the seat before I close the door.

"Take care of yourself because I won't be here to save you next time."

Gripping the door, I lean inside. "What's your name?"

A mischievous smile cuts across his mouth. "Let the fantasy stay a fantasy, darlin'."

I wait until the early morning darkness consumes his taillights and walk to the bar because I'm not allowed back at the trailer until Wesley leaves for the week.

This isn't the first time he's kicked me out in the middle of the night. He does it to remind me he can, but I know better than to stray too far away.

What we have isn't love.

It's familiar and forced.

I don't know how to leave him, and he doesn't know how to let me go. So, we stay in this perpetual cycle of unhappiness and anger, hurting each other even when we don't want to because it's all we have left.

I'M JOLTED from sleep by an invisible terror, my pulse pounding in my ears and sweat beading across my forehead.

The room is pitch black, but the darkness is familiar. Adrenaline courses through my veins, preparing me for a fight that doesn't exist. With shaky breath, I sit up on the pool table, but the room lurches sideways, compelling me to lie back down.

My whole body is sore, and even breathing hurts.

The second time I open my eyes, a figure stands next to me, and I squint to make out that it's Elliot. He's near my feet, typing on his phone, and doesn't realize I'm awake. I push up on my elbows and tug my shirt down where it traveled up on my stomach from tossing and turning. Thank God I keep an extra shirt in my locker and had the forethought to change into it at some point before I passed out.

"Hey," he says when he sees me struggling to sit up. "I was about to wake you up." He assists me off the table.

"How long have you been here? What time is it?" Rubbing my forehead, I downplay how much pain I'm in as we walk to the bar because I don't want him asking more questions than he already will after finding me sleeping here.

He hands me a bottle of water. "I got a notification early this morning, and when I checked the cameras, you were lying on the pool table. You seemed fine, so I just assumed you drank too much."

I don't remember drinking after I got here, but I also don't remember getting here. Everything from last night is a little hazy.

Well, not everything.

"We have cameras?" I chug the water.

Elliot thinks I got drunk and passed out on the pool table, so I'll let him keep thinking that.

"I put them in to keep an eye on things so I can have a life instead of being here all the time."

"That explains why I've felt so much safer at work." I finish the bottle of water. "But if you'll excuse me, I need to get rid of some of this alcohol if I'm ever going to sober up."

There are two bathroom doors, and wouldn't you know it, I pick the right one. I fumble with the button on my jeans, my fingers refusing to cooperate. Lucky for me, I left my zipper down at some point last night. I do my business, wash my hands, and find Elliot in the front room on his phone.

"Feel better?" He shoves his phone in his back pocket.

"I wish. I'm sorry." I sway sideways. "Guess I'm more of a lightweight than I realized." Clamping my eyes shut, I ground myself from the spinning room.

"Easy there." He scoops in next to me and slides his arm around my waist, pulling me to his side. "How much did you drink last night?"

"Apparently too much." My legs wobble when I take a step, and I clutch his arm tighter. "I'm so sorry. I'll make it up to you."

"You don't have to apologize, but I'm wiping the footage because we don't need Jeff crawling our asses about it. I can already hear him bitching about being irresponsible. However, I'm pissed at you for walking so late by yourself. Haven't you heard another woman has disappeared?"

"I don't watch the news because it's depressing," I say.

"Yeah, well, you should be more careful because it can happen to anyone." He guides me toward the front door. "Now, let's get you home so you can puke on your floor instead of mine."

"Have you heard from Wesley this morning?" I'm not sure I can go home.

"I called him when I saw you on the camera, and he said you'd gotten mad and stormed off. Told me to let you sleep it off and bring you home in the morning."

"Yeah." My head feels like it's splitting in two. I've never drunk so much that I felt like this the next day, so it probably has more to do with what happened in the trailer before I ended up on the overpass.

Was the stranger real, or did my mind create him as an excuse to justify failing to carry out my plan once again?

"He had to take off but said to tell you he'll be back in two weeks," he says.

When Wesley comes home, we'll do our dance, and he'll dote on me until he leaves town again, reminding me how much he loves me and hates himself for what he does.

He'll say he doesn't enjoy hurting me, but he loves me so much it drives him crazy sometimes. He never blames me, but it's my fault when he loses control.

He just can't help himself when it comes to me.

5

"That'll be six bucks even," the gas station attendant says as she chews on the metal ring going through her bottom lip.

I toss the cash on the counter and scoop up the bottle of water and Advil. My Converse stick to the tacky floor as I push through the glass door, which is taped with duct tape and cardboard. Per the paper sign, I'm careful not to push on the broken glass.

Brad's cruiser is parked on the side of the building, and he waves me over. I don't wait for an invitation to get in. Nope, I hop in like I'm sleeping with the guy or something, at least according to local gossip.

"I'd ask if you want a ride, but you've helped yourself." He smirks as he puts the car in reverse. "Rough day?" He eyes the Advil as I rip the foil pack open.

"Every day is a rough one." I place the tablets on my tongue and chase them down with a big gulp of water. I can't shake the lingering headache I've had since waking up at the bar two days ago.

The car stops at the edge of the parking lot, and he looks both ways. "Your place or mine this time?"

"You're on duty."

"Since when's that a problem?" Scruff covers his chiseled jaw as he looks at me with those green eyes.

"You know I prefer your place," I say.

Brad's house is small but tidy and not a typical bachelor pad. There's décor and decent furniture, and it smells nice.

"You ready?" He stands from the couch and crosses the room to the bookshelf. "We've got about an hour before I've got to do rounds again."

"No, but you aren't letting me get out of doing it." I lay my head back on the couch and stare at the ceiling. "I don't even know why I'm doing this."

"Getting your GED is the first brick in building a better future for yourself." He plops down on the other end of the couch and pulls a rubber band off a stack of index cards. "That's why you're doing this."

"I just...maybe I've been out of school too long, you know? Like, what if this crap doesn't click?"

"I've invested too much time over the last few months for it not to click. Not to mention risking my reputation because people assume we're having an affair." He shuffles the index cards. "So, you're going to take the exam in Wichita Falls, and you're going to pass. Understand?" He holds the cards up in front of him.

"Yes, sir."

Is it so bad if I go along to make him happy because of the pain I'll cause him soon?

After an hour of being quizzed, I'm grateful he's on duty. Don't get me wrong. I'm thankful for his help, but he has more confidence in me than I do. One night at the bar, I let it slip that I regretted quitting high school halfway through my senior year, and he ran with the information. For all the griping I do, I'm lucky to have him in my life.

I ride around town with him, watching people watch us together. If we're secretive, the gossip will spread faster than Marcy Allen's legs. We don't hide our time together because there's no reason to.

We drive from one end of town to the other three times before Brad declares the town safe, grabs coffee from the diner, and parks at the abandoned cotton gin to watch cars slam on their brakes when they see his patrol car.

We talk about the weather, Lottie's habit of grabbing his ass when she's drunk, and his time in the military, although he skims over the details.

When I ask about the murdered woman, Abigail White, he skirts around the case. He does the same thing when I ask about the latest woman to go missing. His phone rings right before I call him out.

"Slow down." He starts the engine. "I'll be right there." He looks at me. "Buckle your seatbelt." The tires spin and throw dust up behind us.

"What's going on?" Gripping my coffee cup, I reach for his in the cupholder before it tumbles into the seat.

"Jesse Allen's fighting in the motel parking lot." Gritting his teeth, he floors the gas pedal. "I swear to God, if he's in uniform, I'm kicking his ass myself."

IN THE MOTEL PARKING LOT, a fury of fists clash in the glare of headlights as Brad slams on the brakes, leaping from the patrol car and pouncing on the two men. He tears them apart, throwing one onto the gravel and flipping him to his stomach, wrenching his arms back, and snapping on a pair of handcuffs.

"Stay back!" He says to Jesse Allen as he hauls the other guy to his feet.

Once upright, I recognize him.

The stranger from the overpass.

"He fucked my wife last night!" Jesse Allen says over Brad's shoulder.

"Shut up, Jesse!" Brad says and turns to the stranger. "What's going on?"

"He thinks I fucked his wife last night, but I only let her suck my dick." The guy winks at Jesse Allen and spits blood on the ground.

Jesse Allen lunges at him, landing a solid punch on his jaw, then another.

Brad grapples Jesse Allen, shoving him against the patrol car with a loud thud and pressing his forearm under his chin.

"Get in your fucking car," Brad says through gritted teeth. "Now."

Jesse Allen knows he fucked up, so without another word, he glares at the stranger and retreats to his patrol car.

Brad leads the stranger to the patrol car, takes his driver's license, loads him into the backseat, and marches back to Jesse Allen.

I can't hear what Brad's saying, but my best guess is that Jesse Allen is getting his balls busted for fighting on duty.

I twist around, and the stranger slouches in the backseat, his head against the headrest and his hands cuffed behind his back. I feel bad for him...almost.

"Small world, huh?" I say.

He lifts his head and looks past me through the windshield at Brad and Jesse Allen. Brad rants, and Jesse Allen hangs his head.

"Now it makes sense why you didn't want me to take you to the hospital or police station."

"What do you mean?"

"The sheriff," he says. "Did he beat the shit out of you and make you think jumping off an overpass was a good idea?"

"Absolutely not." I shake my head. "Brad's the..."

"Reason someone else felt they had the right to use you for a punching bag?"

My breathing picks up, and my ribcage feels like it's shrink-wrapping my lungs as Brad approaches the car. "Please don't mention the other night." I don't look back at the bleeding stranger.

"You look pretty good compared to the other night. Does he hit you so it doesn't leave marks, or what? That must make him a pro." He smirks.

"Or what," I say.

Brad yanks the door open, and I don't know if the stranger will keep my secret or not.

Inside the patrol car, he eyes the stranger through the rearview mirror. "Going to take you in for disorderly, and Deputy Allen will be dealt with as well."

"That's not fair. You know Jesse Allen started it because he always does. He's fought half the town because of his wife since God made him cute instead of smart," I say.

"Deputy Allen said you threw the first punch." He eyes the stranger in the mirror again.

I twist in the seat to look at him. "Did you?"

"Yeah."

Well, shit.

"What about him being in uniform?" I ask and turn back to the stranger. "Would you have stopped to talk to him if he wasn't a cop?"

"Nope," he says.

"See, he used his authority to entrap him. Of course, he threw the first punch. He felt threatened, cornered like an animal." I twist to the stranger again. "Right?"

"Exactly." A crooked smile emerges.

34

Brad shakes his head as he gets out of the car. He releases the stranger and returns his driver's license. "Don't let me catch you out again tonight, Mr. Brooks. Go to wherever you're going and stay there until you've sobered up, and if you know what's good for you, you'll stay away from Marcy Allen." His cell phone rings, and he turns to me. "Let me get this, and I'll take you home."

When he steps away, the stranger dusts his black cowboy hat off and squats in front of the passenger window. "You know my name now, so you should tell me yours."

"I only know your last name, Mr. Brooks."

"First name's Beau."

"Katie Reese."

"Well, Katie Reese, thanks for getting me out of that jam," he says.

"No problem. Now, we're even."

He stands, drops his hat on his head, and the corner of his mouth turns up. "Oh, no, darlin', we're far from even."

6

I'm high, floating even though my feet touch the floor. I see them but can't feel the wood planks beneath them. Is this what ghosts feel like when they're ghosting around? I don't like depending on something to escape my problems, but here I am, indulging in this temporary peace at every opportunity lately.

"What do you think of Beau and Jake?" Elliot empties his arms of bottles onto the bar. "They seem cool enough. Jeff has taken a liking to them because they drop a lot of money for two drifters."

"Beau's going to keep Brad busy, and I haven't met Jake yet." Thunder shakes the building, causing hanging glasses to clink and rattle. "Do you know why they're in town?"

"Not a clue." He sighs. "But I'm sure they're running from something or someone to be hiding out in a place like this."

A sharp thunderclap reverberates through the building, and the lights flicker for a few seconds, followed by torrential rainfall.

"Shit." Sprinting to the front door, he jerks it open as a bolt of lightning creates the illusion of daylight outside. Heavy wind blows debris inside, and he struggles to slam the door. "This storm was supposed to go around us." He stalks across the bar, holding his phone and mumbling something. "I don't have any service."

I don't have service, either.

But I also don't have a cell phone.

"I left the kitchen window open because I didn't think it would do anything tonight. I'm sure it's flooded already." The scowl on his face must mean he still doesn't have service when he rechecks it.

"Go." I usher him toward the door. "I'll finish up here."

"Are you sure?"

"Get out of here before it gets worse."

"What about you? How are you getting home? You can't walk in this."

"I'll call Brad. Now, go."

"I owe you one."

He runs outside, and the wind catches the door behind him, throwing it back open. Rain comes in sideways, and I'm soaked in seconds as I push the door closed, but the storm pushes back. When did this door get so damn heavy? I lean into the massive wood slab, but the storm proves to be a formidable opponent. Another inch, and it'll latch.

One.

More.

Inch.

A gust blasts the door open, and I slip, landing on my ass and elbows. *Dammit.* Leaves and dry brush mix with the rain, pelting me in the face as I raise my arm to block it.

That's when I get the first twinge of pain in my elbow. *Please don't be hurt too bad.* Rising to my knees, I wince with the slightest pressure applied to my elbow.

One. More. Freaking. Inch.

Beau appears, steps over me, and pushes the door shut with his shoulder.

I go slack, still on my knees with my mouth agape. The floor's soaked. I'm soaked. Beau's soaked.

Beau's here.

His eyes dart around the bar as he takes in the scene. "Are you alright?"

Nodding and unable to utter a single word, I cover my mouth to suppress inappropriate amusement but burst into laughter. This isn't funny. However, I'm beside myself and can't catch my breath. The hiccups. *Great.*

He stares at me like I've lost my mind, and maybe I have, or the door hit me harder than I realize. It could be the weed. What if drugs *are* bad?

Kicking a pile of wet leaves to the side, he grabs my hand and pulls me up from the floor.

"We're closed for the night." I stifle the laughing as much as I can.

"I came to talk to Elliot."

I fight to keep the smile away from my lips. "You just missed him." I can't stop laughing and grab my side to soothe the shooting pain.

"Something funny?" He drops his black cowboy hat on the closest table.

"Nope. Nothing at all. Everything's dandy." I sweep wet hair off my face and blow out a heavy breath. I'm done. I'm good.

I am good.

"Dandy?"

"You have a problem with that word, or what?" I double over, holding my stomach and cupping my mouth.

"Are you okay?"

I wondered how long it'd take him to notice my inability to stop laughing when nothing's funny.

I stand up straight and pull deep breaths in until my lungs steady. "I'm sorry. After the last couple of weeks, it's just..." I fan my chest. "I smoked a joint with Allison earlier and," I laugh, unable to finish.

"You're high?"

The question sends me back into a fit of laughter that causes my eyes to water.

"As a kite." I wipe the corners of my eyes with the heel of my palm. "Hungry, too."

"One of the pitfalls, darlin'." He reaches behind his head and pulls his wet T-shirt off, draping it over the back of a chair near his hat. He pushes his hair away from his face, dragging his hand down his beard to wick water from it. "After about twelve hours, it's not even fun anymore."

"I don't want to be high for that long." I pout.

I don't know if it's the weed or my hormones, but Beau Brooks is way hotter without a shirt. Dark hair covers his chest and stomach, so naturally, my eyes follow it down where it disappears inside his jeans like a flashing sign that says 'look here'.

"Should've thought about that before you did drugs, darlin'." He reaches around me, his bare chest pressing against my dripping T-shirt and his beard tickling my face as he plucks a bottle of whiskey from the shelf behind me.

The heat from his skin reacts with the chill of the damp cotton covering my nipples, and an ache builds in them. "Drugs are bad, or haven't you heard?" His mouth is inches from mine, and I recognize the smokey vanilla scent on his breath from the whiskey we serve. "You're wet."

I hold my breath, or is he stealing it?

He's only there for a few seconds, but it's long enough to imagine what sex with him would be like.

"You have no idea." I pick at the dripping tank top clinging to my stomach and wonder if he can tell I just fucked him in my head. "I've never been this wet with clothes on."

"Well, isn't that a fucking shame?" The corner of his mouth

turns up, a devilish smile creeping in. "That you've never been this wet."

"With clothes on."

My nipples pebble under the drenched tank top, my bra failing to conceal them, and I'm not laughing anymore. I cross my arms over my chest to hide the little traitors, but not before he gets his fill of the treasonous bastards as I flash my own 'look here' sign.

He grabs my arm and inspects my elbow. "Is there a first aid kit around here?"

I recoil from his touch because it's more intense than the scrape. "I'm fine."

"You're bleeding all over yourself." He points to the blood on my shirt. "Where's the first aid kit?"

"The bathroom in the back."

He places the bottle of whiskey on the bar, grabs my hand, and pulls me toward the back. "C'mon."

"I can handle it," I say.

He doesn't acknowledge he's heard me as he hauls me through the saloon doors and inside the tiny bathroom, taking the first-aid kit off the wall and putting the toilet lid down.

"Sit."

"I can do it myself."

"I don't doubt you can."

I sit and stare at the cracking plaster wall while he digs around in the plastic box. There's barely enough room for one person in here, so two makes breathing seem impossible.

He moves in front of me, and my eyes are level with the dark hair trailing into his jeans.

This can't get any more uncomfortable, can it?

He drops to one knee on the stained concrete floor, and I'll be damned if it doesn't become insufferable because now I'm looking into his eyes.

Rivers of honey flow around the dark pupils, mixing with dark brown to create caramel seas. *Wow...being high really does make everything so beautiful.*

"This may sting." The antiseptic wipe burns when he dabs the scrape, and the wound pulsates, sending heat feathering into the flesh around it. "It's not as bad as it looked." He presses a band-aid on my elbow.

"Thanks." Holding my arm to my chest, I experience a newfound sense of embarrassment.

He cups my cheek, and I don't know why, but I lean into his warm palm and close my eyes, inhaling a deep, calming breath filled with his masculine scent. I'm not sure how much time passes. It could be seconds. Could be minutes. Could be a lifetime.

Swiping his thumb under my left eye, his brow furrows.

"Your makeup is running, so someone might see your secret if you're not careful."

"I should finish up." I flee the tiny room, eager to get away because I've never felt more exposed. Those brown eyes saw all of me, including the ugly and sad parts I hide from everyone.

Beau sits shirtless at the end of the bar, drinking whiskey and chain smoking while I flip the chairs up and kill the lights. After I retrieve my messenger bag from my locker in the backroom, he takes that as his cue to leave because he stands, plops his hat on his head, and swipes his wet shirt off the table.

"Need a ride?" He asks.

"I'll walk when the rain lets up."

He strolls across the bar toward the door and calls back over his shoulder, "It's not safe to walk in this."

"Yeah, well, I'm not sure accepting rides from strangers is any safer." I follow him to lock up.

"Were we ever really strangers?" He steps toward me, stopping only inches from me.

"We've never met before, so isn't that what a stranger is?"

He splays his hand over the center of my chest, and I could step back, tell him not to touch me, but I won't.

His brown eyes draw me in, and I can't look away as his tongue darts out over his bottom lip. There's a tiny cut from the fight with Jesse Allen; otherwise, his lips are perfect.

Please don't kiss me.

"We may have never met before, but we were never strangers." He lifts his hand, leaving me longing for the heat again. "Lock up, and let's get out of here." He walks out.

I place my palm on my chest to recreate the warmth, but a chill runs through me instead.

This is bad.

BEAU DIRECTS the truck onto the highway, inching along because the visibility is almost nil. It's a black '95 Silverado, and I only know because my dad had one just like it, except it was blue. This one's in pristine condition, and my dad's wasn't—at least not after the third time he wrecked it after too much to drink.

Beau leans over the steering wheel and squints to see the highway through the downpour as we stop at the four-way intersection in the center of town.

The air conditioner vent flips the green tree-shaped air freshener hanging from the mirror from front to back, and rain pings against the metal cab.

"Where am I taking you?"

Raindrops collect on the passenger window as I stare out. "Take a right at the next stop sign."

"The trailer park?"

"We prefer mobile home estate." A bolt of lightning rips through the blackened sky. "Last one on the left." I point as the asphalt turns to gravel.

He stops the truck and looks around the expanse of mobile homes. "Home sweet home, but I wouldn't rush out yet." He points to the rain hammering down on the windshield as lightning blisters the sky and a thunderbolt claps above us.

"Thanks, but I can't get any wetter." I pluck my sodden shirt away from my stomach.

He reaches for a pack of cigarettes on the dashboard. "You shouldn't say that kind of stuff." He dips his head and lights a cigarette.

Heat flushes over my chest and neck, spreading across my cheeks. "I'm sorry. I wasn't thinking."

"Don't apologize." He cracks his window to allow the smoke out and looks at me. "Words like that from lips like yours are cruel to a man like me."

There's that smile again, and it's good that the seat is already wet.

"I'm sorr-" I stop. "I'm married, so my lips shouldn't matter to you at all."

"Do they matter to the sheriff?"

"He's not my husband."

"That's not what I asked."

I need to get away from this man. I drag the strap of my messenger bag over my head. "Thanks for the ride."

The rain's coming down in a solid sheet, but I throw the door open and run, fumbling with my bag to recover my keys from the heap of disorganized crap inside and fail to notice how close I am to the front door.

I trip on the cinder block and catch myself with my hands, splitting my shin open on the corner of the concrete. *Fan-fuck-ing-tastic.*

Beau appears, soaked by the incessant rain before I've processed the mortifying incident.

"You're just one big fucking calamity, aren't you?" He slips his arms under mine and pulls me to my feet, guiding my arm around his neck and supporting me so I can limp up the remaining blocks.

I'm tempted to look back at my remaining dignity in the mud.

"Go screw yourself if you're going to make fun of me." Hobbling along, I'm irritated and embarrassed because I don't need another man in my life who finds my suffering humorous.

He wipes my muddy keys on his jeans and holds them out, trying not to laugh but doing a piss poor job. "Here."

"I hate you right now." I unlock the door.

"You don't know me well enough to hate me yet." He helps me inside to a kitchen chair.

"Yet?"

"Give it time." He lays his dripping hat on the counter and drops to one knee in front of me.

Rain puddles at our feet, but it doesn't matter because, once again, I'm soaked, he's soaked, and the floor's soaked. Leaning in to examine my shin, his wet shirt molds to his body and draws attention to the flexing muscles in his back and shoulders.

"You may need stitches. Do you have something to flush it out with so I can get a better look?"

"I'll take care of it." My leg gives out when I put pressure on it to stand, so I slink back down on the chair.

"Let me help in case you need to go in for stitches."

"I don't need stitches."

"You might," he says as he stands up.

"I don't."

"You don't know that yet." He boops the tip of my nose and smiles. "So, stop being stubborn."

"Did you just boop me?"

"And I'll do it again." He holds his index finger up like he's going to do it again. "Now, where do you keep your first-aid stuff, Calamity?"

"In the bathroom." I point down the hallway. "Top cabinet behind the door."

He returns with peroxide, snatches the roll of paper towels from the counter, and kneels at my feet. "Looks deep, so this will sting pretty fucking bad." He holds a few paper towels under the laceration and pours peroxide on it.

I grip the edge of the chair and clench my teeth because he didn't exaggerate the level of pretty fucking bad.

"I don't think you need stitches, but you should keep pressure on it while I grab some bandages."

I keep pressure on the weeping wound until he returns.

"Is this going to be our thing?" He drops to his knees in front of me again. "Me saving you all the time?" He flashes a smile as he peels several bandages from their wrappers, taking his time arranging them over the cut. "Not my finest work, but it'll do. Let's give it a few minutes before we wrap it in case you soak them. If that happens, you're going for stitches." He pushes up from the floor and surveys the kitchen. "Got any Advil?"

"Generic." I point to the bottle on the counter by the sink.

"Same shit." After filling a glass from the dish rack with water, he shakes two tablets from the bottle into my palm. "I'd get ahead of the pain if I were you because it'll be sore tomorrow."

It's not the first time I've heard that.

I swallow the pills and pass the glass back to him. "Thank you."

He kneels on the floor again and removes my muddy shoes and socks, positioning my bare foot on his thigh and wrapping his hands around my calf.

The scratches on his arms have all healed except for a few deeper ones. I would've definitely gotten quality DNA under my nails.

"Are you sleeping with the sheriff?" He stares up at me with those honey-laced brown eyes.

"Brad?" I balk.

"It's obvious he has a crush on you, so if you aren't sleeping with him, it's not because he doesn't want you to be." The corner of his mouth curves up into a sly smile.

"He's harmless."

How have I not noticed him making tiny circles behind my knee? How long has he been doing it? He straightens my leg, and my foot travels up his thigh, stopping dangerously close to a place it shouldn't be.

I hold my breath as he covers my shin with the wrap, securing it with a small metal grip. He sits back when he's done but doesn't appear to mind my foot in his crotch. "What about me? Do you think I'm harmless?"

"You're anything but harmless."

"Anything but harmless, huh?"

I'm not having trouble breathing anymore.

In fact, my heart's racing, and my lungs can't steal enough air from the room.

"The word devastating comes to mind when I think about you."

"Well, I'm halfway there if you're already thinking about me." Sliding his hands up my legs, he stops above my knees. "You don't want to know what comes to mind when I think about you."

My skin's on fire, burning and seared under his hands. I should push them away, but I'd rather my flesh blister than not feel the heat.

He inches forward, my feet dropping from his lap to the floor as he advances between my legs and darts his tongue out over his bottom lip. "Would you like me to devastate you?"

I can't take my eyes off his mouth. The way he's sucking his lip between his teeth. The way the corner of his mouth turns up like he has a secret no one knows.

But I recover what little sense I have remaining. "No."

"I think you want to be devastated in every way possible, but you're afraid to admit it," he says.

"You're wrong." I ignore the pulsating pain in my shin and push up in the chair.

"Am I?" He taps his fingers against my skin like he's testing to see if I'll tell him to stop. "Because I don't think I am."

"Is this your thing? Sleeping with married women?"

"Haven't slept with one in my twenty-nine years...that I know of." His fingers slide closer to the bottom of my shorts. "But if you want to pop my cherry for me..."

"What about Marcy Allen?"

"Refresh my memory, darlin'."

"The deputy's wife."

"Oh, yeah, I've never even met her, but the quickest way to get a man to kick your ass is to say you fucked his wife." He winks.

"Why would you want that?"

"Because pain feels better than nothing."

"You should go." I grip the counter to pull myself up and shun the shooting pain as I limp to the door. "I appreciate your help, but I'm not someone you want to get close to."

"Why's that?"

"Because I was born to die," I say.

"We're all born to die, darlin'. It's the living in between that makes it worth it, don't you think?"

"No."

He meets me at the door and leans in, his lips dusting the shell of my ear.

"Be careful, Calamity. I may not be around to save you next time." He straightens his stance and puts his hat on before booping me on the nose again. "Let me know when you're ready to be devastated."

He winks, and then he's gone, the lingering scent of vanilla and oak the only sign he was ever here.

7

Sweat rolls down my abdomen and saturates the waistband of my shorts as I walk along the side of the highway. My lungs press back against the thick humidity, and my chest heaves up and down as I sidestep a massive fire ant mound while cars whoosh by way too close. My shin hurts with every step, the gash threatening to pop open if I put pressure on my leg.

The western horizon has turned black, and charcoal clouds billow overhead, streaking away from the mother cloud like God took a dry paintbrush to feather the edges. The sky up ahead is clear and blue, and there's no sign of anything bad coming.

As I move through the routine of my colorless day, I can't help but wonder what it'd be like living in colors brighter than this stark reality.

I made the right decision last night.

My life has been reduced to this monotonous existence, but at least, for now, it's mine alone to bear.

I turn onto a dirt road to escape the heat-trapping asphalt and the dead skunk around the corner.

Halfway down the glorified alley, an engine hums behind me, getting louder as it gets near, and I edge closer to the ditch as Brad's patrol car creeps up next to me. He leans over the seat and rolls the passenger window down.

"Want a ride?"

"Depends." I continue along the embankment.

"On what?" The car keeps pace with me.

"If you're still worried about people talking." I kick a rock into the ditch.

The car stops. "Get in."

Cute banter isn't worth walking in this heat, so I climb in, and the cold air warrants any rumors that may emerge.

"Thanks. The humidity's a bitch today, and it's like walking with a wet towel over my face." I fall back against the seat.

"That time of year." He concentrates on the road ahead. "So, mind telling me what that was about the other night?"

"What?"

"You coming to the rescue of Mr. Brooks."

I rock my head from side to side. "Jesse Allen's a jerk, and you know he started it. How was Beau supposed to know Marcy's easier to hit than a tumbleweed around here?"

"Beau? You're on a first-name basis with him already?"

"And? Scared the rumor mill might replace you?" I wiggle my eyebrows.

His demeanor changes when we arrive at Austin's. No more witty comebacks or easy smiles. When I ask what's wrong, he brushes me off with excuses about having a lot on his mind because of the murdered and missing women. It's likely the truth, and I'm reading too much into it, as I do with everything.

Inside, Jeff's behind the bar while Elliot and Allison sit cozied up at a table. Beau stands near the pool table with a guy I've never met.

Great, another stranger.

Dark and broody, Beau smokes a cigarette and ignores me.

Maybe I bruised his pride when I didn't drop to my knees last night.

"You're late," Jeff says.

I shove my bag under the counter. "I'm right on time." I point to the clock. "Besides, you told me to come in late tonight to help close up because it's been so slow."

"Don't cut it so close next time. I'd like to pretend having you here is worth what I'm paying you." He drops the towel on the bar and stalks out the front door.

"Sheesh," I mutter as I drape the towel over my shoulder. "Is it too late to call in sick?"

"He's stressed out right now," Elliot says.

"Yeah, well, stressed or not, it's not a pass to be a dick," Allison says.

"It'll get better." Elliot glances over his shoulder to Beau. "Have you met Jake yet?"

It'll get better.

I've heard that before.

I wave, and the slightly taller guy waves back. "Can't say I have." The polite gesture is enough to bring the two men over to the bar.

"Jake Garrison." His hair is lighter than Beau's, and his beard more unruly. "You must be Katie."

"I am."

Beau's gaze meets mine, and he looks away, a trace expression unnoticed by everyone else. His cell goes off, and Jake rolls his eyes as Beau rustles it out of his pocket.

"Five bucks says I know who it is," Jake says.

"Don't," Beau silences the call. The screen lights up again, and he shoves it inside his jeans.

"I think you should change your number," Jake says.

"I don't remember asking what you think." Beau chugs the glass of whiskey and passes the empty glass to me with a nod for a refill but still doesn't make eye contact.

"I'm going back to the motel before you say something to piss me off." Jake puts his hat on. "See you later, love. It was nice to meet you." He walks halfway to the door and turns back around. "Tax his ass if he doesn't behave. Don't take any shit from him tonight."

"We should get going, too," Elliot says as he pushes off the stool.

Allison flicks her eyes toward Beau. "I can stay if you want company locking up."

"He's harmless," I say.

From the corner of my eye, Beau fights a smile as he slides on a stool at the end of the bar.

After they leave, the place is dead. I don't know how we're surviving at this point. I suppose the motel does well enough to float the bar, but how long can it sustain both?

"Rough day?" I ask.

He stares into the whiskey glass. "Something like that."

"I'm a decent listener. I wouldn't say great because my mind drifts, but adequate if you need to get something off your chest." I drag a towel across the bar. "And I can keep secrets."

"It's nothing worth talking about."

"Fair enough. You've got plenty of time to drink your troubles away before I lock up." I leave him alone to wash whatever's eating at him down with the harsh whiskey.

Jeff's office smells like cardboard and coffee. I gather random ink pens from the desk and drop them in the mesh holder. Yellow post-its outline the entire computer monitor, notes to himself about everything.

And I mean everything.

A haircut is due.

Pick up cat food for the stray his wife feeds.

He goes on and on about disliking the feline but stresses when it doesn't come around for a day or two.

A framed photo of his wife and their dog sits on the corner

of the desk, next to a picture of Jeff with his parents and Elliot as a toddler on his wedding day.

Flipping the light off, I close the door and walk out to an empty bar.

Beau's gone.

I check the restrooms and call out for him, but there's no response. He must have left, and it's for the best because broody men are unpredictable.

And unpredictable makes me nervous.

BEAU'S TRUCK is the only vehicle in the parking lot, and I stop when I notice him having trouble unlocking the door. He drops the keys on the ground and almost falls over when he bends to pick them up, catching himself on the truck bed and recovering, but still unsteady.

"You shouldn't drive," I say as I cross the gravel lot toward him.

"I'm fine." He stumbles backward and grabs the mirror to keep from falling, dropping his keys again and making it easy for me to take possession of them.

Snatching them up isn't difficult because his reaction time is almost nil. I'm not known for my quick reflexes, but at least I'm faster than a drunk guy.

"I can't let you drive. Do you want me to call Jake?"

"I'll take my chances." He reaches for his keys, but I step back. "It's forgotten about me, remember?"

"Death hasn't forgotten about you. Maybe you've exhausted it, and it's on vacation." I fumble with the keys to find the ignition key, realizing I don't know what I'm looking for. "Which one starts this beast?"

He sways. "You're the one driving. Figure it out."

"Fine." Yanking the heavy door open, I slide into the driver's seat, buckle my seat belt, and go through the keys one by one until I locate the one that fits. When the engine clanks and rattles to life, Beau dives around the hood and jumps in the passenger seat. I stare at him, clearing my throat.

"What?" He asks.

"Seat belt."

"Yes, ma'am." He buckles up, and his phone wails, cutting through the dead air in the cab. He doesn't answer or silence the call.

"Are you going to get that?" I ask, annoyed with the blaring sound.

"Nope."

As I start driving, he rests his head against the seat and closes his eyes.

"So, what do you do for a living?" I ask.

"My family owns a ranch, but I'm taking some time off." He tilts his cowboy hat down over his face and I take that as the cue he doesn't want to talk.

When I pull into the motel parking lot, the truck seems relieved when I kill the engine, clanking and rattling to sleep the way it woke up. I can't believe it moves at all. Long after the engine's quiet, a vibration remains in my bones from the short drive.

Beau throws his door open but doesn't get out, so I meet him at the passenger door.

"Can you walk without eating gravel?"

"I haven't had that much to drink." He lowers one foot on the ground, and I catch him before he faceplants on the sidewalk. "Okay, maybe I have."

"What number are you?"

"I'm a ten, darlin'." He winks.

"Your room number?"

He points to room three, and I slide my shoulder under his arm, leading him to his room. "Where's your room key?"

"In my pocket."

"Well?" I point to the keypad.

"Well, what?"

"Good, lord." I roll my eyes. "Unlock the door already. You're not light to hold up, and you've had so much whiskey I'm scared I'll catch a buzz standing this close to you."

"You're bossy." He digs around in his pocket and swipes the keycard.

We fall into the room, and I kick the door closed. After guiding him to the bed, I lay my bag on the small table in front of the window.

"Thanks for making sure I got home safe," he says with minimal slurring. "You're the best thing about this place so far." He pumps his fist in the air, but not above his head. "It's a shame you're leaving soon."

"You're so drunk." I laugh.

"I am, in fact, so drunk." With a sharp nod, he falls back on the bed. His legs hang over the edge, and his T-shirt rides up his stomach, displaying the dark hair leading into his jeans. He covers his face with his hat, and I doubt he'll be awake by the time I'm done.

I snag the wastebasket from the bathroom and place it on the floor next to him, along with a few towels in case he gets sick. I put a washcloth and bottle of water on the nightstand—the same protocol I followed for my mom after Dad left her. I put his keys on the table, along with the keycard he dropped on the way in.

He sits up and places his hat on the lampshade, dimming the light in the room. "Devastating. That's what you said I was, but you're wrong."

"I didn't mean it in a bad way, but you're not as harmless as you think."

"You know how I know you're wrong?"

"How?" I ask.

He tilts his head and crooks his finger, prompting me to move closer. "Because a woman like you could easily be the end of a man like me."

Against my better judgment, and because I don't care anymore, I step between his legs, my knees hitting the side of the bed as I look down at him.

"And what kind of man are you?"

I shouldn't be this close to him.

He squeezes my hips, teetering on the edge of sobriety as he stares up at me through hooded brown eyes. "The kind who can't help himself sometimes."

He shouldn't touch me like this.

My heart races when he slips his hands under the hem of my tank top. "You don't understand how dangerous this is."

"There's nothing dangerous about talking." Pushing my shirt up, he exposes my stomach. "If I say I want to taste your lips, those are only words. I might say I want to know what you taste like when you come, but again, just words." His lips hover over my skin, but don't touch me. "I could say I want to hear you say my name when you have an orgasm so powerful you can't remember your own." He kisses my stomach. "But those are only words, and once they pass over our lips," He kisses my stomach again, his lips lingering, "they're gone forever, and one could argue they were never spoken."

My mouth is dry like water hasn't touched it in years.

Something tells me Beau doesn't mind putting his life on the line if it means he gets to have fun. Live fast, die hard. Isn't that what they say? And who is they? No one knows because they're dead from doing stupid shit.

"You're drunk and not thinking clearly," I say.

"This doesn't have anything to do how much I've had

to drink." He runs his palms up my ribcage and stops at the bottom of my bra.

"No?"

"I want you when I'm sober, too."

"You shouldn't."

"I shouldn't, but I do." He kisses my stomach. "I should stay away from you, and I shouldn't make you question your morals because I've thrown mine away."

"Then why do this?"

"Because all the 'shoulds' disappear when I see you, and considering how we met, neither of us has anything left to lose. So, why not do something that feels good?"

Why does this hurt? It should feel good, but it doesn't. It feels tragic. Lovely nothings from lips I'm not supposed to hear them from. Warmth from hands that shouldn't touch my skin. Lust fueling a fire that isn't supposed to burn. It's everything I need after I decided I don't want it anymore.

Prying his hands from my hips, I step back. "This isn't right."

He matches every step I take backward with an advance. "It may not be right, but it doesn't feel wrong, does it?"

I pull the door open and back out of the room. "Goodnight, Beau."

8

"Twenty bucks says I win this one." Jake drags his boots across the floor as he rounds the pool table, leans over, lines his shot up, and misses.

"I'll take your money." Chalking my pool stick, I lean over the table. *Clack*. The eight ball sinks into the right corner pocket, and I hold my hand out.

Jake mumbles as he slaps a twenty-dollar bill into my palm. I've known the guy a week and have already lost count of how many vices he has, gambling being the latest.

I replace the stick on the wall and lean against the pool table while he prepares for another game. "Does having money in your pocket upset you?"

"Yeah, yeah, yeah. You wouldn't be so good if you indulged in the devil's lettuce before the game like I did. I'm at a severe disadvantage."

"Not doing that again anytime soon." I push away from the table and walk to the bar, leaving him to play against himself because he doesn't have any more money to lose, but he'll try winning that twenty bucks back as long as I say yes. "I gained five pounds the last time I smoked because I woke up at six in the morning like a wild raccoon in my kitchen, eating a little of everything and most of a few things."

"You may have gained five, but you were already a nine." He winks.

"Why not a ten?"

"Scores are tied to performance, and I'm in no position to judge that since you're a married woman. Unless you want to put me in that position, in which case, I prefer the bottom," he says.

"Ah, see, it'd never work between us because I prefer the bottom, too. But how open are you to pegging?" I wiggle my eyebrows.

He smiles from the corner of his mouth. "Girl, what do you know about all that?"

"Not as much as you, judging by the smile on your face."

"You two are killing me." Elliot pinches the bridge of his nose to squelch the tears in his eyes. I'm shocked he's maintained his composure until this point.

Around midnight, he and Jake move the fun to Elliot's house, but I stay behind to pump quarters into the jukebox and mop.

Water sloshes on the floor as I dance, pushing the mop under the tables and singing. A glass of Jim Beam is what's for dinner as I dunk the mop in the bucket and drag it over the floor, my pissy mood evaporating with the water.

Until I look up and spot Beau watching me in front of the saloon doors.

My hand flies to my chest, and he's the last person I expected to see because he's avoided me since I rejected him in his room last week.

"How did you get in here?"

"Back door was unlocked. Came to see if Jake was here."

"You missed them by twenty minutes. They were going to Elliot's." Propping the mop in the yellow bucket, I push it toward the back room, toward him. That fucking grin spreads across his lips as he sidesteps to allow me through the saloon doors. "Do you know where he lives?"

"I'm sure I can figure it out."

I step into the bathroom to wash my hands, and he leans his shoulder against the door frame while folding his arms over his chest. "Would you know if you were being devastated?"

"Yes, I'd notice if someone wrecked my existence." I run my hands under the water.

"Is that so?"

"Yeah." Turning the faucet off, I tug several paper towels from the dispenser.

He steps behind me and stares at me through the mirror. "What does devastation feel like?"

There's no 'I didn't know I was holding my breath' moment because I'm aware I can't breathe. I should bolt out of this room and away from him, but I don't.

"I don't know."

"Would it be soft?" He asks, our eyes focusing on each other through the reflection as he gathers my hair over my shoulder and kisses the side of my neck. "Like this?"

My knees buckle when his lips touch me, and he grabs my hips to steady me.

When was the last time someone kissed my neck? Wesley doesn't kiss me at all anymore. He doesn't do anything but take from me.

He looks up through heavy lashes, pulling my ass against his hard cock as he kisses my earlobe and whispers, "Or would it come in forceful like a wrecking ball?"

Nothing.

That's what I have.

Absolutely nothing.

I open my mouth to protest but swallow the words back down because I don't want him to stop.

He unbuttons my shorts, standing me upright and pressing his chest to my back.

"Do you want to watch yourself get devastated?" Muttering against my neck, his breath hot and his beard tickle my skin. He guides my left arm up behind his neck and pushes his right hand inside my panties, his heart thumping against my shoulders as he skims his fingers over my clit.

I close my eyes, and he stops. "You can't enjoy the show with your eyes closed."

As soon as I open my eyes, he starts making tiny circles over my clit, and I whimper under his touch because this is the most erotic thing that's ever happened to me.

I grab his wrist and push his hand lower until he dips two fingers inside me, the warmth and wetness between my legs inviting him in despite my head telling me to stop.

I watch it all, my eyes fixated on his movements because I can't look away.

Curling forward, I clutch the edge of the sink, and he leans over me, his chest pressed against my back, and never misses a beat. He increases the pressure on my clit, and I grind my ass over his cock until he spins me around and kisses me, leaving behind the sweet aftertaste of whiskey as he pulls away.

His devilish grin morphs into a playful smirk as he drags his index finger over his bottom lip and then swipes it over mine. Salty and sweet blend together as our lips combine, and he pushes his hand back inside my panties.

"You can tell me to stop anytime you want," he says as his fingers penetrate me, driving me closer to the release I'm desperate for. "Devastation always feels better when it's begged for." His mouth covers mine. "Beg for it."

"No." I pant.

Tightness pools in my belly, and I grind down on his hand because I've never needed a release as bad as I need this one.

With a final surge, I come hard, my body convulsing as I hold onto his shoulders to keep from melting to the floor at his feet. The small room is hot, and the air's thick as I try to steady my breathing, an impossible feat with his fingers still buried deep inside me.

"Stubborn one, aren't you?" He removes his hand from my panties.

"Sometimes." I press my forehead to his chest while I recover because I don't know what to do now.

My throat tightens, and I can't swallow past the lump in it. I've been unable to cry for a year, and this does it? Not losing my dignity? Not the total breakdown of my marriage? Not coming to terms with the fact that I'm planning to take my life? This? Getting finger-banged in a bathroom by a guy I hardly know?

When I break it down, why wouldn't I cry?

"Okay, when I asked if you wanted to be devastated, this isn't what I had in mind." Beau drags his palms up and down my arms.

I open my eyes, only to stare at the floor because I don't want to look at him.

"I was devastated long before I met you." I sniffle. Devastated is too kind to describe how I've felt for so long. "This isn't who I am. I don't do stuff like this."

"What if I told you this isn't me, either?"

"I'd call bullshit."

"It's true. The married ones cry when it's over, so I usually avoid them."

"You're an ass," I say through my tears. *Don't make me laugh right now.*

He buttons my shorts and wraps his arms around me so

tight I can't move. So, I stop pretending I want to and lay my cheek against his chest, giving in.

And something else happens.

My body relaxes, and I don't fall to the floor because he holds me up.

And fuck me if it doesn't feel nice not to carry the burden of myself for a few minutes.

"You think I'm a nut job, huh?" I mutter against his T-shirt.

"No more than before," he says.

"Ass."

"Nut job."

I pull away and swipe my thumb under my eyes, pretending my makeup isn't running down my cheeks. "I'm sorry. I-"

"Don't."

"Don't what?"

"Apologize for anything."

My gaze falls back to the floor. "I didn't realize how fucked I am until now."

He tips my head back and forces our eyes to meet. "We're all fucked up, and anyone who says they aren't is lying, darlin'."

"This shouldn't have happened," I say.

"You're right."

"So," I shove my hands in my back pockets and rock back on my heels. "We shouldn't let it happen again."

"New boundaries and lines we shouldn't cross," he says.

"Agreed."

"But before we lock these new boundaries in place..." Cupping my face, his lips dust across mine. "I want you to remember this happened every time you see me until you leave for good." He glides his tongue across the seam of my lips, parting them with a softness that shoots straight to my core.

He doesn't grope me or anything else that would allude to this kiss going farther. He's content just kissing me, and I get lost in it—in him.

And no amount of guilt can make me stop.

"Anyone back here?" Elliot shouts from the front of the bar.

"Shit." I jerk away, smoothing my hair down like it'll somehow hide my swollen lips and flushed skin.

"I've got this handled, Calamity." He winks and exits the bathroom, leaving me to compose myself.

I stare at my reflection in the mirror and smile like a madwoman, even though I'll regret this tomorrow.

9

Allison applies red lipstick to my lips despite my reluctance to wear it. I can't stand how it feels, especially the matte kind she's smearing over my lips.

"You're spending too much time on something that'll come off as soon as I eat or drink tonight." I'm turned off by how they feel when I smack my lips together.

"Fat fucking chance. This won't come off for days unless you use an industrial-grade makeup remover." She plucks a tissue from the box on the counter and folds it in half before handing it to me. "Ask Elliot." She winks.

"Eww, gross. TMI." I blot my lips and drop the tissue in the trash bin. "It's sucking all the moisture from my lips."

"Hush." She drags her fingers through the beachy waves she put in my hair earlier. "It's one night and it won't kill you."

"What if continues to suck moisture from my body until I turn into nothing more than a mummified shell?"

"Seriously?"

"What? It could happen."

She performs a dramatic slow clap and bows. "And the award for most dramatic actress goes to Katie Reese." She rises to her full height and fusses with my hair even though she's already locked it in place with a gallon of hairspray. "Dial back the neurosis for the night and have some fun." Once she thinks I'm presentable, she leaves me in the bathroom while she changes into her dress.

I wouldn't have picked the white dress with blue flowers or the sheer yellow cardigan, but Allison's right.

The dress looks great on me.

Left to my own devices, I planned to wear my Converse sneakers because comfort is my priority, but she insisted I borrow her cherry red heels. The hair and makeup are tolerable, and the clothes are gorgeous. However, the shoes may be a point of friction since I'll be barefoot before the burgers are done because my shin is finally healed, and I don't want to bust it open by falling again.

Allison leads me through their crowded house to the kitchen, dragging me to the counter where they've arranged bottles of almost every alcoholic beverage the liquor store offers.

"Start with this." She pushes a red solo cup filled with beer in my hands.

Jeff operates the grill in the backyard, and a small fire blazes in the firepit. Thank God the ground is compact, or these heels would sink, and I'd be on my ass already.

Beau chats with Jeff and Jake, with his back to me, but when Jeff stops speaking mid-sentence and stares, Beau turns around.

I don't like how they look at me as I approach—especially Beau because he sets his attention on me and doesn't try to hide it.

I haven't been able to look him in the eye since I fell apart in front of him three days ago.

"It's a dress, not a second head," I announce to the group.

"You look lovely, Katie." Jeff flips a burger. "Gives me an idea for the bar."

"Please don't make me wear stuff like this."

"Relax. I don't need your mother-in-law up my ass again because she thinks I'm running an unsavory business."

"What did she do now?" I ask.

"Met these guys at the diner and crawled in my ass about entertaining people who could be bad for the town." He points the tongs at Beau and Jake. "Apparently, she just knows they're pieces of shit because of the way they look."

"I thought I looked like a million bucks." Jake feigns hurt.

"Son, at best, you're a cocaine-laced dollar bill from a stripper's thong on a Tuesday night."

A group of us settle in chairs around the fire pit, drinking and listening to Jake share highlights from his youth.

Beau sits beside me, glancing my way occasionally and nothing more while I roast marshmallows. Jeff leaves after everyone's fed, citing old age as his excuse, but I think we remind him of what's at stake if the bar folds.

Allison and Elliot slow dance a few feet away while Jake's all over a blonde I've never seen before, and Beau drinks next to me in a lawn chair.

"You look nice," Beau says.

I lick a smear of marshmallow from my thumb. "You do, too."

"Thanks." He plucks at his black T-shirt. "It has a pocket."

"Pockets are everything."

"Want to get out there?" He tips his beer bottle to the couples dancing in the grass. "All the cool kids are doing it."

Elliot and Allison dance and laugh in their own world while Jake and the blonde make out several feet beyond them.

"Would you jump off a cliff if everyone else jumped?" I arch my eyebrow.

"Depends on how much I've had to drink and what's at the bottom of the cliff." There's that crooked smile. "What do you say, Calamity?"

"I say this is dangerous territory."

"I know."

"Then why ask me to do it?"

"Because I'm not afraid to fall," he says.

"I am."

"I won't let you." He stands and holds his hand out. "And if you slip through my fingers, I'll catch you before you hit the bottom."

The warmth of his hand sends heat through my body as he leads me to a clearing in the yard near Allison and Elliot. Her subtle smile doesn't go unnoticed when he positions his hand on my waist and drapes my arm over his shoulder, holding my other hand close to his chest as we sway to the music.

"So, why are you here?" I ask.

"Seems like as good a place as any other."

"Brad thinks you're running from something or someone. Are you?"

He tucks our hands under his beard and slides his thumb over the back of it. "Not running away from anyone but myself, darlin'."

"We can't do this," I say.

"Why not?"

"You know why not." I'm deeply conscious of his palm splayed across my lower back. "We can't cross the line."

"We've already crossed it."

"Not completely."

"Tell yourself whatever makes you feel better, but the line was crossed on the overpass when you were willing to kiss me." He lays his cheek against my temple and whispers, "The line was crossed when my fingers were inside you."

"Beau." His name comes out behind a breathless sigh. "I'm not worth what you're risking. Why are you doing this?"

I'm treading through treacherous waters, swimming too

close to the deep end because he makes doing the wrong thing so easy that I'm not convinced it's wrong anymore.

He drags his fingertips up and down the back of my hand under his beard, the simple gesture intimate because it hides in plain sight from everyone else. "Do you want the truth?"

"Tastes better than a lie, no matter how bitter it goes down."

"I'm either selfish, or I don't give a shit about the consequences...or a little of both."

Jake staggers over, performing a slow cap with the blonde trailing behind him. Beau clears his throat and releases me, snatching his beer from the nearby table and chugging it in one long pull.

"That was fucking magical to witness. You two moved together like one flawless entity. Ten out of ten," Jake says.

"Thank you. It's been a while since I've danced." I tuck my hair behind my ear.

"I couldn't tell." He drapes his arm around my neck. "Save one for me." He taps my shoulder and points to the side yard where Elliot's waving me over.

Allison's on her knees, and Elliot's holding her hair as she pukes in the flowerbed along the fence.

"Can you grab some water?" Elliot asks.

"On it," I say, digging around in the nearby ice chest and passing a bottle to him.

"Thanks. She didn't eat before she started drinking." He twists the cap off.

"Is there anything I can do to help?"

"Nah, I'm going to get her in the shower, and she'll be good once I get her in the bed." He holds the bottle to her lips, and she pushes it away with the back of her hand.

"I want to sleep under the stars." She falls to her back on the grass. "They're so beautiful."

Elliot laughs. "We can sleep under the stars if you want, babe."

"Lay with me under the stars, Katie." Rolling to her side, she wraps her hand around my ankle. "Please."

Elliot stands, dusting grass from his jeans. "It'll give me a chance to say goodbye to everyone."

I lower myself to the cool grass, tucking my dress under my legs so I don't give anyone a show they didn't ask for. Allison copies me when I position my arm under my head for support.

"Your husband's a fucking idiot." She scowls, but it turns into a smile. "You're beautiful tonight."

"Because of you."

"No, because of you," she says.

"Because of me, what?"

"You're beautiful because of you." Leaning forward, she catches herself from falling face-first on the grass and crooks her finger to lure me closer. "You can fuck Beau if you want to, and I won't tell anyone."

"I have your permission?"

"You don't need my permission. I mean, you can if you want to because he wants to," she says.

"What makes you think that?"

Shrugging, she plucks blades of grass from the ground between us. "I just know these things, Katie. Reading the fuckometer is my gift, you know?"

"Fuckometer?" I laugh and join her, plucking several blades of grass.

"Yeah, and he's in the green when he looks at you."

"Do you think I should?"

"Should what?" She asks.

"Sleep with him?"

She grabs my shoulder and drags me forward. "You should fuck him and tell Wesley that Beau's got the biggest dick you've ever seen because that would serve his cheating ass right." She laughs and falls to her back. "Even if it's only this big." She pinches her index finger and thumb together while squinting.

"I'm going to be sick again." Rolling away from me, she dry heaves because there's nothing left in her stomach.

By the time Elliot returns to take my place, the party has died down and only a handful of people remain.

Beau disappeared at some point, and it's for the best. Regardless of how nonchalant Allison makes it, sleeping with him is a bad idea. If my marriage has taught me anything, it's fantasy trumps reality.

Beau's better off staying a stranger.

After saying a few goodbyes, I go back through the house to leave. Music plays inside, but only a couple of people remain in the house, all of whom I don't know. I stop by the bathroom to grab my belongings and change into my Converse for the walk home because these heels are cute but lethal. And for the first time in a long time, I don't avoid my reflection when I enter the bathroom.

I smooth my hair down while picking pieces of grass and dried leaves from it. My cheeks are warm, flushed red from the alcohol and conversation with Allison. I love her when she's sober, but drunk Allison is hands down more entertaining.

The bathroom door flies open, and Beau rushes in, locking it.

"What are you doing?" I back up until the back of my thighs hit the counter.

"Shhh." He holds his finger in front of that crooked smile.

"What if someone saw you?"

"No one saw me." He steps closer, and it happens in slow motion but at a pace I can't get in front of to prevent.

The smell of whiskey becomes stronger. The tickle of his beard against my chin. His lips force my own to part, and I don't stop him.

He cups the back of my neck, pulling me toward him as his whiskey-laden tongue plunges past my lips, sweeping through my mouth at a dizzying speed. He hoists me onto the counter, guiding my legs around his waist and pushing my dress up. The air in the room becomes thick and hot, leaving us struggling to get enough air because we both refuse to relinquish the other's mouth.

Is this really happening?

"Beg me not to do this." He moans into my mouth, the plea coming on the end of a desperate sigh as his fingers curl into my hips. "Beg me because we're falling."

"You won't let me fall too far."

"That's right, darlin'." He yanks me forward until my ass hangs off the counter as he ravishes my neck. "I'll catch you." He grinds his cock over my panties, bracing himself on the counter with one hand and reaching between us with the other to push my panties aside. I gasp when he pushes two fingers deep inside me. "But who'll catch me?"

"Does it matter? You're not afraid to fall." I hold on to his shoulders as he fingers me with deep and powerful thrusts, sending me reeling into oblivion. He pumps in and out, adding a third finger and stretching me open. The tightness. The fullness. I shouldn't be doing this, but I want more.

"Not if you're what's at the bottom." He smiles against my lips, pumping his fingers faster.

"Beau," I cry out, and he slams his mouth down on mine to absorb the noise. Our tongues battle against each other, neither giving up nor tiring.

"Say it again."

"Beau."

He withdraws his fingers, leaving me feeling empty as he tugs my panties down and kisses the inside of my thigh. "Again," he mutters against my skin.

"Beau." His name rolls over my lips like a lazy summer breeze.

His head bobs between my legs, hungry and eager, as he devours my pussy with an enthusiasm I've never witnessed before. I lean back against the mirror, gasping for air as my lungs burn and my legs shake over his shoulders while clutching his head and pulling his mouth deeper into me.

I can't breathe.

He teases my swollen clit with the tip of his tongue, and it's both pleasure and torture—a delicious blend driving me to the edge. I grind my pussy against his mouth because I need the pressure to alleviate the unbearable ache inside me as he slides two fingers deep, pushing me further into a state of insatiable desire.

He pulls his mouth away from my throbbing flesh, and his eyes lock with mine as he pumps his fingers with an unrelenting intensity.

"Say it again."

"Beau," I whisper.

He drags the flat of his tongue over my clit, increasing the pressure with each pass until my entire body trembles, and I grab his head to guide him, to show him what I want, what I need. Rolling my clit between his lips, he flicks and sucks it while thrusting his fingers in and out of me.

Hot, holy hell.

I clamp down on my lip to suppress my screams as my orgasm explodes inside me, and I see literal stars as contractions spread through every muscle in my body.

I don't know if the earth moved, but I wouldn't be shocked to find out it's been knocked off its axis when I leave this bathroom.

Beau stands, dragging his hand down the length of his beard, and positions himself between my legs. He cups my pussy, capturing my lips with his and delivering a breathy sigh against them as they remain a light feathering of soft flesh against soft flesh.

Every reason I should stop this overwhelms me, but the

words I should say get tangled on the tip of my tongue and swallowed back down.

I don't want to want this or him.

A shudder of uneasiness flows through me, and it's likely nothing. But when he reaches for his belt, my heart thuds inside my chest, my stomach snarls in on itself, and I can't calm the spasms in my core as I turn away from the kiss.

"What's wrong?" He asks.

"Not here."

He runs his hands through the hair on my temples, and I lean into him, my palms flat against his chest, and give in to the hormones hijacking my body. My pussy clenches, and my breasts swell as he devours my mouth, sucking my bottom lip between his teeth with a gentle nip and releasing it.

His heart pounds beneath my palms. "I don't-" The words collide with his lips. "Beau-"

"Make no mistake, you will be the death of a man like me." He lays his forehead against mine, his chest rising and falling erratically. "Give me five minutes to get this to go down, and I'll drive you home."

"I was going to say I don't think the new boundaries are working, but if you'd rather take me home, that's fine, too." I smile.

"Well, considering you just came in my mouth, I'd agree the boundaries aren't working." He kisses me. "And I'm only taking you home if that's where you want to go."

"So, how do we do this?" I ask.

"Do what?"

"Have an affair."

10

Lust and need tangle our limbs together in the dark motel room as Beau presses me against the door. The doorknob jabs me in the back, and I can't see as breathy sighs collide with my lips, sending a stream of desire to my core as my heart hammers inside my chest.

He lifts me, guiding my legs around his waist and holding me against the wall with frenzied movements as he kisses my neck, my lips, and anything else he can get his mouth on.

"Say it," he says on a heavy exhale.

"Beau."

He groans, and our lips connect again as he pulls us away from the wall. We stumble into the side of the dresser and knock the lamp to the floor. Disoriented, I can't make out up, down, right or left.

The kisses are frantic as we give and take, push and pull. My back collides with the wall again, and we slide into the nook housing the sink.

I don't feel like myself because I don't get engulfed by passion, and I don't lose control like this. Except with him, I am that person.

I've gone over the edge but can't tell if I'm flying or falling.

Coolness rushes over the back of my thighs when he places me on the counter and sends a shiver through me. Hands are everywhere. Mine. His.

I don't want tonight to end until I've touched every part of him, and he's touched every inch of me because I don't know if I'll ever do this again.

I push his T-shirt up, and he takes over, yanking it over his head and tossing it aside. It's the first time he's stopped kissing me since stepping inside the room, and his breath is ragged.

"Katie, Katie, Katie." He teases my dress up to my waist for the second time tonight. "You sure can drive a man crazy."

"Pretty sure you're driving yourself crazy." I drag my fingertips through the sparse hair on his chest. "After all, you're the one who flung us over the edge."

I skim my lips over his skin until his hand cradles my head and forces my head back. The room's black, but I know our eyes meet because there's an electrical charge between us when the connection happens.

He sees me.

I see him.

We aren't strangers.

I reach for his belt buckle, the sound of metal deafening in the silent room as his hand covers mine.

"Not yet." He flips the light switch on, and I lean back, supporting myself with my hands on the counter as he dots kisses up and down my neck.

Down to the hollow of my throat.

Down the center of my chest.

Then up again.

His lips crush against mine as he tugs at my panties, and I lift off the counter so he can pull them down. He leans into me, his fingers dancing over my drenched pussy, and I'm so wet it's embarrassing. Kissing my neck, he plunges his finger inside me, removes it, and slides it back in with a second one.

I want him.

He pumps his fingers in and out.

In and out.

In and out.

Oh, God.

He stops.

Oh, God.

"Katie, Katie, Katie." He smiles against my lips. "Lips like yours are cruel to a man like me."

"What kind of man are you?"

"One who doesn't deserve to kiss you." He nips my lower lip between his teeth. "And one who doesn't deserve to touch you like this." He drags his fingers over my pussy. "And definitely one who doesn't deserve to be inside you." He plunges his fingers inside me.

I gasp his name...I think. I'm not sure of anything right now.

Am I dreaming? Maybe I drank too much at the party, and I'm on the grass with Allison, dreaming I'm brave enough to do something so scandalous.

He tries to stop me when I reach for his belt again, but I push his hand away, the buckle clicking and clacking as I open his jeans. I slip my hand under the elastic band of his boxer briefs and encounter wetness on the tip of his cock. Using the pad of my thumb, I spread it over the head and work my palm down the shaft, kissing his chest as I pump up and down.

He grabs my wrist and pulls my hand out of his underwear. "I'm not going out like that tonight, darlin'."

He sweeps me off the counter and spins me around, bending me over the sink and pushing my dress up over my hips. He drops to his knees and nudges my legs apart. Squeezing my ass, he drags his tongue through my pussy from behind, sucking and licking his way to my throbbing clit. Instead of lingering over it like I expect, he stands up.

"I was right." He watches me through the reflection of the mirror.

"About?" I ask.

I look at myself bent over the counter, dress up over my ass with Beau standing behind me gripping my hips. I don't want to see the woman looking back at me, so I lower my eyes because she should be ashamed of what she's doing.

That woman should be, but I'm not.

"You just replaced chocolate milkshakes as my new favorite thing to eat." He leaves me on display while he disappears around the corner, returning moments later with a condom and his jeans hanging low on his hips.

He makes eye contact with me through the mirror again, displaying a devilish grin as he rolls the condom over his cock. "Nervous?"

"Should I be?" I play it cool, but I'm losing my mind. There's still time to throw the brakes on this before it goes any farther.

"Not at all." He grips his cock and drags the head up and down my pussy, coating it with my wetness.

Who am I kidding? I could stop this, but I don't want to. I want to do everything people have accused me of since I moved here.

With a heavy gaze, he presses the swollen head against my entrance but doesn't penetrate me. "There's no uncrossing this line."

"No matter what we tell ourselves, we crossed the line some time ago."

He works his cock in slowly, inch by inch, advancing and backing off until I've taken him completely. Once he's to the hilt, he stills.

"Are you okay?" He asks.

I nod because I don't have words. Seriously, my brain won't format syllables.

But when he pushes the yellow cardigan and dress up further, I don't have the luxury of remaining silent. "Don't."

He kisses my back through the material and doesn't question why I don't want to take it off.

He slides in and out of my clenched pussy with measured strokes, propelling me to the brink of my release once again and igniting a fire I don't want to burn.

But no matter how hard I fight it, the inferno spreads throughout my body—smoldering and suffocating as I grind against him, meeting each thrust with my ass until they get harder and faster, not caring about the craving inside me burning red hot. His balls slap against my clit as he pounds into me, and the sounds of sex are enough to make me climax on their own. Grunting. Panting. Slapping. Wetness.

Tightness coils deep in my belly, and I rock my hips, encouraging him to pick up speed.

I'm almost there.

He squeezes my shoulder with one hand and hangs onto my hips with the other while fucking me over the counter. I've heard about this kind of sex but never experienced it and assumed it was an urban legend—only happening to a friend of a friend's distant cousin that one summer on vacation.

Our eyes lock through the reflection as my climax jolts through me, and my mouth gapes open in a silent scream, sending me spiraling into my own personal oblivion. Our eyes never waver from each other's, making the entire experience so much more intense.

A growl passes through his clenched teeth as his body jerks and his cock pulsates, keeping time with every beat of my heart.

Our bodies are one for a tiny fragment of time.

After a few lazy thrusts, he pulls out and tosses the full condom in the nearby trashcan.

And what do I do?

I remain bent over, my dress up over my ass and my cheek on the cool counter because I'm in shock. I've never had a vaginal orgasm before. I accepted I was one of the countless women who can't achieve them through intercourse alone because I've always needed clitoral stimulation.

Now, as I lay against this smooth countertop, scared to move because I have jelly legs, I can confirm that's not the case.

"Are you alright?" Tugging his jeans up, he doesn't button them or secure his belt.

"Just waiting for the earth to stop spinning."

"Drink too much?" He wets a washcloth in the sink next to my head, and I'm startled when he runs it between my legs from behind.

"Too much dick." I laugh and maybe I did have more to drink than I should have at the party.

"No need to exaggerate for my benefit, darlin'." He holds my panties out. "But please don't stop." He winks.

He pulls my dress down over my ass, smoothing the fabric several more times than necessary. Is he seriously trying to be sly about copping a feel after what just happened?

I slip my underwear back on and face the mirror, smoothing my hair down. Between the messy hair and the smeared mascara, I look like I got fucked in a cheap motel, and I'll be damned—Allison was right.

My lipstick hasn't budged.

Beau's sitting at the small table across the room, enjoying a cigarette by the time I finish.

"So," I sit on the bed in front of him and rub my palms up and down my thighs.

Why does he have to look so hot right now?

He slouches in the chair, shirtless, with his jeans hanging open, and smokes a cigarette. "Don't go getting all shy on me now, darlin'."

He has a point. The man had his mouth between my legs a few minutes ago.

"That was fun." I nod, pressing my lips together. "Learned some new things about myself." I nod again. "Eight out of ten and would definitely recommend."

"Only an eight?"

"There's no room for improvement if I give you a ten out of the gate."

"Does that mean you want to help me get to ten?" Taking a long drag from the cigarette, his eyes lock with mine. "Or are you happy with the eight?"

"We need to establish ground rules even if I'm not going to be here much longer," I say.

"I'm listening."

"I don't want to talk about my relationship with him. It'd be weird and uncomfortable, and this is already weird and uncomfortable enough without adding that to the mix." Leaning over, I slip the red stilettos off. They're gorgeous, but I'm ready to get back into my Converse.

"I don't need to know the details of your relationship. The fact that you're doing this tells me all I need to know."

I grab the plastic shopping bag my sneakers are wrapped in from my messenger bag. "This can't be anything more than what it is."

Get it all out in the open—brutal honesty. I put the shoes on and lace them up. "And we can't be careless because careless is dangerous."

"Got it."

"We can't become invested in each other," I say.

"It'll make it harder to keep things light."

"Exactly."

"That's a long list of 'cant's'." He snubs his cigarette out and stands. "Is there anything you want to add before?" He holds his hand out.

"Before what?" He helps me up from the bed.

"Before I kiss you again."

This kiss is nothing like the previous ones. Those were hungry and bold. This one is sweet. He breaks the kiss and straightens his stance.

"We can hang out for a while if you want, so it doesn't feel so much like a smash and dash."

"It's better I don't." I take a couple of steps backward. "It might lead to us becoming friends."

"What's wrong with being friends?"

"Friends care about each other, and this is about sex." I kiss his cheek and grab the doorknob. "I don't want to ruin a good thing before it starts. Let's have a little fun before we fuck it up."

I feel ashamed and embarrassed but not guilty when I leave the room.

Admitting it was a bad idea to sleep with him is one thing.

Vowing not to do it again is another.

As I walk along the railroad tracks behind the motel, there isn't one iota of guilt swimming around in my conscience.

I smile as I balance on the metal rails, my arms outstretched to prevent me from falling as I move one foot in front of the other.

Why shouldn't I have some fun before my final send-off?

11

The pulsating neon 'OPEN' sign flickers against the diner window, the 'E' barely hanging on for months.

As I open the door, a wave of stale coffee and overcooked bacon hits me, mingling with the pungent scent of last night's regret clinging to me.

The roar of chattering voices and clinking dishes assaults my ears, each sound a needle stabbing the back of my throbbing skull. Familiar faces pack the diner and blur into an unrecognizable sea, their boisterous laughter and lively chatter intensifying the pounding in my head.

Guilt from last night hangs around me like a shroud as I slide onto the cracked vinyl seat in one of the back booths.

Can people tell what I did?

Donna's coughing so violently it sounds like she's hacking up a lung when she brings me a glass of water. This has to be the universe punishing me because I didn't drink enough to warrant this level of misery.

This must be my comeuppance.

I close my eyes and swallow a couple of ibuprofen tablets, willing them to work their magic as I try to tune out the screaming baby in the booth behind me. The lungs on that kid would be impressive if I weren't doing my best not to die.

When I open my eyes, Allison's making her way across the busy diner, looking how I feel.

Blonde hair twisted up in a messy bun with the biggest pair of sunglasses I've ever seen, she stops at the counter and places an order before dredging over to the booth.

"Sorry, I'm late." She plops down across from me and drops her head back against the vinyl seat. "I think I died last night."

"Really?"

"Really. This is my ghost you're talking to."

"If it's any consolation, my head feels like someone put it in a vice." I'm dying to tell her what happened, so I do a quick once-over to make sure no one's within earshot and lean over the table. "I did something after I left the party."

She pushes the huge sunglasses on top of her head, exposing bloodshot eyes with dark circles under them, and leans in. "What did you do?"

"Beau."

"What about him?"

"You asked what I did."

"Shut up!" Her hand flies to her mouth, and she scans the room to make sure no one notices her shock before leaning back over the table. "Are you serious?"

I nod.

"My fuckometer is never wrong. How was it? I bet he's intense in the sheets. You know, the broody stranger thing."

"He knows what he's doing, and I'll leave it at that."

"Well, aren't you a drag?" She rolls her eyes. "Was it a one-night stand, or do you think you two will go at each other every chance you get?"

"We didn't make plans to do it again, but we talked about ground rules, so we'll see what happens."

"Ah." She leans back against the seat as Donna places a plate of greasy food on the table. "I see."

I wait for Donna to leave.

"You see what?"

"It's more than bumping uglies in the sheets, isn't it?" She wiggles her eyebrows.

"There's more to it than the obvious, but nothing profound. He makes me feel good, and he's fun."

"I bet he does." She winks as she plunges a straw into her water.

"Not like that—I mean, yes, like that, but it's more. He makes me forget all the shitty stuff going on."

"That's actually really sweet. Leave it to you to score a guy like that to tryst with. Most of the time, these things just make you feel skeevy," she says.

"Are you speaking from experience?"

She twirls ice in her cup with the clear straw. "I had an affair with a married man, and it didn't end well. But affairs usually don't."

"Did you know he was married, or did he hide it?"

"I knew, which makes it worse because I can't even say he sprung it on me after I'd fallen for him." She pushes her drink to the side.

"Why did it end?"

"He was upfront that he'd never leave his wife, but as it tends to happen, the more time we spent together, the more I daydreamed about a life with him. You know—going on proper dates, spending holidays together, and all the humdrum stuff couples do. I told him I wanted more, and he said he didn't. So, we ended things." She forces a big, fat, fake smile. "But it was for the best because I met Elliot, and I think we have something promising."

"Did you hate him when it ended?"

"At first, but I realized I was the one who broke my heart by allowing myself to get involved with someone unavailable."

I drag my finger around the rim of my water glass. "Am I fucking up? Be honest."

"Life doesn't come with yes or no answers. You're the only one who'll know if you're fucking up or not. Do you feel like that's what you're doing?"

"No, and that's what's messing with my head because it doesn't feel wrong," I say.

"Nothing ever feels wrong when it feels good. Just be careful because these things end as quickly as they begin, and no matter what he whispers in your ear, the odds aren't in your favor. My advice is to take it at face value and nothing more."

"If Wesley finds out, he'll-" My mouth goes dry as I stare across the diner.

True to form, the devil's making her way over, looking prim, proper, and thoroughly pissed.

I straighten my posture, clear my throat, and shoot Allison a panicked glare until she freezes.

"Katie." My mother-in-law stops at our table and waits for me to acknowledge her.

"Hi, Mary. I didn't know you ate here."

"I don't. I came to speak with Mia, but I've missed her." She smooths her hands over the front of her cream pantsuit. "Aren't you going to introduce me?" She looks at Allison.

Mary's the first lady of Seymour, or at least she acts like she is. Wesley inherited her blonde hair, blue eyes, and sense of entitlement. I've never seen her wear anything but a tailored pantsuit, heels, and a full face of makeup. Her skin is radiant thanks to the expensive laser and Botox treatments she gets in Dallas and the facelift she denies having last year.

"This is Wesley's mom, Mary." I smile, though my jaw aches from clenching it. "This is Elliot's girlfriend, Allison."

Mary's demeanor changes like someone flipped a switch and turned bitch mode off.

"I've heard wonderful things about you. Elliot's such a sweet boy."

"I prefer to think of him as more of a man, but..." Allison tisks out of the corner of her mouth. "But I get what you're saying, and I agree he's a great guy."

"Oh, he is, and he's got a good head on his shoulders. I don't see why he isn't in charge of the bar and motel instead of Jeff." She shakes her head. "I'm sure he'd turn them around without welcoming vagrants to town."

"Vagrants?" Allison asks.

"Those boys he's got hanging around the bar. I'm confident neither are making their mothers proud."

"You should come have a drink and conversation with them before judging them," I say, but not to be catty. I sincerely think having some fun might help dislodge the stick she walks around with up her ass.

She ignores me and continues her conversation with Allison. "Where are you from?"

"Canyon."

"Isn't that near Amarillo?"

"A hop, skip, and jump away."

"Maybe consider moving closer if you're serious about your relationship because Elliot's quite the catch, and it'd be a shame if he got away. It's a pleasure to finally meet you." She pats Allison's shoulder and turns to me. "Tell Wesley to call his father since no one ever knows when he'll be home. And I'm sure you'll see Sheriff Harrington before I do, so inform him that he's not to be chauffeuring you around in his department vehicle. We've gotten several complaints about it at the mayor's office."

Her complaint claim is bullshit. It's one of her tactics to remind me she has the upper hand.

It doesn't matter how many times I tell Mary that Wesley never revealed he had a girlfriend, she's convinced I'm the reason he and Mia broke up. She believes it, and because she believes it, almost everyone else does, too.

"I don't think-"

She holds her hand up. "Yes, Katie, you don't think and it's not the taxpayer's responsibility to ensure you have transportation."

We watch her exit the diner, speechless in her absence.

"Wow..." Allison shakes her head. "And suddenly, the idea of marriage isn't as appealing as it was five minutes ago."

"They can't all be that bad."

"Then why do they write books and make movies about them?"

I shrug. "So you'll appreciate having a good one."

"Touché." She nods. "Were you around before Elliot's mom died?"

"No, but I've heard fantastic things about his parents. Brad grew up a few houses down from them and has nothing but good things to say about them. They had to be great people to adopt an infant in their fifties."

"No shit. I can't imagine chasing a crotch goblin around now, and definitely not after menopause."

As we recover from Mary's visit, Beau and Jake walk in. People stare as they cross the room, and some aren't subtle about it.

Beau smirks and Jake appears worse for wear walking behind him as they head toward us. Allison wiggles her eyebrows, and I kick her under the table.

Of course, they stop at our booth.

"How are you ladies feeling this morning?" A smile plays at the corner of Beau's mouth as his attention settles on me. "What about you? You took a pretty hard fall last night."

"You fell?" Allison gasps. "Where? When? What happened?"

Heat rushes to my face. "I slipped, but it was barely noticeable."

He sucks his bottom lip in over his teeth to keep from laughing as he hooks his sunglasses on his shirt collar. "I don't know... looked like you took a good lick from what I saw. I was behind you, so I didn't see it all, but I'm shocked you're not sore today."

"Like I said, I'm fine. Didn't even notice anything happened," I say.

"Join us." Allison scoots to the far side of the booth, and Jake slips in beside her. Beau slides in next to me, and I could choke her.

Jake raises his hand to flag a server down. Donna shows up, seemingly over her coughing fit, with both lungs intact. "A water and," he points to Allison. "Want anything?"

She shakes her head and points to her plate with a mouth full of food.

"What about you, love?"

"I'm fine, but thanks," I say.

He turns his attention back to Donna. "Just water for myself."

"A black coffee and chocolate milkshake, please." Beau shifts in the seat.

Water nearly comes out of my nose, and everyone stares at me.

Everyone.

"Coming right up," Donna says with what I'm assuming is all the pep she can muster post-lung perforation.

Allison grills Beau and Jake about everything from their favorite songs to how they ended up in Seymour, but I'm not part of the conversation because I'm trying not to notice the blue spruce scent wafting off Beau.

It's masculine and everywhere, even drowning out the bacon grease that makes me want to devour a massive BLT. Instead, I want to devour Beau.

His beard hides most of his profile, and inky curls tease his shoulders from under his black cowboy hat. And despite the facial hair, his Adam's apple is pronounced when he swallows, and I shift my legs to quell the pulsing between my thighs.

Turn away now if you know what's good for you.

I divert my attention to Donna as she delivers their drinks.

Beau pushes the water to Jake, keeps the coffee for himself, and slides the milkshake to me. "Consider it a peace offering." He winks.

I rip the paper from the straw and dunk the plastic into the creamy milkshake. If he thinks I'm too embarrassed to enjoy a free milkshake, he's mistaken. I didn't get these hips passing up dessert.

Wrapping my lips around the straw, my cheeks hollow as I work the thick milkshake up the straw.

Sucking and taking a breath.

Sucking and taking a breath.

With a glance here and there, Beau watches from the corner of his eye, and when he shifts in the booth, the bulge in his jeans is apparent before he adjusts himself under the table.

You sneaky little fox.

I bite the straw, and he brings his hand to his mouth, using it to hide his amusement.

Jake says something to me. How long has he been talking to me? I nod and pretend I've heard the entire conversation.

Allison checks her cell phone and crams it inside her purse. "I should go because I want to see my man for a few minutes before he goes to work." Jake stands, and she pushes out of the booth, dropping a twenty on the table. "I'll come by the bar tomorrow night to find out if you suck at pool." She bumps Jake's shoulder with her fist.

Mia enters the diner, and I can't take my eyes off her swollen belly and fuller breasts. How have I not noticed before?

"Earth to Katie." Allison snaps her fingers. "Anybody home?"

I blink a few times. "Sorry. I must've spaced."

"Are you daydreaming over there?"

"Something like that," I mutter and nudge Beau to let me out of the booth. Dropping some singles on the table, I can't bring myself to make eye contact with anyone. "I'll catch you guys later."

Keeping my head down, I focus on putting one foot in front of the other as I sprint across the two-lane highway and into the trailer park. Tears make it hard to see where I'm going, but I've walked this path so many times I can do it with my eyes closed.

I'm such a fool.

Does Mary know? How could she not? And what about all the time Wesley's been spending at his parent's house? Is Mia there? Am I the only one who doesn't know?

It'll get better.

It'll get better.

It'll get better.

I want to believe it will, but how can it if it's only getting worse?

12

I've avoided looking at Brad since we settled in the back booth at the diner.

I stare at my cup of black coffee and nod when he talks, occasionally chiming in with a random 'yes' or 'wow.' The coffee has gone cold, and I haven't raised the mug to my lips once. The place is almost empty, and that alone is odd.

But then again, everything feels off today.

Last night, I went home, drank the cheapest, biggest bottle of wine the liquor store carries, and fell asleep thinking about Wesley and Mia.

He'll have Mia on the east side of town, living in the big, nice house his parents will help them get because they love her, and he'll expect me to remain on the west side in our rusty, broken trailer.

"You know, I didn't invite you for coffee to watch you stare at it," Brad says.

"I should get to work anyway." I slide the mug to the side, and he grabs my wrist.

"Hey." He dips his head and forces eye contact. "That's a joke."

"I'm sorry." My throat tightens as I look at him. He's so concerned about me, but he doesn't know I deserve every ounce of misery I'm feeling right now.

"What's going on?"

I run my fingertips down his glass of water, streaking the condensation. "Life."

He eyes Mia behind the register as he fishes his wallet from his back pocket and drops a few singles on the table. "C'mon. Let's get out of here."

We end up parked near the railroad tracks, where the scenery is depressing. Dilapidated barns and farmhouses mark the horizon, along with rusty old cars that look like their drivers walked away and left them for the earth to consume. What little grass is here is overgrown, and red dirt covers the rest of the land.

"Talk to me. What's going on?"

"Nothing's going on," I say, unable to focus my vision because my gaze falls flat across the landscape.

"Bullshit. Something's eating you up. What is it?"

"Mia's pregnant." Uttering those words aloud makes my stomach drop to my knees.

"And?"

His eyes soften and say everything his mouth doesn't.

The next thing I know, he's got his arm around my shoulder, and I'm sobbing. I'm cold even though it's in the nineties outside, and my mind is paralyzed as I'm flooded with memories from the worst night of my life.

How could he do this? How could he be so careless? Wesley knows how hard last year was for me, and I'm still not over it. I'll never be over it. And for him to do this? Is he trying to see how far he can push me until I break?

"Are you sure it's his?"

"He's never stopped sleeping with her."

"Yeah, but that doesn't mean she isn't sleeping with someone else."

"It's his." My mouth is so dry it hurts to swallow. "I don't know how I know, but I know. I don't know why I'm so upset. It's not like I haven't done things to hurt him, too." I sniffle.

"What could you have possibly done to make this okay?"

I pull away. "Our marriage isn't perfect, but this stings, you know? Like deep. He's never been faithful, but this feels like he's rubbing my face in it because he knows there's nothing I can do about it."

"You can leave."

"And go where? He'll never let me go."

"Men like him are hard to get away from, but not impossible." He reaches across the seat and squeezes my hand. "I'll do whatever I can to help if that's what you want."

Brad's a great friend, but he doesn't understand my situation. Wesley isn't some asshole who'll shred my clothes and cancel my debit card if I leave him. He's nothing like what people think. If leaving him was an option, I wouldn't be entertaining overpasses as my way out.

"You mind dropping me off at work?" I ask, needing to change the subject.

"Why don't we grab some fresh coffee and drive around for a bit?"

"No offense, sheriff, but I'm in the mood for something stronger."

My life stopped last summer, and Wesley's moving forward with his like nothing happened.

FRESH ENERGY that hasn't been here in a long time fills the bar.

People laugh, dance, and shout across the room to one another. I've sold more drinks tonight than in the past month.

And be it the whiskey or the atmosphere, I feel better than when Brad dropped me off.

There's no reason to dwell on Wesley and Mia because neither will be my problem soon.

A blonde waits by the bar for Beau and Jake as they come in from out back, the smell of weed following them in.

"Can I have a hug? Y'all are just too cute." She beams.

"I'd be heartbroken if you didn't." Jake towers over her as he hugs her. "What's your name, sweetheart?"

"Anna." Her cheeks flush when she pulls away. She perches on her tiptoes and throws her arms around Beau's neck, dragging the hug out longer than Jake's.

He taps her shoulder and tries to stand up straight, but she tightens her hold.

"I need my neck back, darlin'."

Beau hangs his arm around her neck and plows through every shot I slide in front of him.

With a nod, he whistles across the bar, leading Jake to pump quarters into the jukebox as he pulls Anna to the dance floor while singing "Women I've Never Had" with Hank Williams Jr. at the top of his lungs.

A glass of whiskey in one hand and Anna in the other, he's relaxed, and she's more focused on him than the music, eating him up with hungry eyes as she slides her body against his.

Jake crosses the room and hauls me to the dance floor, leaving Elliot laughing behind the bar as the song plays out and another starts. He whispers something I don't catch because of the loud music and flicks his eyes to something behind me.

As I turn to see what he wants me to look at, Beau trades places with him and Jake dances with Anna.

"Did you two plan this?" I ask as Beau tucks our hands under his beard, something he didn't do with Anna.

"I'll never tell." He winks and whispers in my ear, "I want you so fucking bad right now."

"You sure about that? You looked pretty smitten with Anna."

"You're the only one I want to take back to my room," he says.

"And what will happen if you take me to your room?"

"I'll lick, suck, and fuck you until you beg me to stop," he says, his lips feathering over the shell of my ear and sending a shiver down my spine. "And those lips..."

"Which set are you talking about?"

He throws his head back in laughter. "Katie, Katie, Katie... what am I going to do with you?"

"Lick, suck, and fuck me until I beg you to stop." I wink and walk back to the bar.

Following with a relaxed stride, he slides onto a stool, tosses a shot of whiskey back, and pushes the empty glass toward me.

"Let me know when you're ready to beg, and we'll get out of here." He winks.

He crosses the room and pulls Anna from her table, dancing with her and staring at me. Does he think he's making me jealous?

Okay, maybe I'm a little jealous, but not because he's dancing with another woman. This sliver of envy comes from knowing how free everyone around me is to live their lives the way they want.

I may not be free yet, but it's coming because I've set it in motion.

13

Fisting Beau's hair, my hips buck against his face as he flicks my clit with his tongue, making me jerk my hands from his head and claw at the flimsy coverlet.

My back arches, and he wraps his arms around my thighs, pinning me in place as he rolls my clit between his lips, applying the perfect amount of pressure as he hums against it.

"Beau!" My body convulses as I come in his mouth, and he tightens his arms around my thighs, kissing my bare mound above my clit while holding me in place. He blows a lazy breath over it and watches the muscles in my stomach tremble. "You're way too good at this." I pant.

He props up on his elbows and skims his lips over my sensitive flesh one last time to watch me squirm before standing to unbutton his jeans. "Maybe you're just easy to please."

"Maybe you're the one who's easy to please. Beau, Beau, Beau." Rising on my knees, I gather my hair on top of my head and let it fall back down. "That's all it takes, right? You just like to hear your name?"

"I like to hear my name on *your* lips." He fists his cock, pumping and priming it.

"What else of yours do you like on my lips?" I crawl to the end of the bed and sit back on my heels as I stare up at him.

"I think you know."

"Say it." I lick my lips. "Tell me what you want me to do."

"I want those cruel lips wrapped around my cock."

I lick the bead of precum away with the flat of my tongue and wrap my lips around the crown before leaning back and gathering my hair over my shoulder.

"What else? Be specific."

He displays that mischievous grin and slides his thumb across my bottom lip. "I want to fuck your perfect mouth, and I want you to swallow every drop when I come down the back of your throat. Clear enough for you?"

"Crystal."

Dragging my tongue along the underside of the shaft, I stop when I reach the head to blow cool air on the sensitive skin. He hisses as I suck him into my mouth, inch by inch until my throat relaxes.

"Fuck." He sweeps my hair away from my face to watch his cock slide in and out of my mouth. "Look at me." With ragged and rushed breaths, he tilts my chin up until my watery gaze meets his. "I want to watch those cruel lips suck me off."

I moan my approval and wrap my hand around the root of his shaft, keeping my eyes locked with his as I jack him off with his cock buried in my throat.

His cock swells, and it's harder to press past my tongue, but I don't look away as I lead him to his climax. My lips glide up and down his cock, matching my pumping hand at the base. He rocks his hips to keep rhythm, and I let him fuck my mouth.

"I'm going to come." He warns through clenched teeth.

Grabbing his thighs, I pull him in so deep I can't breathe as his cock shoots a hot stream down the back of my throat, and his knees go weak as he uses my shoulders to steady himself while I suck him to completion.

"Fuck, woman." He groans as he straightens his stance. "I knew it." His words come out shaky. "I fucking knew it."

I lick my way up his softening cock and lean back, wiping my mouth with the back of my hand.

"You knew what?"

Collapsing against the headboard, he motions for me to join him. "That lips like yours would be cruel to a man like me."

I straddle his lap and place my palms on his chest under his beard. "You consider that cruel?"

"Yes, because I'll spend the rest of my life comparing other women's lips to yours, and they'll never measure up." He drags his hands up and down my bare thighs. "Definitely worth getting my ass kicked for if your husband finds out." He winks.

"I've always wondered what my thing is. Some people are gifted musicians." I kiss his chest. "Or amazing cooks." I kiss him again. "Apparently, mine is giving blow jobs."

"It's giving *me* blow jobs." He kisses me and tucks my hair behind my ear. "That's why I'm going to end up staying in this fucking town longer than I want to."

"Ugh." I sit upright. "Don't joke about that."

"All jokes aside." He moves his hands under my T-shirt and squeezes my breasts. "We're not done yet." He rolls my nipples between his fingers. "I've licked and sucked you, but I promised I'd fuck you, too."

I wiggle my hips over his growing cock. "You think you got it in you to go again?"

The next thing I know, I'm beneath him, and he's reaching across me to get a condom from the nightstand.

Sitting back on his heels, he rolls the condom on before lowering himself between my legs. He pushes into me and slides my shirt up, dropping his lips to my breasts as he rocks his hips.

I tangle my hands in his hair and hold his hot, wet mouth to my breasts as he sucks my nipples, groaning as he pulls out and thrusts back into me harder each time.

"Beg me to come, and you will," he says.

"I'll never beg you for anything." I hook my ankles behind him, pulling him deeper. "Ever."

He braces himself on his forearms and buries his cock in me hard and fast, his jaw clenching and a low growl coming from deep in his chest as he pummels my pussy.

I've never had a man fuck me like this. It's primal and so fucking hot.

I want to taste him.

To touch him.

I want to know him inside and out.

He sits back and positions my legs over his shoulders with that devilish grin as he holds my ankles in the air and pounds into me. A sheen of sweat covers his chest and forehead, but he doesn't stop. He doesn't lose his momentum. He's on a mission to make me beg, and it's one he'll fail.

I reach between my legs and find my spot. *The* spot. I rub small circles on my clit and use my other hand to pinch my nipples, moaning and writhing as pressure builds behind the little bundle of nerves beneath my fingers. I make a V-shape with my index and middle finger, positioning them around Beau's cock and squeezing them together.

He sucks his bottom lip between his teeth as I increase the pressure on his cock. "You're not playing fair."

"Who says I'm playing at all?"

He stops and stands up, yanking me to the edge of the bed and slamming back into me. "You ready to beg me to come yet?"

"Never." I slide my hand over my stomach and back down to my clit, but he swats it away.

"If you come, it'll be because I make you."

"It's my body."

"Not when I'm inside it, darlin'."

A few minutes later, I have what can only be described as an out-of-body experience. Pleasure flows through my bloodstream, leaving me euphoric.

This is better than any drug. I don't even feel like I'm on this planet. It's like a cosmic wave carrying me through time and space to an unknown destination. Wave after wave follows, each less intense than the previous, until my body stops shaking.

Beau's release is much more violent than mine. He grits his teeth as he thrusts, gripping my ankles over his shoulders so tight his knuckles turn white. His cock stops jerking inside me, and he collapses on top of me.

"Sorry, what'd you say?" He mumbles against my sweaty chest.

"I didn't say anything."

"I thought I heard you begging for something."

I slap his shoulder and push him off me. "I can't with you."

"So, you dismiss me after getting what you wanted?"

His phone rings on the nightstand, and I roll onto my stomach as he silences the call and lays it down with the screen hidden. Wesley used to do that before he wasn't afraid of me knowing he was cheating.

Beau sleeping with other women hasn't crossed my mind until now, and I'd be naïve to think it isn't a possibility. After all, he's single and incredibly hot.

Or is he?

The incredibly hot part is evident, but he may also be stepping outside of a relationship, which would explain why my situation doesn't bother him.

"The fact that you're doing this tells me all I need to know."

"I should get going," I say.

Lingering leads to friendship and friendship leads to a connection. Pillow talk is more dangerous than sex.

He snakes his arm around my waist when I twist to roll off the bed, dragging me back to him.

"You're not getting away that easy." He sweeps my hair off my shoulder, nuzzling under my ear and peppering the area with soft kisses. "What made you go to the overpass that night?"

"Why do you think?"

"Why don't you just leave him?"

He had to go there.

He had to ask *that* question.

"Guess it's never crossed my mind." I sit up, searching for my clothes.

His phone rings again, and he rolls away from me to get it. I try not to watch him but can't help myself as I shimmy my jeans up over my hips.

He studies the illuminated screen before silencing the call and laying it down again. He's silent as he puts a pair of jeans on and doesn't bother zipping or buttoning them before settling in a chair in front of the draped window. He dips his head to light a cigarette and watches me finish getting dressed.

I sit on the bed to tie my shoes, and his phone rings again, causing him to curse under his breath. He leans forward and grabs it from the nightstand, holding the button on the side until the screen turns black.

"I have a thing Wednesday morning in Wichita Falls, so I'm going up tomorrow afternoon and spending the night. Should be back in time for work Wednesday, and we can meet up afterward if you want," I say.

"Need a ride?"

"Brad's taking me."

"You and the sheriff spending the night out of town together, huh? People gossip, you know."

"No one knows about it, so I'll know the source if they do." I stick my tongue out.

After pulling a long draw on the cigarette, a heavy cloud of smoke swirls from his nostrils. "You and the sheriff...have you ever?"

"Had sex with him?"

"Been intimate." He smiles.

"People think there's something going on between us, but he's just been helping me study for my G.E.D. I've never cheated on Wesley, if that's what you want to know. You're only the third man I've had sex with, and Brad isn't one of the other two."

"How's that possible?" He asks like he doesn't believe me.

"It's easy. I lost my virginity to my high school boyfriend, and we broke up when we were twenty because we realized we weren't those same kids who had everything in common anymore. I met Wesley right before I turned twenty-three and got married, and there's you—lucky number three. Want to share your entire catalog of sexual partners?"

"Negative." He laughs. "What about the three-year gap? No hookups?"

"Hookups were the last thing on my mind because I was taking care of my mom." I plop down on the bed across from him. "She was sick, I took care of her until she passed, and life went on. Cancer during my senior year, so I dropped out to care for her. Remission a year later, and it came back with a vengeance the following year. We put up a hell of a fight for nearly two years, but in the end, we were both tired of fighting."

"What about your dad?"

"Don't know and don't care because he bailed a couple of years before she got sick. He didn't think about us, so I don't think about him." I walk around the room and check for anything I don't want to leave behind.

"I lost my mom five months ago, and she was sick, too." He flicks his cigarette in the ashtray and watches the smoke rise to the ceiling. "I haven't figured out how to live in a world without her in it."

"Was she sick before she passed?"

"As far back as I can remember."

"I'm not going to say 'I'm sorry for your loss' because it pissed me off when people said it to me. People say time heals, but I don't think it does. Time gives our hearts a chance to catch up with our heads." I haul my bag strap over my head. "It's not fair to let one moment of heartbreak define your entire relationship with her. Cancer took the future I had with my mom, but it can't have the good times before it reared its vile head in our lives."

He meets me in front of the door, his smile not as crooked and his eyes a little more sad. "Do you really believe it gets easier?"

"I do. The sadness will always be there, but it'll hurt less and less until one day you'll only remember the good times when you think about her."

"Do you believe in God?" He asks.

"I believe in whatever brings the peace we need to carry on in a way that would make the people we miss proud." I kiss him on the cheek and walk away.

The field I prefer to walk through is flooded from the previous storm, so I detour along the highway because I'm not worried about anyone seeing me walking at this hour.

Following the white line, one foot after the other, I stretch my arms out and pretend I'm on a high wire.

The moon is full, and stars freckle the clear sky like someone spent endless hours poking tiny holes in the fabric of space for the light to filter through at precise points. The occasional cricket startles me, and a dog barks in the distance, but otherwise, the town is void of sound during these pre-dawn hours.

I lay on the yellow center line and close my eyes. Loose

pebbles dig into my shoulder blades, and the asphalt is cooler than expected, given the sweltering daytime temperatures.

Keeping my eyes closed, I visualize the stars in my mind as I take deep, intentional breaths.

What if a car or truck sped through town and didn't see me until it was too late? The gossip following such a tragic event would be for the books.

A few people will be sad, but most will be shocked. Some will publicly defend my name only to condemn me in private. Most won't care because I'm not one of them.

Tears dampen the hair on my temples as my eyelids flutter open to the pristine sky above.

How did I get to this point?

14

Brad drops his overnight bag on the bed closest to the air conditioner, and I put mine on the bed closest to the bathroom. The room is the same generic room as every other chain hotel room. Nondescript art hangs on the tan walls. Dark wood furniture and beige bedding. Hideous carpet. Nothing extraordinary.

The air conditioner hums under the window, and Brad slides the heavy drapes across the rod and hangs the plastic Do Not Disturb placard on the outside door handle before moving around the room, checking mirrors, and placing a weird lock thing on the inside of the door.

"What's that?" I ask.

"A portable lock. Keeps people from being able to come in even if they have a key." He slides the chain lock at the top of the door in place. "Can't be too careful."

"Paranoid, much?" I sit on the edge of my bed and heel my shoes off.

"Say what you want, but no one's getting in here without me knowing." He glances at his watch and picks up the laminated menu from the table of surrounding restaurants that deliver. "Are you hungry?"

"Not really. My nerves are shot." I walk around the room, checking out the amenities. "What if I don't pass?" I call out as I poke my head inside the bathroom.

This place is nicer than the motel in Seymour because it has name-brand shampoo and conditioner, the ceiling doesn't have water stains, and it smells like cleaning solution instead of pure bleach.

"You'll pass, and if you're not going to eat, you should get some sleep because we've got to be at the college by seven-thirty in the morning," he says as he unzips his bag, dragging a pair of sweatpants out and moving the bag to the luggage stand by the television.

"I don't want to be the bearer of bad news, but you look like you could use some sleep, too." The dark circles under his eyes haven't gone unnoticed.

"Very observant. I'm running on fumes since we found Abigail White's body." He offers a smile, but it's not the one that stops me in my tracks. It's a generic smile meant as a nicety.

Sensing he doesn't want to make small talk, I leave the matter alone.

He leaves to find something to eat, and I shower while he's out. I'm pretty sure he wasn't hungry but needed an excuse to step out while I showered because he's the gentleman I told Beau he was.

When I'm done, steam follows me out of the bathroom, billowing into the room like there's a smoke machine behind me.

"Hot enough for you?" Brad crumples a paper burger wrapper into a ball and drops it in the trash can. How he stays so slim with the way he eats is beyond me.

"Almost." I pull the sheet back on my bed and slip under it, sighing as I snuggle into the pillow. "My God, I've missed crispy sheets."

I'm so used to sleeping on the couch that I'm not sure if I'll be able to sleep with so much space. I tuck the comforter under my chin and wiggle out of my pajama pants because I'm a hot sleeper, and if Brad weren't here, I'd be commando.

He stands from the table and stretches his arms over his head, picking up the sweatpants from his bed and stalking across the room to his bag. He tosses me a stack of banded index cards.

"Keep yourself busy while I'm in the shower."

"Yes, sir."

He emerges from the bathroom wearing only sweatpants. I've never seen him without a shirt, but Allison will have a field day knowing he's flawless beneath that uniform.

"Get any studying done?" He rubs the towel over his wet hair and ignores the water beads on his sculpted shoulders.

I rotate to my side, trying to hide the warmth in my cheeks that's surely evident from checking him out.

"I'm too nervous to focus."

"Then you should get some sleep." He throws the blankets back on his bed, laying on his back with his arm behind his head and the sheet at his waist. "The alarm is set for six." He turns his head to look at me. "Are you going to be a pain in the ass to wake up?"

"No more of a pain in the ass than when I'm already awake." I tuck my hands under my cheek. "Thanks again for bringing me to do this."

I need him to know this wasn't for nothing, and he did everything he was supposed to as my friend because my heart aches when I think about him blaming himself when he gets the news of my death.

My soul died last summer in that trailer, and the decaying

stench trapped inside me is spreading, but I refuse to let it get on the people I care about.

15

Underneath the flickering sign of the struggling motel, Beau and I escape from the world.

The musty scent of damp wallpaper marries a lingering hint of cheap perfume that's impregnated the walls, creating a unique bouquet filling our secluded sanctuary.

Our world away from reality, a place we can live in stolen moments.

A scratchy blanket covers me, and my eyelids flutter as they adjust to the dim lighting in the motel room.

Sitting shirtless in the chair in front of the window, Beau scribbles in a notebook as I stretch out on the bed. I roll to my side and prop up on my elbow, noting that this room isn't as nice as the one Brad and I stayed in last night.

"Do you ever sleep?" I ask.

"Not much these days." The cigarette hangs between his lips as he flips to a new page in the notebook, writing something down as the cigarette dances between his lips.

"What keeps you awake?" I pick at the flimsy coverlet.

"The ghosts won't be quiet."

"Do you have a lot of them?"

"More than I want." Dropping the cigarette in an empty beer bottle, he sits back in the chair, locking his fingers behind his head and stretching his legs out. "What about you? What's whispering in your ear to make you stand on overpasses?"

"I guess I have my own ghosts."

"Everyone has them. Some are just louder than others." He takes a long pull from the bottle of whiskey and hisses after swallowing. "Overpasses and whiskey bottles serve the same purpose. One just gets you there faster."

He stretches out behind me on the bed, his chest pressing against my back as he hangs his hand over my hip.

"Is that why you don't judge me?" I ask.

"I could never judge the second most beautiful tragedy to have ever lived in my world." His voice hints at sadness as he pulls my hair over my shoulder and slides his hand under my shirt, but doesn't travel up past my navel.

"Who's the most beautiful tragedy in your world?"

"My mother." He pushes his hand inside my shorts and rests it on my hip. "You got your question, so it's my turn because I'm curious about something, too."

It's not lost on me that he's changing the subject.

"Shoot."

"What's your middle name?" He kisses my shoulder over the thin cotton shirt.

"That's what you're curious about?"

"It is." His words muffle against my shoulder as he reverses the kisses toward my neck.

"I don't tell anyone that. Sorry."

His lips skim the shell of my ear. "Is it that bad?"

"I still haven't forgiven my mom."

"It can't be that appalling," he says.

"It's Blue."

He lifts his head. "Like the color?"

"Katie Blue Asher became Katie Blue Reese." I press my lips

together. "Told you it was horrendous, and now you have to swear you won't tell anyone."

"I swear." He makes an 'X' over my heart.

"You can't pull a fast one over on me. You crossed my heart, not yours. Do it right, or I'll never tell you anything else."

I'm on my back with him kissing me, but he doesn't linger before propping himself up on his elbows.

"That's because yours is more important, so it means more if I promise on yours. Mine doesn't mean shit. And for the record, it's a beautiful name."

"Don't do that."

"Do what?"

"The lovely nothings—the trivial flattery. That's not what this is about, so let's not cheapen our sleazy affair with compliments."

"They aren't for nothing." He tilts his head to the side with a relaxed smile. "They make you smile and turn your cheeks red." He kisses me. "But mostly, they make you smile." His lips linger on mine, and then he rolls onto the bed. "I have another critical question." He splays his hand over my lower stomach, and I know he can feel the scar through my shirt.

He's never questioned why I don't take my shirt off, but I know he's curious.

"Ask away."

"The scar on your stomach…what happened?" He skims his fingertips across the scar through the thin cotton.

"Are you sure you want to know?"

He nods.

"Fine." I roll back onto the bed. "A raccoon jumped from the dumpster when I was taking the trash out one night and attacked me with a rusty knife. He ran away, and they never caught him. There was a three-day search, but it's like he vanished into thin air. The police thought he was affiliated with a local raccoon gang, but they couldn't prove it because none of his little raccoon friends would give him up."

"Yeah? A raccoon?"

"It was wild. No one's ever seen anything like it, and I still have nightmares about him coming back to finish the job because I went to the police."

"Well, now I'll be more cautious taking out the trash." He spreads his palm flat on my stomach.

"You should because I have it on good authority that they have an underground syndicate operating in this area."

"Good to know because one can never be too careful." He pushes his hand down the front of my shorts, searing the inside of my thigh as he skims over my flesh. Our eyes remain focused on one another despite my urge to look away. "Is it okay if I touch you like this?"

"Yes."

He inches farther down, stopping when his fingertips touch the waistband of my panties. "Is it okay if I touch you here?"

"Yes."

"And what about here?" He strokes the cotton fabric over my pussy. "Is this okay?"

"Yes."

He pushes up from the bed and covers my mouth with his as he slips his hand inside my underwear. My hips grind against his nimble fingers as he sinks them deep inside my pussy, and I clench down on them, the feeling of needing to be full overwhelming.

"Do you like me touching you here?" He pants into my eager mouth while pumping his fingers.

"Yes."

I hate how I feel when I'm with him because I love how I feel when I'm with him. He makes me believe I'm the only woman in the world. Allison says that's what affairs are supposed to do —create unrealistic ideals of two people. If this were an actual relationship, we'd never be able to maintain this intensity, which is why I don't want us to ever be more than we are now.

I don't want to ruin the best, worst decision I've ever made by trying to turn it into something it's never supposed to be.

As quick as it started, his fingers are no longer inside me, and he's lying next to me again. He lifts my hand to his mouth and kisses it before placing it on my stomach. "I want you to make yourself come."

"I can't," I say, still working to reclaim my breath. "Not while you're watching."

"Why not? You like to watch, and maybe I do, too." He guides our hands down my stomach and leans closer to my ear, whispering, "Show me what you do when no one's looking."

"I don't...I can't..." My protest spirals into a nosedive, diminishing outright as he pushes our hands down farther.

"We'll do it together." He slides our fingers through my wet slit. "Wet your fingers."

I dip my finger inside my channel and close my eyes as I move in and out of myself while he covers my hand, guiding it over my clit and making those tiny circles, but he doesn't touch me. I'm pleasuring myself.

"Are you going to keep going if I remove my hand?" He removes his hand and splays it over my stomach as I rub my swollen clit. He leans over me and kisses my neck while I masturbate next to him. Turning my face into his chest, I move my fingers faster. "Does it feel good?"

"Yes," I pant.

"Do you like making yourself feel this way?"

"Yes." Words are harder to force out now.

He drags his hand up and down my inner thigh. "Then relax and enjoy the ride, darlin'."

I concentrate on the tightness coiling inside my core, twisting and tugging as I rub my clit. Meanwhile, he kisses the side of my neck and massages my thigh, sending my body into sensory overload when he bites my nipple through the sheer T-shirt.

That's when I feel it.

Pressure starts low in my belly and travels deeper until it bursts free with the aid of my fingers. My back arches, and I squeeze Beau's arm as my body convulses with the powerful orgasm slamming against my core.

He crushes his lips against mine, absorbing the cries and moans as I shudder through the remnants of one of the most pleasurable experiences of my life.

"Hi." He smiles from ear to ear when I open my eyes.

"Hi."

He pulls the blanket over me and snakes his arm under my neck, the other around my waist, pulling me flush with his chest as he lays his cheek against my temple.

"Katie, Katie, Katie." He nuzzles against me. "A woman like you is cruel to a man like me."

"What kind of man are you?" I snuggle into the pillow.

"The worst kind." He slaps my ass, shattering the euphoria. "Let's play a game."

I SIT across from him and chew the inside of my cheek, my hands tucked between my legs and my knee bobbing under the table.

Why did I agree to do this?

He lights the joint he swiped from Jake and puffs it, passing it to me before we start.

"Repeat the rules back to me again." He holds the smoke in his lungs and taps the deck of cards with his middle finger.

"We each draw a card, and the lowest has to answer a question of the winner's choosing." I suck the smoke in and choke.

We each draw a card and lay it face up for the other to see. He has a three of hearts and I have a seven of clubs.

"Where are you from?" I ask.

"Wichita Falls, born and raised." We pull cards again and flip them over. I win again with a nine of spades.

"Do you have any brothers or sisters?"

He takes a hit from the joint and passes it back to me. "Two brothers and one sister, all younger." We draw cards again.

"Finally." He smiles at his king of hearts over my two of diamonds. "Does your husband hurt you often?"

"Geez," I pass the joint back to him. "Straight for my jugular, huh?"

"Is there any other way?"

"All the time." I draw a two of clubs and prepare to answer another question because it feels strange speaking about things I've spent so much time hiding.

Beau pulls from the deck, and as I suspect, he gets a nine of clubs. "Why doesn't the sheriff help you if you two are such good friends?"

"It's not that easy."

"Truth." He leans back in the chair. "That's the rules."

I gather my hair over my shoulder. "Wesley's dad is a judge, and Brad will lose his job if he goes after Wesley. The bar will go under if I tell Elliot or Allison because my mother-in-law will get their license pulled. So, I don't want them to know because it's not worth it. Besides, it'll be my word against his, and my word means nothing in this town."

His nostrils flare, and he sits up straight, pulling a card from the deck—two of spades.

"Whose phone calls are you avoiding?" I ask.

"Cassie, my ex. My family ranch is going bankrupt, and she wants me to help save it, but I don't want to."

"Why not?"

He draws a card, and I follow—queen of hearts for him and three of diamonds for me.

"Why does everyone tiptoe around him and his family?" Beau asks.

"I don't know."

I win the next draw. "Do you think you'll ever get back together with your ex?"

"I'd rather chew off my foot."

I'm two for two when we draw cards again. "Why don't you want to help save your family's ranch?"

He pushes the chair back and moves around the table, pulling me up from my chair. "This is stupid. Let's just talk. Can we do that?"

Climbing in the bed, he lies on his back and tucks me into his side. "I want you to talk to me because you want to, not because of some stupid game," he says.

When this ends, I want us to look back on this time and think about slow dances and making love instead of sad stories and heartaches neither of us caused.

Cars passing by on the highway break up the silence in the room, and the air conditioner rattles under the window. I pluck at the dark hair on his chest as I drape my leg over him and nuzzle into his side. I drag my fingertips up and down his stomach, stopping at the waistband of his boxer briefs. "Tell me your secrets, and I'll tell you mine."

"Bargaining with me now?" He looks down with a smile.

I shrug. "What have you got to lose?"

"You go first," he says.

There's a sudden hollowness in my stomach. "What do you want to know?"

"Are you still planning to take your life?"

"Yes."

"Is there anything I can say that will change your mind?" He asks.

"No."

"Why?"

"Why not? I don't have anything to live for, so why continue this tragedy for an entire lifetime?"

"Sometimes it's not about you. It's about the people you're leaving behind and what it'll do to them."

"I'm nothing to people around me, unremarkable and meaningless. They'll be upset for a while, but they'll be better off without me in the long run," I say.

"Trust me, you have no idea what it'll do to the people you leave behind." He shifts away from me and sits up on the edge of the bed with a blank stare toward the window. "We should get you home before it gets too late." His voice cracks as he pushes off the bed and rushes to put his clothes on while avoiding looking at me.

Allison's voice in my head reminds me this will end as abruptly as it began, and all signs point to her being right.

16

The road in Beau's rear-view mirror is thick with red dust as we cruise down the desolate gravel roads on the outskirts of town, the scent of earth permeating the cab of the old truck.

I didn't grow up in Texas, but I've lived here long enough to understand dirt gets everywhere, and keeping it at bay is impossible.

Stars dot the clear sky, and he keeps me tucked next to him with his hand on my knee while humming along with songs on the radio.

This feels more right than anything before, but it's the most wrong thing I've ever done.

Propping his arm on the open window, he steers the slow-moving truck with his left hand. With his right hand, he makes those tiny, calming circles on the inside of my knee as we creep down the darkened road.

He navigates the truck behind an abandoned grain mill, parking in the shadows and killing the engine.

"I don't think anyone will bother us here," he says.

"I feel like I'm seventeen again."

"I'm glad you're not because I wouldn't be here." He stretches his arm across the back of the seat and twists to face me, pulling my leg into his lap.

"What are your plans after you leave here?" I ask.

"Jake and I aren't the kind of guys who make plans." He massages my calves.

I bunch my hair up and lean against the passenger window to hold it in place. "Tell me about your life before."

"Before what?"

"Before you hated it so much."

"Who says I hate it?"

"Context clues." I smile.

Dragging me to his lap and turning me around, my back becomes flush with his chest, and our legs entwine across the length of the seat as he snakes his arms around me, tugging my shirt up until a sliver of skin peeks out for him to make the tiny circles on. "What do you want to know?"

"Do you miss it?"

"Every fucking day." He lays his cheek against my temple. "I'd give anything to have one more day with my mom so I could ask her everything I'll never get to and tell her all the things I wish I could tell her now."

"Like what?"

"Like where she stashed the porn magazines she confiscated from my room when I was thirteen, and I'd tell her I never liked her pancakes because they were always undercooked in the center."

"That's what you'd do with one more day?"

"I'd ask her what I should do about the ranch." He squeezes me, kissing my temple. "And I'd ask why she left us."

"What happened to her?"

"She suffered from the same affliction as you," he says.

"Did she..." I can't bring myself to say it.

"Yes."

I twist to look at him. "Will you tell me more about her someday?"

"If you're still around to have a someday." The bitterness rolling off his tongue is undeniable as he shifts behind me, nudging me forward. "But enough about that shit show."

He slides to the middle of the bench seat and hauls me on his lap.

I'm sure it's difficult knowing someone plans to take their life, and there's nothing you can do about it. His mother's death complicates this for him, but there's nothing I can do to help him with those demons when I have my own.

I straddle him and hold his face in my hands, brushing my thumbs over his cheeks and staring into his brown eyes.

How did I not notice the sadness in them before?

"I hate to break it to you, but this *is* the shit show. You. Me. This whole fucked up purgatory we pretend is our lives. We're stuck in a limbo of not wanting to live and grasping at anything to feel alive."

"Are there days you're glad you woke up?" He asks.

"Yes, the good ones."

His lips are soft against mine, and his beard tickles my chin as his tongue sweeps inside my mouth, a weak hint of vanilla from the whiskey he drank earlier remaining. "They'll all be good ones someday if you stick around."

"And you'll stop hating your life someday, too."

"Katie, Katie, Katie," he says against my lips. "I already hate it a little less." He kisses me again. "Maybe you can help me figure something out since we're tackling serious subjects." He rocks my hips over his growing erection. "How's it possible you turn me on so much?"

"It's the forbidden fruit thing."

"How can you be forbidden fruit if I've already eaten you?" He pops the button open on my shorts and lowers the zipper.

I move onto the seat next to him and take off my shorts and

underwear while he frees his cock from his jeans and puts a condom on.

Lowering myself over his lap, my pussy cocoons his thick shaft as I slide back and forth over it. Slick. Hot. Hard. The swollen crown rubbing my clit sends me close to climaxing in seconds.

I use his shoulders to steady myself as he fists his cock and positions it for me to ease down on, and no matter how wet or ready I am, he stretches and fills me beyond what I think I can take, leaving me whimpering as I take all of him. The fullness sets in, and my pussy contracts around him, still wanting more —always wanting more because I'm becoming greedy when it comes to him.

He slams his mouth over mine as my hips rock, and the small space turns hot and humid, sweat dampening us as we race to our releases.

"What you do to me, woman." He clenches his jaw as he pushes my shirt up, jerking my bra down and pulling my nipple inside his mouth, sucking and biting as he splays his hands on my back to hold me close.

I don't release his shoulders because I don't want to lose my rhythm. I push him away from my breasts and grind against his hips. *I'm so close.*

Digging his fingers into my flesh, he thrusts his hips upward and collides with my hips every time they come down. Frantic. That's the only word that comes to mind. We're both desperate for a release.

An electric jolt shoots through me as I cry out when the head of his cock strokes the perfect spot at the perfect angle, and he takes over, bouncing me up and down, slamming into me over and over. No slowing down. No catching our breath. Over and over until my entire body seizes, and I cry out his name inside the dark cab.

"Say it again." He works my hips, pushing and pulling them back and forth.

"Beau!"

"Ah, fuck!" Clamping his eyes closed, he clenches his teeth to get through it as he rides the wave of his climax through to the end.

Finally, he opens his eyes and smiles. "Have I mentioned I love when you say my name?"

"Once or twice." I'm an exhausted blob of spent sexual energy, my limbs useless as I melt against him. "But I can stop if you want me to."

He plants a deep, wet kiss on my lips. "I don't want you to ever stop calling out my name when you come."

I push him back against the seat. "Okay, but won't it be weird for a guy whose name isn't 'Beau'?" I climb back into the seat beside him and redress because that's what you do when you have sex in the cab of a truck like a hormone-driven teenager.

"Guess you'll have to stick with guys named 'Beau' from now on." As he zips his jeans and scoots back behind the steering wheel, he dips his head to look at the mirror. "Are those headlights?"

Blue lights blind me when I stretch to see out the back window.

"Fuck," he says.

I struggle not to hyperventilate as I scamper to the opposite side of the seat, trying to establish as much distance between myself and him as feasible because there's nowhere to hide, no explaining this away.

I tuck my hands under my legs to conceal their shaking, and bile hangs in the back of my throat, ready to spew any moment because only an idiot wouldn't know what we're doing out here this time of night. Condensation on the windows will give us away to whoever approaches the door, even if we deny it until our last breath.

"Relax," he says as he rolls down the driver's side window. "It'll be okay."

I nod but don't believe him.

"Mr. Brooks." Brad's voice fills the truck cab before he's visible. The shock on his face is unmistakable when he lowers his head and peers inside. "Katie."

Relief surges through me, but I'm not out of the woods.

"Everything all right?" Beau asks.

"Yeah, just checking to see who's parked out here at this hour." Brad eyes me through the open window.

"I didn't know parking was a crime," Beau says.

"We're taking extra precautions because of the recent case. Can't be too vigilant, you know?"

Beau nods. "Agreed."

"I'll let you two go on about your business." Brad turns to walk back to this patrol car but backtracks after only a few steps and leans in the window. "Can I speak to you in private, Katie? It'll only take a second."

Dry brush scratches my ankles as I trek to where Brad waits by the tailgate, and Beau stretches his neck to see us in the rearview mirror, otherwise granting us the privacy Brad requested.

"Are you kidding me?" Brad props his hands on his hips.

"What?" I cross my arms over my chest.

"That's all you're going to say. What?"

"What am I supposed to say?"

"Gee, I don't know." He curls his lips over his teeth with a sharp breath while shaking his head. "How about I wasn't fucking some guy I hardly know in his truck?"

"Fine. I wasn't fucking some guy I hardly know in his truck. Better?"

"Did all the conversations we've had not register? I'm

busting my ass to look out for you, and you do something this reckless?"

"You're trying to control me like he does. Telling me who I should and shouldn't talk to. Who I should and shouldn't be seen with. When and how I get to and from work. Your motivations may be different, but your behavior's the same." My chest is tight as I cross my arms over it.

"Do you grasp how bad things will be if Wesley finds out? He's barely tolerable when you aren't doing anything wrong. What if it'd been Ricky or Heath instead of me who rolled up on you two?" He throws his hands in the air. "Shit, Ricky's all over Wesley's nuts, and Heath's looking for a reason to have Wesley in his pocket. Do you think either would hesitate to call him the minute they drove away?"

I drop my gaze to the gravel below, my chin to my chest as heat rushes to my cheeks. "No."

"No, they wouldn't, so you're damn lucky it was me out tonight and not one of them." He gnaws at the inside of his cheek. "How long have you two been doing this? And be honest. I'll find it insulting if you lie to me because you're horrible at it."

"Not long."

He pinches the bridge of his nose. "As if your life wasn't bad enough, you add this to it? What's going through your head?"

"You really want to know?"

"Please enlighten me."

"Do you know how exhausting my life is? I live in a constant state of hopelessness, but I don't feel it when I'm with him because he doesn't know anything about me. He hasn't been fed the lies everyone else has, so he sees me for me and not what he's been told to see me as. I don't have to worry about him losing his job if I spend too much time with him or his business going belly up if the wrong person thinks he's helping me too much. I have to keep everyone at arm's length, but not him because he's had one foot out the door since he got here."

His expression softens, as does his tone. "An affair, though?"

"I don't expect you to understand."

"I don't need to understand, but I care what'll happen if Wesley finds out because he's not known for being rational." His voice cracks, but he recovers before he thinks I noticed. "How well do you know this guy?" He flicks his eyes toward the truck.

"Well enough."

"Yeah, well, the last guy you knew 'well enough' turned out to be a total pain in my ass." He hugs me, stunning me because he's not big into physical affection. "I'm sorry. I just...you know how bad this could turn out."

I step back. "I know what's at risk, and the dice are mine to roll. I don't care what happens to me as long as he doesn't get hurt." I flick my eyes toward Beau.

"Since when do you gamble?" He leads me back to the cab and opens the door.

"Since I realized the odds of winning are zero if I never play."

He closes the door and leans in the window. "You two need to keep this behind closed doors because I'm likely the only person who doesn't care that you're doing it." He slaps the door and walks back to his patrol car.

Beau smiles. "Busted, huh?"

"Yep." Pressing my lips together, I nod. "Busted."

"Is he jealous or what?"

I cut my eyes at him. "Or what."

"Want to go back to the room?"

"I can't tonight. He's coming home in the morning."

17

Wesley holds my hand as we approach Elliot's house, and my heartbeat matches the anxious fluttering of moths around the porch light.

My fingers tighten around Wesley's hand while my mind whirls with endless possibilities of how easily tonight can spiral into disaster since he's already gotten mad at me for forgetting to put on the earrings he gave me.

Elliot called and invited us over because he's unaware of the potential storm brewing. Little does he know that beneath our public smiles lays a private world lived in chaos and fear.

And that's my fault because I hide the truth from him like everyone else.

We've always looked good together, and things appear normal if people don't look too close.

The backyard is lit by lights strung through trees and across the porch. People are scattered around, and I stretch my neck to see if Allison's here. I don't see her, which is a good thing because Wesley doesn't like me hanging out with her.

Wesley mingles, and I settle in an empty lawn chair with a warm cup of keg beer that tastes like shit. As I watch him talking with a group of people near the fire, something familiar takes root in my mind.

Wesley impressed everyone the first time he walked into the diner I worked at in Jackson. At six-foot-three, his blonde hair and broad shoulders were difficult to miss. My co-workers whispered and giggled like schoolgirls as they watched him, but I'd been uneasy when he sat in my section.

Was my gut warning me back then? If it was, I tuned the signal out when he looked up at me with those glacial eyes.

I became his the moment he decided I would be.

"I'm going to be back Thursday, and I'm gonna take you on a proper date." He'd told me that day when he paid his check.

He kept his word, coming back the following Thursday as promised. He took me on a date, a picnic and ice cream, and behaved like nothing less than a gentleman, ending the date with a peck on the cheek. An onlooker might've thought a boy had never kissed me before because of how giddy I was when he left.

After that day, no one could convince me Wesley wasn't my Prince Charming come to rescue me from my woeful small-town life.

For the next three months, my stomach fluttered every time his rig pulled into the parking lot because it'd only be a few minutes before he walked in with that schoolboy grin after a long week of nightly phone calls.

Wesley was everything I wished for after my mother died, and when I met him, I knew God heard my prayers and delivered him to me to ease the blow of taking her.

He was perfect, and he chose me.

When the company he worked for assigned him to a new route, I didn't hesitate to accept his proposal because I couldn't bear the thought of never seeing him again.

We eloped on a Wednesday morning and arrived in Seymour to start our new life by Friday night.

Three years ago, I sat in this same spot and wondered what would happen if he woke up one day and decided he didn't love me anymore. As a newlywed, I shouldn't have been thinking about that, but it happened to my parents—life was great until one day, it wasn't.

All because someone changed their mind.

I was so worried about him changing his mind that it never occurred to me that I might change mine.

Now, I do my best to avoid thinking about the early days because they are cruel reminders of what we've become.

"Penny for your thoughts?" Brad's voice startles me as his tall, slender frame comes into view wearing jeans and a button-up shirt with the sleeves rolled halfway up his forearms, surprising me by how much younger he looks when he's not in uniform. "Maybe a nickel because those are heavy thoughts." He lowers himself in the chair next to me.

"What are you doing out? I didn't think you ever had fun." I smile.

"Thought I'd stop by and say hello since I never get out and have fun. Don't remember the last time I saw you two out together." He eyes Wesley across the yard.

"It's been a while."

"When does he leave again?" He asks.

"Tomorrow morning."

"Want to come over when I get off tomorrow? I'll cook dinner."

I shift in the chair and stare out over the yard. "Can we raincheck it?"

Now that I've decided to exit stage left, I don't want to waste any more of his time.

"You know how to find me if you change your mind." He smiles.

Wesley sees us talking and leaves the group.

"Sheriff." He juts his arm out and shakes Brad's hand.

"Wesley." Brad nods, looking up at him. He's one of the few people Wesley doesn't intimidate, and it drives him insane that Brad's not afraid of him. Maybe he should be since Wesley's wider than he is smart. "How long are you home?"

"Long enough to remind everyone Katie has a husband."

"Mmm..." Brad nods, pressing his lips together. "Is this the part where you bang your fists against your chest and drag her off by the hair?"

Wesley narrows his eyes, and red splotches break out on his forehead.

"Nah, she knows who she belongs to, and I ain't worried about you, sheriff." He winks at me. "You two enjoy your conversation." He turns his back to us and waves to someone on the opposite side of the yard as he stalks off.

Wesley isn't jealous the way people think. He doesn't care if I have male friends because having control over every aspect of my life doesn't mean he'll exert it. He just needs to know he can if he chooses.

"I really don't like him," Brad says, eyeing Wesley.

"Have you ever?"

"No, I don't think I have." He cocks his head to the side like he's deep in thought. "Yeah, no, never."

"You know why he doesn't care that I hang out with you, right?"

"Not a clue."

"He thinks you're gay." I fight against a smile.

"Good. Let him keep thinking that." He winks.

I end up by myself under the big tree drinking shitty beer until my bladder becomes full. I scan the yard to let Wesley know I'm going to the bathroom, but don't see him.

Now that I think about it, I haven't seen him since Brad left an hour ago.

I ask a few people if they've seen him, but everyone says no. I even check the side of the house and the shadows for him.

Eventually, I navigate through the sea of people inside the house, and a drunk guy points to the back bedroom.

I push down the hallway and stop at the last door on the left, knocking on the hollow door of the guest room. When I twist the brass doorknob, someone from inside slams it in my face and engages the lock.

A few seconds later, the door swings open, and Wesley smiles.

"Hey, babe. I was just coming to get you."

A woman behind him stares at me with big green eyes lined with black eyeliner, matching her inky, straight hair. She shares an eerie resemblance with Mia.

"Come on in." Grabbing my hand, he pulls me inside the bedroom and locks the door.

"What's going on?" Focusing on him, I try to ignore the Mia clone.

He slouches in front of me and slips his arms around my waist. "This is my friend, Ashleigh, and she's in town for the night, so I thought the three of us could hang out."

He kisses the side of my neck, and I pull back. He hasn't touched me in months, and I've never heard of anyone named Ashleigh.

Holding my back flush against his chest, he waves her forward, palming her hip to bring her closer. As she enters our little bubble, he steps back, leaving us standing shoulder to shoulder. "You'll like it. I promise," he says from behind me.

"Wesley, I don't want to-"

The glare I know all too well falls like a curtain over his face as he lowers himself into a chair by the bed. "Get on the bed."

Ashleigh gives me a sympathetic smile as she takes my hand and climbs onto the bed. I look back at Wesley and follow her.

"We'll go slow, and I promise you'll enjoy it," she says as she drags her fingertips over my collarbone and down my arms.

I don't want this.

I don't want this.

I don't want this.

"Wesley, I don't want to do this." My voice hitches.

"Don't be nervous," she says and slips the straps of my sundress off my shoulders, looking at him like she's waiting for him to tell her to stop or keep going because what I say doesn't matter.

His large frame towers over us as he dips his knee onto the bed and slides his arms around my waist from behind, palming my breasts over the dress and squeezing them while he nuzzles under my ear.

"Don't you want to make me happy?"

"Yes, but-"

"Then don't overthink it." His hands roam over my body, keeping me in place as Ashleigh hooks her finger over the elastic band of my sundress between my breasts. "There's nothing wrong with having fun," he says, and she pulls the material down, exposing my bare breasts.

Instinctively, I raise my hands to cover myself, but Wesley pushes them back down, and I twist to look at him because I need him to see I'm not okay with this.

"Wesley, please. I don't want to do this."

"It'll be a lot worse if you don't." He tightens his grip on my wrists. "Yes or no. Decide."

A sob catches in my throat. "No."

He pushes me to the floor, and I scramble to the other side of the room, pulling my dress back up as I go.

"We could've had fun, but you're turning this into a thing like you always do." He shoves Ashleigh to her back on the bed. "Get back over here," he says.

I don't want this, but what I want has never mattered, and my feet are unsteady as I cross the room.

"Get behind her," he says.

"Wes-"

"Did I fucking stutter or are you just too stupid to understand what I said?"

I position myself against the headboard with my legs spread around Ashleigh, and she lays her head in my lap as she unzips her jeans.

This isn't happening.

Wesley yanks them off before pushing his down and exposing himself, locking his gaze with mine as he penetrates her.

I know better than to look away.

Moaning and whimpering, she grabs my arms above her head as my husband pounds into her, his movements growing more powerful until every thrust impacts me with the top of Ashleigh's head hitting my stomach.

My eyes remain locked with his as he makes me watch him fuck her. I blank out, my gaze falling flat as I leave my body and go somewhere safe.

I check the fishing line for movement and rake my fingers through the cool grass next to my leg as a dragonfly lands on the surface of the still water and flies away right before another one lands in the same spot.

A breeze shuffles the bluebonnets growing along the water's edge, and I think I have a nibble on my line, so I tilt my head to detect movement of the clear filament and wait for confirmation.

Nada.

Nothing.

Zilch.

Oh, well. At least it's quiet here.

Wesley's deep growl rips away my tranquility and propels me back into this hell that's only beginning.

INSIDE WESLEY'S TRUCK, I turn away from him, making myself as small as possible against the passenger door as I white-knuckle the handle.

"I'm sorry." My bottom lip trembles.

The truck stops at the four-way intersection in the middle of town, and Wesley's expression is blank as he looks ahead.

"You're sorry, huh?" He grips the steering wheel, twisting his hand around it.

The traffic light blinks yellow, and there aren't any other cars on the road, so he could've started driving if he wanted.

I stare ahead into the darkness because that's where Wesley likes to be. He can hide what he does to me in the shadows because I won't tell.

"Yes, I'm sor–"

I don't even see his hand leave the steering wheel before his clenched fist connects with the side of my head.

My head ricochets off the glass, bouncing back to center before the pain registers. Buzzing in my ear throws my balance off, and everything sounds like I've dunked my head underwater.

I don't know what comes over me, but I open the door and hurl myself out of the truck. I don't know where I'm going, but I don't want to go home with him.

I run, but my legs give out, and I collapse onto the asphalt, crawling on my hands and knees to get away even though we both know I won't. Maybe being able to say I tried will alleviate some of the guilt that'll follow when he's done.

I didn't just lay down and take it this time.

My head throbs as he yanks me up from the highway. "You wanted a fight, so that's what you'll get." He squeezes my jaw with one hand, shaking me. "You're lucky no one saw that shit." He looks back over his shoulder as he shoves me in the truck.

Once we're home, he's on me before the front door latches,

yanking me around the room by my hair and throwing me onto the couch.

"I'm sorry, I'm sorry, I'm sorry." I pull my knees to my chest.

"Don't ever embarrass me like that again!" He wrenches me to the floor by my ponytail. "You fucking understand?"

I prepare for the unavoidable and fold in on myself because fighting back makes it worse. The initial blow comes as a kick, but my legs prevent it from reaching my abdomen.

"Sometimes I wish I'd never met you." He drags me to the middle of the floor and flips me onto my stomach, pressing his knee against my lower back before wrapping his hands around my neck.

My hands aren't my own as they battle to pry his from my throat. My skin burns as I hook my fingers between his hand and my neck.

His grip is too strong, and my knees dig into the carpet, but I can't get away because he's too heavy. His calloused hands wrap around my neck with an ease that isn't fair.

I'm fighting to keep my life while he's taking it away with minimal effort.

The pressure in my head builds, and my peripheral vision transforms into a dark, narrowing tunnel as the song on the radio in the background fades away. I kick, or at least I think I do, but my legs are too heavy, and Merle Haggard sings underwater.

I'm going to die listening to Merle Haggard tell me this is the way love goes.

But, as usual, Wesley releases me and jumps back, leaving me coughing and gasping for air as he paces the room.

"Why do you do this?" He squeezes his head as he crosses the room. "Why do you make me do this to you? You push, and you push until I lose control!" He punches the wall, his fist leaving a hole in the wood paneling.

"You made me watch you fuck another woman. I fucking

hate you." I force the words out even though it feels like I'm swallowing gravel. My head pounds when I try to stand, and I catch myself on the corner of the couch, sliding back to the floor.

I don't know where this courage is coming from, but if he's going to kill me, I wish he'd just get it over with.

"Oh, *you* hate *me*?" He kicks me in the chest, and I fall on the floor, hitting my head on the edge of the coffee table as I go down. "You fucking hate *me*?"

He delivers repeated blows to my ribcage until I'm facing the couch, and that's when he starts in on my back. "You were nothing when I found you, and you'll be nothing when I'm done with you."

I make myself as small as possible.

It'll be over soon.

Begging him to stop doesn't work. He won't stop until he's done—when he thinks he's gone too far, but it's never far enough.

"Why do you make me do this?" He punches the wall over and over in rapid succession. "Why do you make me do this to you? Why do you make me like this?" He leans over me. "Why can't you be happy?" His salvia peppers my face as he rants. "Would it kill you to just be fucking happy for once?"

I attempt to crawl up on the couch, but a blow to my back stuns me, and I don't feel the second or third one.

He pulls me up from the floor, hauls me to the bedroom, and shoves me on the bed, pressing my face into the pillow as he pushes my dress up and rips my underwear off.

"Don't," I mutter into the pillow.

"I'm your fucking husband." He binds my wrists over my head with one hand and unbuckles his belt while climbing on me from behind. "I fucking own you, so you don't get to tell me no."

His hot breath turns my stomach as he grips the back of my head and tries to enter me, but he can't get hard.

I'm not sure how long he tries to penetrate me, but tears dry in the corners of my eyes as I stare at the wall. Finally, he stops, but not because he's done.

He flips me to my back and climbs over me, holding a pillow over my face. I thrash under him, kicking and pulling because I can't breathe.

I can't breathe.

Oh, God, I can't breathe.

It's finally happening.

I BOLT up on the bed and throw the pillow off, disappointed that I'm gasping for air.

Wesley's passed out next to me, his legs dangling over the edge with his pants around his ankles, and I'm naked from the waist down, semen all over my thigh and lower abdomen.

He's fucking useless.

Fighting back was instinct.

It doesn't mean I don't want to die. I just don't want that asshole to be the one to take my life when he's taken everything else from me.

I'm careful not to wake him as I ease to my feet. The floor dips, and there are two of everything.

A pounding in my head makes me want to throw up as I feel for the wall in the dark hallway, steadying myself until I reach the bathroom and turn the shower on, not bothering to take my dress off before stepping in. I want to scream as the hot water rolls over me, but I cover my mouth to deaden the sound of my misery.

A loud thud comes from the hallway, and the bathroom

door flies open, bouncing off the wall. Wesley yanks the shower curtain back, grabs my arm, and pulls me from the running shower.

"Get your shit and get out."

"Where am I supposed to go?" I ask, water dripping from the soaked sundress.

"Don't know and don't fucking care." He shoves me into the bedroom. "You've got five minutes."

"Wesley, please. It's two in the morning."

"Four minutes."

I'm crying so hard it's difficult to see as I pull on denim shorts, an old T-shirt, and scoop up my worn-out Converse.

Wesley's heavy footsteps come down the hallway, and he's so big he blocks the light when he stands in the door frame. He grabs me by the bicep and pulls me through the trailer until we reach the front door.

"Where am I supposed to go? I don't have money to get a room, and I can't call anyone." I sniffle.

This isn't the first time he's done this—thrown me out in the middle of the night and expected me to fend for myself until he decided it was time to come home.

"Actions have consequences. You didn't want to fulfill your duty as my wife, so why should I give a fuck about where you sleep tonight?" He pushes me out onto the cinder block steps and slams the door in my face.

My hair is still dripping wet, soaking my T-shirt as I sit on the blocks and put on my shoes, unsure of where I'll sleep tonight.

18

Wesley leans over the pool table, eyes the eight ball, and misses the shot. He spins around on his heels, punching the air as he circles the table for a better vantage point.

Elliot's up but preoccupied with his phone and doesn't notice Wesley take the extra shot. After the successful follow-up, Wesley lays the pool stick on the table, grabs his beer from a nearby table, and pumps quarters into the jukebox.

I sit at a table across the room because my side and back are killing me after sleeping in the back of Wesley's truck last night. I don't know why I provoked him because I knew better. What did I expect to happen? I deserved it after what I've done, and my guilt will manifest in color: Red. Purple. Yellow.

"Good book?" He leans too close.

I nod, closing the book and pushing it aside because he doesn't care what I'm reading.

He brushes my hair back over my shoulder. "Do you think you can switch to a different shampoo or soap, or whatever that smell is?"

"It's probably my shampoo. It was on clearance at the grocery store. It's lavender and va-"

"It doesn't smell bad, but it doesn't smell good, either." He kisses the back of my hand. "And you're way too pretty not to smell delicious."

"I'll pick something different up the next time I'm at the store."

There's a loud bang on the front door, and Elliot sprints across the room to open it. A few seconds later, Beau and Jake stroll in.

Jake's all smiles and laughter, but Beau doesn't crack the faintest facial expression. He hangs back, following on Jake's heels as they walk across the bar.

Beau has me twisted into one big, needy knot when he's near, but I don't get him. He can have any woman he wants, and he's chasing one who's as unavailable as it gets.

From my observations, he's an instant gratification kind of guy. No thinking about tomorrow. No thinking about consequences. For guys like Beau, the moment they're in is the only thing that matters.

I'm envious.

What would it feel like to live for today? Most of my days are spent in the past, reliving grief so I won't forget it. And if I'm not in the past, I'm daydreaming of a tomorrow that won't come because I plan to make sure it doesn't.

"This is Beau and Jake," Elliot says.

Jake presents his hand to Wesley. "Jake Garrison."

"Wesley Reese." He turns his attention to Beau and holds his hand out. "Katie's husband."

"Beau Brooks." He remains expressionless, not acknowledging me or shaking Wesley's hand.

"Why don't you grab everyone some fresh drinks?" Wesley says to me.

I fetch beers for them, but Beau declines his and asks for a glass of whiskey as he slides onto a stool at the bar.

After half an hour, all four men are sitting at the bar and I should be getting paid.

The mood seems light. Laughing. Joking. No one's being too serious. Occasionally, I catch Beau's eye, but it's subtle, and no one notices.

Wesley's demeanor shifts after a couple of hours, and gone is the easy-going guy having beers with friends. He's talking less, which means he's thinking more and getting in his head, his reality molding to his paranoia. It's taken years to recognize his pattern, and as scary as it is to witness, I'd pick this over the sudden outbursts I don't see coming because I can cut this off at the head sometimes. Redirect him. These aren't the bad ones.

It's the ones I don't see coming that knock me on my ass.

"Are you getting hungry?" I ask him. "Because I'm starving."

"Maybe after a couple more." He holds his beer bottle up. "Turn the television on. I want to check the score on the Rangers game."

"Who are they playing this week?" I stretch to turn on the television behind the bar.

"Houston." He slides his empty bottle across the bar. "You guys enjoying the show?" He asks the group.

"What show?" Elliot asks.

"That one." Wesley points to me as I hand him another beer. "One of you is looking at her ass every time I look up."

"Well, it *is* a nice ass," Jake says.

Wesley slams his beer bottle down on the bar. "The fuck did you just say?"

"Wesley, please." I step forward. "Don't. He's just joking." I grab his forearm and snatch the beer bottle up. "Let's just go home."

He yanks his arm away, and I fall backward with a loud crackle of glass breaking.

"Dammit! Are you okay?" He rushes around the bar and wraps his hand around my arm, pulling me up because my palm's bleeding from the broken bottle. "Let me see it."

"It's fine." I hold it close to my chest with my other hand.

"How bad is it?" Elliot leans over the bar.

"If there's a way to get hurt, you'll find it, won't you?" Wesley shakes his head, ripping a few paper towels from the dispenser.

"It's not that bad." My hands rattle the paper towels I take from him. "I think a piece of glass may be lodged in it."

"Let's clean it up." He sounds genuinely concerned, but he isn't.

Once in the small bathroom, he locks the door and pulls the first aid kit from the wall.

"I'm sorry," I say as I sit on the toilet lid.

"Sorry for what?" He digs through the kit. "How can you be sorry when you can't even tell me what you're sorry for?" He pulls out the small bottle of alcohol we keep in the cabinet.

I stare at the floor because I don't know what to say that won't make this worse.

He grabs my hand and pours alcohol on the gash. I try to jerk it back, but he tightens his grip.

"This..." He squeezes my palm. "Is your own fucking fault." Instead of using disposable tweezers, he uses his thumbs to milk the shard of glass from the cut.

I bite my bottom lip to suppress tears because the glass isn't coming out. He's moving it around and pushing it deeper. The blood goes from a trickle to gushing as he makes the wound worse and forces my hand over the sink.

"Don't make a fucking sound."

He pours the entire bottle over the wound, and my knees buckle as I grip the edge of the sink, biting my lip to transfer the pain somewhere else.

It hurts so fucking bad, and the burning sensation dulls into a thousand tiny needles pricking my skin. My pain tolerance has grown considerably thanks to him, but I'll never get used to the feeling of molten lava being poured under my skin.

"Clean yourself up, and let's go." Releasing me, he drops the empty bottle in the trash can.

He slams the bathroom door, and I hear mumbling outside but can't make out what's being said or who's saying it as I run cold water over my hand to flush the remaining alcohol out.

I sit on the toilet lid, grab a pair of disposable tweezers, and dig around in the wound for the piece of glass. It's hard to see what I'm doing through the tears, but it's not physical pain causing them. It's wondering what I did to deserve this.

There's a knock on the bathroom door a few minutes later, and Beau calls through the door, "Just checking on you."

I don't answer immediately because I don't want him to know I'm crying.

"You okay in there?"

"I'm fine." I choke out as I wrap my hand in several paper towels and open the bathroom door. "I'm okay. I can't get the piece of glass out, so it won't stop bleeding, which makes it look worse than it is." I smile, but the sentiment falls short.

"What am I going to do with you, Calamity?" He steps inside the small room and takes the tweezers from me. Holding my hand up, he tilts his head and studies the wound for a few seconds. "He's intense." I hold my breath as he brings the tweezers to the cut.

"He can be." I barely feel the tweezers as Beau fishes for the piece of glass.

His brow furrows as he focuses on his task. Not looking up, he says, "I don't like him."

"I don't either."

His eyes flick to mine, and a sleek smile comes into play. "I guess that's good for me, huh?" He holds the tweezers up. "Got it." He wipes the sliver of amber glass onto a paper towel and passes it to me. "Crazy, isn't it? Something so small causing so much pain?"

I nod and drop the paper towel in the trash.

"You sure you're okay?" He moistens a paper towel and cleans the blood from my hand.

"Would it be okay if I come to your room tomorrow night after work?" I ask as he dries the wound.

I've decided to do it after my birthday, so I'd like more time with him since that day is coming soon.

"If that's what you want." He places a bandage over my palm and looks up through his dark lashes. "Is it?"

I nod, holding my throbbing hand to my chest. "I should get back out there."

19

In the quiet solitude of the trailer, the world outside doesn't include me.

I can't shake the feeling of being an observer of my own life, watching as the oblivious and uncaring world leaves me behind.

I settle on the couch in front of the window, reaching over my head and tugging the pull cord to raise the blinds by a couple of inches because I want to watch the weather while I prepare for my death.

My birthday is Saturday, so I only have a few days to get things in order.

As I sift through a small cigar box of memories, I don't know what to do with them. No one wants my childhood photos or the handwritten notes my mom slid under my door as peace offerings when I gave her the silent treatment as a teenager.

There's one of Mom, Dad, and myself, and it's the only picture I've ever seen of us together.

The next is of my mom and dad before I burst onto the scene. They looked young and carefree because they were.

My least favorite is of me and mom right before she died because she looked so frail.

Last, the most important, is the one I cherish the most.

Mom's eighteen, and I don't know who's taking the photo, but she's dancing in a field of wildflowers with thick, wavy brown hair down to her hips and a pale pink dress on. Eyes closed, she's smiling with her head tilted to the blue sky, and the sun washes across her flawless skin, revealing how beautiful she is.

Life hadn't started beating her down yet. I tear up thinking about what was coming down the line for that unshackled spirit and how sad her life would become.

She deserved so much more than this world gave her.

I watched the rain fall on my mother's fresh grave as the heavens wept over her passing. The smell of damp earth and fresh flowers stood out as the wind whipped through the graveyard, carrying the familiar scent of her perfume, a reminder of her absence and an unspoken testament to a bond that was ours, leaving me struggling to comprehend why no tears would come.

I don't know why I couldn't cry. I wanted to. She was the only person who loved me, and I couldn't shed a single tear.

She'd be so disappointed if she were here to see my life now.

I tuck the other photos back in the box and keep the picture of my mom, slipping it inside my messenger bag.

A truck door slams outside, and the chihuahua next door loses his mind, barking until he chokes. Poor little asshole wants so badly to be intimidating.

Elliot stalks up the cinder blocks to my front door, and I greet him before he can knock.

"What are you doing here?" I ask as I open the door.

He remains outside, which isn't like him because he usually makes himself at home, going straight for the refrigerator.

"There's money missing, and Jeff's hellbent on finding out where it went." The urgency in his voice is as desperate as he appears.

"You two are the only ones with access to the safe."

"If you borrowed money, just tell me, and I'll tell him there was a misunderstanding. We can fix it before it spirals into something bigger because I know it's been tight for you guys lately."

"I'd never steal from you."

"No one's suggesting you stole." He runs his hand through his hair. "Maybe you borrowed it without us knowing."

"I'm not a thief, Elliot."

"Let's go talk to Jeff and clear this up together."

"There's nothing to clear up because I didn't do anything."

He takes a few steps toward his truck and waits for me to follow. He's not asking me to come with him.

WHEN WE ARRIVE at the bar, Elliot lingers inside the truck after he's killed the engine while I peer out the window, struggling to control my emotions. Brad's patrol car is next to the front door.

Did Jeff call him before even talking to me?

"Just tell the truth," Elliot says and exits the truck.

The building's quiet, except for the ice machine kicking on as I walk by the bar. Whispering voices come from Jeff's office, and I glance back at Elliot. He urges me forward with a sharp nod.

Jeff's office is dark, and the overhead light comes on, blinding me. As my eyes adjust to the brightness, there's a collective 'Happy Birthday' shouted, and Allison rushes me, flinging her arms around my neck.

"Happy birthday, Katie!"

I scan the room over her shoulder. "What's going on?"

Beau and Jake stand against the wall with smiles, and Brad stands near the window. Jeff reclines in his desk chair, and I whirl around to Elliot sporting a mile-wide smile as he drags me into a hug.

"Surprise," he laughs.

"We wanted to do something for your birthday, and we thought a small, no-fuss party would be perfect. It's a few days early because I won't be here Saturday." Allison beams, her excitement contagious. "I know you don't like making a big deal about it, so we got creative." She smiles at Elliot.

"You ass." I smack Elliot's shoulder. "How could you do that to me?"

He rubs his arm, feigning injury. "It was Jeff's idea. He said that'd be the only way to get you here without making you suspicious."

I narrow my eyes on Jeff. "So, you're the ass, huh?"

His laugh is hearty and from a deep, healthy place in his belly. "Happy birthday, kid."

I surrender a massive sigh and push my hair away from my face. "You guys all suck, but thank you."

Jake gives me a lazy side hug. "Don't be mad at me. I only went along because they told me to. Happy birthday, love."

"Thanks, but I'm not showing you any mercy on the next game of pool."

Beau crosses the room and gives me the same lazy hug, winking as he pulls his arm away. "Happy birthday, barkeep."

I'm the only one who notices his fingers graze my lower back and linger longer than they should. The not-so-innocent touch creates an instant throbbing between my legs as my body remembers what those fingers feel like inside it. He smiles as he raises his beer to his lips, pleased by his influence on me.

"Happy birthday, Katie." Brad throws a nod of his head but doesn't move from the spot he's in.

"Were you in on it, too?" I ask Brad.

"Only for about three hours." He smiles. "I didn't know anything until I ran into Elliot at the gas station."

"So, Jeff," I call from across the room. "Do I get my birthday off?"

"No," he says. "But you can have today and tomorrow off if you pull a double on Saturday and come stock on Sunday."

"Sorry." Elliot shrugs. "I tried, but he told me no, too."

"Saturdays have been pretty lucrative, so you've got yourself a deal," I say.

What I expected to be a horrible situation turned into something less grim. My birthday isn't a day to be celebrated, but it's better than what I thought would happen.

Allison slides onto a stool beside me and presents a cold beer. "Please don't be mad at anyone else because it was my idea."

"I'm not upset." My eyes water, and my throat tightens. "It's just unexpected." No one has done anything like this for me since my mom was alive.

She was the last person to make a fuss over it. Even though she was bedridden, she talked a group of neighborhood kids into blowing up dozens of balloons and hanging them all over our apartment. The chick living downstairs picked up the cake for her in exchange for some of her painkillers.

That night, when I got home from my shift at the diner, she'd fallen asleep, so I went to bed because I didn't want to celebrate without her. She was still sleeping when I woke up mid-morning, and I never celebrated that birthday or one since.

I'm overcome with emotion when I think about how mad everyone in this room will be at me this time next week.

They won't understand why I do it, and I hope they never will. They'll wonder if they could've said or done something that might've changed my mind, but nothing will stop me. I don't like the idea of leaving them with the guilt, so maybe I'll leave a note telling them why it has to be this way. They're going to say, *'Why didn't she just leave him?'* or *'She could've come to me'.*

This isn't my first choice.

It's my last resort and the only way I'll ever have control of my life again, no matter how short the time will be.

"Oh, don't do that. If you cry, I'll cry, and I'm wearing shitty mascara, so it'll run everywhere. Don't do that to me." Putting her arms around my neck, she squeezes me as she rocks from side to side. "Ugh, I love you so freaking much," she says through gritted teeth like she's fighting the urge to squeeze me to death.

She tunes into Beau laughing with Jake at the pool table. "Are you guys still?"

"As far as I know."

"Is the sex amazing? I mean, it must be to risk getting caught, right?"

"We aren't in high school. I'm not divulging that."

"There's nothing wrong with sharing the deets with your bestie." She walks backward away from me with a smug smile, luring Elliot to the middle of the room and hanging her arms over his shoulders as they dance.

Beau chats with Jeff and Brad in the corner, his gaze locking with mine for a fleeting second before redirecting his attention back to the conversation.

I'd give anything to dance with him like I did at Elliot's party. The way he held me. His scent. The way he kept my hand to his chest so I could feel his heart beating.

I feel the most guilt when I look at him because he lost his mom the same way. I don't know the details because he won't talk about her. Regardless, it's strange that he doesn't try to talk me out of it. He knows what I'm planning and seems along for the ride, no matter how short it is.

"Want to get out there?" Jake startles me.

I blink several times as if the action will banish thoughts of Beau from my mind. "I, um, sure."

He leads me to the dancefloor and rests his hands on my hips while I lay mine on his shoulders. I haven't felt this rigid since my junior prom when I danced with James Holden and let him feel me up later that night under the bleachers. We both denied it afterward and still do to this day, but I'm unsure why. He was popular, and I wasn't exactly unpopular.

"Will that husband of yours come after me for dancing with you?" Jake asks.

"No, he's out of town for a couple of weeks."

"He's gone a lot, huh?"

"Yeah, during the week, but he picks up extra routes, so sometimes he's only home every other weekend to two."

"I see." He nods. "Guess that gives you and Beau plenty of time to sneak around when no one's watching." His statement throws me off balance, but his grip tightens, and I recover instead of falling. "Relax, love. I won't out you guys."

"When did he tell you?"

"He didn't." He spins me around and pulls me back into our rigid stance. "You just did." He winks. "I had a feeling something was going on between you two."

"How?" I rack my brain to find a moment that stands out. Were we careless at some point? I can't believe we were so thoughtless. First Brad, and now Jake.

"There wasn't any one thing," he says. "It was a lot of little stuff and how I know him better than he knows himself."

"Oh..." Beau's deep in conversation with Jeff and doesn't notice me looking at him. "Are you mad at him?"

"Why would I be?"

"Because I'm married."

"There are plenty of people pissed at him because of how he lives his life, but I'm not one of them. I trust he knows what he's doing, and if he doesn't, I'll back him up when it's time to get his ass kicked for whatever dumb shit he's done."

"I don't want him to get hurt because of me."

"He will, though, because you're fire, love." He glances at Beau. "And he can't play in the fire without getting burned."

The song ends, and he bows in front of me before joining Elliot and Allison as a third wheel for a few humorous moments.

I go straight to the bar, twist the cap from a new beer, and turn it up. My head swims with panic because I don't want to be fire, and I don't want to hurt Beau.

Beau approaches from my left with a cocky grin. "Having fun?"

"I was."

He leans his hip into the bar and raises the beer bottle to his lips, pausing before taking a drink. "But you aren't now?"

"Jake knows." I watch for his reaction, but there isn't one.

"Took him longer than I thought it would to figure it out. Guess he's off his game."

"He said he knows you better than you know yourself."

"That's true."

"He also said you'll get hurt because of me."

"That," He turns his back to the room and pulls an ashtray across the bar. "He's not right about."

I keep my attention on the room. Allison sits in Elliot's lap at a table near the stage while the men stand in the office doorway, laughing at something someone said.

"You admitted he knows you better than you know yourself."

He lights a cigarette and turns back around, supporting himself against the bar with his elbows. The cigarette dangles between his lips, but a smile still takes shape. "I fuck myself more than anyone else ever could, so if I get hurt, chances are it'll be my own fault. But there's no reason to think about something that won't happen."

"You can't play in the fire without getting burned," I repeat Jake's ominous statement.

"The fire makes us feel alive, though."

"What does getting burned do?" I ask.

"Hurts like hell and leaves a scar."

"Then why risk getting burned?"

"Because you got to dance in the flames." His lips spread into a cunning smile. "For every push, there's a pull. For every up, there's a down. For every pleasure, there's pain. Everything comes at a cost because nothing's free, so you've got to decide what's worth the price you'll have to pay."

"How do you know what's worth it?"

He stands up straight and downs the remaining beer he's nursed during our conversation, sliding the empty bottle along the bar behind me so his fingers can graze my shoulder blades as he retracts his arm.

"I don't know. You tell me. Is it worth it?"

Elliot approaches and grabs a couple more beers. "Are you guys good over here?"

"Yeah, Katie has a headache." Beau takes my beer and places it next to his empty bottle. "You should take some aspirin before it gets worse."

"There's some in the first aid kit in the back," Elliot calls back as he meets Allison in the middle of the dance floor.

"I don't have a headache," I say.

"Yeah, you do," he says as he walks toward the saloon doors leading to the back of the bar.

I don't know what's going on, but it's apparent I'm supposed to go to the back. Do they have another surprise planned requiring me to leave the main room? I follow him to the employee restroom, where the first aid kit hangs on the wall, and pause before entering the small space.

"What's going on?"

"It's in here, isn't it?" He points inside the small room like he hasn't used the first aid kit on me in this very room twice before.

"Yes, but I don't need it." Folding my arms over my chest, I stretch to look over the saloon doors. No one even noticed we left. "You can drop the act now."

"Fine," he says, pulling me inside the restroom.

Pressing me against the cool wall and crushing his lips over mine, he distracts me from the pain caused by the pressure on the bruises on my back.

The act is lustful, and need radiates off him in a way I didn't know possible. Splaying his palms flat on the wall next to my head, he backs away every time I try to touch him, but the kiss remains deep and shows no sign of ending.

But stopping is precisely what we must do, so I push against his chest until he raises his head.

"We can't do this here." Panting, my breathing ragged and broken. "It's too risky."

"You're right." He steps back.

I glance at myself in the mirror to establish I'm not disheveled—only flush, swollen lips and rosy cheeks—and he coils his arms around me from behind, resting his chin on my shoulder.

"I have a surprise for you, but I've got to get you out of town tonight to give it to you." He eyes me through the reflection. "Tell everyone you have a headache, and I'll offer to drive you home."

"How far out of town are we talking?"

"Forty-five minutes, tops."

"Won't it be suspicious when you don't return?"

"Not if I casually mention I'm on my way out of town after I drop you off."

"I don't know."

"What don't you know?" He asks.

"Maybe this isn't the best time."

"Can we compromise? I don't remember if that's in your rules or not."

I pinch his arm, and he winces. "What are you suggesting?"

"If you hate my surprise, I'll bring you straight back, no questions asked. You say leave, and we leave."

"You're wasting your time and gas because I'm going to hate it. That's what I do. I hate stuff, especially when someone puts a lot of thought or effort into it. Just hate it." I bunch my nose up like I've smelled something rotten.

"Why don't you go hate having that headache so we can get out of here?" He slaps my ass.

I stick my tongue out, and he copies me, sticking his back out at me.

He leaves the small bathroom, and I check myself to ensure I don't appear guilty of something I shouldn't have been doing.

I hate a lot of things about my life, but Beau Brooks isn't one of them.

20

Moonlight pierces the dense canopy of trees as Beau maneuvers his truck with familiar ease down a path less traveled where eager tree branches and brush claw at the truck's sides.

Dim dashboard lights illuminate Beau's face as he focuses on the path ahead, and a cool breeze sneaks in through the open window, bringing an earthy scent of pine and damp moss.

Forty minutes on the road felt like a lifetime, yet it was only when we veered down this narrow dirt pathway I felt a twinge of excitement as the headlights sliced through the darkness.

A sudden turn reveals a serene lake within a grassy clearing, its tranquil surface reflecting the stars overhead.

"What is this place?" I stretch my neck to take it all in.

"Friend of mine owns the land, and it's ours for the night."

"Are you serious?"

"As a heart attack. Since we can't celebrate your birthday on Saturday, I thought this would be the next best thing."

My anxiety dissolves as he silences the engine, leaving an undercurrent of intrigue in its wake.

Trees creak and sway as a mild breeze nudges them. The

lake reflects silver moonlight, and dragonflies skim the water while frogs croak in the distance.

Beau leads me by the hand to a sandy area near the water's edge where a tent is set up and preparations for a small fire.

"Did you do all this?" I ask.

He releases my hand and lights the bundle of firewood. "I drove up earlier to get it ready." Standing, he dusts his hands over his jeans. "What do you think?"

"It's like a dream." I throw my arms around his neck and kiss his cheek. "But how did you know my birthday was coming up?"

"Elliot and Allison were talking about it yesterday, and I may have been eavesdropping when they were planning their surprise party." He smiles.

"What would you have done if I refused to come with you?"

"Had the perfect spot to lick my wounds and nurse my pride back to health." Squeezing my hips, he steers me to the tent. "Check out the inside. One-star amenities, but the staff is exceptional."

Blankets and pillows fill the interior, and strands of tiny, battery-powered amber lights hang suspended across the top to create a soft glow.

"Beau," I gasp, spinning around to find him holding a plastic supermarket bag.

"It's not a birthday cake, but it works better out here than a cake."

I open the bag and smile—graham crackers, chocolate bars, and marshmallows. "You thought of everything, didn't you?"

"I just tried not to forget the important stuff." He winks.

We settle in chairs around the fire, make s'mores while drinking beer, and listen to music streaming from his phone while sharing stories and laughing.

It's difficult to wrap my head around the fact that we have separate lives to return to tomorrow.

I can't name the song playing when we dance by the lake, but I'll never forget it. The surrounding trees rustle, but I can't pinpoint which direction the breeze blows from as I lay my ear against his chest to memorize the rhythm of his heartbeat. Inhaling, I hope I don't forget his scent after a lifetime of not taking it in passes in a few days.

"Why are you doing all this?" I'm not prepared to see his face if he lies to me, so I don't look up. "What's in it for you?"

"Fate led me to you." He drags his palm up and down my spine. "Fate wanted me to find you because it knew I needed you before I did. And as far as what's in it for me? That's easy." Releasing my hand under his beard, he positions his index finger under my chin, forcing my gaze up. "A connection."

"A connection?"

"You're not the only one who's lost." He lays his cheek against my temple. "You've turned into a bright light keeping me from being swallowed by the darkness."

"How can I guide you out of the darkness when I live there, too?"

"All I know is I feel better when you're around and worse when you're not." He lifts his head and smiles. "It's not complicated."

When he kisses me, it's different from the nights we steal away together in his motel room. His lips are soft, and the kiss is intricate like he's planning each movement. His tongue grazes mine every time it slips between my lips, slowing down the precious time we have tonight.

Inside the tent, pillows and blankets are arranged under the delicate amber radiance of the tiny lights. Cozy and inviting, it doesn't scream seedy adulterous affair.

I sit on my knees with my feet tucked beneath me while he powers his cell off and tosses it in the corner with his hat.

"No need for that. Unless you want to listen to some music? I can put something on."

"No, I like the sound of nothing out here."

He positions himself in front of me on his knees and rests his palms on his thighs. His dark hair is pulled into a low pony-tail, and without the hat and sunglasses he hides behind, I can study his brown eyes.

They're kind eyes but haunted by things he's never talked about.

He points to the top of the tent. "We'll have to close it if it rains."

A mesh screen provides a view of the night sky over us. Stars gather around the full moon above us, and when I look at Beau, he's staring at me.

"What?" I ask.

"Just admiring how beautiful you are."

"We've been over this." I tuck my hair behind my ears. "You don't have to do that."

"Do what? Compliment you?" He laughs and tickles me.

His fingers dig into one of the more tender bruises, and I shriek.

Startled, he jumps back as I wrap my arms around myself, tears rolling down my cheeks thanks to the sharp pain in my side.

"Fuck." Palming the back of my head, he pulls it to his chest and caresses it. "I'm so fucking sorry. I didn't realize I grabbed you so hard. Fuck, I'm sorry."

This is it.

This is when my real life spills into the ethereal world I've created with Beau and stains it.

Things won't be the same after this, but I can't let him think he hurt me. I can't allow my wounds to bleed onto him. Humili-ating or not, I'm not letting him carry an ounce of guilt that belongs to Wesley.

I push away from him, and the confusion on his face leaves

my heart in pieces. Blowing out a heavy breath, I fan my face with my hands to dry my cheeks. "I'm sorry."

"No, no, no." He reaches for my hand, but I keep it out of his reach. "It was my fault."

There won't be any more hiding behind smiles and witty banter once he sees me as the damaged creature I am.

Maybe Jake has it wrong. Maybe Beau's fire, and I'm the one who'll be left scarred because I'll never forget the look on his face.

"I told you I was devastated long before I met you," I say, forcing the lump in my throat back down.

The sooner he sees the truth, the sooner he can take me home, and we can move on like this—like we—never happened.

I turn my back to him and grip the hem of my tank top, lifting it over my head. He's never questioned why I don't take my shirt off during sex. *Breath. Inhale. Exhale. Repeat.* I've never shown anyone. I take a deep breath and unlatch my bra, releasing it to the bedding surrounding us.

My impulse is to cover myself, to hide, but I don't. Everything I've worked so hard to conceal is on display. *Inhale. Exhale. Repeat.* Beau knows Wesley hits me, but he's not aware of the extent of the abuse because I've never let him see it before tonight.

When I look over my shoulder, he's staring at my back with his lips pressed together and brow furrowed. "When?"

"Afer Elliot's party Sunday night."

"Is it always this bad?"

"It's been worse, but it's not always this bad."

"Is that why you never take your shirt off?"

I nod.

"I need a minute." He leaves the tent, and I choke back tears.

This is why I insisted on rules, why we weren't supposed to

spend nights together at lakes. No matter how faint, a connection is there now, and he feels obligated to be the good guy.

Luckily for him, I don't expect good guys in my story.

I get dressed and fold the blankets because the quicker I get everything packed up, the faster we can enjoy an awkward drive back to Seymour.

By the time I've stacked the pillows and blankets by the tent opening, Beau still hasn't returned. I draw my knees to my chest and tilt my head back to view the stars overhead, wishing on the brightest one even though this wish won't work.

I should've made up an excuse not to be alone with him until my back was healed. I knew better, but I haven't been making the best decisions—especially when Beau's involved.

I just want to go home.

I find him sitting on the tailgate of his truck, and he turns when he hears me approaching, his eyes landing on the bedding under my arm.

"What are you doing?"

"Packing up so we can get going." I shift them from one side to the other. "Do you want me to put them in the cab or the back?"

"Do you want me to take you back?"

"I assume you're going to."

"Why?" Sliding off the tailgate, he walks toward me. "You think I'm done with you?" Taking the blankets from me, he tucks them under his arm. "Can I share a secret since you shared one with me?"

"Of course."

"I don't regret this affair, so don't think that, but I've been feeling guilty because it'd kill me if you were my wife and doing this behind my back. But now, I'm glad I'm fucking his wife, and if sleeping with me helps you get back at him for doing that, I'll keep doing my part to help."

"At first, that's what it was about, but not anymore. I don't think about him when I'm with you."

"We should talk about this, but let's not give him tonight. Okay?"

Tears prick my eyes, and I nod.

We spread the blankets back out in the tent and zip ourselves inside. He's quiet, but so am I. Perhaps we don't know what to say, or we've said everything we needed to.

We sit across from each other again, but this time he practices caution like I'm a wild animal, and maybe that's how he regards me now—a mistreated creature with crippling anxiety.

Cradling my face with both hands, he sweeps his lips over mine. Without deepening the kiss, he raises his head and kisses the tip of my nose.

"Don't get in your head, okay? I want to be here...with you... right now. And if you haven't figured it out by now, I don't do anything I don't want to do."

"You're a good guy, so of course you'll say that." I offer a weak smile.

"I'm not the good guy you think I am, but I'd never do the things he does. I may break your heart, but I'll never break your body or spirit."

"Why do you assume you'll break my heart?" I wrap my hands around his wrists and pull them to my lap.

"I break everyone's heart eventually. It's inevitable." He pulls my shirt above my head; his movements are slow and controlled as he reaches around me and unclasps my bra, throwing it and the shirt behind him. He kisses me and leans back. "Lay on your stomach."

"Beau, I don't-"

"Please."

I lay face down on the blanket, and he moves on top of my legs, straddling me below my ass. I cringe when he kisses my back, planting my hands on the blanket and attempting to push myself up. "Please, don't."

"Shhh." He kisses me between my shoulder blades. "I'll stop if it hurts."

"It doesn't hurt, it's...embarrassing." I lay my cheek against the blanket.

He spends a few minutes kissing my bruised back, and without a word, he convinces me I don't have to hide them from him anymore.

He stands and strips out of his clothes while I flip to my back to watch him. He lays down beside me on the blankets and props himself up on his elbow, dragging his fingers from the hollow of my throat down between my breasts and circles my belly button, settling on the scar next to it.

"That's for the conversation we're having later." I push my fingers through his hair at his temple.

"Fair enough." He flicks one of my nipples with his tongue and latches onto the plump flesh, sucking and twirling the rosy peak. His skillful tongue manipulates the swollen bud while he massages my other breast, squeezing and molding it to the shape of his hand.

There's a throbbing between my legs. Pulsating. Hot. Achy. Shifting to relieve the building pressure backfires when the action enhances the desire to bear down.

My swelling breasts press against his bare chest as he leans over me, and my nipples harden when they come into contact with his warm skin. I can't catch my breath as he nudges his way between my legs. Despite his erection pressing against me, the kiss remains mellow and mindful. The tense muscles in his shoulders make me wonder if he's restraining himself because he thinks he needs to be careful with me now.

Lifting my hips to reach his, I rub my pussy against his straining cock through the jeans I still have on because I've never needed to connect with anyone like this before. But as the need to connect with him teeters on the verge of intolerable, he rolls off me.

"Can I give you a lovely nothing for your birthday that you won't protest?" He asks.

"If you insist."

His hand travels down my stomach and between my thighs. "You're the most beautiful," he rubs the denim over my pussy, "woman I've ever known." He unsnaps my jeans. "On the outside," he pushes his hand inside my panties and cups my pussy, "and the inside." He plunges a finger inside me, only to withdraw it and force my body to pine for his touch again.

My heart throbs as he sits up and tugs my remaining clothes off, leaving me raw and exposed in every sense. He glides his hand between my legs, and my knee falls to the side as he moves his fingers through my soaked slit, plunging two inside me.

"You've blown my fantasy of you out of the water each step of the way," he says against my lips as he drives his fingers in and out of me. "My imagination hasn't held a candle to the reality of you."

I don't care if his words are true because they're lovely, even if they mean nothing.

"You're almost there." He pumps his hand faster.

My nerves jolt awake when I surrender to him and experience an intoxicating surge of pleasure as my body convulses, bearing down on his fingers to ease the pulsating pressure.

He kisses my neck and mutters against the delicate skin under my ear, "See, the lovely nothings aren't for nothing."

"You used them against me." I pant.

"But did you enjoy them?"

"Yes."

The tension in my stomach returns, expanding with every trace of his soft lips. How's this possible? I experienced a mind-shattering orgasm, and my body craves to do it again. It's beyond wanting him inside me. I need to feel him there. I reach down and wrap my hand around his cock.

"Yeah?" He smiles.

"Yes."

"I'll give you anything you want, darlin'."

My legs fall open, and he positions himself between them, sitting back on his heels and ripping a condom foil.

I grab his hand. "I want to feel you."

"Are you sure?" His gaze is heavy, and the swollen head of his rigid cock presses against my entrance. "This is another line we can't uncross."

"None of the lines mattered after we crossed the first one."

I don't want to ruin the mood by mentioning I'm not concerned with consequences because I won't be here this time next week.

He presses forward, the head of his cock spreading me wider as he eases in and out, expanding and stretching my pussy with his thick shaft.

I can't help but appreciate how handsome he is as he inches deeper inside me. I can tell his jaw's clenched through his beard by the way he presses his lips together as he steadies over me, probably because he's afraid to hurt me while he takes his time sinking into me. Using slow, measured strokes to weave our bodies together, he withdraws and advances farther with each unhurried thrust.

"You always feel so fucking good," he says through gritted teeth as he pumps in and out of me, propelling me to the brink of my release once again. But this time, he doesn't pull me back from the threshold or pick up momentum. He doesn't penetrate me deeper or harder. Instead, he maintains his steady pace, unhurried and deliberate. Torturous.

He's not fucking me.

For the first time, he's making love to me.

My throat tightens as he moves over me, showing extreme

care with smooth movements as he slides in and out, his eyes give away what he's fighting to hold back.

He wants to fuck me, but he won't tonight.

My heart pounding in my ears muffles the sound of heavy breathing in the tent, and I clench my eyes shut. A lump takes shape in my throat as he pumps his hips against mine, driving his cock deeper with every stroke, and I hang onto his shoulders as I open my eyes.

The stars above are so picturesque I could be persuaded to believe they were placed there just for me to enjoy during this moment. They blur into little white streaks as tears overflow from my eyes with the realization they were.

I deserve to be part of this world, not a shadow watching everyone else experience it.

Death enters my body, and every emotion, good and bad, gets expelled all at once. The hate, the pain, the regret—my soul purges it all, and I tremble as the negative energy flows from my body and returns to the universe because it's not mine to carry anymore.

I've spent months planning my death and didn't expect it to happen like this.

Beau lifts his head, and the horrified expression on his face crushes me as he pulls back, creating space between us.

"Don't stop." I pull him back down. "I need this." I press my lips to his out of desperation, fearing he'll stop and leave me in purgatory. "Please, don't stop."

His eyes dart back and forth, no doubt searching for an explanation. I don't know if he finds what he's looking for, but he wipes the tears from the corners of my eyes and kisses my forehead as he begins moving his hips again—pushing and pulling, up and down, in and out.

Everything comes at a cost because nothing is free.

There's no sudden jolt of electricity coursing through my body this time. No spasms. A sensation spreads from my core like warm water through my veins. Almost like I've gotten the warmest, tightest, comforting hug from the inside out. Every thrust pushes the warmth farther out until it consumes me. My heart feels like it's going to burst from my chest as I cry out, gripping Beau's shoulders like he's the life jacket I need to survive this tidal wave.

While I'm working to make sense of the way I'm feeling, he lets out a primal groan that sounds like it's on the verge of pain, but I know it's not. Seconds afterward, his cock tightens, and he pumps his seed out over the course of a few heartbeats.

He stills over me and opens his sleepy eyes, his lungs driving out an exaggerated breath. "Katie, Katie, Katie."

Lying on top of me with his cheek pressed to my chest, his heart batters against the inside of his chest with such force I feel it on my stomach. We're both a sweaty mess, and the air is heavy and muggy.

Falling next to me onto his back, he braces himself on his elbow with an enormous smile and leans over me, splaying his hand over my lower stomach and tracing his fingertips over the scar below my navel.

"What really happened here?"

I'm relieved he's asking about the scar instead of me crying during sex...again.

"I was jumped by a gang of skunks about a year ago, and their smell made me pass out. I woke up with this and have no idea what they did to me."

He cocks his eyebrow up. "A gang of skunks?"

"Yeah, they're vicious little bastards." I nod. "And quick. I never saw it coming."

"Well, if you ever see them again, point them out, and I'll execute revenge on your behalf because no one hurts my girl and gets away with it."

Sirens go off in my head, and he must notice the flash of

panic in my eyes because he moves his hand from my stomach to the blanket between us.

"It just slipped out." He pulls me down next to him. "I know I shouldn't say stuff like that."

"The other night, you said you haven't hurt me yet, but that implies you will." Fingering the black hair on his chest, I wait for him to say he won't.

"I cause suffering to everyone I care about. The more I care, the worse it'll be for you." He drags his palm over my hip, but it feels different now. Shallow. Like he's going through the motions. "So, if that gang of skunks comes after you again, you're on your own."

He laughs.

I laugh.

But something big happened tonight.

21

I died last weekend at the lake.

Well, the part of me that idealized death as an escape died when I realized not wanting to live in this world anymore doesn't mean I want to die.

I want to eat ice cream until I make myself sick. I want to adopt a cat, maybe a dog—just not a chihuahua. Maybe I'll pass my GED exam and take some college classes.

I deserve to live a life that makes me happy. I deserve more than this world has given me, and I'm going to fight for it.

I want to do what my mother wasn't able to.

I'm hit by a heavy curtain of heat the moment we step out of the truck at the fairgrounds, and the scent of fried food sends my stomach into a riot.

Beau practically drags me across the parking lot, kicking his way through a carpet of discarded tickets and candy wrappers, oblivious to my hunger after springing the last-minute trip on me when I found out Wesley wasn't coming home for another week.

The sullen grey sky is ominous, but rain isn't in the forecast —not that the weather reports around here can be trusted because Texas weather is as unpredictable as Beau's sudden whims; it's all educated guesses and high hopes.

We play the ring toss game, eat funnel cakes, and guzzle lemonade while kids chase each other and couples walk hand-in-hand, clinging to won prizes and paper tickets.

It's difficult to wrap my head around how much living I've missed since getting sucked into trying to survive Wesley's world.

"I'm going to go find a bathroom." Beau kisses my cheek, startling me because we're in public.

As I step under a pavilion to wait, a man's voice comes from my left. "Excuse me, I think you dropped this."

He's holding my driver's license.

"Thank you." I tuck it back inside my small crossbody bag. It must've fallen out when I was looking for my lip gloss a few minutes ago.

"Travis." He holds his hand out. "And you're Katie, right?"

I step back.

"Your ID." He points to my bag. "That's how I knew your name."

"I'm sorry." *I'm such an idiot.*

"Hey, you can't be too careful these days."

Travis is a handsome guy, notably in his late twenties or early thirties, wearing a backward baseball hat that allows me to see his green eyes. Tall, slender, and dark scruffy hair with a beard cut close that doesn't conceal his jawline the way Beau's does.

A young girl shrieks as she chases another girl in front of us, and Travis winces, rubbing his ear.

"Good thing I've got two of these." A guy selling candy apples walks past us. "Want one?" He points to the passing vendor.

"Thank you, but no."

"You sure?" He arches an eyebrow. "I mean, it's a candy

apple from a sketchy-looking guy passing through town, so you know that'll be the most delicious thing you've ever put in your mouth." He licks his lips with a half-cocked smile, and I'd bet money he has more on his mind than a candy apple.

"Travis!" Beau says as he stalks toward the pavilion. "Hands off!"

"You know Brooks?" He asks.

I take a few steps to the left, away from Travis, and brace myself for Beau's approach. I'm cold despite the heat clinging to the night air. I wasn't doing anything wrong, but what if I stood too close to him? Or talked to him for too long?

"This is one motherfucker," Beau points to him as his feet falter to a stop in front of us, "you are not allowed to talk to."

"I'm sorry." I direct my gaze to the ground and clasp my clammy hands over my stomach.

"Jesus, Brooks," Travis says. "Nice to see you, too."

Beau positions himself next to me, his stance wide. "Is he bothering you?"

I shake my head, and even though I'm looking up, I don't make eye contact with anyone. I stare past everyone because it's the easiest way to get through this.

"We were having a pleasant conversation until you barged over here." He lights a cigarette and holds the pack out to me.

"I don't smoke," I say.

He passes them to Beau, who takes one and tosses the soft pack back to him. He dips his head and lights the cigarette. "I had to see if you were making a move on my girl."

"Well, I'll be damned. Cassie finally got knocked off her throne as the woman in your life?" Thick cigarette smoke billows from his nostrils, and the humidity suspends it in the air. "I guess hell finally froze over."

Sweat beads down the back of my neck, my ears are ringing, and my mouth is dry. This is what Wesley did. At first, he teased other men when they talked to me. Then, it wasn't funny anymore, and everyone stopped talking to me. If someone made the mistake of speaking to me when Wesley didn't think they should, it was my fault.

"You okay?" Beau asks me.

I nod. "I'm fine."

"You sure? You're pale." He settles his palm on my lower back, and I flinch.

"I'm going to walk around for a bit." I smooth my hands over the front of my sundress.

Stepping out from under the pavilion, I remind myself it's one foot after the other as I go left toward the Ferris wheel. *One foot after the other.* Gulping air, I blow out staggered breaths as I walk farther from Beau.

Will it always be this way?

The corn maze is past the carousel, and I purchase a ticket because I need to disappear for a little while. Thick corn stalks surround me, and straw crunches under my feet as I move deeper into the living puzzle.

As I turn at the first right, someone grabs my arm from behind, and I spin around with my hand raised in the air, ready to hit first and let someone else ask questions because I'm not sticking around. As my fist comes down with momentum I can't stop, Beau catches my wrist in mid-air.

"Easy there, killer."

Fear threads around my lungs and through my heart, the tugging making it hard to catch my breath. "How did you find me so fast?"

"I followed the sound of the straw because I know this maze like the back of my hand. I've gone through it every year since I was six." Releasing my wrist, he sweeps my hair off my shoulder, causing me to flinch again.

"I'm sorry I talked to him for too long. I didn't mean to upset you."

"Travis?"

I nod.

"I don't care that you talked to him." He reaches for my hand. "We've given each other shit every chance we've gotten since elementary school." He threads our fingers together and guides me deeper into the maze. "Is that why you left? Because you thought I was mad at him?"

"At me." A loud thunderclap rumbles overhead.

"Why would I be upset if someone flirts with you? And don't say he wasn't flirting because I know Travis." He bumps my shoulder with his arm.

Another loud crack jars the darkened sky. "Because he wouldn't have had the opportunity if I hadn't talked to him."

We veer left and immediately right again. I have no idea where we're going, but I trust Beau does.

"Katie, Katie, Katie." Singing my name, he positions my arm inside the bend of his elbow as we walk. "You're beautiful, and men flirt with you because they can't help themselves. I know I couldn't."

Turning again, the path gets narrower and he turns into me, pushing me into the wall of corn stalks—only it isn't a solid wall. It's a small nook, maybe three feet wide by five feet deep, hidden away in the thickest part of the passage. He must know this maze like the back of his hand because I would've never noticed it. With my back against the stalks, he stands so close I can't move.

"I'm not like him," he says.

Tears well up in my eyes. "I know."

"I don't think you do." He dries my cheeks with his fingertips. "If you did, you wouldn't have flinched when I touched you." Back-to-back thunderclaps overlap, and the smell of impending rain rides in on the western winds.

He takes his black cowboy hat off and plops it on my head. "Someday, you'll know."

Another someday.

He kisses the hollow of my throat as he slides his hand under my dress and up my outer thigh. "Someday, you'll know nothing he does to you is your fault." He moves his hand to the edge of my underwear. "Someday, you'll know it was never your fault." He leans his shoulder into mine, pushing my panties to the side and slipping his hand inside them. "You'll know it was never your fault." I close my eyes as he pushes his fingers inside me and uses the weight of his body to pin me in place. "It was never your fault."

A loud crack overhead releases a roar of summer rain over us as I hold onto his shoulders and get finger-banged. We're soaked in seconds, but he doesn't stop.

His mouth covers mine as his hand makes circles over my clit and creates the friction I need. The downpour lashes against my skin, stinging while the chaos of the frantic kisses make it easy to believe Beau.

Someday.

I grab his hand as my orgasm ripples through me, stilling him because every nerve in my body ignites, and his touch is too much. He lays his forehead against mine, rain still rushing down over us.

"You're wet."

"I've only been this wet with clothes on one other time in my life." I smile.

"Well, isn't that a fucking shame?" He drags his fingers across my lips so I can taste myself.

Unexpected and unstoppable.

If I had to describe Beau Brooks, those two words come to mind.

He guides me deeper into the maze, and it's raining so hard he's just a silhouette in front of me as I follow him through the twists and turns.

Lightning flashes on the heels of a thunderclap, illuminating several wooden benches in a small clearing as we turn a corner. He pulls me over to one and hauls me into his lap.

"One last ride before we go?" He pushes his hands under my sundress.

"What if someone finds us?"

"You really think anyone is coming in here right now?" He flicks his eyes toward the sky. "Besides me." He flashes a smile that makes me melt. "I hope."

"Do you think a person can be conditioned to believe they aren't worthy of being treated well?" I ask.

His features appear much softer in the moonlight. "I think if someone tells you something enough, you'll start to believe it as the truth. Doesn't mean it's true, though. It only means they're good at manipulating your thoughts."

"Do you ever feel like you'll never be good enough no matter what you do or how hard you try?" I ask.

Palming my hip, his eyes narrow. "My brothers are the sons every father wants because they've never strayed too far from the ranch, and their entire worlds revolve around it. They eat, live, and breathe keeping that place running. Then there's me. The one who doesn't want anything to do with it, and they can't understand why."

"Why don't you?"

"Because I can't break a horse like Jack or frame a house as fast as Jace, and no matter how much effort I put into something, my dad thinks I should give more. My all isn't enough, and I don't have more to give because I'm unwilling to sacrifice everything the way they do."

I smooth my fingertips across his cheek, and he turns into my palm, closing his eyes and inhaling a deep breath. His lips find my palm, and after a few delicate kisses, he lifts his head, our eyes meeting again.

"Why are you so easy to be with?" He asks.

"Because I don't expect anything from you."

"Or we were never strangers." He slides his palms up and down my thighs, his cock twitching to life against my pussy.

I lean over and capture his mouth with a quick kiss. "Or we were never strangers." I smile against lips I've grown fond of kissing.

He reaches down between us and frees his cock as I pull my panties to the side, adjusting myself over him so he can line himself up at my entrance.

I think he's going to go slow, but he thrusts up, impaling me with his entire length at once. Gasping, I fight the natural reflex to pull up off it because it hurts when he plunges deep inside me.

Leaving me panting with each advance, I fall forward, spreading my palms flat on his shoulders as I find my bearings and rock my hips without Beau's help.

"You okay?" He asks.

"Yeah, it's just intimidating sometimes."

"I thought we weren't exchanging your lovely nothings anymore." He cocks his eyebrow, the corner of his mouth turning up.

"They aren't for nothing. They make you smile."

He curls his hand around my nape, pulling me down and straining to meet me halfway for a kiss as we struggle to catch our breath. "*You* make me smile."

I ride him unapologetically, not thinking about my squishy hips, the softness of my lower belly, what my hair looks like, or that my breasts are more than his hands can hold. The way he makes me feel drowns out the negative voices telling me I'm not good enough. He looks at me like I'm the most beautiful woman he's ever seen, and sometimes I believe him.

"Slow down." His words come out ragged. "I'm close."

I force my inhibitions aside and press two fingers in his mouth. Groaning, he sucks them and watches me squeeze my breasts as I slide the slick fingers around my swollen clit.

"Fuck," he says and strains to sit up straight, only to fall back against the bench. "Yeah, just like that."

His enthusiasm arouses me, and I rub my clit faster while he guides my hips over his cock because I'm useless as I climb to the peak of my satisfaction.

He loses control before I reach my climax, his body tensing and convulsing as his cock pulsates inside me. He hangs his head back, his neck straining as he rides out his climax and goes lax beneath me.

Moments later, I come undone by my own hand, and my pussy clenches his cock as my orgasm ripples through it, pulsing and squeezing until I collapse against him.

"That's it. I'm keeping you." His breathing is uneven and heavy.

"Maybe I don't want to be kept."

"Oh, you'd want me to keep you, darlin'." He drags his palm up my spine.

"Full of yourself much?"

"Not at all, but if I keep you, you'll always be full of me."

The more time I spend with Beau, the more unbearable my time with Wesley becomes.

I'm free when I'm with Beau because he doesn't expect anything from me I'm not willing to give. I don't have to watch what I say or worry my tone may upset him.

He doesn't give me that 'Are you going to eat that?' look when I show up at his room with a pint of ice cream after a hot day. And dare I say it, but I think he finds my squishy hips attractive because he's constantly squeezing them when we have sex.

What we're doing is wrong, but when the guilt creeps in, I convince myself I'm not hurting anyone because Beau's passing through town and this heat wave will last longer than our affair.

My hair clings to my chest as he pushes the strands over my slick skin and behind my shoulders. Spreading his hands over my back, he pulls me closer and presses his lips between my breasts before releasing me back to my upright stance.

"This is nice, huh?"

"Sex with you is always amazing," I say.

"No, I mean it's nice not worrying about who we may run into and enjoying each other's company outside the motel room," he says.

"I've had a lot of fun, minus the freakout I'd like to never mention again."

"Life could be so different if you leave town with me."

"I can't."

He lifts my hand to his mouth and kisses my knuckles. "It's scary, but that's what he wants you to feel. Call his bluff. Leave with me."

"And do what? Follow your coattails? We barely know each other. Eventually, I'd like my life not to be a series of poor decisions followed by even worse ones."

He laughs, cupping my face in his hands. "You'd do whatever the fuck you want to do, darlin'. That's the point of getting away from him." He claims my mouth again, smoothing his tongue over mine and backing away. "It'd be awesome if you kept doing me, but if you don't want to, that's cool, too. Still be the best sex I've ever had."

"Shut up." I thump his shoulder. "I don't want to leave one man just to be under another one's thumb."

"If you're going to be under anything of mine, it won't be my thumb." He winks, and there's that smile again. "Katie, Katie, Katie."

The rain has lightened to a drizzle. "Beau, Beau, Beau."

"Tell me you'll at least give it some thought."

"I'll give it some thought."

And that's the first time I lie to him.

22

It's been a week since Beau asked me to leave town with him, and the question hangs between us like a restless ghost haunting every moment we're together.

He hasn't said anything about it, and I can't help but wonder if his silence is born from regret or if he's accepted my avoidance as an unspoken refusal.

There are so many people tonight Elliot slings drinks with me in the trenches. We start at opposite ends of the bar and work our way to the middle, doing it all over again after cheesy high-fives. A group of truck drivers keep to themselves by the pool tables, and a bunch of twenty-something guys haggle each other at the dart boards, along with a few women working the room.

A typical Saturday night.

The night, like most Saturday nights, goes by fast. The crowd clears out after the live music ends, but enough people remain to make the tips worthwhile.

Beau and Jake take up at a table near the back with a blonde and a redhead, and since Elliot and I are taking turns working the floor, it's my turn to go to their table.

The redhead has her hand on Jake's thigh under the table, and the blonde keeps hers on her lap. She shoots me a snarky smile and scoots her chair closer to Beau's when she notices me checking them out.

I slide the bottles to the guys and hold my tray against my hip.

"Can I get you ladies anything? We've got dollar drafts, and if you want something sweet, I've been told I give out the best blowjobs in town." I wink.

Beau chokes on his beer, coughing and banging his chest. "Fuck." He grumbles as he tries to catch his breath.

Jake smacks his back. "Forget how to swallow?"

He clears his throat several times. "Went down the wrong pipe."

"Do you know how many carbs are in the blow jobs?" The blonde asks.

"Not sure." I shift my weight from one leg to the other. "I think they're mostly protein."

Beau whispers in Jake's ear, and I have a good guess what it is when Jake drops his head on the table in a fit of laughter.

The blonde orders two blow jobs, and the redhead requests a draft. Elliot makes the delivery to their table on his way to take his break, and my attention drifts to Beau's table more than it should.

A guy from the dart board group slides onto a stool, crossing his arms over the bar.

"You know, I've been here for hours, and you've given me most of my drinks, but I don't know your name," he says.

"It's Katie. Bud Light drafts, right?"

"That's us."

"How many can I get you?" I grab a glass.

"None." He waves his hand to stop me from pouring. "We're ready to close our tab."

"No problem." I run his card and pass him the receipt to sign.

"Buybacks?"

"Sorry." I smile.

"It's all good." He points to the tip line. "How much should I leave?"

"That's up to you."

"The service is excellent." He leans forward. "And the bartender is hot as hell."

I point to Elliot sitting at Beau's table, laughing with the group. "Yeah," I nod. "Elliot's something else."

Jake walks past us to the back and rolls his eyes, so I assume he overheard the conversation, or at least the cheesy part.

"How about your number, and I'll leave a worthwhile tip?"

"My husband might have a problem with that, but all tips are worthwhile and appreciated."

"No ring." He points the pen at my left hand. "If you don't want to give me your number, what about some ass, and we won't pretend like I'll call you tomorrow. My truck's parked out back."

"Has that line ever worked?"

"We're going to find out, aren't we?" He winks. "What do you say?"

"I'll pass."

"C'mon, you've been teasing every cock in this bar all night in those shorts. Why not follow through?"

I lean over the counter. "How about you pay your tab, and we'll pretend you're not a misogynistic asshole?"

"You've been prancing around with your tits pushed up to your chin, and you act offended when you get the attention you want? Maybe you should blow me for that tip."

"Apologize, settle your tab, and leave." Jake's voice booms out of nowhere.

The guy spins around on the stool. "Excuse me?"

"I didn't stutter. Apologize, pay your tab, and get the fuck out." Jake steps closer to him. "Was that clear enough, or do I need to draw you a fucking diagram?"

"Who do you think you are?" The guy jumps to his feet and stands chest-to-chest with Jake.

Beau approaches. "Everything alright over here?"

"Tell him what you think she should do for her tip." Jake jerks his chin toward me. "Go on. Tell him."

Several men from the guy's group surround him, and his confidence grows.

"I told her to suck my dick." He squares his shoulders and puffs his chest out. "But if she won't, one of you pussies can do it for her."

Beau punches him in the mouth, sending him flying backward onto a table. Beau fists the guy's T-shirt and kneels on his chest, delivering repeated blows to his face while Jake throws punches against any of his friends trying to stop the fight.

The back of the guy's head bounces off the broken tabletop with every strike, and Elliot charges across the bar, slamming into Beau's side and knocking him off the poor guy.

The room falls silent, and everyone freezes, waiting to see if the fight will resume.

Beau stands, swiping his thumb over his bloodied lower lip. "Since you're down there." He unbuckles his belt.

Elliot yanks the guy to his feet and pushes him to the bar. "Settle your tab and be on your way."

"I'm not paying for shit." He spits on Elliot's chest. "You're lucky I don't press charges."

Elliot speaks through clenched teeth, "Pay your bill, or I'll break your fucking hand."

"Fuck you." He tries to push him back, but Elliot tightens his grip on his blood-stained shirt.

"Fuck *me*?" Elliot raises his eyebrows and steps back. "Yeah, sure. Fuck me."

Marching around the bar, he retrieves the hammer we use to tack license plates to the wall and rounds the corner of the bar with it at his side.

The guy doesn't notice Elliot approach from behind, but he stops moving when Elliot lays the hammer on the bar next to him. Elliot leans into the bar next to the guy and flicks his eyes to the hammer.

"I can't let you disrespect my bartender, damage my property, skip out on your tab, and insult me. Pick one. Right or left. Doesn't matter to me." He lifts the hammer.

"Okay, fine!" He can hardly hold the pen to sign his name because his hands are shaking so badly.

Elliot escorts him and his friends to the front door with notice they're banned from returning. He breezes back to the bar where Beau and Jake stand over the aftermath and puts his hands on his hips, laughing as he studies the busted table.

"Jeff's never leaving us home alone again if you two keep trashing the place."

"You can take the damages out of my pay," Beau says.

"Mine, too." Jake offers. "But it should be a seventy-thirty split because Brooks threw the first punch."

Beau slaps Jake's chest with the back of his hand and gives him a 'what the fuck' look.

"First of all, neither of you works here, and replacing it is just another tax write-off." Elliot waves his hand in the air and picks up pieces of wood.

The bar's empty when they finish hauling the busted table to the dumpster. After locking the front door, I pour four shots of whiskey, and we celebrate another Saturday night in the books, despite the hiccup at the end.

"Dude, I thought you were really going to crack that asshole's knuckles." Jake hoists himself onto the stage, his long legs dangling to the beat of the music from the jukebox.

"I was." Elliot turns the light off over the pool table.

"You were not." I melt into a chair because tonight kicked my ass.

"He thought I was, and that's what matters."

"Jeff will have a stroke if he finds out you did that," I say.

"Where do you think I learned that trick from?" Elliot laughs. "Don't let the grey hair and lack of amusement in his personality fool you. My brother was ruthless in his prime."

"You know, I believe you. It's in his eyes," Beau says.

"And you two." Elliot points his bottle in each of their directions. "What's with the fighting?"

Jake shrugs. "It's fun."

Beau nods. "It really is."

"What the fuck ever." Elliot pushes his chair back. "It's been a shit day, so I'm going home to get some sleep because Allison will be back from her parents in the morning." He crosses the room and grabs his phone from the bar. "See you guys later."

"Your eye's starting to swell," I say to Beau after Elliot's gone.

He touches the top of his cheek. "Guess it is, huh?"

"Awe." Jake pretends to pout, pointing to his eye, which is already changing colors. "We're going to have matching shiners."

I find a couple of Ziploc bags in the back, fill them with ice, and take them to the injured warriors, handing one to Jake first. "It'll keep the swelling down."

Beau looks up at me from the chair when I present his ice pack. "You're not going to ice it for me?" He winks as he slides his hand over my ass.

I glance back to Jake.

"Fucking do it already." Jake moans. "I don't give a shit."

Beau pulls me down on his lap and smiles against my lips. "He doesn't give a shit." I hold the ice pack on his cheek. "Do you think he would've done it?" He asks Jake.

"He was about to fuck that guy up." Jake holds his ice pack over his eye. "Zero doubt about it."

"No joke." Beau runs his palm up and down my back while I hold the ice pack on his eye.

"He'd never do anything that barbaric." I refuse to believe the Elliot I know could do something so brutal to someone over something so insignificant.

Jake announces his departure before Beau's money is up in the jukebox, saying he's walking back to the motel to get some fresh air, but I don't think that's why he wants to be alone. Okay, maybe not alone, just not around us.

I straddle Beau's lap and drape my arms over his shoulders. "We should be more discreet around Jake."

He runs his hands up and down the outside of my thighs. "Why? Did he say something?"

Yes, but I'm not telling you he thinks I'm taking you down in a fiery inferno.

"No, but I don't think he's okay with this."

"He doesn't give a shit about who or what I'm doing." He kisses me.

"He cares more than you realize, and he's worried you'll get wrapped up in my drama." I kiss him. "And I don't blame him because that's what a good friend should do."

"What drama?" He squeezes my hips and rocks them over his strained cock. "You alleviate the symptoms of an otherwise boring existence."

"Is that right?"

"Absofuckinglutely." He kisses the side of my neck. "But speaking of drama..." He clears his throat. "Have you given it any thought?"

"It's all I've thought about." I play with the bottom of his beard, a spark of guilt kindling in my chest that I'm not prepared to deal with yet.

I'll be honest with him, just not tonight.

We share an undeniable attraction, but we aren't star-crossed lovers. This is supposed to be a snippet of fun in an otherwise miserable life.

"You don't realize what you're asking me to do."

"Pretty sure I do."

"I'm not the girl you risk everything for, Beau. There are things about me you don't know because you haven't known me long enough to find them out."

"Like what?"

"Nothing I want to talk about tonight."

"Keep your secrets if you need to." He slants his mouth over mine and tastes like everything I've grown to love. Sweeping his tongue over mine, he nips my lower lip and raises his head.

"What would I have to say to get you to spend the night with me?"

I chew the inside of my cheek. "Wesley will be back in the morning."

"Then we should get you home."

"I can come to your room for a while." I push up from his lap. "I just can't fall asleep."

"Let's raincheck it." He keeps his hand on my lower back as we walk to the door. "You need to get some rest before he gets back, and I've got to go buy a new pack of smokes because I lost mine. Could've sworn I left them on the bar earlier." He pats the front pocket of his jeans.

"You lose more cigarettes than you smoke." Locking the door, I follow him to his truck parked on the side of the building.

"Maybe I'll quit one day."

"You should because they're not good for you." I climb inside his truck.

"Neither are you, darlin'." He winks.

23

Daylight bleeds into night, and Wesley's almost finished the eighteen-pack of beer he started the afternoon with.

He sits in the recliner across from the couch and texts someone, his lips pursed into a thin line like he's annoyed, so it's probably not Mia. He doesn't notice me watching him and realizing how different I see things now.

I used to wonder how women let themselves get into abusive relationships. I used to say I'd never stay with anyone who mistreated me. But I stayed because I didn't recognize the abuse until it was too late.

Like when Wesley wouldn't let me wear my favorite sundress because he didn't like how his friends looked at me when I wore it. Or when he insisted my name didn't need to be on the bank accounts because it was too much hassle. I could use his debit card because everyone here knew he was my husband. Or when he demanded we sell my car and use the cash for a down payment on something newer we never got.

It got harder to make excuses when he started dictating my daily life.

Eat this...better not eat that.

Wear this...I'd rather you not wear that.
Go here...I don't want you going there.
Don't talk to them...don't buy that.
I'd prefer you do it this way.

I thought he was looking out for me. He wanted me to be healthy and look my best. He didn't want me going to unfamiliar places, and he knew people here when I didn't.

When I discovered his infidelity, he convinced me I drove him to it because I wasn't in tune with his needs. I was too inexperienced.

So, I tried to fix us by fixing myself. I went on a crash diet and did everything my mom did for my dad, striving to be the perfect wife. I gave in to the things he wanted to do in the bedroom until he went too far. He promised to never do it again, but it came with a price. My inability to give him what he needed became his free ticket to be with other women because they could give him what I couldn't.

"I'm going to ask you something, and you need to be honest with me," Wesley says, staring at his phone. "Do you think I'm stupid?"

"Of course not." I cover myself with the blanket from the back of the couch. "Why would you ask that?"

Minutes pass before he speaks again, giving my stomach plenty of time to tangle into knots.

"Why have you been hanging out with that Brooks guy at the bar so much?"

My lips are so dry they crack when I speak, "I don't hang out with him. He's just there all the time."

"So," He looks up at me. "You *do* think I'm stupid."

"No, I don't."

A curtain of rage falls over his face, and his blue eyes become darker than I've ever seen them. He leaps out of the recliner and clenches my jaw in his big hand, leaning closer until the heat from his breath collides with mine as his lips curve into a cruel smirk.

"You think you can do anything in this town without me finding out?" He touches his nose to my lips and inhales my fear, staring at me with cold eyes. "I'm your whole fucking world."

I close my eyes, my chest deflating because everything comes at a cost, and nothing is free.

"That's what I fucking thought." He presses his index finger against the center of my forehead and pushes my head back against the couch. "You forgot every breath you take belongs to me." He walks down the hallway to the bathroom.

As soon as the bathroom door latches, I grab his phone from the recliner, and it's impossible to steady my hands as I struggle to figure out the four-digit code to unlock it. It's not his birthday or mine. I enter the pin assigned to his debit card and nothing.

"Who are you calling?" Wesley's voice booms from the hallway.

How did I not hear the bathroom door open? Those fucking hinges scream to the heavens any other time. I drop the phone on the chair, and he picks it up, tapping the screen before handing it to me.

"There you go. All unlocked."

I refuse to take it because this is a trap.

"Go ahead. Make your call." He thrusts the phone toward me.

"I don't want it."

"Take the fucking phone, Katie." Squeezing the nape of my neck, he slams the phone against my chest, holding it there until I take possession of it. "Make your fucking call."

"I don't want to call anyone."

"Sure you do." He tightens his grip around my neck. "Call Elliot and see how fast I get their liquor license revoked. Or maybe you want to call Brad since you two are so fucking close these days. I'll have his badge before he finishes the paperwork to take me in." He leans closer to my ear. "But remember one thing." He sniffs my hair. "No one will believe you. And if they do, I'll still be home before lunch and pissed about spending my morning explaining what a complete fucking idiot my wife is to my dad. You'll have to live with ruining their lives." He crosses his arms over his massive chest and waits for me to make the next move. "How do you think that'll go? You think people avoid you now? Call someone. I fucking dare you."

I place the phone on the arm of the chair and submit to him because I don't know what else to do.

He reaches into his back pocket and flashes a handful of plastic ties before yanking me up by the arm and shoving me down the hallway to the bedroom.

He pushes me to the floor and brings my wrist to the leg of the footboard. "I don't know what to do with you yet, but I've got other shit to take care of before I have to leave again." He secures my wrists to the bed.

"I'm sorry, Wesley." I cry as he cinches the plastic around my wrists. "Please don't leave me like this."

"You're always sorry, Katie." He pushes up from the floor with a heavy grunt. "Have you ever thought about not doing shit to be sorry for?"

Minutes.

Hours.

I'm not sure how long I've been locked in the bedroom.

It's nighttime, and sweat drenches the hair on my nape. The ties on my wrist are gone, and Wesley bangs around in the kitchen. My hand goes to my stomach, but there's no blood this time. No cramping. No praying.

The door is cracked open, so I crawl to the chest of drawers and grab the top, pulling myself to my feet. I inch the door open, and the hasp is flush on the wall again, the padlock keeping it flat. Stepping into the hallway, I can't see Wesley, but I hear him.

The dance.

I keep my back to the wall and slip into the bathroom. The relief when I sit on the toilet is indescribable. I don't think the stream of urine will ever stop, but it does, and I wash my hands, avoiding my reflection.

"You're finally awake." Wesley's voice makes me cringe, and I jump back against the bathroom wall. He stands in the door-way. "You hungry?"

I nod.

"Of course you are." He rolls his eyes. "I picked up a pizza." He leaves me in the small room by myself. "I've already eaten. Gotta hit the road," he says on his way to the kitchen.

My legs are unsteady as I follow him. He stands with his back against the counter and watches me as I fill a glass from the tap and chug it. Water dribbles down my chin, dripping onto my chest. After the second glass, I slow down because I don't want to make myself sick.

"Done?" He asks.

I nod, wiping my chin with the back of my hand.

"This was more for you than me." He pushes off the counter. "I don't like doing that, and the fact that I don't do it more often should prove it." He unplugs his phone from the charger on the bar. "I called Elliot and told him you're not coming in."

I keep my back to the sink because I don't want to take my eyes off him. I don't know why. It's not like I can stop him from doing whatever he wants to me.

"Can you wrap your little brain around how easy it'd be to make you disappear?" He zips and unzips various pockets on his duffle bag on the counter. "I could've left you in there, and no one would notice until you were a stench in the air because it only took one phone call to make sure no one misses you." He lugs the bag over his shoulder and returns to the kitchen, not stopping until he's inches from me. "No one will miss you, Katie. No one."

My gaze falls to the floor. This isn't the dance. We've reached another morbid milestone—the one where he doesn't pretend to be sorry anymore.

"So, since you made us go through this again...do you know your place?"

I nod.

"Where is it, Katie?"

"Where you tell me it is." My voice is barely audible, and dizziness sweeps over me. It's not from my injuries. It's him. Standing this close to him makes me ill.

"You don't work at the bar anymore. I told Elliot you quit. We'll get your last check in the mail because you're not allowed to go back there. People are talking, and I don't like what they're saying."

"Do you want me to find work somewhere else?"

"Your place is in this house from now on, and I'll provide whatever I think you need. Mom will take you to the grocery store every week. You shouldn't need to leave more than that, and if you do, I'll make the arrangements." He tilts my head back and forces me into eye contact. "And if I so much as hear you've waved at that motherfucker on the street, I won't be so nice the next time." He kisses my forehead. "I love you. Don't forget it." The screen door slaps against the frame as he leaves.

I drop to the floor and lean against the cabinet with my head in my hands, pleading and begging for mercy from anything, or anyone, bigger than me—even though I don't deserve it anymore, and I'm not sure I did before.

This is how he'll keep me here. Isolation from the rest of the world. No money and no way to make it. No transportation. No friends. I'm his prisoner, and I handed him the keys to lock me up every time I gave in to his demands. Every time I hid the bruises. Every time I believed him when he said it'd never happen again.

He used to say we were fated to be together forever, and now I think he's right.

24

I push the plate of pizza to the middle of the kitchen table and lower my head in my hands, inhaling a deep breath to center myself.

The last two days have been hell.

Beau and I are done. There's no question about it. Wesley suspects something's going on between us, and I've got to squelch the suspicion by cutting all ties with him because I don't want to put him in Wesley's sights anymore than he already is.

I move to the couch and slide down, pulling an afghan over my head. What would happen if I walked out the door and kept walking? Walked past the diner. The gas station. The bar. Just kept walking. How far would I get? Far enough? How far is far enough?

There's a bang on the door behind my head, and I don't move. Whoever it is shouldn't be here, and I don't want to see anyone because I need to wallow until I figure out how to dig myself out of this clusterfuck. But they bang again.

When I open the door, Beau's got his arm in the air like he's about to knock again.

"You can't be here," I say, stretching to see if anyone's around that may tell Wesley.

"Elliot said you quit the bar."

I move away from the door and lower myself onto the couch, fighting the pain running rampant in my body. "He doesn't want me around you anymore, so you shouldn't be here."

He crouches on the floor between my legs and snakes his arms around me. "Let's just go."

"Beau," I sigh, sweeping my hands through my hair. "I ca-"

"You don't have to love me or even like me all that much. Just let me take you away from here, and then you never have to see me again if you don't want to."

"He'll find me no matter where I go."

"I'll make sure he doesn't." There's so much hope in his eyes that it makes this that much more painful. He really thinks he can save me, and that's the cruelest thing that could've happened to him.

"You don't know him. He'll never stop. He'll do whatever it takes to find me...and you if I leave with you." I squeeze his hand. "It's better this way."

"Better for who?"

"Everyone."

"Not for you and not for me." He pulls his hand back like my touch burns, and it should.

After all, I'm fire.

"I'm sorry." I pick at my cuticles because I don't know what else to say.

He paces the living room, keeping his hands on his hips and his head tilted to the ceiling. His shoulders slump, and he hangs his head.

"I can't watch you stay here knowing what he does to you, so Jake and I are moving on." His voice shifts to a flat, emotionless tone with a slight shake of his head as he stares at the carpet.

He kisses the top of my head, lingering as he inhales, and I think he may change his mind. When he lifts his head, dull eyes stare back at me.

"Take care of yourself, Calamity." Head down, he walks to the front door, pausing before exiting. "And stay off those overpasses." He offers a half-hearted smile.

Then he's gone.

25

The next day, the scream of the alarm clock shatters my sleep, and daylight slices through the narrow gaps of the flimsy blinds behind the couch, a reminder of another day in paradise.

Groaning, I reach out from my cocoon of blankets, my hand blindly searching for reprieve from the snooze button. With the heaviness of a man sentenced to death, I sit up and brace myself for Mary's imminent arrival.

After all, it's not every day your enemy gets assigned to chauffeur you around town. An unlikely alliance, Mary and I are bound only by our shared contempt for our roles in this charade.

I wander down the hallway to the bathroom to take a shower because I smell like vomit, sugar, and alcohol. I use all the hot water to wash away the malaise, but it doesn't work. Steam loosens the tightness in my chest, but coughing doesn't expel anything. I turn the water off and sit in the bottom of the tub, breathing in the steam, hoping it'll loosen whatever's hurting my chest.

Is this what a broken heart feels like? No, that broke a year ago and didn't feel like this.

This must be what a broken spirit feels like.

I towel dry my hair, twist it into a messy bun, and brush my teeth, refusing to look in the mirror while doing any of it because I can't tell the woman looking back how monumentally fucked she is now. She'll figure it out soon enough on her own.

I don't want to leave the house because I don't want to see the world going on like mine hasn't been pummeled by a blonde-haired, blue-eyed asteroid. The bitterness and rage don't compare to the absolute hopelessness and defeat I feel.

There's a honk outside, and I peel the blinds apart to see Mary's sleek Mercedes parked in my driveway.

I pep myself up as I jog around the front of the luxury sedan. *Don't let her in your head.* When I open the door, she scrunches her nose like she's smelled something rancid.

"Hey." I greet her as I slide in the seat.

"Just the grocery store?" She asks as we drive out of the trailer park.

"Yes."

Riding in silence might be uncomfortable for some people, but in this situation, it's ideal because we don't have anything productive or pleasant to say to one another.

When we arrive at the grocery store, I expect her to go in with me because I don't put it past Wesley to have her chaperone me.

"Coming?" I pause before opening the door.

"I'd rather not." She swipes her phone screen, not bothering to look at me. "Make it quick because I've got other errands today."

Clamping my mouth shut, I exit the vehicle.

Don't let her in your head.

Top hits from the eighties play over the sound system in the grocery store, and Cyndi Lauper's voice comforts me as I roam up and down the aisles.

Since Wesley took my debit card and most of my cash, I have to stretch the twenty-dollar bill he overlooked in my bag until I get my last paycheck from Austin's.

I grab a small jar of peanut butter, a loaf of bread, and a half dozen eggs, calculating the total in my head to see if I have enough for a package of sandwich meat and chips. It'll be cutting it close, so I nix the sandwich stuff and opt for a small box of microwave popcorn instead.

My head hurts as I stand at the register and stretch my neck to see what's holding up the line.

A woman my age, possibly younger, with a baby on her hip, swipes her card repeatedly, but the transaction declines each time. The only thing on the conveyor belt is a pack of diapers. That's it. She isn't stocking a pantry or feeding a neighborhood, only trying to buy a pack of diapers—and not even a big one.

Despite the cashier's blatant annoyance, the woman insists on swiping her card again. The baby babbles, unaware of his mother's embarrassment, as it chews on its chubby hand.

"Do you want me to put them back on the shelf?" The cashier asks.

The young mother nods as she shifts the baby to her other hip, her eyes glassing over as she pushes her card into her back pocket.

"Hey, I haven't seen you in so long," I say with a big, fake smile as I step forward. "How've you been? The baby has gotten so big." She's confused and trying to figure out where she knows me from, but she won't because she doesn't.

"I've been okay." She plays it off with an uneasy smile.

"That's great." I nod. "That one gave me trouble last week, too." I point to the keypad. "I can spot you the diapers, and you can pay me back the next time I see you."

"Thanks, but-"

"I insist." I push my twenty-dollar bill into the cashier's hand. "It's a good thing I ran into you like this because it gave me time to realize I forgot something." The cashier passes my change back to me.

"Thank you," the woman says as I follow her around the register on my way back to the aisles. "I thought I had enough."

I wave to the baby on her hip, still drooling on his tiny fist. "That's the story of my life."

I return everything to the shelves and pick up a bag of dry beans and a couple of onions.

Back out in Mary's car, she gawks at the sole plastic bag in my lap. "That's all you got? I spent more money on gas bringing you here." She shakes her head as the car stops parallel to the highway. "A wasted trip."

"I got what I needed."

Don't let her in your head.

"I don't understand why Wesley doesn't cut his losses, but I suppose he loves you. For whatever reason, I haven't figured out yet." She huffs.

With my legs slanted toward the door, I stare out the window and watch trees blur into different shades of green. I press my knuckles against my lips to hide their trembling, but can't stop the falling tears when we pass the bar.

Beau's truck is there, loaded with their stuff. He's not bluffing. He's leaving.

It's better this way.

"Oh, enough with the alligator tears. Those only work on the fools interested in what's between your legs," Mary says.

Don't let her inside your head.

I can't lash out at her because I'm already on thin ice with Wesley. Maybe it's time for an earnest conversation. There's nothing wrong with talking. As we pull into my driveway, I grip the plastic bag close to my stomach.

"Why do you hate me?" I ask.

"I don't hate you. I've just never liked you."

"You know what he does to me, don't you?"

Her face contorts with fury. "What? Provide for you? Love you?"

"Don't play dumb, Mary. You know why I wear long sleeves in the summer. You know your son better than anyone, right? It's the one thing you boast about all the time. No one knows Wesley Reese better than his mama."

She puts the car in reverse, giving me my cue to get out. Back to the shitty trailer I live in. Back to the miserable life I can't seem to escape from.

Thunder rumbles in the distance, and the storm is approaching faster than usual for this time of year. The sky is black, and the wind has picked up. Chimes play erratic songs throughout the trailer park, and humidity hangs thick in the air because it's rained every day for a week.

There's comfort in knowing the world cries with me now.

WIND CHIMES SWING in volatile circles, and dark clouds churn in slow motion with lightning illuminating their ominous presence.

Thunder booms as I sit on my tiny back porch, watching white streaks rip through the black sky. Gusts whip my small apple tree back and forth, and I hope it doesn't sustain damage from the violent thrashing.

After losing my baby last summer, I needed to do something to cope with the grief. I read a book that suggested planting a tree, so I did.

And in a way, it worked because I spent all my time caring for the sapling. It didn't need so much hands-on care, but I did.

Everyone told me it'd never grow because the land was too dry, but I watered it until the roots grew strong.

Looking around the enclosed yard, I appreciate the paradise I created in my hell, cultivating and tending the barren dirt until it became bountiful soil.

There were so many times my back screamed from pulling weeds and planting seeds, but I watered on the days I didn't feel like it and ran outside like a lunatic to cover delicate plants when the surprise frosts came.

No one can say I didn't tend my garden.

The wind picks up, and I move inside because my heart is too heavy to enjoy anything that brings me joy.

I don't have any freedom left or the ability to create it. My dreams of leaving Wesley went from something I could do if I tried hard enough to something unattainable, regardless of my efforts.

I have to depend on him for everything, but I can't depend on him for anything.

I straighten the blankets on the couch and lay down because I'm done with today.

Rain erupts from the sky, and I lean over the back of the couch, pulling the blinds open. I can't even see the trailer across from mine. The rain battering against the metal roof becomes deafening.

A loud clap startles me, and a distressing boom follows like a bomb exploded in my backyard.

I rush to the back door, throwing it open for the wind to catch. My apple tree is split down the middle, splayed open like an unlucky fish at the market. My ribcage tightens around my lungs, and I'm soaked to the bone as soon as I step off the porch. The rainfall is so dense I can hardly see the tree as I fall to my knees, weeping for my loss a second time.

Hands grab me from behind, and I scream, but the storm

masks any sound I make as I twist around, trying to get away from whoever's behind me.

"Get up!" Beau hauls me to my feet.

"What are you doing here?"

"I'm not done with you!" He says over the downpour. "We are not done!"

"Please go!" Rain veils tears flowing from my eyes.

"Not unless you come with me." He reaches for my hand.

I push his hand away, knocking us both off balance, and we land on our asses in the mud. "He'll kill me if I leave! You've got to go! You can't be here!"

He crawls to me through the mud and sits back on his heels. "He's going to kill you if you stay!"

"Leave." I push against his chest.

"Not without you." He rests his palms on his thighs and holds steady in front of me, not caring that it's raining or that we're sitting in a mud puddle. "If you want me to go, make me. Do to me what he does to you, and maybe I'll hate you the way you hate him. That's the only way I'm leaving without you."

"Go." I press, but he doesn't waver.

"You can't hurt me."

I push, unable to control my sobbing.

"Harder, dammit! Stop holding back! Do it and fucking mean it! You take it and take it because you're scared. You believe you're as worthless as he makes you feel. If you want your life, fucking fight for it!"

I freeze.

I ball my hands into fists and bang his chest. I hate him. I hate Wesley. I hate myself. I hate being alive. When I no longer have the energy to fight, I fall onto him sobbing. "I'm so sorry."

"Don't fucking apologize." He molds his arms around me. "You fought back."

I fist his drenched T-shirt and wail, "I'm so, so, so sorry."

"Shhh." His hand glides up and down my back. "Don't cry."

He carries me inside the trailer and lowers me to my feet in the short hallway. My gaze remains on the floor because I can't look at him.

"I need you to look at me." He lifts my chin, and I open my eyes. "You didn't hurt me, but you're stronger than you look." He winks. "You did what I wanted you to do. You needed to get that shit out because you'll end up kicking a puppy if you keep it bottled up."

"I don't feel any better than him." I sniffle.

"You're nothing like him." He glances back to the bedroom. "What do you want to take with you?"

"I never wanted you to rescue me. You don't have to step in and save me because I can't do it myself."

"I don't do a single fucking thing I don't want to do. Remember? And I'm not trying to save you. I'm helping you save yourself." He glances around the trailer again. "Now, what do we need to grab?"

"I don't have any money."

"We'll figure everything out once we get you out of here. One bite at a time, okay?"

I nod.

"Now, for the last time, woman...what do you want to take?"

"Just some clothes, but I need to talk to Brad before I go."

"How does tomorrow night sound? Jake's cousin is picking him up in the morning, and I'm meeting with Jeff to square up our tab for the last couple of weeks. We can be on the road before sunset, and I'll drive until you tell me to stop." He rubs his thumbs over my cheeks.

I search for a reason I shouldn't leave with him and can't find one.

"Okay."

"That settles it." Bending, he hooks his arms behind my knees and lifts me up.

I wrap my arms around his neck. "What are you doing?"

"You're not staying another night here if I have to burn this fucking place to the ground to make sure of it. Do you understand? Never again." He twists the doorknob and kicks the door open.

"What if someone sees you carrying me outside?" I twist to get down, but he tightens his hold.

"Oh, they'll have way bigger things to gossip about soon, darlin'." He winks.

26

Beau sleeps next to me, and the motel room is quiet, save for the distant hum of semi-trucks passing on the highway and the lullaby of the air conditioner.

Stale cigarettes and the musk of old linen linger in the air, a testament to the transient souls who've passed through this room seeking refuge from life's storms. The world outside continues its relentless spin, but in this moment, time seems to hold its breath for us.

As I lay listening to Beau's steady breathing and feeling unfamiliar tranquility, I wish for a pause button—a superpower for the weary soul to freeze fleeting moments of peace and keep them safe from the unforgiving march of time.

If I were granted one wish, that would be it—to live within the confines of this moment forever.

He flips to his side and curls his arms around my waist, wrapping his legs around me until I'm unsure where my body ends and his begins.

"You're still here." His voice is groggy as he nuzzles my hair.

"Did you think I'd sneak out while you were sleeping or what?"

"Or what." He pulls me on top of him so I'm straddling him and rubs his palms up and down my thighs with a sleepy smile. "I thought you might've changed your mind about leaving with me."

"I haven't, but if you've changed yours, I understand."

"I don't change my mind." He squeezes my hips, digging into my hipbones and sending me doubling over in a fit of laughter as I squirm to get away from him. I make it to the edge of the bed, but he pulls me back to the center and holds his hands up in front of him.

"I swear I'm done," he laughs.

It's difficult to catch my breath because I can't stop laughing. "Ugh, I hate you right now." I blow little puffs of air out to regain my composure. "You know I'm ticklish."

"I do." He displays a mischievous grin. "That's why I tickle you."

I slap his shoulder. "In that case, you're an asshole."

Staring at me with a solemn expression, his eyes narrow. He crosses his arms over his chest, shifting his expression from annoyed to impatient. "Well?" He asks.

"Well, what?"

"I'm waiting for you to say something untrue."

"You're a lousy lover."

"I am, huh?"

I nod and pull my lower lip between my teeth. "The worst."

He pushes my T-shirt above my breasts, and I anticipate his touch, but he denies me with a crooked smile as he positions himself over me again. "So, what would an excellent lover do?"

"An excellent lover wouldn't have to ask."

"Ouch." He nips the side of my neck, kissing and sucking until he reaches my earlobe. He sucks it between his lips, teasing it with his teeth, and drags his lips across my jaw. I part my lips to kiss him, but he pulls back.

His eyes lock with mine as he reaches down between us,

spreading my pussy with his fingers. He avoids the one spot he knows will give me the most pleasure and plunges two fingers inside my channel.

"Am I doing this right?" He grins as he works his fingers in and out of me.

"Yes." I grip his biceps and stretch my neck.

I want to kiss him.

I want him to kiss me.

He slows almost to a stop. "Or should I go slower?" He watches me, waiting for me to beg him to keep going.

I won't.

Two can play this game, and he'll be just as frustrated when it's over.

"That isn't doing anything for me." I lie.

"Damn, I thought I had it in the bag." He pokes his bottom lip out. "Guess I am a lousy lover." He descends to the foot of the bed and stretches out on his stomach, kissing my inner thighs, and raises his eyes to meet mine.

"Maybe this will do something for you." He flicks my clit with the tip of his tongue, sending a jolt up my spine.

I grip the pillow above my head, squeezing it while he suckles the sensitive bud. I'm aware of every taste bud on his tongue when he sweeps it over my clit.

He's really great at this.

He holds my legs over his shoulders as he edges me closer to my orgasm with his tongue.

I'm almost there.

I lift my head, and he watches me with those beautiful brown eyes. I drop my head back on the bed, preparing to come undone any second. My legs tremble, and he tightens his grip to still them. I cry out as my climax approaches.

He lifts his head and smiles. "That not doing it for you either?"

He stands from the bed and wipes his hand over his mouth,

dragging his palm down the length of his beard while I wait for his next move. How much longer is he going to keep this up? The better question is how much longer *can* he keep this up?

Not long if I get my way.

I crawl to the edge of the bed, lick the bead of precum off his strained cock, and look up at him. His gaze is heavy and dark as I wrap my lips around the head, inhaling a deep breath as I pull him into my mouth again.

I take him as deep as I can, the head of his generous cock sliding past my tongue and into my throat. The muscles in my throat tighten around him in response to the invasion, causing him to groan and fist my hair with both hands.

He watches his cock slide in and out of my mouth, moaning every time I take him to the hilt and enjoying the view of me sucking him off. His cock swells and tightens, indicating he's close to his orgasm.

I release him and sit back on my heels, wiping my mouth with the back of my hand.

"You weren't into that, were you?"

He grabs my head and kisses me with so much force I think my lips may bruise when he's done. He rolls me to my stomach and pulls me up on my knees, and I barely have time to find my balance before he plunges into me with one powerful stroke and releases a guttural growl.

He holds me in place while plowing in and out of me. It's so fast, so powerful, that I don't feel my orgasm building. It just crashes over me like a tsunami.

I cry out, gripping the coverlet and anything else I can get my hands on as his hips pound against my ass. I almost topple over a few times, but he catches me and tightens his grip. His breathing is erratic, and the strokes are hard and even until the warm rush of semen fills me, and we both collapse on the bed.

His chest rises and falls against my back, and we gulp air into our overworked lungs. He kisses my shoulder and rolls away. As much as I love his touch, I'm glad because I'm hot, sweaty, and can't breathe.

We stare at the ceiling for a few minutes, neither saying anything because we're too busy fighting for our breath to waste it on words.

"Wow." He blows a heavy breath out. "That was a lousy way to start your day, huh?"

"The worst."

He turns his head to the side and smiles. "Are you really leaving me to go see other men?"

"Yes, but then I'm all yours if you still want me."

"Oh, I want you again right now, but you need to get this over with so we can leave tonight."

I shower and kiss him goodbye despite his attempts to lure me back to bed with promises of sex and food.

I POKE my head inside Jeff's office, knocking on the door to be polite. He's plugging away on the keyboard when he glances up and returns to his task.

"What brings you by?" He keeps his attention on the monitor. "We don't open to the public for another twenty minutes."

I lean my shoulder into the doorframe and cross one ankle over the other. "I'm meeting Brad, and I wanted to talk to you before he gets here."

He removes his reading glasses and lays them on the desk. "About?"

"It wasn't my choice to leave you short-handed."

He rocks back in the chair and threads his fingers together behind his head. "I knew who you were married to and what came along with him when I hired you, so it didn't blindside me."

"Have you found anyone yet?"

"I've had a few people interested, but one can't work after nine, one can't do weekends, and the other is as flaky as a biscuit. Pretty sure I've fired her from the motel before, but I'm not positive because her hair's a different color now. Believe it was pink or blue or some shit like that back then."

"I may have the solution to your problem." I smile.

"And what would that be?"

"Jenna."

"From the diner?"

"She's looking for a second job and wants something in the evenings because she likes the morning shift there, so it'd be perfect for you both."

"Tell her to come by."

"I'll pass the message on." I take a deep breath because it's time to get on with it. "Which brings me to the other reason I came by today."

He walks to the coffee bar his wife set up for him. "Do I want to know?"

"In case I've never said it, which I don't think I have, thank you for giving me a chance when no one else would."

"You don't have to thank me for anything. I hired you to do a job, and you did it most of the time."

The bell over the door dings, and Brad crosses the room in jeans and a red button-up shirt, so it's safe to assume he's off duty.

"Mind if I serve us a couple of beers?" I ask.

"Go on before I change my mind."

"About what?"

"Something." The clicking of the keyboard keys begins again. "Pull the door closed, will ya?"

I grip the doorknob and pause, taking in the scent of coffee and cardboard one last time. I never imagined I'd miss walking in on Jeff hunched over his cluttered desk, pecking away at the keyboard, and guzzling cups of black coffee. He urges me out of the office with a dismissive wave.

"Hope I'm not late," Brad says as he pulls a chair from a table and sits down.

"Only if I expected you to be early." I snatch two beers from the cooler and join him, sliding one across the table to him. "I've had a lot of coffee with you but never a beer, and we should change that."

"I agree."

He tries to suppress his amusement when I inform him I'm leaving town with Beau tonight. There's an 'I told you so' written all over his handsome face, but he keeps it to himself, allowing only the faintest smirk to turn the corner of his mouth upward.

"It's not like you think," I say.

"I didn't say anything."

"You don't have to because it's all over your face."

"There's nothing on my face." He rubs the stubble on his chin. "I take that back."

"I'm not running away with him. He's helping me leave. There's a difference."

"You don't have to explain anything to me." He pulls a white envelope from his back pocket and slides it across the table. "Suppose it came just in time."

I listed his address as my mailing address because I couldn't take the chance of it coming to the trailer and Wesley finding it.

"Is this what I think it is?" Ripping the envelope open, I scan the paper inside.

It's stupid to feel so emotional, but I could cry. All those nights studying have paid off. It's not a high school diploma, but it's the next best thing, and my mom would be happy. She was beside herself when I had to quit school after she got sick, so I hope this makes up for it.

"Thank you for pushing me to get this."

"That was all you. I only made flash cards."

"And stayed up late helping me study, which could've ruined your reputation. And drove me to Wichita Falls to take the test. And paid for the hotel room. And pushed me to keep going when I wanted to give up." I owe him more than he'll ever admit.

He asks about my plans after I leave, and I concede I don't have any. The only thing I know for sure is that I'll be happy. Things might be difficult, but I'm ready for the challenge.

"Why did you come back when you got out of the military?" I've always wondered and may never get another chance to ask. "You could've gone anywhere and came back here. I don't get it."

"Gee, thanks."

"You're different from most people here. That's all I meant."

"It's home." He shrugs. "And I wanted to make a difference. You know, change things for the better."

"Have you ever thought about leaving?"

He sips his beer. "I like knowing the people I'm taking care of—the good and bad ones. What about you? Do you ever think about going back to Jackson?"

"I've never given it much thought because I don't have family there anymore. Is it still home if the roots are gone?"

"It's familiar."

"It *is* familiar." I nod. "But part of me wants something new. A fresh start in every sense."

"Fresh starts are okay, but be careful because, at some point, you're just running away from things you don't want to deal with," he says.

"You're not old enough to dish out such worldly advice."

"I'm older than you." He winks. "By a decade."

"That's not a lot."

"Hey, there's a lot of mileage crammed in that decade." He winks. "So, what's the plan for running away with Beau?"

I scrunch my nose up and stick my tongue out. "He's picking me up around six, and we're hitting the road."

"And you're leaving for good?"

I nod.

"What about Wesley? When's he due home again?"

"Not until the weekend," I say.

"He's going to lose his shit when he realizes you're gone."

I pick at the paper label on the beer bottle. "I know."

He pushes away from the table and stands. "I guess this is it, huh?"

"I suppose it is."

I hate goodbyes, so I say I'll see him around even though it's not likely. I jog across the room to catch him as he nears the front door.

"Miss me already?"

"Can I ask a favor from you?" I ask.

"Sure, what's one more?"

I narrow my eyes. "Haha." I clear my throat. "Will you keep an eye on Mia? You know, the baby and all? It's only a matter of time before he does it to her."

"One step ahead of you."

"Thank you."

He hugs me. "You still got my number?"

"I do."

"Keep in touch. I'd like to know where you land after this."

"*If* I land. I may wander the earth for the rest of my life."

"*When* you land."

I glance at the clock and should've started walking to the diner twenty minutes ago. I run outside and wave Brad down as he pulls out of the parking lot. When he stops, I lean in through his passenger window. "Will you drop me off at the diner?"

"Get in."

ELLIOT AND ALLISON sit in a booth near the front window, snuggled against each other and laughing before they notice I've arrived.

"Hey, guys." I slide onto the bench across from them. "You two look cute and cozy."

Elliot shrinks away from the compliment, but Allison beams. "You're super cute today, too."

She's sweet but a liar because I look like crap.

I've barely wrapped my fingers over the edge of the depression I've been in to pull myself out since Wesley stripped away what's left of my independence.

I couldn't sleep last night, staring at the motel ceiling, wondering what'll happen next, and imagining every scenario I can think of—none of which end well. The only one I haven't played out in my mind is the one where everything goes as planned.

There's no point because it's the most farfetched one.

Allison tells me about wanting to leave her job because her boss is rude and inconsiderate. I fill her in on, well, nothing. I don't have much to say, at least nothing I can share. I want to tell them tonight's my last night here, and I'm finally leaving.

No more wishing and hoping.

No more praying and daydreaming.

I want so badly to share it with them, but my gut screams not to. *Don't jinx yourself.*

An hour later, Elliot reminds her they have plans to watch a movie, and I walk out with them because I want to get back to the motel before it gets dark. Once outside, Allison realizes she's left her cell phone on the table and rushes back inside.

I wish I could say goodbye to him, but I can't because I don't know who to trust anymore. So, I just hug him.

"Don't ever change. You and Allison are the only reason this place doesn't totally suck."

"You're giving us too much credit." He laughs.

I step back. "I'll never be able to thank you enough for everything you and Jeff have done for me."

"If this is about that night, I erased the footage so he didn't see you like that."

"I can't believe I let myself get that bad." I stare down at the white gravel parking lot.

"How'd you feel the next morning?"

"Like absolute shit. Might be the worst hangover of my life."

He kicks a few rocks around. "Yeah, well, that's not shocking."

Allison jogs out of the diner, waving her cell phone in the air. "Got it."

Elliot's eager to get going, so I say a quick goodbye. I didn't think there'd be so many emotions. I expected excitement, nervousness, and happiness—but not sadness. At some point, the good things got swallowed up, lumped together with the bad ones I've been trying to escape.

I'll miss the good things.

I take in the sky, painted orange and pink, as the sun disappears below the horizon. Fall is around the corner, and the evenings are cooling down. Inhaling the crisp air, I close my eyes.

This is it.

I decide to grab burgers to take back to the room, and when I go back inside to place my order, Mia watches me like a hawk.

I sit in the back booth because it has the best view of the highway to watch passing cars while I wait. This time, I don't experience the deep ache in my chest as cars leave town because the unbearable longing to be one of them isn't present.

Mia approaches, and I sit up straight, preparing for whatever bitchy comment she's saved up since we saw each other last. "Mind if I join you for a minute?" She asks.

"Be my guest."

As she sits across from me, picking at chipping polish on her fingernails, I don't feel the anger toward her that I'm used to. Her short black hair isn't as shiny, and her pale skin appears ashen now. I can't put my finger on what's different about her, but she isn't behaving like the Mia I know.

"Wesley said you know." She stares out the window with a blank expression. "About the baby."

"I do."

"I didn't do it on purpose. I was on the pill, but..." Her voice softens and fades out.

"Accidents happen." I glance toward the kitchen to see if my order has come out yet, but it hasn't.

She chews her bottom lip until it bleeds, but even then she won't stop worrying it between her teeth. "He told me some stuff, and I was wondering if it's true."

"Like what?"

"Mind if we walk outside?" She asks because Donna's staring at us and probably thinking hell has frozen over.

Out back, Mia pulls a pack of cigarettes from her apron. "You don't smoke, do you?"

"No, and you shouldn't either...at least not right now."

She lights the cigarette and leans her shoulder into the brick wall. "Wesley said you were pregnant last summer."

"I was." I sweep loose dirt back and forth with the toe of my shoe and watch the pattern emerge. "We didn't tell anyone, though. Just his parents."

"He told me what happened."

"What does that have to do with anything?"

Her hand shakes as she pulls a long drag on the cigarette. "No, he told me *what* happened. How you lost the baby."

I snap my head up. "What did he tell you?"

"He said he made you lose it." Her voice quivers. How much did he tell her, and how did he spin it? *If I know Wesley, it was an accident.*

"Did he tell you about this?" I pull my shirt up and show her the scar on my stomach.

"Mmm hmm." She nods.

"What did he tell you happened?"

"He said he needed to make sure it was gone."

Holy shit.

He told her the truth.

"I still don't know what that has to do with anything," I say.

"I think he's going to hurt us, too." She paces. "He says he doesn't want kids. And if he'll do it to you, what will stop him from doing it to me?"

"Nothing. You need to get away from here and away from him. I don't have to tell you what kind of man he is because you already know. The only thing I can tell you is he's capable of much worse than you can imagine."

She pulls the cigarettes from her apron again and puts a new one between her red lips.

"He says you pick fights with him. Treat him like crap. Says you've threatened to tell everyone what happened if he leaves you."

I pull the cigarette from her mouth. "These are bad for the baby."

I hold my hand out, and she places the pack in it. "This baby's going to have a shitty father, so the least you can do is give it a mother who'll always do what's best for it."

I toss them in a nearby trashcan, snuffing the lit one out on the bottom of my shoe and crumpling it into the trash. "If you want your baby to be safe, disappear before it's born, and never let him know where you are."

"Please don't tell him I said anything."

I adjust my bag strap over my shoulder. "Despite what Wesley told you, I've never been your enemy, Mia."

27

My bag's on the couch, and I can't stop obsessing over the clock as I pace the living room, unable to sit down.

Beau should be here any minute, and I'll finally say goodbye to this town forever. He dropped me off to pack a few more things while he wraps things up with Jeff, but I barely filled my bag because I don't want anything from this place.

I pull a bottle of water from the refrigerator and chug it, running my fingers over the four perfect indentions on the freezer door.

That was the first time Wesley got physical with me. He didn't hit me, but he punched the refrigerator beside my head and told me I was lucky.

I felt lucky.

In the living room, a framed thrift store print of a bear cub hangs by the window, the only picture they had big enough to cover the busted paneling. That was the first time he put his hands on me.

We'd argued about the dress I wore that evening, and he slammed my face against the wall. I was stunned into silence, and the argument ended. All the arguments ended after that.

He backed me into a corner, and I've cowered to him every day since.

The doorknob rattles, and I sprint to let Beau in, but Wesley's large frame towers over me when I open the door.

He's not due home for three days.

My hope pummels to the ground, shattering into a thousand pieces at my feet.

He stands in the middle of the living room and eyes my bag on the couch but doesn't say anything. Instead, he grabs a beer from the refrigerator and sits in his recliner, popping the tab on the can. He plucks the remote from the table and takes a long drink of the beer.

"Don't just stand there." He motions for me to sit on the couch and turns the television on.

I watch him instead of the television, sliding my bag under a blanket and hoping he doesn't notice.

"What are you doing home? Is everything okay?"

He stares at the television. "Needed to take a few days off. Is me coming home unannounced a problem?"

"I'm just surprised to see you."

"I guessed that by the look on your face when you opened the door." He takes another drink of beer. "Were you expecting someone else?"

"I wasn't expecting anyone." I glance at the clock over the television. It's almost six. I need to warn Beau not to come. "I didn't plan to cook tonight because I'm trying to skip a few meals so these hips will stop spreading." I pinch my hips. "Do you want me to walk to the diner and get you a burger?" Maybe I can catch Beau to warn him.

"Later."

"I was just about to go pick up some laundry detergent because we're out, and I'm assuming you have clothes you need washed before you head out again." Standing from the couch, I smooth my shorts down.

"Sit back down."

"I can take your truck to make it faster."

"Sit." The muscles in his jaw flex.

How am I going to warn Beau if I can't get away? Maybe he'll see Wesley's truck in the driveway and keep driving.

"Since when do you pack a bag to go buy laundry detergent?" He eyes the blanket with my bag under it.

"Those are some clothes that don't fit anymore. I was going to see if Elliot's girlfriend wants them."

He crosses the room and lifts the blanket. "Let's see what you're giving away."

I want to puke. Like all over him, the couch, the ugly orange carpet. Everywhere.

He removes my clothes and drops everything on the floor at his feet, flipping the bag upside down. "That all?"

I nod.

He crouches on the floor in front of me, and those blue eyes see every lie I've ever told him.

"Tell me the truth, and we can work through this."

He knows.

I don't know how, but he does. Did Brad tell him? He's the only person who knew about the plan to leave tonight.

I glance at the clock. It's fifteen past six. Beau's late. Why is he late? Did Wesley already get to him?

"I don't know what you're talking about."

"You know exactly what I'm talking about." He cradles my face with his large hand and rubs his thumb over my cheek. "And you need to get that idea out of your head because leaving isn't an option unless you want to go be with your mom. I'm willing to pretend this didn't happen on one condition."

"What?"

"I want to hear you say it." He slides his hand up and down my arm. "And I'll know if you lie to me."

"I'm not sure what you want me to say."

His hand flies across my cheek. "I want you to admit you've been fucking the guy I told you to stay away from!"

I cover my burning skin with my hand. "You're not happy, either."

"I'm very fucking happy, Katie. You're the one who can't be happy. You're the one always trying to leave." He paces in front of me.

"What about Mia and all the others?"

His thick neck vibrates with laughter. "What about them? They scratch an itch, but they don't mean anything."

"Mia's having your baby."

He drops to his knees on the floor and positions himself between my legs. "She's only good for one thing, and that baby probably isn't mine."

The way he tucks my hair behind my ear would be endearing in a different situation.

Tears spill onto my lap when I look down at him. "Wesley, please, just let me leave. Please."

He rises from the floor and kisses my forehead before leaning over the back of the couch to peer out the window.

"That's not an option," he says.

He's calm, calmer than I've ever seen him, and sits next to me, raking his fingers through the length of my hair. "Your hair's one of the first things I noticed about you. The way it teased the top of your ass when you walked away the first time I saw you in the truck stop."

"Please." My entire body trembles because an even-tempered Wesley is more terrifying than a raging Wesley.

He leads me down the hallway to the bathroom, and my legs feel like noodles as he sits me on the edge of the bathtub. My knees bounce, and my hands clatter against the tub as he rustles around in the cabinet over the sink and pulls out scissors.

He leans into the mirror and pushes his blonde hair around

in the front. "It's about time for a trim. What do you think?" He eyes me through the mirror.

"Maybe."

"Stand up," he says.

I'm not convinced my legs will support me, but I stand.

He positions me in front of the mirror and stands behind me, pulling a brush through the length of my hair, and I wince every time it scrapes over my shoulders.

I focus on him through the reflection because he wants me to maintain eye contact. If I go along with it, maybe he'll spare Beau. I don't care what he does to me, but Beau doesn't deserve the fallout from this.

This is my hell, and I'm the only one who should be burned in it.

"Does he like your hair, too?"

I remain silent because this is part of his game.

"Does he appreciate how beautiful it is? How long it took me to get it to this length when you were trying to cut it all the time?"

I don't dare utter a sound.

"What man wouldn't?" He secures my hair at the base of my neck with an elastic and another about six inches down from the first. He spins me around by my shoulders and smooths a couple of flyaways on top of my head. "Perfect." He rotates me back to the mirror. "I think I did a pretty good job."

"You did."

"Look at me, Katie." He picks up the scissors. "I'll slice your fucking ear off if you blink."

I stare into his menacing eyes as he pushes the blades through my hair above the bottom elastic. His eyes glaze over, absent of emotion—at least none I recognize. He seems to have gone somewhere else in his mind, and the only time his expression changes is when the scissors nick the skin between my shoulders.

Please keep driving, Beau.

He lays the scissors on the counter and holds the butchered hair in front of me. "I wonder if I could make something out of it. Seems a shame to throw it away." He pushes me closer to the mirror. "Do you really think someone else wants you?" He thumps the back of my head. "Maybe we'll shave the rest off later."

My eyes swell with tears, but I don't close them.

He forces me against the wall, compressing my windpipe with his calloused hand.

"Did you think I wouldn't find out?"

My eyes feel like they're bulging, and I try to pry his hand away, but he's too strong. My vision tunnels before he releases me, and I collapse to the floor, coughing and gagging.

I scamper across the linoleum to the hallway, but he grabs my ankle and drags me back kicking and screaming. It's for nothing when his fist comes down on the side of my face, and I fall on my back, the room spinning.

I hear his zipper and feel him yank my shorts and under-wear off. I will my body to fight back, but another blow to my temple leaves me struggling to stay conscious.

"Please don't," I say through panicked tears.

He forces himself between my legs. "Don't what? Take what's mine? You're mine. This," he grabs me between the legs, "is mine. You had no right to give it to someone else." To my shock, he stands up and disappears from the room.

Now's my chance.

I gather the energy to stand and poke my head from the bathroom. He's in the kitchen rummaging through drawers, so I bolt across the hallway to the backdoor and fumble with the latch at the top.

He charges across the trailer and tackles me. "Oh, no, you don't."

I kick against the carpet as he drags me to the living room and tosses me onto the couch.

"If I see you move a finger, I'll snap your fucking neck." He goes to the kitchen and opens the drawer next to the stove. "Remember how easy I said it'd be to make you disappear?" He pulls a knife out and slams the drawer. "Poof...gone."

I pay close attention to the blade in his hand as he approaches me.

"Take your shirt off."

I lift it over my head. Only in my bra and nothing else, I shiver, but it doesn't have anything to do with the lack of clothing.

He sits beside me and traces my collarbone with the knife tip. "Did you actually think you were leaving?" The blade's cool against my skin as he runs it underneath my bra strap. "Leaving me to be with him?"

"I wasn't leaving you for anyone." My voice cracks. "I was just leaving."

"Stop lying!" He springs up and drags me to the floor, yanking me up to my knees by my arm. "I want the first thing he sees when he walks in is you sucking my dick so he'll know who you belong to." He unzips his jeans again.

My teeth are clenched so tight my jaw aches as he taps my cheek. He hooks his fingers inside my lips, trying to force my mouth open, but I keep my jaw shut.

"Open your fucking mouth!"

A knock on the door draws his attention away from me.

God, no.

Another knock.

When Beau calls my name, Wesley holds his finger over his lips and whispers, "Don't make a fucking sound."

My heart races as he unlocks the door.

"Stay outside, Beau!" I say, and Wesley lunges for his duffel bag.

Beau rushes inside and freezes when Wesley presses a gun to the center of his chest.

"Slow down, cowboy. She's not ready to ride off into the sunset with you just yet."

Beau's eyes dart back and forth between us as Wesley pushes the barrel of the revolver into his chest, forcing him to sit in the recliner and keeping the gun pointed at him while picking the knife up from the carpet. He tosses it down the hallway but never takes his eyes off us.

"You can do whatever you want to me, but let her leave," Beau says.

How is he not freaking out right now? There's a gun pointed at him with a maniac behind the trigger.

"Can't do that, cowboy." Wesley shakes his head. "You know why she's the one I picked to marry?"

Beau doesn't engage with him.

"It's because she has the tightest pussy I've ever stuck my dick in. But you already know that, don't you? You know how sweet and tight her little cunt is, don't you? Is that why you're trying to steal what's mine?"

I plead with Beau not to answer using my eyes, begging him to let Wesley ramble. I don't want him to react because that's what Wesley's counting on—a reaction.

Beau doesn't respond, and he presses the gun to his temple.

"Wesley, please stop!" I wail. "I'll stay! I'll stay!"

He snaps his head back to me, fury filling his eyes. "What makes you think I still want you?"

"Then let me go, and you'll never have to see me again." If my tormented pleas could only reach the part of him I pray is still there. "I'll leave town and never come back. I swear."

"But then you'd get what you want, and that's not how this works. I told you what would happen if you betrayed me. I made it clear what I would do to you and the piece of shit you cheated on me with, didn't I?"

I nod.

"Didn't I?" He shouts.

"Yes." I sniffle.

His eyes remain locked on me as he presses the gun against Beau's temple. "I hope it was worth it."

My chest heaves up and down. "Please, don't, Wesley!" I sob. "Do whatever you want to me, but don't hurt him. I'm the one who betrayed you…not him. Punish me because I'm the one who hurt you."

He looks down at Beau. "She has a point, but you knew she was married, so that makes you just as guilty, doesn't it?"

"If you're going to hold a gun to a man's head, you better be ready to pull the trigger," Beau says.

"Oh, I plan to, cowboy. Don't you worry," Wesley says. "But I want you to see the mess you made first."

Wesley keeps the gun pointed at Beau as he grips the back of my neck, squeezing as he pushes me forward.

"You see him?" He shakes me like a rag doll. "You did this. You're the reason he's going to die tonight, so you're going to watch. This is your fault."

This has to be a nightmare, and I'll wake up soon.

"Don't you dare close your fucking eyes until he takes his last breath. If I see your eyes closed, I'll blow his fucking brains all over the wall." He turns to Beau. "Same goes for you, cowboy. Her brains will be all over this carpet if I see your eyes closed."

Beau clenches his jaw, and the vein in his forehead bulges. I don't know what he's thinking, but I regret every moment we've shared, every word we've spoken to each other, and every touch we've exchanged.

I wish I'd never met Beau Brooks on that overpass.

I've got to get control of this because all the wishing and praying in the world won't save us if I don't.

"I'll make it up to you," I say.

"You expect me to believe you?"

Unable to look at Beau, I keep my attention on Wesley.

"He doesn't mean anything. I was lonely, and things got mixed up in here after last summer." I point to my head. "I want to get better, but I don't know how to stop being so sad all the time."

I'm a piece of shit for bringing that up to save myself, but I don't know any other way to reach him. If he's capable of guilt or regret, that's the one thing he'd take back because he knows he went too far last summer.

He blows an exasperated sigh to the ceiling. "You have a knack for fucking shit up, don't you, Katie?" Jerking me back onto the couch, he sits next to me but doesn't allow the gun to waver off Beau.

"I still want a family with you." I pull his free hand over my stomach. "I made a mistake, but it's not too late. The doctor said it's unlikely, but it could happen. What if we could have a second chance to get this right?"

"I don't know." He blows out a weighted breath. "I don't know."

"What can I do to prove I want to stay?"

He gnaws at his bottom lip. "You're going to do it."

"Do what?"

"You're going to shoot him." He stands from the couch. "You're going to prove how much you love me and how little he means to you. We're going to say he raped you, and you shot him." He grabs my bicep and drags me back to the floor. "Get on your knees."

I position myself on my knees, and he circles like a vulture, stopping in front of me and looking at Beau.

"Get up, cowboy."

Beau does as he says and looks like someone has death punched his soul, regret written all over his face in his solemn expression.

Wesley directs him to stand in front of me with the gun pointed at him.

"Let's get this over with," he says as he flicks his eyes toward Beau's belt.

I nod, tears streaming down my cheeks as the realization of what I've got to do to save myself sinks in.

Under Wesley's direction, I fumble with Beau's belt buckle, and my hands shake so badly I can hardly unbutton and unzip his jeans. I want to look up to express how sorry I am, but I can't. I'm just trying to survive, so I keep my eyes straight ahead, eyeing the denim as I sit on my knees on the hideous orange carpet. He releases an audible gasp when I tug his jeans down a few inches.

"Lay down." Wesley rolls the gun in my direction.

"Wes-" I try to talk him out of this.

"Lay the fuck down!" He says. "Don't act like fucking him is upsetting!" I ease back on the carpet and spread my legs.

"Now, saddle up, cowboy. Time to put some DNA where it shouldn't be if this is going to be believable."

"No," Beau says.

"C'mon now. Don't get shy on me. If you can do it behind my back, you can do it in front of me." Wesley presses the gun to Beau's temple. "Fuck her, or I'll put a bullet between your eyes right now."

"Pull the trigger," Beau says, unblinking.

"How about this?" Wesley leans closer. "Do it, or I'll put a bullet between *her* eyes."

Curling his bottom lip over his teeth, Beau glares at Wesley.

"You're getting to go out with a bang before the bang." Wesley laughs. "That's more than most men in your situation get."

Lowering himself between my legs, he rests his forearms alongside my head as he pushes into me. My body convulses, and I can't catch my breath.

Is this really happening?

Laying his cheek against my temple, he whispers, "Pretend we're at the lake." He thrusts in and out of me, the motions mechanical and unfamiliar. Sobbing, I shut my eyes and try to calm myself. "That's it," he says. "It's just me and you."

Dragonflies dance across the still water, and frogs croak in the background. Cat's tails sway along the edge.

I need to stay here a little longer.

It's almost over.

A rabbit emerges from the tall grass and bounces around the lake, disappearing past the tree line.

He comes a few minutes later, the act uneventful and dull. He stills over me and sits back on his heels, glaring at Wesley as he tucks himself back inside his jeans. "Happy now?"

Wesley's face is red, but what strikes me is the massive bulge in his jeans because watching us turned him on.

"Get on your knees," he says, and I do it.

We sit face to face on our knees while Wesley circles us, waving the gun around.

"You two have no idea how satisfying this next part will be." Producing a pistol from his waistband, he hesitates before handing it to me. "You do this, or I put one in you both. Got it?"

Nodding, I take the gun.

Can I go through with this, even if it's the only way I walk out of here tonight?

Wesley's mad. Insane. Seething and foaming at the mouth with wrath. Brushing against the window, he drags the curtain panel open far enough for me to see the destroyed apple tree.

He's robbed me of my past, isolating me from everyone I knew before him and taken my present, not allowing me to exist from under his thumb. If I don't do this, he'll take my future, too.

Everything comes at a cost because nothing is free.

My hands tremble, but I'm not sure if it's because I'm

pointing a gun at a man's chest or if it's because there's one pointed at me.

Please forgive me for what I'm about to do.

"Look at me," Beau says, his voice calm. "Do what you need to do to save yourself, but promise me you'll make it count because I won't be here to save you next time. Okay?"

I can't.

I can't do this.

I can not do this.

"A woman like you was always going to be the death of me." Beau dips his head and forces our eyes to meet. "Go ahead, darlin'. Devastate me like I knew you would." He winks.

"I'm sorry." I squeak the words out. "I'm so sorry you got mixed up in this."

"You love him, don't you?" Wesley asks.

I refuse to turn away from Beau when I answer. "No."

Beau's lips tighten into a thin line, but I won't shy away from this like a coward because I made this mess.

Wesley takes a couple of steps to the left but keeps the gun on us. "At an angle, so it looks like he attacked you on the floor. Prove a stranger means nothing, and I'm your everything."

Crying, I hold the gun up, and it's heavier than I expected. How did it come to this? My hands tremble so bad I'm afraid I'll drop the gun as I peer up at Beau, our eyes focusing on each other's.

"We were never strangers," I whisper as I increase the pressure on the trigger.

"No, darlin', we weren't." He winks, shredding my heart into a million lifeless tendrils.

The sound of the gunshot is deafening as Beau falls to his knees in front of me, pinning me to the carpet.

28

Beau lunges forward, snatching the gun from my hand as Wesley lies on the floor, clutching his bloody thigh.

"You fucking bitch! You shot me!" Wesley's fury fills the room as blood soaks his jeans.

Beau kicks Wesley's revolver into a corner and tosses his phone to me. "Call an ambulance." He yanks his leather belt from his jeans and ties it around Wesley's leg, cinching it tight while I'm on the phone with emergency services. "Grab all the towels you have." Leaning over Wesley, Beau presses down on the gaping wound.

Wesley struggles against the pain, his cursing blending with Beau's commands until I only hear muffled voices above the ringing in my ears. Beau fights to keep Wesley stable, and time seems to slow as we wait for help to arrive.

In the bathroom, I sweep towels from the shelf into my arms and drop them on the floor next to Wesley. Beau covers the hole in Wesley's leg and continues applying pressure while I grab the blanket from the couch to wrap up with.

I stand over them because I don't know what to do. I don't

want him to die, but I don't feel an overwhelming sense of duty to save his life, either.

"Ugh! I can't believe you fucking shot me! You fucking cunt!"

Beau leans forward, increasing pressure on the wound. "Don't make me regret helping you," he says through gritted teeth. "I'm only doing it so she doesn't have to live with taking your life."

Wesley's head falls back on the floor with a thud. "How long have you been fucking my wife, cowboy?" Even from a distance, the beads of sweat developing on his forehead are evident.

"Now's not the time for that conversation."

Wesley turns his head to the side and stares at me with bloodshot eyes. "How long, Katie?"

"Almost the entire time he's been here."

"Fucking whore."

Beau puts his weight on Wesley's wound again, causing him to clench his jaw as he groans in pain. "You probably tasted my dick on her lips once or twice, asshole."

"You two deserve each other."

"And you deserve this!" I hurl myself toward him. "I fucking hate you!" I bang my fists on his chest. "I hope it hurts like hell!"

Beau drags me off him from behind kicking and screaming, the screams piercing the stagnant, metallic air in the room, but I fight to get back to him. I want him to suffer, to endure the anguish that's consumed me on this very floor.

Beau has my back to his chest and my arms pinned to my sides, but my spirit remains unbroken with fierce defiance. "I fucking despise you!"

"Calm down," Beau says. "He's not worth it."

"Yeah, calm your fat ass down." Wesley pushes up on his elbows, sweat soaking his shirt collar, and staggers to his feet, falling into the front door and yanking it open to hold himself up.

"No!" I thrash against Beau, but he squeezes me tighter. "You're not getting away with it this time."

"Like you can fucking stop me." The sirens are louder with every passing second he stands there. "You did the right thing because I was ending you both tonight. Watching you take his life was just the icing on the cake. This isn't over because you're still mine and will be until I decide I'm done with you." He limps out of the trailer, the door slamming behind him.

Beau and I lunge for the door but for different reasons. I try to pull it open, but he slams it shut and locks it, standing in front of it.

"Let him go."

"It's not fair that he's getting away with everything again."

Squeezing my shoulders, he forces me to look him in the eye. "Chasing him will only get you hurt. If you want to make sure he doesn't get away with this, be around to tell your side of the story."

Blue lights come into view through the blinds as a small crowd gathers in the yard, and Jesse Allen talks to a few onlookers as Brad arrives.

"I'm going to talk to them. Let Brad come to you, okay? Don't come outside," Beau says.

Jesse Allen and Brad talk to Beau for a few minutes, and I prepare for the ass-chewing I'm about to receive as Brad stalks across the yard. He steps inside the trailer and stands with his hands on his hips as he surveys the room.

"I take it Wesley didn't take the news well."

I shake my head.

"Are you alright?"

"I'm fine."

"You don't look fine."

"Thanks."

"Well...what happened?"

I pull another blanket over myself because I still feel exposed. "Wesley showed up instead of Beau. He knew about the affair and my plan to leave tonight."

"How'd he know? Who'd you tell?"

"You're the only one I told."

"Do you think Beau told someone, and they told Wesley?"

"The only thing I know is when he got here to pick me up, Wesley held us at gunpoint, threatened to kill us, and I got my hands on the gun," I point to the pistol Beau left on the kitchen counter, "and shot him in the leg."

"*You* shot him?"

"I didn't want to kill him. I just wanted him to stop." I scowl at Wesley's blood on the carpet. "But with hindsight being twenty-twenty, I wish I would've aimed higher."

"Any idea where he might go with that kind of injury? He knows we'll be checking the hospital, so I doubt he's stupid enough to go there." He follows my gaze to the bloodied carpet. "But he's got to go somewhere if he's bleeding that bad, and he may be that stupid."

"Maybe Mia's or his parents? Those are the only people he goes to when he needs something."

"I've got guys at their places and the hospital." He stares at Wesley's blood on the floor. "Beau said he took off in his truck, so I've got the state police keeping an eye on the highways out of town, too."

"What are you going to arrest him for? I shot him, so he'll claim he's the victim."

"One thing at a time, okay? They'll take you to the hospital to get checked out, and I need to talk to Beau again."

"I don't need to go to the hospital."

"It's about documentation, so we can charge him with as much as possible."

Brad leaves, and I zone out, unable to tear my attention away from Wesley's blood on the hideous carpet as flashing lights from the patrol cars illuminate the room.

My carefully woven web of secrets has come unraveled for the world to see.

29

The delicate, pale fingers of sunrise caress the horizon as I stare out the motel room window. Gripping the blanket wrapped around my shoulders, fear and relief have worked their way into my bones, but guilt settles on me like a suffocating second skin because there's no turning back.

What's done can't be undone.

I couldn't sleep last night. Wesley's hands on me, his vile words, the smell of blood and gunpowder consuming the tiny trailer—it was too much. I'll never forget the sound Wesley made as he fell to the floor after I pulled the trigger.

My instinct to survive was stronger than any moral restraint I possessed up until that point.

A hot tear slips down my cheek when I think about every blow from him. Every bruise. Every cut. Every broken bone. The way he hovered over me like a vulture waiting to pick over my carcass after he took what was left of my life.

Beau's asleep in the bed, his peaceful features illuminated by the early morning light. Will he be able to look at me the same way after last night?

We've barely spoken since checking into the motel, and he's

done his best to avoid me. He showered and fell asleep within half an hour of getting into the room.

As the sun continues climbing, I can't shake the feeling that our escape was too easy. I can't tell if my paranoia is justifiable or born from living under Wesley's tyranny for so long.

He's never been one to go down without a fight, and nausea churns in my stomach as I recall the way he stared at me with those soulless eyes, almost daring me to pull the trigger like he knew what I planned to do.

It happened so fast, like watching myself in a movie, removed from my actions, until the deafening click of the gunshot echoed through the trailer and snapped me back into my body.

I have no remorse—only a numbness deep in my soul that I'm scared has eaten any happiness I had left.

I want to believe I can heal myself, but moments like this make me question if people like me ever get better. Are we destined to create new wounds while tearing open the old ones because healing them takes too much work?

It's easier to pretend they aren't there at all.

The pain in my chest radiates outward like a spreading ink stain as I look over at Beau again.

Thinking about how close we came to losing our lives makes me ill, but the strange sense of detachment creeping over me when I look at him hurts more.

Why did he pursue me when he knew my situation and how fucked up it was? Does he have some kind of savior complex? Did swooping in like a knight in shining armor feed his ego? Is his plan to win me over before unleashing his insecurities on me the way Wesley did?

It'd make sense because he doesn't have to work to break a woman down if she's already in pieces.

Why didn't I leave as soon as the abuse started? Why did I stay and let it escalate?

I've asked myself those questions a thousand times, and the answer is I didn't realize what was happening until it was too late because that's what abusers do. They start out doing things you don't recognize as abuse.

He didn't start by bashing my face into the refrigerator because that would've made me run immediately.

My abuse started with snide comments disguised as love.

The first time he hit me was the physical manifestation of what he'd been doing to me emotionally and verbally for months.

We'd been invited to a party for one of his friends, and he was late coming off the road, so he called and told me to meet him there. I'd purchased a new pink dress, the color Wesley preferred me to wear, and tucked it away for a special night since we didn't go out often.

Everything seemed normal all night. Wesley doted on me the way he tended to do in public, and I was happy because he was happy.

His mood shifted as soon as we got in the truck to go home, and he didn't speak to me the entire drive.

Once inside the trailer, he screamed about how slutty I looked and how I embarrassed him in front of his friends.

My make-up was too heavy.

My heels were too tall.

The dress was too short and tight because I'd gained a few pounds.

Even my hair being down pissed him off that night.

I apologized for making him uncomfortable around his friends. *"I'm sorry. I only wore this because I thought you liked it."*

I never expected him to grab the back of my head and slam my face into the wall. As blood poured from my nose, I cried and apologized more.

He made me take the dress off, grabbed a knife from the

kitchen drawer, and sliced it to shreds before tossing it into the trash.

"You're my wife, not some whore I want my friends jerking off to when they get home."

Afterward, he went to bed, and I sat at the kitchen table with an ice pack on my face, crying because I believed what happened was my fault.

The following day, he gave me flowers and told me how sorry he was for what had happened. He said he loved me so much that he wanted to protect me from the world. We cried together as he apologized and swore he'd never do it again.

And I stayed.

I should've left, but I didn't.

It was months before he hit me again.

I don't remember what set him off the second time, but I remember the next day.

Flowers. Apologies. Crying.

But even that didn't last.

The flowers stopped, and the apologies came less often. I covered the bruises with make-up or clothes, hiding them because I was embarrassed that I let myself become a statistic. I was humiliated and ashamed that I was too scared to leave him. By the time he stopped hiding his infidelity, I prayed he'd fall in love with one of them and leave me.

Why didn't I leave as soon as the abuse started?

Because it was subtle until it wasn't.

30

The motel room is steeped in the acrid scent of stale cigarettes from Beau's chain smoking. I've pretended to be asleep for the past hour because I don't want to talk to him.

It's childish, but I don't know what to say. I watch him through half-closed eyes while he types on his phone so he doesn't notice I'm awake.

He sits shirtless in the chair by the window, his back against the peeling wallpaper and his face lit by the harsh glow of his phone. An occasional sigh punctuates the rhythmic tap-tap-tap of his fingers on the screen as he interacts with a world beyond these four walls.

I'm not sure how long I slept after Brad delivered the news this afternoon; Wesley got away. His truck was found wrecked outside of town, with no sign of him.

He left, and I lost track of time as my body succumbed to exhaustion. My mind reeled from the devastating news that he's still on the loose.

The room spun as my legs gave out, and I would've crumbled under my emotions if Beau hadn't prevented me from hitting the ground. When my stomach couldn't handle the stress anymore, he held my hair back as I retched into the toilet because fear consumed me. All I could think about was Wesley returning to finish what he started.

The details of how Beau cleaned me up and carried me to bed are hazy, as if they were a dream. Dread and despair ran rampant through my mind as I drifted into a restless sleep brought on by physical and mental exhaustion.

I deserve a lot of things, but he's not one of them.

I don't deserve someone who cares for me like he does because I'm not sure I can do the same. At one time, I could have. But now? I don't know. He should be with someone who can love and trust him without hesitation.

He needs to be with someone who isn't me because the destination of my life has gotten farther away with every wrong turn. I'm so lost I don't think I'll ever find my way back because I can't even remember where I was going.

Beau stretches his arms over his head and rises to his feet, unbuttoning his jeans and draping them over the back of the chair. I remain motionless as he climbs into the bed behind me.

Normally, he'd mold his body to mine and hold me as we fall asleep. He doesn't do it this time, and I'm grateful. I should acknowledge him, say something. Ask how he's doing because we've both been through hell.

But I don't.

31

I squirm beneath the shadow moving on top of me, and I can't get away because it's pressing me into the couch. I dig my heels into the cushion when his mouth smothers mine, and I bite his lip, tasting blood.

My cheek is on fire after his hand flies across it.

He leans back, but only far enough to push my shirt up over my breasts. I bang my curled fists against his chest and shoulders, but it excites him more.

"Stop!" I scream.

He seizes my face with one hand, squeezing my jaw and covering my mouth with his again. His hot breath makes me want to vomit when he sucks my nipple into his mouth. He bites it, and I slap the side of his head to stop him.

"Stop, Wesley!"

"Shut up." He slaps me again.

He slides his hand inside my panties, and I clench my eyes shut.

I don't want this.

It burns when he shoves his fingers inside me because my body isn't ready. My flesh tears as he moves his sandpaper fingers in and out, treating my body like an object for him to use and manipulate at his discretion.

I don't want this.

It'll be over faster if I go along with it.

I turn my head to the side and pretend I'm on a beach somewhere. Water laps at the shore, and seagulls squawk overhead. I drag my feet through the hot sand.

I like this.

The sun blazes high in the sky, and the seagulls become louder. They're giving me a headache.

My skin's on fire, but there's no shade to seek out. It's blistering. Painful.

A seagull drops from the sky onto the beach with a loud thud, and blood drips from its beak. The smell of burning feathers inundates my nostrils.

Ripping.

Tearing.

It hurts so fucking bad.

He yanks me to the floor on my knees and rams his dick in my mouth. I push against his thighs. I can't breathe, but he doesn't care. He fists my hair to hold my head still so he can shove his dick down my throat.

Tears stream down my face, snot runs from my nose, and I feel vomit coming up. I struggle to pull back, but he buries himself in my mouth and leaves nowhere for the vomit to go but back down my throat and spewing from my nostrils.

His body jerks as he comes in my mouth.

His sweaty palms are still on me. I feel them on my skin as I fling the blanket away, and I can't get off the couch fast enough. I can't get away from the sensation because it's under my skin. It's Wesley.

He's everywhere. He's always going to be here. With me. On me. Inside me. Part of me.

I fight to break free from the arms wrapped around me because I can't go through that again.

"It's me, Katie." A calm voice whispers in my ear. "You're safe. You're safe."

I blink several times while my eyes adjust to the dark room. How long have I been awake? When did I get out of bed?

The tension in my body melts away, leaving me weak and sagging against Beau's chest. His heart beats hard against my back, a result of an adrenaline rush, even though his voice is unbothered.

My legs give out, and I slide to the ground with his arms guiding me onto the dingy carpet. Trembling starts in my hands and travels up my arms until my entire body shakes, and I lurch over, my stomach twisting in knots because I haven't eaten in over twenty-four hours.

Beau sits beside me and drags his palm up and down my spine, not speaking because his presence is best served in silence.

Proving once again that I don't deserve him.

I press my hands to my face, trying to contain the over-whelming tears. My mind is a relentless projector, replaying intrusive thoughts of a gruesome scene where Wesley's bullet ripped through Beau's skull like a memory.

I lunge to my feet, slamming into the edge of the toilet, but my body can only dry heave with nothing left to purge except burning acid. Each convulsion wracks me with sobs, the smell of bleach burning my nostrils until I'm gasping for breath between heaves.

Beau grips my arms above my elbows from behind. "C'mon. Get up off the floor."

I jerk my arms away. "Leave me alone!" I wail. "Get away!"

"You're upset."

"No shit," I say through tears. "Just go...please."

"We should just leave," Beau says.

"We can't." I push myself up off the floor. "Brad said he'd let us know when we could go."

"He can't stop us, and he has my number if he needs to talk to us."

"I told him I'd wait until he says we're clear to go." Since he isn't leaving the room, I will. I push past him and rummage through my bag next to the sink for my toothbrush.

"There's nothing a simple phone call can't resolve." He leans his shoulder into the door frame. "I say we go before the sun rises."

"Why aren't you listening when I tell you I don't want to leave yet?" I lock myself in the small bathroom.

I sit on the bathtub's edge and stare up at the ceiling. I want to cry. I want to scream. I want to...I don't know what I want.

The room door closes, the lock engages, and Beau's heavy footsteps move around the room, growing louder until there's a knock on the bathroom door. When I unlock it, he opens it with caution.

"Hey." He steps inside the cramped room.

"Hey."

He sits next to me and pulls my hand in his lap. "I didn't mean to upset you."

"I'm sorry I overreacted. I know you're trying to help."

"That's all I've ever wanted to do."

"I don't want to go until Brad says it's okay because I need to be done with this place for good once I leave. I never want a reason to come back."

He releases my hand, puts his arm around my shoulder, and pulls me to his side. His body is rugged and masculine, but his energy is gentle and soothing. "Then we'll stay."

I'm happy with him, but I don't want to love him because love makes people vulnerable and closes their eyes to truths. It makes them see good in others when it doesn't exist. Worst of all, it convinces people it doesn't do any of those things.

I wasn't supposed to fall in love with a stranger.

I shouldn't know his scent or that he has different smiles for different situations. I shouldn't know he isn't a morning person or that he hates tomatoes. I shouldn't know how soft his lips are or how warm his skin feels. I shouldn't know that his presence in a room is enough to make me smile.

But I can detect his scent in a room he's been in as soon as I enter it. His smile gives away when he's being polite and when he's genuinely happy. The left side of his mouth curls up more when he lets his guard down. He likes the taste of tomatoes but not the texture.

I shouldn't know these things.

But I do, and I'm tired of fearing and fighting my way through life.

So, I'm giving up and giving in.

I throw my arm around his neck and bury my face in the bend of his neck. It shocks him, but he wraps his arms around me and pulls me into his lap. His skin soaks up my tears until my pain is part of him, too. He runs his hand up and down my back but says nothing.

He just lets me be.

His eyes hold no judgment or pity when I kiss him through my tears. He holds me like he's afraid to let go, and the more I cry, the tighter he squeezes.

"I'm so sorry for everything. I wish I would've jumped off the overpass that night before you came along, and none of this would've happened." I try to pull back, but he doesn't give an inch, forcing me to stay close.

"Please don't say that."

"Why? No one would've missed me." Wesley's words echo in my head.

"Me." He pulls back so I can see his eyes. "I would've missed you."

"You didn't know me, and if I weren't such a coward, you would've never had the misfortune of meeting me."

"I may not have known you, but I would've missed you. I

would've spent the rest of my life pining for something because you're that something. I would've spent my days and nights searching for something I'd never find." He presses his lips to my forehead. "I would've missed you...even if I didn't know it was you I felt the loss of."

I keep my eyes closed and my forehead against his lips as I inhale a deep, intentional breath. "You should leave town because things will get messy now that everyone knows about us."

"Look at me." He waits until I open my eyes to speak. "Why would you say that?"

"Because it's the truth."

"According to who?"

"You deserve someone better. Someone who can give back instead of always taking. That's all I do. Take, take, take because I have nothing to give. Maybe I will someday, but you can't spend your life waiting on a maybe. I don't know if I'll ever be able to cleanse my body and mind of him, and it terrifies me." I avert my gaze to the wall, but he palms my cheek and drags my attention back, forcing me into eye contact again.

"If you want me to go because you don't want to be with me anymore, I'll wish you well and leave as soon as day breaks. But if you want me to go because you think you don't deserve me, I'll leave after breakfast, and you've had time to decide you're going with me." He smiles.

"I'm serious, Beau."

"You're right. You don't deserve me. You deserve someone better." He touches his nose to mine. "I don't want to be without you, but if that's what you want, I'll leave because I want you to be happy. But you have to mean it if you say it because it'll break my fucking heart, and I won't be able to do this again if you change your mind."

I wrap my arms around his neck and burrow my face in the

side of his beard, breathing in the spruce scent. "I don't want you to go, but I'm scared for you to stay."

"Why does me staying scare you?"

"What if I can't move forward because he's always in the back of my head or in my dreams? How can I be with you if part of me is still with him?"

I wait for him to say it'll get better with time. For him to say Wesley's presence will fade, and it won't feel like any of this was real. When I'm older, there'll be a gap in my twenties anytime I try to recall memories, and it'll seem like a bad dream I could've sworn was real but wasn't.

I wait for him to say those things, but he doesn't.

PRYING my arms from his neck, he stands and turns the shower on. Steam fills the small room as he pulls his shirt over his head, drops it in the corner, and tugs mine off the same way.

As I stand under the hot water, the bruises and cuts on my skin throb in protest. Part of me wants to hide, to disappear into the shadows where no one can see me because no one can hurt me when I'm invisible. There, I'm alone. There, I'm safe. I wrap my arms around myself to shield my breasts as the hot water lashes my back.

"Will you wash my beard for me?" Beau holds the shampoo out, catching water in his palms and splashing his face.

I dispense a dollop of shampoo on my palm and rub my hands together. I expect him to close his eyes when I drag my soapy fingers through the length of his beard, but he watches me as I lather it up.

"Do you think you'll ever shave again?" I make small circular motions with my fingertips against his cheeks, working the soap into the follicles.

"If I have a good reason." He tilts his head back so I can work the suds under his chin. "But it'd have to be a damn good reason."

I slide my hands down his neck and rest them flat against the dark hair on his chest. "I can't imagine you without it."

"My mom's the only person to ever cut my hair, and I let it go after she died. She's still the last person to cut it if I don't cut it." He holds my hands to his chest and presses his lips against my forehead before trading places with me so he's under the shower.

His dark hair stretches past his shoulders as he washes it, and I think I love his shoulders. Defined. Strong. I like the way they flex when he moves. His slender frame is muscular in all the right areas, proving it isn't fair how someone who drinks all their calories and chain smokes has a better body than someone who tries to be conscious of their health.

That someone isn't me, though.

I'm the last person to judge anyone's eating habits, considering I spent a sizeable chunk of my late teens binging and purging so I wouldn't gain those thirty pounds back.

He guides me back under the water. "Tilt your head back."

The hot water hitting my sore scalp hurts and feels amazing at the same time. I don't think Wesley pulled any hair out, but I bet it'd be black and blue if I could see it. Beau massages the shampoo, and I wince because any touch is too much.

"Sorry. It's sore."

His nostrils flare as he tilts my head back and rinses my hair. "That's good enough for now."

He holds my hand above my head and twirls me around like we're dancing and washes my back, sliding the washcloth over the globes of my ass and out over my hips. Spinning me around again, he moves the slippery cloth over my collarbone and down my sternum between my breasts, circling them from the bottom and gliding the soap over my nipples. He doesn't linger on them despite the erection indicating he may want to. I gasp when he drags the cloth between my legs, grabbing his shoulders to steady myself.

Trying not to smile, he sinks to his knees in front of me and positions my foot on his thigh the same way he did in my kitchen the night I busted my shin, running the washcloth from my thigh to my ankle and repeating the ritual on the other leg. When he's done, there isn't an inch of my body untouched by his hands.

He holds my hips and kisses the scar next to my navel. He clenches his eyes shut, inhaling and exhaling against my wet skin but not breaking the connection.

"What happened last summer?" He asks.

"I was four months pregnant, and Wesley decided he didn't want me to be, so he beat and stabbed me." I touch the scar. "I ended up with an infection from an incomplete miscarriage that'll keep me from getting pregnant again...at least that's what the doctor thought when he used the term 'highly unlikely'."

Water droplets hang from his eyelashes when he looks up with brown eyes full of compassion and love. I urge him to his feet because I don't want him on his knees anymore.

"In the trailer, that wasn't us. I didn't want to do that," he says.

"I know."

"I was scared if I didn't, he would-"

"I wasn't there. I went to the lake." My heart aches as I wrap my arms around his neck because he's become one more person Wesley has hurt. "I didn't mean anything I said. I was just trying to diffuse the situation."

"Your skin's clean of him now, and it'll never be touched by his hands again." He lays his palm over my heart. "I can't wash away what he left here or here, though." He kisses my forehead. The bruise around my eye and the one along my jaw draw his attention, and he traces them with his fingertips, his eyes narrowing.

I wrap my hand around his wrist. "They'll heal."

"They're the last ones you'll ever have."

"Bold statement, considering I'm a walking calamity."

"Yes, you are." Our wet chests slip and slide against each other. "You're free now, and no one will ever hurt you like that again. You'll come out on the other side of this and fill the world with light you don't think you have." He skims his palm up and down my spine, the left side of his mouth curving higher than the other with a haphazard smile.

"I'm scared of what this will turn us into. What if we wake up one day and are strangers?" I ask as I step from the shower.

"That can't happen."

"How can you be sure?"

He follows me out of the shower and kisses me. "Because we were never strangers."

"Take me to bed," I say against his lips.

"Are you sure?"

"I want to feel something good, and you're my something good."

He swings my legs around his waist, gripping my ass as he carries me across the room, where our soaking-wet bodies fall onto the bed. He's already between my thighs when we land, hovering over me as he slides inside me, driving deep to the hilt and pausing before easing back out.

He's making me feel something good. He makes everything good. I don't know what comes over me, but I'll regret it if I don't say it.

"I want to love you."

It comes out wrong.

He lifts his head, the left corner of his mouth curling higher than the other side. "Yeah?" He pushes his entire length inside me and stills, the width of him stretching and filling me. "Well, I'm a lovable guy."

He kisses the side of my neck and almost pulls out, leaving only the tip in before plunging back in and repeating the torturous act. Sinking to the hilt, he pulls everything but the head out and pauses. "So, what's stopping you?"

"I'm scared it'll hurt."

"Love doesn't hurt if you do it right." He advances back inside me with slow movements. "It only hurts if you're not ready and force it." He withdraws his cock from my body. "If you do it right, it's the best feeling in the world." He lunges forward again, hitting the spot he knows will make me come undone. "Remember how I said a woman like you is cruel to a man like me?"

"I recall."

"Well, you've done the cruelest thing a woman can do to a man like me." He kisses me and pulls back. "I've fallen in love with you, and if our path leads nowhere, I need you to know this was real for me, and you mattered."

Guilt seizes my heart.

Those three words carry so much weight I can't pick them up. Words have the power to change people, and not always for the better. Wesley changed after I confessed my love for him.

Those three words left me vulnerable because I craved to hear them after I lost my mom, and Wesley knew it. Like so many other things, he ruined this for me, too.

"I don't know if I can give you that," I say.

"I'll never ask for more than you can give, and I'm willing to wait because you'll love me eventually."

"How can you be sure?"

"Because I'm extremely fucking lovable." He sweeps his tongue inside my mouth, and I hook my legs around him, pulling him in deeper.

"I don't need you to love me. I just don't want you to hate me like you do him."

He sucks my nipple inside his hot mouth, swirling his wet tongue around the stiff bud as I grip his head, twisting my fingers in his dark hair as I hold his mouth to my breast. An intense urgency builds between my thighs, and I raise my hips to meet his.

"Beau," I say because I don't have enough air in my lungs to do anything else. His hips rock back and forth, and I hang onto him while he fucks me hard. He pulls back and slams into me, driving his cock as deep as it'll go over and over.

His chest slides across my breasts, the sparse hair rubbing against them until they feel raw. But I love it. His beard drags against my skin, and I love it, too.

He growls through clenched teeth, climaxing as his body tenses and jerks. His cock pulsates, pushing his seed out until there's nothing left, and he collapses on top of me.

"Cruel, I tell you. Cruel." He rolls onto the bed next to me. "Give me five minutes, and I'll be ready to go again." He stretches his arm out, inviting me to his side.

I snuggle against his chest, throwing my leg over his. He makes those tiny circles on my hip as he hums a song I don't recognize. Without warning, he sits straight up and stands from the bed.

"With everything that's happened, I forgot to give you something." Crossing the room, he rustles through his bag and returns with a small brown paper bag dangling from his index finger. "I was going to give it to you once we got on the road, but..." He shrugs. "Shit happened."

I push up into a sitting position, and he drops the bag in my lap, not giving me a chance to refuse it. I lift the white iPhone box out and stare at him.

"You need a phone," he says. "It's a necessity, not a luxury."

"This is too much. I can't." I lower the box inside the bag. "I don't need one this expensive." I hold the bag out to him, and he tucks his hands behind his back, shaking his head. "This is too much." I put the bag on the bed since he won't take it.

"I added it to my account, but we can switch it to your own whenever you're ready. You need to be able to call for help if you end up in a dangerous situation."

"I agree, but not with a thirteen-hundred-dollar phone."

He takes the box from the bag and rips the seal off. "There's nothing wrong with having nice things." Teasing the box open, he powers the phone on.

"Says the guy who drives a thirty-year-old truck."

"It has sentimental value." He rustles through the brown bag and drags out a case and screen protector. Apparently, he thinks of everything. "Besides, I can afford a new one. I just don't want one."

He's right.

If I ever fall in love again, it'll be with him.

32

There are lucid moments between waking and sleeping when I feel like I'm floating and nothing bad has ever happened. A flash of euphoria. Contentment. Peace. Suspended in a time where reality and dreams flirt with each other.

It's here, in this liminal space, where I exist as an echo of who I was and a glimpse of who I'm meant to be.

Beau's stretched out on the bed, one arm behind his head and the other resting over his stomach. He hasn't slept much the last couple of days, so I curl my arm around the lumpy pillow and keep my distance because I don't want to wake him.

I want to be still with him for a little longer.

His profile is perfect. He has a perfect nose and perfect lips that go lopsided when he smiles. I want to touch him but won't because he needs to rest.

I roll to my back and stare at the stained ceiling tiles. A mildewy smell lives in the room, and I don't know if it's from the threadbare carpet, the dingy drapes, or the peeling wallpaper. The stench could be from all three—the ideal mix of stale cigarette smoke, shitty air flow, and humid summers.

But when I turn my head to my right, perfection sleeps next to me.

However, Beau isn't perfect. He's flawed like every human, and I can't ignore those flaws.

I ignored so much with Wesley, and I won't do it again.

Beau drinks and smokes too much, doesn't get enough sleep, and intense emotions cause him to shut down. He has walls up he won't acknowledge.

As if he senses my staring, he rolls to his side and pulls me against him, nuzzling his nose in my hair. "Are you hungry?"

"I don't have much of an appetite."

"Will you try?" He asks.

"Do I have to?"

"You don't have to do anything, but it'd be a good idea."

He's right. I need to eat something because I can't puke all day and night if I don't put something in my stomach. "I can't make any promises, but I'll give it a shot."

"Thank you." He stands and pulls his jeans on, the brass buckle jingling as he cinches the belt around his slim waist.

"We're leaving the room?"

"Not much here to eat." He pulls on a black T-shirt. "Some fresh air might be good for us since we've been cooped up in this room for two days, and I can't take another shitty delivery pizza."

I rummage through the garbage bag I crammed clothes in when Brad took me from the trailer and find a pair of denim shorts and a light blue cotton tank top.

I close myself inside the tiny bathroom to change because I don't want him to see the bruises on my body. When I step out, I avoid my reflection as I sweep my choppy hair into a low bun. The bruises on my arm look worse today than they did yesterday.

"Do you have a flannel or hoodie I can borrow?" I call to Beau as I dig through my purse for my concealer.

He walks across the room with a lazy swagger. "We've just gotten out of triple-digit days." He wraps his arms around my waist from behind.

"I assume that's a no."

I lean over the counter and dab concealer along my jaw. The tender bruises hurt like hell, especially when I blend the makeup over them.

"Don't," he says as he watches over my shoulder.

"Don't what?" I pat the makeup across my jawline.

He runs a washcloth under the water and wrings it out in the sink. He takes the tube from my hand, sliding it to the corner of the small vanity.

"What are you doing?" I reach for the make-up, but he blocks me.

"Let people see what he did to you." He wipes the makeup off my jaw, and I wince. "Don't hide it anymore."

"I can't go out in public like this."

"Why not? The truth is out, darlin'." He takes my hand. "And it's setting you free."

"I'm GETTING THE PANCAKES." Beau pushes the laminated menu across the table. "Are they good?"

"Yeah, coffee sounds great." I scan the menu, but the words jumble together because my eyes won't focus. I've stared at it for at least five minutes. That's five minutes of not looking up to see everyone gawking at us.

I recognize most of the faces, even the ones whose gazes dart away when our eyes meet. Their scrutiny is unyielding even as they pretend not to stare. The diner pulses with whispers, and I don't need to hear the conversations to know what they're saying.

Whore.

Had it coming.

Deserved it.

They're not wrong.

"Hey." Beau hooks his finger in the menu fold and pushes it down on the table. "Fuck what they think."

How's he so nonchalant about this? His name is on the tips of their tongues as well.

"Let's get something somewhere else," I say.

"We have just as much right to be here as they do." He spins the menu around. "Now, how about those pancakes? Or what about French toast? We need carbs and sugar if we're going into battle against the righteous." He winks.

"The blueberry oatmeal is my go-to." I point to the menu.

He waves his hand in the air to flag a server over and folds his arms over the table. Donna takes orders from tables surrounding us but lowers her gaze to the floor every time she walks past our booth.

Several new groups enter our section and are promptly assisted. Beau twirls a fork between his fingers and taps it on the tabletop, cutting his eyes at Donna when she passes us once again.

"Let's leave. We can grab something at the gas station," I say.

He ignores me and stretches to get Donna's attention.

"We're wasting our time because they're not going to serve us." He can stay here all day if he wants, but I don't want to be gawked at anymore.

As I pull my messenger bag strap over my head, I see Jeff walking across the crowded diner.

"Didn't expect to see you two." He smiles like he does when he doesn't know what to say in awkward situations. "Figured you'd both have tucked tail and left town already. Mind if I join you?"

"You'll ruin your reputation if you sit with us," I say.

"Oh, that's been ruined for a long time." He motions for me to scoot over and sinks down next to me. "Hell, most of them have been trying to shut the bar down for over a decade." He nods to the man staring at us from across the room. "Between us, knowing how much it pisses them off is one reason I keep it open." The man diverts his gaze to his cell phone. "Have you ordered yet?"

"Can't get anyone to take our order," Beau says.

Jeff whistles loud enough to get Donna's attention, and she's at our booth in less than thirty seconds.

"How you doing today, Donna?" Jeff asks.

"What can I get you?" She doesn't look in my or Beau's direction.

"I'll have a coffee, black, and they're getting..." He wags his finger between Beau and me. "I think they want something to eat."

She tucks the yellow pencil over her left ear. "I'll grab your coffee and take their order when I come back."

After Donna's departure, an awkward silence overtakes the three of us. I don't know how much he's heard about what happened.

"So, you two, huh?" He studies us. "I was surprised but not shocked."

"I didn't want to hurt Wes-"

Jeff interrupts. "I was surprised you shot him because I didn't think you had it in you, but I'm not shocked someone finally put a bullet in him. And as far as you two go, I had my suspicions."

Harold joins us, with Donna hovering in the background. He's a middle-aged, balding hanger-on who tries to be in the know, part of the inner circle of the Seymour happenings, but he'll never be more than an interloper because he isn't from here. Same as me. The difference is I've never wanted to be one of them.

"How's it going today?" He extends his hand, but Jeff doesn't shake it. "Listen, I hate I'm in this position, but I can't get involved. You know Thomas and Mary loaned me the money for the renovations last year."

"I remember." Jeff nods. "It was after you almost lost this place because of some bad luck at the casino, right?"

Harold's ears flush red. "Yes, I hit a rough patch."

"Like we all do from time to time." Jeff takes the coffee from Donna, pours a few sugar packets into the mug, and takes a sip. "Because none of us are without faults, correct?"

"I can't get mixed up in this." He glances around the diner like he's scared someone will see him talking to us. "I've always liked you, Katie, so I hope you understand this isn't personal."

I'm not upset. I don't think so, anyway. I feel bad for Harold if he's in Thomas and Mary's pocket because that's the worst place he could've ended up. He's a fly caught in the spider's web, and there's only one way it'll end for him.

"Can we at least get something to go since we've been sitting here for so long?" I ask.

He looks down at the tabletop. "It'd be best if you just leave."

"Ah, for fuck's sake." Jeff slams the ceramic mug on the table and pushes out of the booth.

Anyone who wasn't staring at us before is now.

"You're in my bar crying to Katie about your wife threatening to leave you because you can't get it up every time I turn around. I've heard you ask the girl for 'advice,'" he does air quotes, "and anyone with balls knows what you're doing. If she wanted to, you wouldn't have hesitated to sit in Beau's position even for a night." He drops a few dollar bills on the table. "So, don't stand here and pretend like what they've done is so damn unimaginable it prevents you from serving them your shitty food." He storms off, leaving Harold, along with everyone else in earshot, shocked.

Beau slides from the booth, and I follow his lead, placing my hand in his when he holds it out. He tips his black cowboy hat to Harold.

"You had to know you never had a chance." He winks.

I can only imagine what's being said inside when we meet up with Jeff in the parking lot. He's leaning against the back of his truck with his arms draped over the side.

"I'm sorry, Katie. No one in there has any right to judge anyone because these people forget they have secrets too, and I hear everything when lips get loose on Saturday nights." He shakes his head. "Harold's wife is sleeping with Marty from the post office, and Donna's daughter just had a baby with a man who won't leave his wife." He huffs. "And don't get me started on Donna."

"It's nothing I wasn't expecting." I sigh, but now I'm curious about Donna. "They'll never have to see me again once Brad gives us the green light to go."

"You guys want a drink?" Jeff asks.

"Do you have to ask?" Beau squeezes my hand.

"You shouldn't take our side because the bar's barely hanging on as it is," I say.

"Kid, the bar's been taking on water for a while. You two will just be the iceberg to finish her off." He yanks his truck door open. "Follow me over. I'll call Elliot and Allison to meet us there."

ALLISON CHAMBERS IS HABITUALLY LATE.

I've never known her to be on time for anything, and it drives Elliot crazy because punctual could be his middle name. When people say opposites attract, they're talking about those two.

She barrels through the front door twenty minutes later than Elliot told Jeff they'd be here, wearing oversized sunglasses that hide her blue eyes. She brings the heat in with her because her introduction makes the room warmer.

"Sorry, we're late." She slides her sunglasses on top of her head. "I just…" She fans her chest with her T-shirt. "There's no excuse. I'm just fucking late. It's who I am. Allison-I'm Fucking-Late-Chambers."

Wiping salt granules off the bar, she dusts her hands together before pulling a beer from the cooler and plopping back down. She twists the cap, eyeing Beau across the room talking with Jeff and Elliot.

"Are you two okay?" She asks.

I pick at the paper label on my beer bottle. "As okay as we can be considering."

"I'm pissed at you. You understand that, right?" She eyes me over the rim of her bottle before taking a drink. "I'm glad you're okay, but I'm mad at you for not coming to me before it got that bad. Why didn't you trust me enough to tell me what was happening? I could've helped."

"Because there was nothing you could do. You would've ended up hurt, too."

"Yeah, right. You were too kind. I would've aimed for his head and left him drooling or dead."

"Hurting him was never part of the plan."

"Yeah, well, even the best-laid plans don't always work out, do they?"

She falls quiet, which isn't like her. I dip my head to force her eyes to meet mine.

"Hey." I squeeze her arm. "There's nothing you could've done. I didn't want you to get caught up in it because we both know you would've made a scene."

"I would've made a scene." She nods. "A big one."

"I know."

"You should've told me instead of keeping it to yourself. Even if I couldn't help, I could've at least carried some of it for you because I know that crap was heavy."

"It was, but it was mine to carry."

She throws her arms around my neck and squeezes. I return the gesture, and we remain like that for a few minutes before separating. When I see her face again, her eyes are watery and red.

"Are you one of those people who cries when they get angry?" I ask.

She presses her fingertips into the corners of her eyes. "No, I'm one of those people who cries when they realize they almost lost their best friend."

She's right.

Wesley could've shot us before we knew what happened, or he could've fired back when I shot him. But that's not what happened.

"But you didn't. I'm still here even though some people wish I weren't." Reluctantly, she gives up a smile. "Now, let's pretend things are somewhat normal. Please?"

"Fine." She sniffles. "You want normal?"

"Yes."

"Okay." She clears her throat. "You never told me if he was any good in the sack."

"It feels wrong talking about something so personal."

"You're in love with him, aren't you?"

"No. I don't know. I care about him a lot, but I'm not sure it's love."

"You can lie to yourself and everyone else, but you can't lie to me." She nods and flicks her eyes over my shoulder.

I twist to see Beau and Elliot walking toward us.

"Are you ladies good over here?" Elliot takes up next to Allison.

"I think so." She snakes her arm around his waist.

Beau stands next to me, not as close as Elliot to Allison, but close enough that it'd be suspicious if the entire town didn't know the truth about us.

The front door opens, and everyone's attention snaps to the three men stalking across the room, led by Hazard Rogers.

Yes, Hazard is his real name.

His dad thought giving his son a unique name would set him up for a life of greatness, but Hazard's only claim to fame is being the best meth cook in Baylor County—or the worse, considering he's blown up two trailers in the time I've been here. The only other thing he's known for is being Wesley's best friend in high school. If you ask me, a cool name was wasted.

"We're closed, fellas," Jeff calls out to the trio.

"Looks open to me," Hazard says as he slides onto a stool.

"We're just trying to get a few beers, and we'll be on our way," Jimmy Mooren says.

"You boys behave, and you're welcome to drink as long as you like." Jeff pops caps from three beers and slides them across the bar. "Understand?"

Hazard performs a sloppy salute and the other two laugh at his antics. Monkey see, monkey do with these three.

Jeff disappears to his office, which isn't shocking because that's where he'd rather be most of the time. He doesn't care for crowds, regardless of how small they are. That's why Elliot's in charge of the front of the bar, and Jeff sticks to the business side. It works because Elliot's great with people—even assholes named Hazard.

I chat with my friends and pretend Hazard isn't staring a hole through me.

I smile, even laugh, to show him he doesn't bother me. Does he think I'll cower because of a glare? They must not know Wesley well because if they did, they'd know nothing they can do to me holds a candle to what he did.

But like with most bullies, when staring doesn't work, he

ratchets up the intimidation by talking loud enough for me to overhear the vile things he's saying to his minions. I'm used to Wesley's worshipers making my life miserable, but it bothers Beau and Allison.

"Ignore them," I say. "They're trying to get a rise."

"It's working." Allison glares at the men.

"They're not worth it." I remind her.

Hazard winks and follows it up with a cocky grin, irritating Allison further.

"She's right. They're not worth it." Elliot rubs her back.

Hazard slides off his stool and walks toward us. Beau stiffens next to me, and Allison stares daggers through him during his approach, which doesn't help the situation. She's like a guard dog, fearless even though she should be scared because Hazard lives up to his name in one regard.

Most people he fights don't fare well. In that respect, his father got it right. His son is certainly not good for anyone who crosses him.

"Relax." Hazard raises his hands. "I just wanted to come over and meet the man with balls big enough to steal my best friend's wife." He holds his hand out, and Beau glares at him. "C'mon, I'm fucking with you." He slaps Beau's shoulder.

"Don't touch me," Beau says.

Hazard holds his hands up. "Calm down, man. I'm trying to be friendly. You know how to do that, don't you?"

Beau doesn't take the bait.

"No one wants you here, so why don't you leave?" Allison says.

"You're a rude one, aren't you?" Hazard shakes his head. "Not sweet like Katie here." He lays his calloused hand on my shoulder.

I shrug his hand off me, but Beau's livid.

"Put your hands on her again, and mine will be on you," Beau says.

"Oh, you want to go?" Hazard steps backward, inviting Beau to the middle of the floor with a wave. "Come on."

Beau puts his beer down on the bar, and Elliot puts his hand on Beau's chest. "This is what he came for, so don't give him the satisfaction."

"Listen to him so I don't have to embarrass you in front of your lady," Hazard says.

"Elliot's right. Ignore him." I say.

Beau takes a deep breath and turns his back to Hazard, kissing the top of my head. "Let's go."

"I'll call you," I say to Allison as I slide from the stool.

He slips his arm around my waist, palming my hip as we walk toward the front door. Neither us notices Hazard approaching until he's in our faces, chest to chest with Beau.

"Only a pussy steals another man's woman."

"Funny, I don't remember her being married to a man, only a low-life piece of shit," Beau says.

"Watch what you say about my friend."

"You know what? You came here for a fight, so let's go," Beau tosses his hat onto a nearby table.

I wedge myself between them and put my palms against Beau's chest. "It's not worth it."

"Listen to the bitch." Hazard laughs. "It'll save you from getting your ass handed to you."

"Apologize to her," Beau says.

"Fuck you and fuck her."

Elliot appears next to Hazard. "You need to get out of here."

"You're siding with them over someone you've known your whole life?"

Elliot sighs. "I don't want this shit on my doorstep."

"I'll go because I got respect for you and your brother." Hazard glares at us. "Not because of them two."

"Thank you," Elliot says, rolling his eyes as he walks back to Allison.

Beau's nostrils flare and his face is red, his chest vibrating with anger he's trying to rein in. He's not an angry person. This is one more example of how I'm not good for him because he wouldn't be in this position if not for me.

I try to keep Beau focused on me, but no matter what I do or say, he's laser-focused on Hazard's every move.

"Hey, Katie," Hazard calls from behind me as he approaches.

I spin around to keep my eyes on him. "Yeah?"

"If you were looking for dick, you should've looked closer to home." He grabs his crotch. "I've got something better for you to suck, you filthy little slut."

My hand flies across his cheek, and, in the same breath, he slaps me, knocking me into Beau.

The entire scene is chaotic as Beau shoves me to the side, and Elliot runs across the bar. Hazard steps to Beau, itching for the fight he came for, and I end up behind Hazard, screaming at Beau to stop while Elliot rushes to get in between them.

Everything happens so fast.

Beau pulls his arm back, and his fist cuts through the air toward Hazard's jaw. Hazard shifts to the left, dodging the blow, and I see the horror in Beau's eyes as he realizes what's happening and that he can't stop it.

33

A dull ache pulses at my temples as I sit up on Elliot's couch, a cruel reminder of last night spiraling out of control.

Everything comes flooding back. Hazard. The fight. Beau's panicked stare as he realized he'd lost control in the worst possible way.

Light spills out from under the swinging kitchen door, and I pick up a muted conversation from the other side, but I can't make out what's being said. As I swing my legs over the edge of the couch, I attempt to stand, and a wave of dizziness pulls me back down as I let out a groan, half frustration and half pain.

Allison breezes through the swinging door, dark circles under her eyes and hair a mess.

"You're awake." She sits next to me and holds her hand out. Two ibuprofen tablets sit in her palm, and I love this woman. I take the glass of water she offers and chase the pills down.

"Where's Beau?" I ask.

Before she answers, there's a look, and I can't tell what it is.

"I'm not sure. We brought you here because Brad wanted

him to calm down somewhere else. He was pretty upset."
There's that expression again.

"Brad?"

"Elliot called him because we were worried you might have
a concussion."

"Would you mind giving me a ride to the room?"

Allison glances at the kitchen and back to me like I may not
have noticed. "Maybe hang out here for a bit."

"What's going on with you?"

"Nothing."

"Bullshit. You're acting weirder than usual."

"I'm worried about you. That's all."

I bunch the blanket up in my lap. "There's no reason to be
concerned. It was an accident."

"Everyone saw what happened. No one thinks he did it on
purpose." She chews her bottom lip and stares down at her lap.

What's going on that she doesn't want to tell me? This is so
far beyond her typical behavior that she must know it's
obvious.

Elliot appears from the kitchen with Brad on his heels. Both
men look at me the same way Allison's looking at me, and it's
infuriating.

"Why are you guys acting like someone died?" I ask.

"No one died," Elliot says.

I turn to Brad. "Will you give me a ride to the motel?"

There's a subtle exchange between them, and he walks to
the door. "I'd be happy to. Care if we grab some coffee on the
way?"

"I don't mind." I scoop my messenger bag up from the chair
beside the couch and follow Brad outside.

Inside his patrol car, I buckle up and break the silence.
"Have you heard from him?"

"Not since I sent him to cool off." He inserts the key into the ignition, pausing before turning it. "Beau aside, I need to talk to you about something."

"Okay, you guys are freaking me out. What's going on?"

"Let's get coffee first."

"THIS TASTES LIKE SHIT." Brad opens his car door and pours his coffee on the dirt road. "Does yours?" He pulls the door closed.

"Tastes like it always does to me." I follow the rim of the paper cup with my index finger.

"Really?" He pushes a stack of paperwork around on the dashboard and rummages through the console. "Has it always tasted this bad?" He peels the foil from a piece of chewing gum that's seen better days.

He's seen better days, too.

He's sporting a five o'clock shadow that's moved into the next day, and his clothes are rumpled like he slept in them.

"Never mind. Don't answer that because it's the only place to get a cup in a hurry, so don't ruin it for me." He pops the gum in his mouth, chews twice, and spits it out the window.

His phone rings, and he steps out to take it, pacing behind the car and running his hand through his hair. He pauses and closes his eyes like he's trying to recall something. I've never seen him so stressed. He's always in control but appears to be struggling to maintain it.

After the failed attempt at a cup of coffee and avoiding what he wants to talk about, he takes me to the motel.

Sticking around long after I expect him to leave, he paces the room and pulls the heavy curtains back every few minutes, emitting a neurotic energy unlike him.

"You don't have to babysit me," I say.

"Not babysitting you." He stares outside. "Just hanging out until Beau gets back."

"I've texted and called, but he isn't answering his phone."

"I'm sure he's just sleeping it off in his truck somewhere, and he'll be back soon enough."

"This was all my fault. He didn't do anything wrong. He tried to help Wesley after I shot him. He saved his life because I would've let him bleed to death before calling an ambulance." Anger sizzles under my skin thinking about it. "I wanted him to feel the same helplessness I've felt on that floor."

"He's not getting away with anything this time." He leans back in the chair. "Why didn't you tell me it was that bad?"

The horrified look on his face when I told him the truth of what my marriage to Wesley has been like is something I'll never forget.

"Wesley was my problem, and I didn't want you catching fallout from helping me."

"I'm sorry if I ever made you feel like you couldn't come to me."

"You've been a great friend, and that's why I didn't tell you. It wasn't worth everything you could've lost."

"Your life and well-being are more important than a job." He narrows his eyes, anger creeping into them. "I don't give a shit about losing a job."

I linger by the vanity counter, leaning my shoulder against the wall. "Have you slept at all?"

"If I'm being honest, I don't remember." He pinches the bridge of his nose. "I dozed off at my desk earlier, but I don't know if I imagined it or if it really happened." There's a slight smile, and I'm not sure he has the energy to fully form one.

I sit on the bed across from him. "Do you think Thomas and Mary know where he is?"

He peeks through the drapes over his shoulder. "I'm sure of it."

"How are they going to cover this up?" I can't imagine what's going through Mary's head, knowing she may not be able to get Wesley out of this one.

"They're not." He releases the thick fabric and leans forward, resting his elbows on his thighs as he clears his throat. "So, when I said there was something I needed to talk to you about...I have some questions about your marriage."

"What kind of questions?"

"The personal kind, that as your friend, I don't want to ask."

"Are you asking as a friend, or is this in a professional capacity?"

"I assure you I wouldn't ask if I didn't have to." He produces a small notepad and pen from his back pocket and lays it on the table. "Did you ever see anything suspicious in Wesley's truck or rig? Like something you thought was odd but didn't think much about it at the time?"

The ink pen clicks. The air conditioner hums in the background. My heart beats in my ears. "Nothing stands out."

"What about his behavior? Has he said or done anything out of character?"

"That's hard to answer because his mood is always unpredictable. One minute, he's happy and laughing, and the next, he's using my face as a punching bag."

"Okay, so if he's a moody asshole in general, are there times he's nicer than normal?"

"Only when he hurts me. He's always extra attentive the next day, sending flowers and stuff like that...until he stopped pretending to be sorry."

Brad scribbles something down. "Given the crimes, I need to ask some intimate questions."

"Crimes? What's going on?"

"I don't think you're the only woman he's hurt." He flips to a new page in the notepad. "In the bedroom," He clears his throat, and it's obvious he's uncomfortable. "Does Wesley have any preferences that aren't normal to you? I understand normal is subjective, but I'm talking about anything that makes you uncomfortable."

I tuck my hair behind my ear. "He likes rough sex. I don't consider myself a prude, and I get that people enjoy different things, but he takes everything to the extreme."

"How so?"

"He can't finish unless he's choking me, and there were a few times I lost consciousness."

"Often?"

"Often enough." I clear my throat because the air in the room seems dryer now. "He forces me to look him in the eyes the entire time because he likes watching the light fade out." A hard lump makes it difficult to swallow.

"You should have come to me."

"And say what?" I sniffle. "It was my word against his, and he would've denied everything."

Asking for his help would've been pointless, and he would've felt responsible and helpless when Mary and Thomas swooped in to clear Wesley's name. They practically own this town, and anyone who thinks differently is either delusional or brave beyond measure.

And Brad isn't a delusional man.

With a heavy sigh, he rises from his seat and strides toward the door. "Stay vigilant," he warns, his eyes glinting with a mix of exhaustion and anger. "Plenty of his supporters are looking to even the score, and I don't have the patience or energy to deal with their stupidity. If I could spare the bodies, I'd post someone outside, but I don't, so I can't. When Beau gets back, tell him I need him to swing by the station and sign a few papers."

"Brad," I follow him to the door. "What's he done?"

"I think he's connected to Abigail White."

My hand flies to my mouth to disguise an audible gasp. "You don't think he...did he?"

"I don't want to assume anything. We've taken samples of his blood from the carpet in the trailer to send off for DNA testing. We should know more once it comes back."

"I need to sit down." I guide myself along the wall until I reach the chair and table. "Did they know each other?"

"A friend of hers said she'd been talking to a guy in town who matches Wesley's description, and he's the only one in town who drives a truck like she described. Do you remember ever seeing her?"

"No, I...I don't." A hard knot forms in my stomach because the thought of Wesley killing someone confirms my worst fears.

If he's capable of taking someone's life, he won't make an exception for mine.

"There's something else, but you're not going to like it, either."

"Geez, you're just full of fun today, aren't you?" I rub my temples, keeping my eyes closed so the room won't spin.

"Thomas wants a meeting with you."

"No way." I shake my head. "Not happening."

"I'll set it up for this afternoon and go with you. I think you should hear him out."

"I shot his son."

"All the more reason to see what he has to say."

34

A cloud of red dirt forms on the road ahead, and I recognize Thomas Reese's truck in front of it. The black Dodge stops next to us, blocking the road. It's a good thing only farmers use these roads, but I suspect that's why Thomas chose this location.

Brad lays his cell phone on the seat between us. "Ready to do this?"

No, I'm not ready to do this.

I round the front of the truck as Thomas exits his. He's aged a decade since I saw him last. When I look at him, I see Wesley in thirty years. The two men are built the same and carry themselves in the same manner.

"Thanks for doing this." Thomas shakes Brad's hand.

Brad leans back against his truck door and hooks one ankle over the other. "Don't thank me." He jerks his chin toward me. "She's the one who agreed to come."

Thomas looks at me, but I don't know what's going through his head. He doesn't say anything, just offers a slight nod of acknowledgment.

The three of us stand around, no one knowing what to say. I keep my distance, staying in the front of the truck so there's one less corner to get around if I have to run.

"Have you heard from him?" I break the ice.

"No." He shakes his head and crosses his arms over his broad chest. "I've tried calling his phone, but it goes straight to voicemail. I assume the battery is dead, or he's turned it off."

"So we can't trace it," Brad says.

He's lying. There's no way Wesley wouldn't have called Mary or Thomas by now. He knows he's in deep shit, so they're the first ones he'd call for money or help fleeing.

"Or that," Thomas says.

"I'm not trying to be a bitch, but why did you want to see me? What could you possibly have to say to me that you couldn't have said over the past three years?"

I can't look at him. He looks too much like Wesley, and it's making my skin itch.

"The press has gotten wind of what's going on, and I wanted to ask you not to speak with them because the police haven't proven that Wesley has done anything. The court of public opinion has the strongest influence on a person's guilt or innocence, and I want him to get a fair trial if it goes that far." He glances at Brad.

"Do you think he's innocent?" I ask.

"It doesn't matter what I think."

"It does matter." I take the baseball hat off, freeing my mangled hair from the elastic so he can see it. "This is what he did." I tug on the uneven locks that used to be at the top of my ass and are now at my shoulder blades. Without the hat, the sun shines on my jaw.

"This is what he did." I lift my tank top above my belly button. "This is what your son did." I point to my scar. "And you helped him get away with it like you always do."

Thomas turns his head and refuses to look at it. He was

there the night Wesley did it. He called Thomas, panicked because he thought he killed me.

They hatched the plan to put me in the bedroom for a few days. If I made it out, great. If I didn't, they'd tell everyone I bled to death during a miscarriage. Cremation. No funeral. No questions. Wesley could play the part of a grieving husband and father-to-be.

"Yeah, I heard you and Wesley that night. I heard it all and suffered in that bed for three days, hoping to die. You're no better than him because you've fed the monster inside him." I bite tears back because he will never see me cry again. "I don't understand how you can condone his behavior. It doesn't make sense."

"That's because you're not a parent."

"Yeah, well, thanks to your son, I'll never be one." The words burn like venom on my tongue, but I've got to bite him or risk poisoning myself.

"Look, I didn't come here to rehash everything Wesley's done wrong in his life, and we can all agree you're not innocent in all this, given recent revelations. Can't we?" He narrows his eyes.

I cross my arms over my chest and raise my chin. "You're right. I had an affair. I cheated on him. But if we're tallying things, ask me how many women Wesley slept with in the last year alone?" I grind my teeth, fury burning red hot in my chest. "Ask me how many times he's taken me to the emergency room in Wichita Falls because he doesn't want anyone here to know what he does to me. Ask me, Thomas." I fist my hands at my side. "Ask me."

Brad steps between us and grabs my shoulders, dipping his head to look me in the eye. "Calm down." He inhales deeply and blows it out steadily. "Breathe."

I nod and choke back tears. Sadness and hurt didn't cause these tears. These tears are made from anger. "I'm sorry."

Thomas plops a brown envelope on the hood of the truck. "There's everything you need to start your life over."

I look at the envelope and then to Brad. As if he can read my mind, he reaches for the envelope. He pulls a stack of papers and a thick white envelope out.

"The requirements were met to waive the waiting period for the divorce to be finalized. I filed it with the court yesterday. As of eleven yesterday morning, you got what you wanted. You're a free woman," Thomas says.

"I never wanted any of this."

Brad holds the papers out to me, but I don't need to see them. He pushes them back into the envelope and holds the sealed white envelope up. "And this?"

"Is ten thousand dollars." Thomas looks at me like I'm supposed to thank him for it.

"You're trying to buy my silence?" I ask.

"I'm paying a debt I owe." He glances at his watch. "You never deserved my son, and he never deserved you. Interpret that how you want. I'm trying to help you salvage something from the last three years of your life. Don't let pride ruin the only positive thing coming from this."

"Does Mary know you're doing this?" I ask.

"What do you think?"

I take the white envelope from Brad and toss it past Thomas' head into his open truck window. "I don't want anything from you."

"So be it." There's a slight chuckle with the statement. He gets inside his truck and starts the engine, looking past Brad and locking his eyes on me. "I'd appreciate it if you'd be discreet around town while you're here. It's one thing for everyone to know but another for you to rub it in everyone's face."

"What? You think we're going to go at it on the courthouse lawn or something? Do you really think so little of me?"

"You shot my son, Katie. I don't want to think of you at all anymore." He rolls the window up and drives away, leaving a cloud of red dust in his path.

"Do you think he knows where Wesley is?" I ask Brad as I scoop the brown envelope off the hood and climb into the passenger seat.

Brad slams his door and starts the truck. "Without a doubt."

His phone rings, and he frowns when he glances at the screen. "Let me take this, and then we'll head back to town." He exits the truck.

I pull the divorce papers from the envelope and see words like 'dissolution' and 'final' as I skim over them.

I'm free.

He doesn't have anything to hold over me anymore. I thought I'd feel more. I don't know what I expected, but whatever it was, it was more than this. I still feel like a prisoner. Like he's going to pop up any minute and drag me back inside that trailer.

Wesley knows the police are searching for him, and he knows I'm the closest thing to him they have. If he says he'll find Beau and me to finish what he started, I believe him.

Now more than ever, I believe he meant it when he said he'd never let me go.

This piece of paper doesn't mean anything to Wesley. In his mind, I'm his and always will be. The realization hits me.

This won't ever be over.

Not unless he's arrested. But then what? He'll pick up where he leaves off if he's found innocent.

I shove the papers inside the envelope to keep them from getting tear-stained. I'm so tired of crying because of him. But no matter how much I cry, there's always another reason to shed tears when it comes to him.

Will I ever heal? Will I ever go a day without crying because of Wesley?

Beau wants to replace all my terrible memories of Wesley with good ones of him, but it doesn't work that way. I can't just turn them off. They'll be here, lurking in the dark corners of my mind to remind me of what can happen.

The driver's door opens, and I swipe my cheeks.

"What's wrong?" Brad asks as he hurries to get inside the truck.

I shake my head, scared to speak for fear that I'll break down even more.

"Did something happen?"

"No." I sniffle and swipe my fingertips under my eyes. "It just gets overwhelming sometimes when I think about everything that's happened."

To my shock, he leans over the console and hugs me. He doesn't do this. He's not a hugger. He's hugged me twice in two years. He palms the back of my head, and I turn my cheek on his shoulder.

"After I got out of the military, I had a hard time unseeing things that happened while I was deployed. It used to keep me up at night and made me drink way more than I should have."

"What did you do to make it stop?"

"Nothing. It hasn't stopped. I still think about every person I couldn't save."

I lean back and chase another tear away with my fingertips. "If you're trying to make me feel better, you're not doing it right."

Fine lines crease in the corners of his eyes as he smiles. "Those memories will never go away because they're a part of you now. The only thing you can do is accept the role they play in your life. Like the good things that happen to us, the bad ones are important, too. Everything we go through shapes us into who we are today and who we'll be in the future." He leans on the armrest and turns his wrist up. "See that?" He points to the three-inch-long faded scar where a watch would sit if he wore one.

"What happened?"

"I couldn't deal with the memories, so I tried to become one." He rolls his arm over to take the scar out of view. "It's the lowest I've ever fallen, but I don't regret it because I had to fall to get back up."

"Does seeing the scar remind you of how low you fell?"

"It reminds me of how high I've climbed. Instead of being embarrassed or ashamed, I made it part of my story. You've got to learn how to stop thinking about how low you fell and start thinking about how high you've climbed." He reaches over and dries my cheek with his thumb. "And how much higher you're going to go."

The moment is intimate, like two lovers, and I see it for the first time. The reason people think something went on between us. He cares about me. Not the way people assume, but he cares about my well-being for whatever reason.

I fall back against the truck seat and turn my head to him. "Do you know Beau thinks something went on between us?"

He shakes his head and buckles his seat belt. "That's ridiculous. Why would he think that?"

"I don't know. Maybe because you're nice to me."

"I'm nice to you because I like you. But you are, I mean were, a married woman, and I'm not that kind of guy, so nothing would've ever happened."

I raise my eyebrow and smile. "The kind of guy Beau is?"

He nods and laughs. "Yes, that kind of guy."

"Thank you." I look out over the cotton fields. "In case I haven't said it."

"For what?"

"For everything you've done that you didn't have to and for being my friend because I don't have many of them."

The truck stops at the end of the dirt road, and he hesitates before pulling onto the pavement that leads back to town. "If you consider me your friend, why didn't you trust me enough to come to me sooner? I could've helped you."

Because Wesley was irrational and would've hurt anyone who cared about me.

"Because I considered you my friend."

35

I'm glad Brad didn't fight me when I asked to be dropped off at the bar instead of the motel room because it felt like the walls were closing in on me as soon as I opened the door.

I still haven't heard from Beau even though I've called and texted him all day. His things were undisturbed, so it didn't appear that he'd returned to the room while I was out with Brad.

As I processed Brad's suspicions about Wesley, my mind went to a terrible place.

He's not a good man, but a killer? I thought his anger was only directed toward me because I wasn't a good wife. I thought there was something about me that set him off.

"I just can't help myself when it comes to you."

An overhead lamp is out, so the bar is dimmer than usual, almost setting the mood for my despair with the mix of cigarette smoke and the faint scent of spilled beer. The only other person here, an older man at a table near the empty stage, seems content with his own thoughts and doesn't pay attention to anyone else.

I order a whiskey from Jeff and take a big gulp, welcoming

the burning sensation traveling down my throat. I need it now more than ever to calm my racing mind and the uneasy feeling in my gut that something's off.

Well, something more than the obvious.

Jeff slides onto the stool next to me, a fresh cup of black coffee in hand. "Didn't think I'd be seeing you tonight."

"Didn't think I'd be here tonight." I offer a weak smile. "But I needed to get out of the room, and this is the only place I could think to go where I wouldn't have to explain myself."

He emits a soft chuckle. "I would ask if you're feeling alright, but I'm sure you're tired of people asking that, aren't you?"

"You have no idea."

"I'll ask something else then." He sips his coffee. "Is the reason you're here related to Beau being MIA?" He tries to act like he isn't staring at the bruise around my eye.

"Have you seen him?"

He shakes his head.

"Do you think he'd leave without saying goodbye?"

"I stopped assuming things about people a long time ago." Raising the mug to his lips, he pauses and eyes me from the side. "His stuff still here?"

I nod.

"Then he's probably just lying low until his pride recovers."

We don't talk for a few minutes, and it's a silence I'd never get with Allison or Elliot. I can't mention anything Brad said about Wesley, so I let Jeff continue to think Beau's the only reason I'm hiding away here.

"People are going to have a field day with this one." I mindlessly spin the glass tumbler and point to my eye.

"Yeah, they'll have fun at your expense, but someone else will do something stupid, and they'll move on. That's how this machine works." Jeff laughs. "Hell, Elliot was the topic of conversation for months after he came back from college until the Stevenson boys got caught breaking into the pharmacy, and that was more tantalizing."

"Why were they talking about Elliot? Dropping out of college isn't newsworthy."

A simple hand motion dismisses my question. "It's not important. Just remember, no matter what they're saying, they'll be saying it about someone else soon enough."

"I don't know. I did something pretty scandalous."

"Don't flatter yourself. There's always a bigger, better scandal around the corner." He smiles. "C'mon, let's get you out of here before you get all mopey and shit."

Jeff drops me off at the motel, and when I step inside the room, all of Beau's things are gone. I walk around, opening drawers and searching for anything of his that may still be here.

But there's nothing.

There isn't a goodbye note or even a 'fuck you' scribbled on the back of a receipt. There's no proof he was ever here.

He's just gone.

36

Time is strange right now because it's lost its rhythm, each second stretches into eternity while the hours slip away like wisps. Beau's absence is a gnawing void. His laughter no longer fills the room, and the corner where his suitcase stood seems more like a silent tombstone.

The room is shallow without him, empty, a carcass of its previous self.

My head pounds and my stomach snarls in on itself because I haven't been able to eat anything in days. It'll take half an hour, tops, to walk to the diner and back. I'll take my chances on getting served there before going to the gas station.

When I pull the motel door open, bright red painted letters greet me on the outside of the door.

W-H-O-R-E

B-I-T-C-H

S-L-U-T

I get a small bucket from the front desk and position myself on my knees, dunk the sponge in the soapy water, and scrub the door. Maybe whoever did it was paying homage to The Scarlet Letter and tried to be poetic by using red paint.

Who am I kidding?

Wesley's friends don't read.

I dip the sponge in the bucket and scrub as staring strangers walk by. I think about calling Brad, but what good would that do? He's got too much on his plate as it is. Besides, defacing a door doesn't scream imminent threat. If anything, the message it sends is that Wesley's friends are cowards.

I stretch to reach the top of the door, scrubbing until my shoulders burn and sweat breaks out on my nape. When I'm done, I pour the red-stained water into the parking lot, mesmerized by the resemblance to the blood-soaked carpet in the trailer.

I scream when Wesley pulls the trigger, and Beau slumps over on the couch. I rush to him, not caring if Wesley pulls the trigger again.

I scream as I shake Beau, but he doesn't move, and blood seeps from the center of his chest, soaking his T-shirt and running over my fingers as I put pressure on the gaping gunshot wound. The bullet hit his heart, and he's not waking up.

Wesley laughs from behind me as I sob, pointing the gun at me, but I don't care. I want to die because he'll never let me be free. He'd rather see me dead than without him, and I'd rather be dead than with him.

"Pull the trigger! Do it!" I scream.

"Oh, no, Katie Bug. I love you." He steps closer with a smile.

I try to scream when he touches my cheek, but nothing comes out. I think Beau's eyelids flutter, and I pray I'm wrong. Maybe he's still hanging on.

I run to the front yard with Wesley on my heels, but he's not trying to stop me.

I need to get help for Beau.

People are everywhere, watching us in the front yard, and I scream for someone to help me, but they just watch as Wesley pulls me to the ground. No matter how loud I scream or how hard I cry, no one helps me. They all just stare as he rapes me in the grass.

He leans back to climax, and I'm able to grab the gun from him. It happens so fast. The metal is cold against my lips as I pull the trigger.

"You okay, lady?"

I jump, blinking several times as my eyes struggle to focus on the adolescent boy beside me on the sidewalk.

"Yeah, I'm fine." I clear my throat.

"Do you want me to get my mom?" He asks.

"No, I'm okay." I shake the bucket one last time. "Thank you, though."

I return to the room and close the door, dropping the bucket at my feet and laying my head back against the door. My chest is tight, and I can barely breathe as I force intrusive thoughts out.

I'm pretending to be strong for everyone because I don't want them to worry. I've tried to convince myself I can handle what Wesley's done to me, but I'm not strong.

Everything around me is falling apart.

I'm falling apart.

37

I pull a worn baseball hat down over my eyes and take a deep breath as I open the diner door.

The sun is low on the horizon, so the hat isn't to shield my eyes. The mindless chatter ceases to a dull quietness, and I feel the stares as I approach the counter.

"You know you're not supposed to be here," Donna says.

"You guys are the only place to get food besides the gas station. I just need to put an order in to go, and I'll be out of here." My voice is low, and I tug the hat lower as if it'll protect me from prying eyes.

Donna pulls her small pad from her apron and drops it on the countertop, huffing as she clicks the ink pen. "What do you want?"

"A burger, no mayo, and a small order of fries."

"We're out of burgers."

"Umm...a chicken sandwich?"

"Out of chicken, too."

"The BLT?"

"Sorry, out of the B and the L." She places the notepad in

her pocket and clicks the ink pen over and over as she stares at me, smacking that fucking gum. "No one wants you here."

Everyone looks away because they don't have the guts to look me in the eye while judging me. I turn back to Donna and pull the hat off.

"What about Wesley? Is he welcome here?"

"I don't know what to tell you," she says.

I lean over the counter so only she can hear me. "People talk, and I know your daughter likes to give Wesley a blow job every year for his birthday. So, maybe step down off your high horse." I put the baseball hat back on, tugging it low over my eyes again.

"There may be some burger patties in the back if you still want one."

"You know what, I'm good. But thanks anyway."

As I walk, the highway ripples in waves and the sun creates a mirage I wish were real. I've dreamt more about leaving Seymour than anywhere I'll go because the destination is inconsequential.

A truck roars past me and blows cool wind that makes me shiver. I keep my head down, watching my feet as I walk.

A loud ding alerts everyone when I push the glass door open at the gas station. I take a sharp right down the chip aisle to the coolers on the back wall.

As I stand there, I look up at the large mirror in the corner and notice people staring and whispering. On my way to the register, I grab a couple of bottles of water, a pack of sour gummy worms, and a pint of chocolate ice cream.

The door chimes again, and Marvin and Lendall James enter—two people I could've gone the rest of my life without seeing again and been fine. The brothers grew up across the street from Wesley and are as loyal to him as they were in high school.

"Well, if it isn't Katie Reese," Marvin says as he stands in line behind me.

"Nah, that's Katie, the whore." Lendall laughs.

"Same thing." Marvin stands so close his breath hits the back of my neck. "If we would've known you were giving it out to everyone, we might've taken our turn."

I place my items on the worn counter and ignore the two idiots. "Can I also get two fried burritos?" One of them, I'm not sure which, snatches my hat, and I spin around, reaching for it. "Leave me alone."

Lendall smiles, but it isn't friendly. It's something sinister. Something bad.

"Wesley didn't want a wife who spreads her legs to strangers, so we don't always get what we want. Do we, sweetheart?" He plops my hat on his head.

"That'll be sixteen dollars," the cashier says.

I push a twenty dollar bill across the counter, sweeping my stuff into my arms. "Keep the change."

"Careful on your walk," Marvin calls out as I leave.

Gravel crunches under my feet as I trek through the parking lot, and the occasional sharp edge pushes into the soles of my Converse. I pause at the side of the two-lane highway, look both ways and cross into the parking lot of the abandoned movie rental business.

I chug a bottle of water as I walk around the back of the building and pass through a small patch of grass to get to the narrow dirt road behind the businesses. Wildflowers nearing the end of their season reach for the setting sun along the banks, and an occasional wild rabbit sprints from one side to the other.

An engine revs in the distance behind me, and I move closer to the ditch. I look over my shoulder as the sounds get louder, and a jacked-up Ford races toward me, red dust billowing at the rear like flames.

Lendall James shouts the word 'slut' through the passenger window as it passes, and I lose my footing, sliding down the embankment. Marvin pulls across the road, backs up, and turns around.

They watch me climb up the bank, the sand collapsing between my fingers every time I get a grip on it. Tiny pebbles dig into my palms until I reach level ground.

Marvin revs the engine, and the metal beast rocks like it's itching to be set loose for eight seconds. They're trying to scare me. Intimidate me. They're proving their loyalty to Wesley.

I stand in place as the truck barrels toward me, throwing up a thick cloud of dirt in the air. It veers to the right at the last minute, and a beer bottle flies from the window.

I turn away, and the glass shatters against the back of my head as they speed away. Pieces of amber fall around me, but it doesn't hurt like they hoped it would, so the joke is on them.

I've had worse.

I stare at the pint of busted ice cream liquifying and mixing with sand at my feet. *"Your fatass didn't need to eat that anyway."* Wesley's voice echoes in my head as I squat to pick the soggy cardboard container up, along with the burritos that ants have already found.

I stand up, kicking everything into the ditch, and return to the motel.

Brad's patrol car is parked in front of the room, and my gut tells me he's bringing more bad news because that's all he has these days.

As soon as I walk in front of my room, he spots me and ends a phone call as he gets out of the car.

"Where have you been? I've been worried out of my goddamn mind." He slams the patrol car door.

"I walked to grab something to eat." I enter the room with him on my heels.

"I told you not to leave this room."

My bottom lip trembles because I've disappointed him after everything he's done for me. "I went to the gas station because I've got to eat."

"You walked that far alone?"

"Yes, but-"

"What the hell were you thinking? You should've called me, and I would've taken you."

Tears blur my vision, but I blink them away. "I said I'm sorry. I shouldn't have walked that far by myself. I wasn't thinking."

He leans his back against the door, letting his head follow as he folds his arms over his chest. He closes his eyes and inhales.

I walk over to him, unsure if I should, but he doesn't open his eyes. "I'm sor-"

"Don't." He interrupts my apology, still refusing to look at me. "Do you know how worried I was when I got here and you weren't here?"

"No."

"Out of my fucking mind." He grits his teeth.

"Do you hate me now?" I ask.

He opens his eyes but pins his gaze to the ceiling instead of looking at me. "Why would you think I hate you?"

"You won't look at me."

"I can't look at you because I need to be mad at you right now." He sucks his bottom lip between his teeth. "And if I look at you, I won't be able to stay mad. So, let me be angry for a while because it's better than what I've felt since I got here and couldn't find you."

"I'm going to shower while you stay mad." Sweat trickles down the back of my neck after walking all over town.

I close the bathroom door and lay my clothes on the towel

rack while undressing. Brad has every right to be pissed at me because walking to the store alone was idiotic on my part.

Hugging my body as the hot water rolls over my shoulders and down my achy back, the thick steam swirls around me and makes breathing difficult. I lean under the water, scrub my palms over my face, and open my eyes.

Blood-tinged water pools in the bottom of the tub, and I raise my hand to the back of my head. It doesn't take much probing to find the wound. Maybe an inch long, not huge. My marriage taught me head wounds appear worse than they are. Nothing to panic over, so I wash my hair and rinse it until the water runs clear.

I finish my shower and get dressed, fully expecting Brad to be gone when I exit the small bathroom, but he's sitting at the table on his phone. I want to talk to him, but I give him space because that's the only thing I have to offer anyone these days.

I brush my teeth, and when I lean over to spit in the sink, I catch him watching me through the mirror.

I can't read him, so I don't try.

Instead, I untwist my hair from the towel, remove the crappy blow dryer from the wall, and flip my hair upside down to dry it.

Brad taps my shoulder, and I bolt upright, my hand flying to my chest as I turn the blow dryer off. "You scared me."

He holds my hair towel in his hand. "What's this?"

I take it from him and kick it under the sink. "Nothing. I scratched my head."

I don't want to lie, but I also don't want to say what happened because he's already mad at me for putting myself in a dangerous situation. The last thing I want to do is confirm he had a reason to be concerned.

"Scratches don't bleed like this." Moving around me, he inspects my scalp for the injury. "What the hell did you hit?

There's a gash deep enough that you may need a couple of staples."

"It's not that bad." Raising my fingers to his, I push them away from the wound and smooth my hair over it. "Even the tiniest cut gushes on a head."

"Yeah, but I looked at it, and it's not a tiny cut. If it were tiny, it wouldn't still be bleeding. What did you hit your head on?"

I push around him, gathering my toiletries and shoving them in my bag. "I don't remember."

In a blur, he's in front of me, chest to chest, and looking down at me.

"That's not how this works anymore. No more lies. What happened?"

I curse myself because I can't stop fucking everything up.

"Someone threw a beer bottle at me on my walk back. It's fine, though. I swear."

His face flushes red, and he's about to say something but stops and begins tossing my things in the bags scattered around the room.

"Get your stuff together. You're leaving." He moves around the room in a frenzy.

"What are you talking about?"

He stops and looks me in the eye. "You're not staying here by yourself anymore. I'll let Jeff know, but right now, your job is to get anything you don't want to leave behind because we're leaving as soon as I put these bags in the car."

"I don't have anywhere else to go."

"You don't want to be here, so why the hell are you fighting so hard to stay? Beau's gone, and it doesn't look like he's coming back."

"Slow down." I hold my palms up. "You're making this bigger than it is. I'm fine."

"You're fine this time, but what about next time? What then?"

Even Brad knows repercussions are coming like a storm churning over the ocean. The pressure is dropping, the waves are battering the shore, and it's only a matter of time before this storm makes landfall.

Wesley will take my life before this is over.

38

Twisting ramen noodles on my fork, I drop them back in the styrofoam cup because I'm not hungry. Not even a little, so I'm not sure why I made them.

Brad's guest room is too quiet, its silence only broken by the occasional drip from the leaky bathroom faucet across the hall. I've been here for a week and can't get used to it.

I strain the broth from the noodles in the bathroom sink and toss the rest in the trash.

I crawl under the sheet, and the pillow I took from the motel smells like Beau, so it's easy to pretend he's next to me with his scent still here—the only thing he didn't take with him.

If he could leave without saying goodbye, I'm glad I didn't love him. If he did that, I'm happy he's gone.

But I'm not happy.

I'm sad and angry and hurt and scared. I'm a lot of things, but happy isn't one of them.

Damn you for making me think I might love you.

I've called his phone, but it's always off, and the calls go straight to voicemail. Out of desperation, I reached out to Jake.

His phone rang the first time with no answer, and each subsequent call went to voicemail.

It's like Beau dropped off the face of the earth, and the message he's sending is loud and clear.

We're over.

I keep trying to convince myself there's no way he'd leave without saying goodbye. I fall asleep every night expecting to wake up to him climbing into the bed behind me with whiskey on his breath.

But that doesn't happen.

My rational brain says I need to get on with my life because he's getting on with his. My aching heart says there's a chance he'll walk through the door any minute with an explanation.

I spend endless hours watching the door, thinking there'll be a knock any minute. I'll open it, and he'll be standing there with that smirk. Every hour without that knock, my brain convinces my heart that we're waiting for nothing.

He made up his mind and I'm left to accept his decision.

I call and text him every time I wake after drifting to sleep. It's pathetic, but I can't stop myself even though the result is always the same.

No answer.

Unread messages.

I want him to pick up the phone and tell me to stay put. Wait. He'll be here soon. But that's not what I get.

I get silence.

I force myself to shower and pull Beau's pillow to my chest when I lay down. I don't know what makes me do it, but I redial his number, hoping the result will be different this time.

It's not.

When I dial Jake's number, it rings, and I bolt up in the bed, my heart racing because this is the first sign of life I've had. After the third ring, he answers, and my throat tightens.

"Hello?" He asks a second time.

My words get trapped in my throat, and he ends the call.

My hands shake as I press the green button on the screen again.

"Hello?"

"Jake." My voice trembles.

"You shouldn't have called, love."

There's rustling in the background, and I hear Beau talking. I can't make out what he's saying, but he's laughing. *He's laughing.*

"Please let me talk to him. I know he's there."

"That's not a good idea."

"I need to know what I did wrong."

"You didn't do anything wrong, love."

"If he won't talk to me, put me on speaker so he can at least hear what I have to say."

"I can't do that, love."

"Why?" I sob. "I don't understand."

"I'm sorry, love. Take care of yourself." I hear him lift the phone from his ear.

"No, no, no." I wail. "Don't hang up!"

The line falls silent, and I fumble with my phone. I call Jake back, but it goes to voicemail.

I hurl the phone across the room and curl up on the bed, distraught and sobbing, Beau's words haunting me as I cry myself to sleep.

He is the worst kind of man.

He made me fall in love with him only to toss me aside like I'm nothing, like I don't matter. I knew he'd devastate me from the start, but I never expected it to be like this.

Wesley was monstrous to his core, and that's why I was prepared for the heinous things he did to me. But Beau went out of his way to convince me he was nothing like him. However, he's just as cruel.

He brought me back to life and made my heart beat in a

way I never thought it could again. And now, he's standing at the end of the knife plunged into the barely beating organ, twisting it to make sure I suffer as much as possible.

For that, I'll never forgive him.

This summer was one of the hottest on record in Seymour. We broke records for the most consecutive triple-digit temperatures, and my affair with Beau kicked off much like the heat wave.

It was scorching from the start, all-consuming, and impossible to escape. We ran hot like the days and even hotter than the nights.

The sweltering temperatures are pulling back, allowing cooler autumn temperatures to take their place. The leaves on the trees are changing and will soon trickle to the ground, their lifespan ending.

With grace, this season will step aside so the beautiful things it created can draw to a close when their time is up.

My affair with Beau changed colors like the dying leaves, grinding to a halt as suddenly as it started, as Allison warned me it would.

And, like the summer, our time is up.

39

Ninety-three days.

That's how long it's been since I've seen Beau's face or kissed his lips. Ninety-three days since my body touched his.

Today marks the first day of three hundred and sixty-five days that I won't cry when I think of him. If I can make it one whole year without shedding another tear over him, I can go a lifetime.

As the leaves turned from green to orange and red, dread settled over me. I felt it coming for weeks but told myself I was fine because I'm in a better place than I was three months ago. I held onto the dwindling summer days, clinging to the late hours because I didn't want them slipping away while I slept. But as with every season, I couldn't make it stay any more than I could've made Beau stay.

It was always going to be this way.

The past few months have been the hardest of my life. But as fall passes with winter on its heels, I've let myself rest and grieve the loss of my life as I knew it.

The good and bad parts have finally been put to rest.

I struggled to let go of my identity as Wesley's wife in

Seymour, but the more time that passed, the easier it got to separate myself from him. I never intended to stay here, but things didn't work out as I hoped after Beau left.

I never heard from him again; a communication I was desperate for morphed into something I no longer desire.

I kept the cell phone he gave me because I can't afford a new one yet, and to be honest, I expect the line to be turned off once he realizes he's still paying for it.

I spent the last weeks of summer sad because of him, mourning a bond that was never there. He would've never disappeared from my life if it were real, as he claimed. The night Jake answered his phone cemented what I feared most when I heard Beau laughing in the background.

I never mattered.

Our relationship was one-sided, just as my marriage to Wesley had been. I ate the lovely nothings from Beau's hand because I was starved for affection and intimacy. I saw only what he wanted me to see. Even with people saying he'd break my heart, including him, I ignored the warnings like I had with Wesley.

That revelation led me to spend most of my days angry. Angry at him for reviving my dead heart. Angry at myself for believing I mattered. Angry I dreamt of him, waking up with tears dried in the corners of my eyes.

Resentment clogged my heart, and I tasted bitterness when I spoke about him. The more I vented my unhappiness, the more unhappy I became. Watching my friends laugh and be carefree made me start to hate them, too, and I realized what a horrible, angry person I'd become.

That's when I decided to take Brad's advice and started seeing a therapist who suggested I was projecting my feelings for Wesley onto Beau because I never allowed myself to heal from that relationship before entering a new one with Beau.

She said my subconscious saw the two as one, unable to separate my feelings for Wesley from my feelings for Beau.

She wasn't wrong, but I'm not sure she was right.

I hated them because I loved them, and they hurt me worse than anyone else. It didn't matter if I agreed with her; she made me realize that, even though they hurt me, I didn't have to keep letting them hurt me. I could move on anytime I wanted and take my power back. So, that's what I did. I let it go. The hurt they caused. The anger I felt. The love I had for them. All of it.

I still get a sense of impending doom when I think of the leaves changing colors, but I'm trying to see fall as more than a time of dying.

When the leaves flutter to the ground, I imagine winter around the corner. A time for rest. A time to prepare for growth. Don't get it twisted, though.

I didn't change into an optimist. I just figured out every season has a purpose.

My season with Wesley taught me to be strong when I didn't think I could.

My season with Beau taught me to trust again when I didn't think I should.

My season alone has taught me to move forward even if I don't know where I'm going.

A lot has changed, but much has stayed the same. I'm working at the bar again, thanks to Jeff's reassurance that people would get over themselves. Most have. There are still people who practically spit when they see me, but mostly, people ignore or forgive me.

The most significant change has been moving in with Brad. I didn't want to but left with no other options, I accepted the invitation to stay in his extra room with gratitude because I'd be able to save money to move. I should have enough to leave soon if things keep going well at the bar.

Sometimes, I kick myself for not taking the money from

Thomas because I could be long gone if I had. Brad reassures me I did the right thing because anything from the Reese family comes with strings attached.

Living with Brad is easy. He's tidy and quiet, and we get along great. We take turns cooking dinner, and I'd be a liar if I said I didn't feel safer living with him.

It's been three months, and still no word on where Wesley is, so sleeping under the sheriff's roof is the only reason I'm able to sleep.

As the fire dies down, I sit around the metal fire pit in the backyard. I'm tired, but I can't fall asleep without smoking a joint most nights since it's the only thing blocking the nightmares. I try not to do it when Brad's around because, well, he's the sheriff.

I light the joint, pulling the smoke into my lungs and holding it as long as possible. I close my eyes and think about Beau telling me I was a bright light keeping him from getting swallowed by the darkness.

"Wherever you are, whatever you're doing..." I lay my head back and blow a plume of smoke up to the dark sky. "You're an asshole."

A knock from the backdoor startles me, and I bolt up straight in the chair. *Shit.*

Brad smiles as he crosses the yard. "I thought I smelled something illegal."

"It's medicinal, I don't do it often, and I thought you were already in bed."

"It always is, they never do, and I wasn't." He sits in the chair next to me. "You're old enough to know better." He holds his hand out, and I pass the joint to him like a teenager getting busted. He takes a hit, and I stare in disbelief as he blows the smoke out. "But so am I."

"Am I so high I imagined you smoking weed?" I ask.

He passes the joint back to me and slumps in the chair, stretching his long legs out and hooking them at the ankles.

"I haven't smoked since before I joined the military. I used to grow a few plants back in high school. Nothing major. Just enough for me and my friends because the local stuff was shitty and overpriced."

"Shut up!" I throw my hand over my mouth because it came out way louder than I expected. "You were a drug dealer in high school?"

He retakes possession of the joint, holding it between his thumb and middle finger as he wags his index finger. "Not a drug dealer. I grew a few plants for me and my friends." He takes a long drag and passes it back to me.

"So, you *have* done fun stuff before." I finish the joint and lean back in my chair. The two of us mirror one another as we stare at the sky.

"I do fun stuff all the time. The whole town just doesn't know about it because I don't make an ass of myself when I do it."

"That's a low blow." I poke my bottom lip out.

"That's for all the old man jokes." Scruff covers his chiseled jaw as he looks at me with those green eyes.

"Fair enough."

He turns his head to the side, and as he's about to speak, a scream comes from the neighbor's upstairs bedroom. He holds his finger to his lips, turning his ear toward the house, and I burst out laughing as the woman screams again. Moans follow the scream, along with the occasional use of the word 'fuck'.

I point to the window. "She's apologizing for being a nag." At least that's what she said when we met at the mailbox this afternoon.

"She's very vocal with her apology." He twists his finger in his ear and winces. "That's all Mick's going to hear for a while."

"I'm sure he has zero complaints." I pull my legs up to my

chest and wrap my arms around them, resting my chin on my knees.

He opens his mouth to speak at the exact moment the neighbor screams, *"fuck me harder"*, and his eyes get huge. He shakes his head and blinks several times, clearing his throat. "It's going to be hard to look them in the eye from now on."

"She said they're leaving for Colorado in the morning, so it won't be hard for long."

"From the sound of things, it won't be hard much longer tonight, either." He laughs.

I stand and extend my hand to help him up. He places his hand in mine, and I use my body weight to lean back, pulling him up from the chair. I tumble forward, almost falling face-first into his chest.

"You don't weigh anything. When's the last time you ate?"

"Spaghetti about five hours ago." I lead the way to the house through the back door.

"You moved spaghetti around on your plate for half an hour, but I don't remember you eating any of it." He opens the refrigerator and pulls out the casserole dish containing the leftovers.

"Most people don't catch onto that." I sit down at the kitchen table.

"I've made a career noticing what most people don't." The microwave dings, and he places a plate of steaming pasta on the table in front of me. "Now, eat." He sits across the table and laces his fingers behind his head. "At least half, and I'll get off your case...for the night."

"For the night?"

"I don't like seeing you like this."

"Now, it feels like old times again." I stab the mound of pasta and twist the fork, lifting the fork to my lips and blowing on the spaghetti. "You lecturing me about my life choices."

He gets that smug look I've seen a hundred times on his face. "Well, make better choices, and I won't lecture you."

I stick my tongue out and stab the pasta again. "We smoked together, man. You were *so* close to being fun."

"More eating and less talking because I'm tired and ready to get this over with."

"I've heard that's common when you're almost forty."

He sucks his bottom lip in while shaking his head. "Are you going to be a smartass the entire time you live here?"

"Probably."

"Maybe I'll start working more."

I shrug my shoulders. "Your loss. I'm a fucking riot. But I understand a man of your age might not appreciate the excitement of a younger woman."

"Ten years." He shakes his head. "I'm only ten years older than you."

"Yeah, but you said it yourself. There's a lot crammed in those years."

He slides the chair back and stands up, stretching his arms over his head. "Your room or mine tonight?"

"Ugh...can't we skip tonight?"

"Nope." He walks through the living room, pausing at the base of the staircase. "Finish your food, and I'll get everything ready."

"Yes, sir."

40

I lay in my bed staring at the ceiling like most mornings after we stay up all night stripping wallpaper from the bedrooms that must've been applied with the world's strongest glue.

We've worked for weeks and only completed the guest room, leaving our bedrooms to tackle. It's my least favorite thing about my life right now, but it's the least I can do since he lets me stay here.

A loud whack comes from outside my bedroom window, and there's another one every few seconds.

I walk to the window and spot Brad in the yard. He's chopping firewood, shirtless, and I can't stop staring at him. Did I mention he's shirtless?

I give him grief about being older, but he's in better shape than any other man I've seen shirtless—at least the ones I've seen in real life. The ones on television and in magazines don't count because I'm sure their abs are photoshopped. But not Brad's. He has an eight-pack, and the way his jeans hang on his hips reveals he has *the* V.

That's it.

I'm taking a shower because I'm staring at Brad. *Brad*. The man who has done more for me than anyone else. Someone I can call day or night, and he'll drop what he's doing to help me.

I don't take a cold shower because I'm not at that point yet. However, I take one that leaves my skin flushed red from the heat.

I dress in my comfiest flannel button-up shirt and worn jeans, blow-drying my hair because it's too cold for anything wet on my body.

My hair has grown to the middle of my back again, and I keep telling myself I'll cut it, but I haven't. I only hated it long because it wasn't my choice for it to be that way.

The back door opens and closes downstairs, so I slip into the ridiculous bigfoot house shoes Jeff gave me as a house-warming gift when I moved in here. He said I'd need them because the floors in these old houses are always cold, and he wasn't wrong.

I come face to face with Brad in the living room as he stacks firewood by the wall. Thankfully, he's wearing a shirt now. He takes one look at me and laughs.

"What are you wearing?" He stares at my house shoes.

"Oh, these? You like them?" I point to my feet.

"They're the tackiest things I've ever seen." He finishes piling the firewood up. "This should get us through the next few nights without turning on the heater. It's supposed to dip below freezing after midnight."

"Are you still going out with your 'friends' tonight?"

"Cute." He wipes his hands together. "Just making sure you have plenty for the night because I'm not sure how long we'll be out."

"Thanks."

All kidding and banter aside, I appreciate how he looks out for me. He's responsible like that. Always paying attention to the little things most people wouldn't think of.

He stops at the base of the stairs and looks back over his shoulder. "Still time to change your mind if you want to go."

"Look at me." I wave my hand over myself. "Do I look like I want to trade this to be out there tonight?" I follow him upstairs, and that's where we part ways. I go left to my bedroom, and he goes across the hall to his room.

I'm deep into a documentary about killer kids when there's a knock on my bedroom door. "It's open," I call out.

Brad brings the smell of man with him while wearing dark jeans, a long-sleeved plaid shirt with rolled up sleeves, and a white undershirt peeking out from the undone top two buttons. His hair is still damp, and he didn't shave, but the look works for him. I've never known him not to have at least a day or two's worth of stubble.

"Wanted to let you know I'm taking off." He stays close to the door. "I'll lock up on my way out."

"Have fun. But not *too* much fun." I wiggle my eyebrows and get an eye roll in return as he leaves the room.

I slide down on the bed and reach for the remote on the nightstand. As I press the search button, there's another knock on the door, and Brad pushes it open without waiting for the go-ahead.

"Forget something?" I ask.

"My friends are waiting outside, so you've got ten minutes to get ready."

"Ten minutes to get ready for what?"

"To go out." He surveys my room. "You need to get out. You can't just sleep and work. It's not good for you."

"I wasn't going to sleep all night. I planned to Netflix and chill."

"Alone?"

"Yes, alone. Netflix and chill means something else to some people, but I literally watch Netflix and chill."

He opens my closet, steps inside, and pulls the string on the ceiling to turn the light on. "Still, you need to get out and have some fun." He comes out carrying a pair of jeans and a blue turtleneck I've never worn. He lays them on the bed and walks to the door. "See you downstairs in five."

"You said ten."

"Yeah, five minutes ago," he says as he leaves the room for the second time.

I shake my head as I slide off the bed and close my bedroom door to change.

Ten minutes later, I'm downstairs, and Brad's in the driveway standing next to a black Tahoe. When I step onto the porch, he sprints to meet me before I step off the first step.

He scans me up and down, glancing over his shoulder toward his waiting friends. He stares at the brown off-the-shoulder crop top sweatshirt I'm wearing. "You look..."

"Hot. Amazing. Beautiful. Gorgeous." I hand my purse to him and slip my denim jacket on. "Any of those will make a girl's night to hear."

"Cold." He passes my purse back to me. "What happened to the turtleneck? It looked warm."

"Look at me." I place my hands on his shoulders, thanks to the height advantage from standing on the top step. "A crop top isn't the end of the world."

"Then why have the turtleneck? Why give the impression you care about being warm when it's cold outside?"

"See this?" I point to my jacket. "It's a magical gadget that allows people to wear anything they want and remain warm when they put this on over it. The best part is you can slip it off anytime you want. For instance, you're inside a business, and they have heat. You can look cute without compromising your comfort. Then, when you have to brave the outside elements, slip it back on. Easy, right?"

"You've made your point." He tugs my jacket closed over my stomach like the sight of my bare midriff is offensive. "Let's go."

He opens the door for me and four guys occupy the Tahoe —two guys in the front and two in the middle bucket seats. One guy in the middle row offers to sit in the back with me because his legs aren't as long as Brad's, but Brad declines and settles next to me, cramped in the third row.

"Guys, this is Katie." He buckles his seatbelt. "Driver's Bryce. Passenger's Grant." He wags his finger between the two guys in the middle from left to right. "Ryan and Nick."

"Which one is Ryan, and which one is Nick?" I look back and forth between the two men.

The blonde guy on the left twists in the seat and smiles. "Ryan." He points to the other guy. "Nick."

Ryan is clean-cut, his blonde hair is trimmed neat, and not a single strand is out of place. He's fit and trim like Brad but more tan and clean-shaven. He has a boyish smile thanks to adorable dimples and perfect teeth. His blue eyes glimmer even in the dark vehicle, and he's wearing a crispy white shirt with the top two buttons left open, allowing a few light chest hairs to peek out, and a pair of black slacks pressed to perfection. This guy looks way more put together than anyone I expected Brad to be going out with.

To the right, Nick sits glued to his phone. He isn't as tall as Ryan or Brad, but still easy on the eyes and dressed far more relaxed than Ryan in jeans and a T-shirt. He has hair barely darker than Ryan's, but it's a disheveled mess. He's more in line with what I expected Brad's friends to look like. Laid back. Casual. Not dressed to the nines like Ryan.

"Nice to meet you, Ryan." I look at Nick. "And Nick." I stretch my neck and call out to the guys up front. "Nice to meet you guys, too."

Grant throws two fingers up to acknowledge me while catching my eye in the rearview mirror, and Bryce does the same as we pull away from the house.

Grant stands out because of his jet-black hair and piercing

blue eyes, which stand out thanks to his olive skin. From back here, I can't see much more. The same goes for Bryce. Red hair and fair skin are all I can make out.

Ryan twists around in his seat. "It's nice to finally meet you, Katie. Brad's told us nothing about you, and now I see why." He winks.

Is he flirting?

My palms are sweaty, and a cold sweat blooms on the back of my neck. I'm not prepared for flirty.

Fun, I can do.

Flirty, I can't.

Brad leans over, whispering in my ear. "Relax."

I nod and take a deep breath. *Relax.*

Sounds easy enough. People do it every day, right?

Relax.

WHEN WE WALK into Austin's, Elliot waves from behind the bar, and Allison shrieks, leaping off a bar stool and running over to me. She throws her arms around my neck, rocking us back and forth.

"You look freaking adorable!" She pulls my denim jacket open to see the crop top.

"Thanks." I tuck my hair behind my ear. "Dad thinks I'm showing too much skin." I jab my thumb over my shoulder toward Brad and the men trailing behind him.

"Not the daddy vibe I'd expect from him." Allison laughs.

"What about whose dad?" Brad asks upon approaching from behind.

"Nothing." Allison hooks her arm in my elbow and leads me to the bar. "The usual?" She asks.

I nod, and Elliot slides a glass of whiskey to me. I lift the glass to my lips, take that first burning sip, and suck a cooling breath through my teeth. I used to hate the taste of whiskey, but now I hate it for a different reason.

It reminds me of Beau—the smell, the heat, the way it hurts. Drinking is more like punishment than pleasure these days.

A stupid ritual I don't enjoy but can't stop.

Ryan steps up to the bar and leans his shoulder into mine. "Do we need to watch out for you later? Does whiskey make you frisky?" He winks, and there's a look in his eyes.

He's flirting, and I don't hate it.

I lean my shoulder into his to mimic him and answer, "Guess you'll just have to wait and find out, won't you?"

From the corner of my eye, Brad raises his beer to his lips, smiling as Ryan flirts.

Allison rounds the end of the bar, leaning over it in front of Brad, Ryan, and myself. "How old are you, sheriff?"

"Why?" Brad asks.

"Curious is all."

He cuts his eyes at me. "Thirty-six."

"That's like the new twenty-six. And you're in great shape, so I would've never guessed you're almost forty."

"And that's my cue to go." Ryan spins around on the barstool, sliding off and joining the others at the pool table.

I tap my index finger against my chin. "Almost forty...wow."

"Don't," Brad says.

"What? I wasn't going to say anything," I say.

"Good. It'd be in your best interest not to." He raises his beer bottle to his lips and narrows his eyes before walking away to join his friends.

Allison's mouth falls open. "Jesus, how have I never noticed how hot he is? That authority figure thing. The older guy thing."

"There's so much wrong with every word that came out of

your mouth." I shake my head. "First of all, you're practically married, so cool it. Second, it's Brad. *Brad*. Third, he's probably one of those 'missionary is too spicy' guys because he's so uptight about everything."

"Honey, that look in his eyes just now...there's something wild inside that man."

Brad and his friends play pool and darts while Allison and I chat over too many drinks. She and Elliot eventually disappear to Jeff's office, doing what I can only imagine a newly engaged couple would do alone.

It's only when I'm alone that the night takes a turn.

I sit alone at the table Beau preferred because he could see the entire room from it. It doesn't take much for my mind to go back to the summer.

The warm nights riding around in his truck with the windows down and late hours staying up in his room making love. For a while, the memories make me smile. But, like so many other nights when I'm alone, the sadness creeps in.

It sneaks in behind the memory of him washing Wesley off my body in the shower. He was so gentle, and I felt how much he cared about me.

Was that a lie?

That moment meant so much to me, and when I think about it now, I question it. I question everything. I'm not sure if anything with him was real.

Every kiss was a sin, and every touch was forbidden. Yet, there I was, sinning away without a care in the world.

But that's not true.

I did care.

I cared about Beau. I cared about hurting Wesley. I cared about what he'd do to Beau if he found out about the affair. I didn't go into it with blind disregard for everyone around me like Beau did. I turned myself inside out for him and showed him the ugliness I hid from the rest of the world.

I don't want to be here, having fun and laughing like I'm okay because I'm not.

I sneak out back where I can be alone with my sadness without explaining myself to anyone. I lean against the cool brick and stare at the night sky.

I thought I was over Beau.

I tell myself I don't care where he is or what he's doing. And to a degree, it's true. But I can't let go of the anger that comes from the way he left. Was I so irrelevant he couldn't tell me he was leaving?

I have so many questions, and I'm trying to come to terms with the fact that they'll never be answered.

The back door swings open, spilling light from inside across the darkness, and Allison steps out.

"I thought you might be out here." She treks over to me, standing beside me on the brick wall. "I need to tell you something, and you have to swear to keep it to yourself."

I hate when she does this.

"Okay."

"I don't know if I'm doing the right thing." She stares up at the blank night sky. "My heart's screaming marry him, but my head's like 'hold up'." She rolls her head to the side. "Elliot's a great guy, and I'd be a fool not to marry him, right?"

"I'm the last person you should seek relationship advice from. I shot my husband, and my lover abandoned me in the middle of the night, never to be heard from again. That nagging feeling could have more to do with you than Elliot. It doesn't matter how great of a guy he is if you don't think he's the one."

"That's the thing, though. Until we got engaged, I knew he was the one. Everything's just so muddled in here." She points to her temple. "I can't pinpoint where this is coming from."

"It's just stress from planning the wedding. What if you downsized it? No one said you guys have to have a huge, elaborate wedding. Run away and elope or have a small ceremony with close family and friends."

"We're going to scope out venues in Dallas, but he's only doing it to appease me. He's set on having the wedding here in the church his parents attended." She scrubs her palms over her face. "I get it. It's sweet, but I don't want to get married in this town, surrounded by people who talk shit behind my back and smile in my face."

"Who's talking shit about you?"

"People."

"Be specific."

"I overheard a lady at the diner telling the lady she was eating lunch with that I was only marrying Elliot for his money."

I burst into a fit of laughter. "What money?"

"If he's wealthy, he hasn't told me about it yet."

"People think he got money when their parents passed away because I've heard the rumors about his dad having money stashed all over their property. Apparently, he didn't trust banks. But I can assure people the bar wouldn't be struggling if that were the case."

"Right!" She slaps the front of her thighs. "Like, why in the hell would Jeff live off antacids and blood pressure meds if he had a secret stash of money lying around?" She lays her arm around my shoulder, leaning her temple to touch mine. "You always know what to say to make me feel better."

"I know this will go against sister code, but I have to say it. It's your wedding, and most women dream of this day, but it's his wedding day, too. He may want to get married in the church his parents attended because it's the closest thing he has to them being there."

Her eyes glass over. "I've been such a controlling bitch with this wedding stuff."

"They don't call you guys bridezillas for nothing."

"I'll cave if he really wants to do it here, and I don't care if you're only there for the ceremony, you're not getting out of being my maid of honor because you're my best friend and the wedding is in three months. Besides, I don't have time to find anyone else." She stretches her arms over her head, yawning and eliciting one from me afterward.

"If you're going to have the wedding in Seymour, why bother looking at venues in Dallas?"

"Umm, a week of being spoiled in Dallas. Duh. You and I know any venue I have in mind will laugh when I tell them we need it in three months." She steps inside the bar. "Wanna get out of here and go to my place? I've got some serious shit I need to talk to you about, and I'd rather not do it here."

"More serious than you having cold feet and admitting people think you're a gold digger?"

"Way."

"Let me tell Brad I'm leaving."

ELLIOT AND ALLISON'S house is only ten minutes from the bar, but it's the longest ten minutes known to man when you're waiting for something to be dropped in your lap.

Allison's been quiet since we left, keeping our conversation minimal as we cruise to the north side of town.

"So, how's it going living with the sheriff?" She asks as she parks in their driveway.

"He's easy to get along with."

"Have you seen him naked yet?"

"No." I roll my eyes.

"Pity." She shakes her head. "Bet he's a sight to behold."

I follow her inside, dropping onto the couch while she grabs a bottle of wine from the kitchen.

"I can't help but get the vibe you're pushing me to sleep with Brad," I call out.

"Oh, God, no." She scrunches up her nose as she hands me a wine glass. "That's a terrible idea. You two are total opposites."

"Then why are you hyping him up?" I hold my glass out, and she fills it to the brim.

She cocks her head to the side. "Am I?"

"You kind of are."

"Hmm." She looks around like she's lost in thought. "I didn't realize I was. But admit it, that bit of grey hair on his temples and chin is kinda hot, huh?" We both laugh out loud, and she scoots back on the couch, pulling her knees to her chest, her mood shifting.

"Look, I want to show you something that's going to upset you, like a ton, but it's the band-aid you need so you can move on."

"What are you talking about?"

"Beau."

"What about him?" I become defensive at the mention of his name.

"The way things ended with you guys...I think that's why you're having trouble moving on. You didn't get closure. He didn't rip the band-aid off."

"I'm not having trouble moving on."

"You arrived at the bar with a group of hot men and ended up sitting by yourself all weepy."

I don't answer because she's making up things that aren't true. I'm fine. I'm over Beau. Beau who?

"Fine." She pulls her cell from her back pocket and swipes the screen. "Here." She shoves the phone in my hands. "Look."

I stare at the screen, and my chest tightens.

It's the first time I've seen his face since that night at the bar. I don't have pictures of him, and if I did, I would've trashed them. I thought I remembered him, but as I stare at the screen, I see him the way he really was, and it breaks my fucking heart all over again.

His warm brown eyes. The dark beard is a little longer. Seeing his smile, higher on the left side, rips me to fucking shreds because I know that smile and what causes it.

Genuine happiness.

There's a beautiful blonde at his side, and he's happy.

I toss the phone in Allison's lap. "Why show me that?"

"Because you need to see it."

"Why? Why do I need to see him with her?" I leap from the couch and head straight for the kitchen because that's where the other bottle of wine is.

He's fucking happy.

She follows on my heels. "You need to see he's moved on."

I twist the metal cap from the cheap bottle of wine. "I'm not stupid." I fill my wine glass, chug the entire thing, and refill it. "I didn't mean anything to him." I choke on sadness I didn't notice tiptoeing in, but I won't cry over him again because I've got to make it one whole year.

She moves in to hug me, and I step back.

"Not right now." I hold my hand up. "Please."

Her expression falls, and damn her for being so honest. She knew this would sting and did it anyway.

"I'm sorry. I just...I wondered how someone could disappear the way he did, so I looked him up online. He doesn't have a profile, but I stumbled onto hers through dumb luck and a lot of snooping around." She winces but won't hold the truth back because she's an excellent band-aid ripper off-er.

I nod, sucking my bottom lip between my teeth so I don't break down. "What's her name?"

"Cassie Caldwell. From what I can tell, they go way back."

"She's his high school sweetheart," I say.

"If you want, I can make a fake profile and troll her page."

I smile even though it's fucking agony. "That's unnecessary."

"You sure? Might be fun."

"I'm sure."

She moves in closer, and I don't stop her from hugging me this time. "He didn't deserve you."

"Maybe he did."

She holds me at arm's length and furrows her brow. "What's that supposed to mean?"

"Maybe I was his karma."

"You are no one's karma." She cocks her head to the side like she's thinking and smiles. "Okay, maybe you were Wesley's karma, but that's a totally different situation. Apples and peaches."

"It's oranges."

"What is?"

"The saying is apples and oranges."

"Whatever. You know what I mean."

The rest of the night consists of us drinking wine, watching cringy conspiracy theory videos online, and listening to random songs that make us laugh or cry.

It's what I needed, even though I didn't know I needed it.

41

The following day, I wake up on Elliot and Allison's couch with a horrendous headache. I don't know if it's me or what, but the hangovers seem to be getting worse these days.

I sit up, rubbing my forehead and squinting against the sun bleeding through the blinds behind the couch. I don't even remember laying down last night.

The last thing I remember was Elliot showing up with a new bottle of wine after Allison called and begged him to pick up "just one more."

After that, lights out.

Elliot jogs down the stairs. "Did I wake you?"

"No, the sun's an asshole." I look around the living room for my phone.

"I put it to charge in the kitchen when you passed out." He plops down in the chair and scoops the television remote up from the coffee table. "You went pretty hard last night. Everything okay?"

"Yeah, just stupid crap." I fall back on the couch, pull the blanket up to my chin, and pretend to be interested in whatever he's watching. "Is Allison still asleep?"

"Nah, she had to run some errands."

"Oh."

"No worries, though. You can stay as long as you want." He drops the remote on the table with a loud clack. "Hungry?"

"Not even a little. Just the word makes me want to hurl. I need to get home because I have a lot to do before work tonight." I sit up, wincing when I shift on the cushion because I'm sore. "Hey, did I bust my ass last night?"

"Not that I'm aware," he calls from the kitchen. "But anything could've happened before I got here. I went to bed right after I got home, but you two stayed up." He pokes his head from the other side of the swinging door. "At least have a cup of coffee before you go."

"Maybe," I mumble as I stand up.

I manage to finish an entire cup of coffee and help Elliot load suitcases in his truck for their trip to Dallas.

"Three months, huh?" I lug Allison's suitcase from the edge of the porch steps across the yard. "Are you getting nervous?"

"Nah." He reaches for the bag I'm struggling with and tosses it in the truck like it weighs nothing. "I don't get nervous about stuff like that." He slams the door and dusts his hands together. "What about you? How are things going?"

"Things are good. I can't believe it, but they are."

"It must be weird living with Brad." He squints against the midmorning sun as a car speeds by. "He's cool, but I'm not sure I could share a house with him."

"Technically, he's sharing his home with me," I say as we walk back inside the house. "And living with him isn't bad. It's kind of nice. He cleans up after himself, and he's hardly ever home."

"No word on Wesley?"

"Not a peep. I don't want to jinx myself, but I think he's realized I'm not worth the chase."

"And the other one?"

"Nada."

"Good. Maybe it'll stay that way." He pulls me into a hug. "You deserved better than the way he treated you. Better than both of them."

"I got what I deserved for what I did. I hurt a lot of people, including you and Allison." My cheeks get hot even though I'm shivering when I think about how hurt they were when they found out I'd lied to them about everything.

I damaged my relationship with them, and thinking about it makes me ashamed all over again. I push tears from my eyes and turn around when the front door slams.

Allison marches across the room with Brad on her heels.

"No, no, no!" She waves her finger at me. "I know why you're crying, and he's not worth it. Stop right now because he's dead to us. You hear me? D.E.A.D." She stops in front of Elliot. "Did you bring him up? I told you not to bring him up."

He rolls his eyes as he digs the keys from his pocket. "You didn't say which one I wasn't supposed to bring up."

"Neither of them." She huffs. "Both of them are dead to us. Deceased, Elliot. And if you make her cry again because of them, you will be, too."

I laugh through tears and look at Brad. He shoves his hands in his pockets and rocks back on his heels, pressing his lips together and looking at me from the corner of his eye, grateful not to be in Elliot's shoes.

After saying our goodbyes, Brad and I stand in the front yard and watch them drive away.

"What are you doing here?" I ask as I scoop my bag up from the porch step.

"Thought I'd come by and see if you needed a ride home."

"Thank you." I climb into his truck. "Are your friends still in town?"

"They took off this morning. I think you broke Ryan's heart

when you left with Allison last night," he says as the truck starts moving.

I think about what Allison said last night, specifically the part about me not being over Beau. While I disagree with her, I can see how she might think that.

"Is he a nice guy?"

"Who? Ryan?"

"Yeah."

"Nice enough." He shrugs. "You think that's a good idea?"

"What?"

"Getting involved with someone so soon after..." The truck comes to a stop in our driveway. "You know."

"Who says I want to get involved with him? Maybe I want to use him for a good time." I wiggle my eyebrows.

Brad starts a fire when we get inside because fall has barely settled in, and it's already being nudged out of the way by winter. Picking the iron poker up, he moves the logs around, introducing more oxygen to the embers, and remains silent.

"Hey, I was halfway joking." I place another log in the fireplace. "I thought it might be nice to hang out with someone new. Someone who doesn't know about all the bullshit...at least not until I tell him."

"You're an adult. You can do whatever you please."

"In my defense, I didn't expect you to have friends, and I certainly didn't expect them to be cute." I try to break the tension with our usual banter.

"You're going to make me do it, aren't you?" He stares into the fire.

"What am I going to make you do?"

He stands upright and places the iron back in the stand. "You're more than welcome to hang out with Ryan."

He avoids my question, and I let it go because he doesn't do anything without purpose. "You said I should lie low until

Wesley's caught, or at least until you get a lead on where he's at."

"You'll be out with a decorated sniper, so I'm sure you'll be okay."

"I shouldn't. Last night was pushing it."

"Suit yourself. You'll be missing a good time." He walks to the kitchen, pulls a bottle of water from the refrigerator, and returns, twisting the cap off.

"Yeah, okay." I roll my eyes. "I'm assuming guys your age wrap things up by what...nine? Ten if you want to push it to the limit? Guys your age tire early since you wake up at dawn."

He takes a big drink of water. "You're one to talk, Ms. 'I'm Staying Home So I Can Read'."

"Yeah, well, I'll still be awake long after you go to bed." I tilt my chin up and smile. "That's the power of youth. Endless energy." I curtsey and turn to the staircase, stopping halfway up and leaning over the railing.

"Ten years," he says.

I make a gun with my index finger and thumb, aim it at him, and pretend to look through a scope. "Yeah, but you said it yourself. There's a lot of mileage in those ten years."

I pull the imaginary trigger, leaving him feigning injured with his hand over his heart as I march up the stairs.

42

—————

"Coffee?" I ask Brad as I lift the carafe from the coffee maker.

"I don't have time." He pops a mini bagel between his teeth as he buttons his uniform shirt.

"Got a ton of paperwork to get through before my vacation starts this afternoon." He guides his belt through the loops on his pants, securing his firearm on his hip. "The sooner I get it done, the sooner I'm in Dallas for a week with no one calling me to complain about grass clippings on the highway or dog shit on the sidewalk."

"What are you going to do all week?" I pour a splash of creamer into my coffee and lean against the kitchen counter.

"Not a fucking thing." He takes my coffee mug, sipping it on his way to the front door.

"You ass!"

"I owe you!" The front door slams, and I laugh as I make a new cup of coffee.

Brad may be starting his vacation this afternoon, but I've got to work all week, which is why I'm taking advantage of my day off today.

After coffee, I engage both locks on the front door and head upstairs to shower and get dressed. A scalding shower, a pair of torn jeans, and an oversized sweater later, I'm staring at Wesley's piercing blue eyes.

Inside my walk-in closet, behind my clothes, there's a secret Brad doesn't know about.

It's where I've compiled everything I can find about the missing women and Wesley. I sit in here at night when I can't sleep, staring at the wall, berating my brain for not making the connection I know is there. It's the least I can do since I failed to recognize how dangerous he truly was.

I thought he was only my monster, but the entire world should've been afraid of him.

I spend most of the day mulling over documents and photos I've examined for the past three months. My brain hurts.

I bury my face in my hands, rushing a frustrated sigh out as I push my hands through my hair. I don't get it. Everything inside me screams I know something that can break the case wide open, but my brain has hidden it away so well I can't access it.

So, I come to this room and stare at these ramblings, hoping something will spark that buried memory and set into motion an inferno that won't stop until it reaches Wesley.

The hardest part is knowing I was married to him for three years and never knew him. If anyone could piece this together, it should be the person closest to him. I used to think that person was me, but maybe I'm wrong.

What if there's someone else? Someone he shared the depraved details of the heinous acts he committed? It wouldn't be a stretch. He could've found someone who shares his desires. It happens all the time. Some women are drawn to men like Wesley. They see the darkness inside him and want to be the one to guide him out of it or be the one to feed it.

I grab my notebook and write down every woman I know about. There was Oklahoma, Denver, and Amarillo. I lay the pen down and pinch the bridge of my nose.

I don't know their real names.

I referred to them by where they lived because I didn't want to know anything more about them. The more I knew, the more real they became. In my fucked up mind, that kept it from hurting so bad.

"Katie?" Brad calls from the stairs.

Shit. He wasn't gone as long as I thought he'd be.

"Up here!" I shove the notebook inside a plastic tote. Scrambling to my feet, I slide the hangers to cover everything and step out of the closet as he enters my room.

"You alright?" He asks.

"Of course. Why wouldn't I be?" I smile. "Just putting away some laundry."

"Laundry, huh?" He bends down and picks up a piece of paper that must've fallen when I rushed out of the small room. He flips it over and studies it. "Why do you have a copy of Abigail White's driver's license?"

Fuck.

I can't think of a lie to explain this, so I only have one option. Tell the truth.

"I took it from the files you brought home and made a copy." I wince, waiting for him to blow up. I shouldn't have done it, but in my mind, the ends justified the means.

"You do understand that's classified information, right? As in, private? As in, not for public consumption?"

"Yes." I stare at the floor, feeling those daddy vibes, and not in a good way. "I'm aware."

"Because I want to trust you, I'm giving you one chance to explain what you're doing with it."

I twist the doorknob of my closet, step inside, and push my clothes to the side, exposing my secret.

I watch for his reaction as he stares at the walls covered in newspaper clippings, notes, photos, and anything else that might help. He drags his palm over his mouth and blows out a loaded breath. I can't tell what he's thinking. He's shocked, but I don't know if it's a good shock like 'Look at all the hard work you've done' or a bad shock like 'What is wrong with you?'.

He steps up to the plastic tote and thumbs through a notebook, catching sight of the stack just like it below. He pulls random notebooks out, peeking inside them, and returns them to the tote.

"You did all this by yourself?"

"It's what I do when I can't sleep."

"Remind me again what would've been so bad about scrapbooking or painting?" He stares at the photos of the missing women tacked to the wall. "I mean to each their own, but this doesn't scream healthy."

"Scrapbooking and painting won't help put Wesley behind bars."

"And you think doing this will?" He points to the photos.

"If I can figure out the link between Abigail and the other woman, maybe I can link Wesley to one of them. I'm missing something, and I know it's here." I tap my temple. "I've just got to see the right picture. Read the right report. Hear the right song. And it'll click. I know it will."

"There is no link between them. They lived separate lives. They ran in different circles. From what I can see, the only thing they have in common is Wesley."

"That's what you think, but look at this." I flip through the pages of one of my notebooks. Where is it? I flip to the back and back to the front. Then, I start over and repeat the process. *I know it's in this one.*

He squeezes my shoulders from behind, stilling my arms at my sides. "Stop."

"Give me a minute because I think I may have-"

He spins me around. "I believe you, but this isn't healthy." He releases me and steps back. "Let me make a phone call. Stay put."

Several minutes later, he returns with a smile. "Okay, are you in the mood to compromise?"

"Do I have a choice?"

"Not really." He flashes that million-dollar smile surrounded by three-day stubble. "When vacation is over, we're putting our heads down and picking through this wall until we come up with something. I'll bring my case files home, and we'll add them to what you've put together. No more sneaking behind my back, okay? Maybe if we combine forces, we'll figure this thing out."

"You're not mad?"

"I'm impressed. If I'd known you were this tenacious, I would've hired you as my deputy instead of Jesse Allen. You ready for the catch?"

"No."

"Good. Here it is. You need to get away from here, so you're coming to Dallas with me for the week." I open my mouth to protest, but he holds his hand up. "I called Elliot, and he said it's fine. Ryan has a spare room, and he doesn't mind you coming for reasons I'd rather not think about." I open my mouth to speak again, and he holds his hand up. "Trip's paid for. You've got the time off work. No excuses."

"I don't know what to say."

"How about thank you and I'll be ready to go in an hour?"

43

"This is where Ryan lives?" I crane my neck to see farther up the long, winding driveway past the iron gate. Cattle occupy the rolling green pastures on both sides of the driveway and congregate around several small ponds in the distance.

"He inherited it from his grandparents." Brad punches in the code, and the gate swings open.

"This place is amazing. I'd take in every stray animal that crossed my path if I had this kind of space."

"Luckily for Ryan, he doesn't have your bleeding heart."

"Or unluckily for him."

We top the hill, and the view takes my breath away. An enormous house—no, it's not fair to call it a house—a massive brick mansion sits in the middle of lush, manicured grass.

A four-car garage is attached to the right side of the house, and a detached three-car garage is to the left. Why does anyone need that many cars? A white Mercedes sits in the driveway next to a newer model black Chevrolet truck. Who has seven garages and parks outside? Amber lights illuminate the house's exterior, creating a warm, inviting glow around the perimeter.

"This is a joke, right? Are we squatting here because the owners are out of town?" I ask.

"How would I have the code if I was a squatter?" He puts the truck in park.

"I just..." I look around the estate. "I expected something on a smaller scale. But now I have an overwhelming urge to ask if you know who shot J.R."

He swipes his cell phone off the dashboard. "This is one of the largest cattle ranches in the area, so it's safe to say Ryan and his family don't do anything on a small scale." He throws the truck door open.

A light comes on, and Ryan appears in a doorway to the right of the garage, crossing the driveway with long strides.

"It's about time." He slaps Brad's shoulder. "Gang's here already." Turning to me, he says, "I think you're going to like it here."

"He said it's an annual guy's week," I jab my thumb over my shoulder at Brad, "so thanks for letting me tag along. I promise you won't even notice I'm here."

"Oh, don't do that to me. I want to see you as much as possible while you're here." Ryan pulls his bottom lip between his teeth, and heat flushes up my neck.

Brad clears his throat. "We're starving."

The inside of the house is more impressive than the outside. The door Ryan emerged from leads to the kitchen, and entering it is like walking on the set of one of the cooking shows I used to watch with my mom. The appliances are stainless steel, and the countertops are black granite with specks of gold. The floors are wood—not the stuff that's made to look like wood. I've never been in a kitchen this nice. I'm sure it cost more than my childhood home in Jackson.

"Where is everyone?" Brad places our suitcases at the bottom of the staircase off the side of the kitchen.

Ryan removes a casserole dish from the refrigerator. "They're in the pool." He kicks the door closed.

"In this weather?" I ask, shocked because I saw my breath when we were outside.

"Indoor pool." Brad grabs a bottle of water from the refrigerator.

"Hope you brought a bikini, Katie." Ryan squints at the knob on the oven as he rotates it to the right.

"I didn't."

"Even better."

"We'll go into town and pick one up." Brad tosses the water bottle cap in the trash can.

"I doubt you'll find one this time of year." Ryan slides the casserole dish in the oven. "Give it half an hour, and we can grub."

"That's plenty of time to settle in our rooms." Brad grabs my hand and pulls me toward the staircase.

The second level of the house is just as gorgeous, with the same wood floors and white walls. A loft wraps around the living room and follows a staircase down on the opposite side, forming a U-shape of open space looking down over the living area.

I follow Brad across the landing, and instead of following the railing around, he continues straight, down a small hallway. At the end of the hallway, there's a sharp left turn and a much smaller staircase. We take another left that opens into a narrow hallway up the stairs. Four wooden doors line the narrow passage, two on each side.

"There are other rooms, but I want you by mine." As we pass the first door on the left, Brad points to it and stops at the second one on the right. He lowers the suitcases to the floor, pushes the bedroom door open, and nudges my suitcase inside the room with his boot.

"A private bathroom." He points to a closed door to the left of the room. "All four of the rooms up here have them."

"You could've warned me, you know?"

"About what?" He pulls the curtains closed on both windows.

"All this." I sweep my hand through the air. "I wasn't expecting a place like this. It's too..." I touch the pillowcase. It's the softest linen I've ever felt. "I don't belong in a place like this."

"Well, not with that attitude you don't." He laughs. "It's just a house. Four walls and roof."

"This isn't just a house. From what I've seen, it's the size of a small village."

"Take your time and settle in. I'll text when dinner's ready."

I STRETCH out in the bed, feeling rested from tip to toe, until panic sets in. I fell asleep. I snatch my phone from the nightstand to check the time, and it's almost nine. There are several texts from Brad from over an hour ago.

Dinner's done

You going to eat?

I'm assuming you fell asleep. Who's the old one now?

I'm sorry. I did fall asleep

You're awake now so come eat

I'm not hungry

You haven't eaten all day

> Are you keeping tabs on my eating
> habits now?

If you aren't going to eat, get dressed and
come down. We're going out

> What if I don't want to?

Five minutes or I'm dragging you out of
that bed

> You wouldn't

Test me

I stare at the ceiling as I tick the minutes down in my head.

Three

Two

One

Heavy footsteps ascend the stairs, and I bolt up in the bed.

> I'm on my way down

The footsteps stop and grow fainter.

> You're an ass sometimes

See you in five

I wash my face, brush my hair, and pull on torn jeans and a hot pink crop top sweatshirt. It's cold, and I should wear something else, but the crop top will irritate Brad, and he deserves it.

When I descend the staircase, all eyes are on me from the men standing in the living room. I recognize everyone from their visit to Seymour. Ryan and Brad stand near the fireplace, Grant and Bryce lounge on the couch with their cell phones, and Nick stands near the French doors with his phone to his ear.

"He would've done it." Ryan sips from a glass of amber liquid.

"I know." I shoot Brad a foul look as I stop on the last step. "Where are we going?"

"Not sure yet," Nick says as he plops down on the couch near Grant. "Somewhere that has booze and babes."

"Your days of scouting babes are over." Grant pops Nick's chest with the back of his hand. "Have been for a long time."

"Yes, and thank you again for that," Brad says to Nick.

"Why are you thanking him?" I ask Brad as the group migrates toward the front door.

"That's a story I don't feel like telling right now."

I pause at the threshold after everyone else has exited and look up at him. "Will you tell me later?"

"Are you going to ask again later?"

"I might."

"Well, then, I suppose I might tell you." He grins as he holds the door open for me. "You look nice," he says as we walk to the waiting Tahoe.

"Nice, but cold?" I bump his arm with my shoulder.

"You're an adult. You have a weather app on your phone, and if you're unsure of its accuracy, you can step outside to see for yourself. If you choose to wear inappropriate clothing for the season, I assume you know what you're doing."

"That was painful for you, wasn't it?" I climb in the Tahoe and move to the third row.

"Not at all." Brad follows me, stretching his long legs between the second-row captain's chairs.

"Liar."

He reaches between us and holds my hand, resting them on the black leather seat between us.

"Okay, you got me. Am I such a bad guy for wanting you to be warm when it's freezing outside?"

I look at our hands and then back to him. "No, you're not."

"Then stop acting like a brat when I suggest it." He releases my hand and stretches his arm across the seat behind my head.

"Yes, Dad."

Ryan spins around in the center-row seat and cracks a smile. "Dad or *Daddy*?"

"Mind your business." Brad thumps the back of his head. Leaning over, he says in my ear, "See the can of worms you're opening up."

I look up at him, unable to stop smiling. "What did I do?"

"What did you do?" He shakes his head. "That's the scary part. You have no idea."

44

The small bar reminds me of Austin's, but this place seems more cared for. All the neon signs work, and the pool tables look brand new. No peeling felt or stains. It's dark, like most bars, but the vibe isn't as depressing as Austin's. This place is full of life and people living it.

Our group takes over a couple of tables in the back because the guys insist on not having their backs to the door.

Brad maneuvers me to an inside chair, cramped between him and Ryan, and clears his throat when I remove my jacket and drape it over the back of the chair.

Women gawk at our group, probably wondering how I ended up surrounded by all these handsome men who look like they could rip someone's throat out.

It's nice to be envied, and not the one people feel sorry for.

A petite redhead stops at our table to take our drink order, and I catch her ogling Brad when she doesn't think anyone's looking. "What can I get you guys?" She asks.

Grant starts with his order, and she makes her way around the table, smiling and laughing when every guy but Brad and

Nick flirt with her. Brad orders a whiskey on the rocks and I second his order for myself.

"You sure you don't want it with a Coke?" She asks.

"I'm sure. In fact, let's nix the rocks," I say.

"You want it straight? No coke? No ice?"

I nod.

"Alrighty." She scribbles on her notepad. "Good thing you're with all these strong guys in case one of them needs to carry you out of here later." She winks before walking away.

Brad's eyes are fixed on her ass as she exaggerates the sway in her hips, and I smack the side of his leg with the back of my hand.

"What?" He laughs.

"A little discretion goes a long way."

"Was I not being discreet?"

"Not even a little bit."

"I'll apologize when she brings our drinks. Would that make up for it?"

"Just look without being obvious." I lean into him, saying in his ear, "Want me to hook you up with her?"

He pulls back, his eyes suspicious. "You know her?"

"No, but women trust other women. I could put in a good word for you."

"Appreciate it, but I can manage my personal life just fine."

"Suit yourself." I shrug.

As the drinks flow, the group reminisces about their past lives—well, everyone but Brad shares stories of their pasts.

I learn Ryan is not only a ruthless divorce attorney, but he was also a sniper in the military. Whereas Ryan enjoys retelling his greatest hits, Grant is reserved with his. His demeanor is like Brad's. Closed off. Guarded. They keep people on a need-to-know basis, and no one needs to know much about either of them.

Grant speaks very little, but he's invested in the conversation, listening, and giving his friends undivided attention. He hasn't been glued to a cell phone all night like Nick and Bryce. He chimes in to call Ryan or Nick out if they remember events differently than him, but otherwise, he's quiet. Not as reserved as Brad, but he could give him a run for his money.

Brad drapes his arm over the back of my chair and leans close when he sees me watching Grant.

"All those Secret Service guys are like that," he whispers with a smile. "They're conditioned to be seen and not heard."

"What about the Homeland Security guy?" I flick my eyes toward Nick, who sits beside Grant and types at a maddening speed on his cell phone.

"I don't have a handle on him anymore." Nick catches us looking at him, and Brad raises his glass. "He's settled down with a baby on the way, so he's changed a lot." He sips the whiskey. "As he should have."

"That's kind of sweet."

"If that's what you want." He downs the rest of his drink, waving the glass in the air to get the server's attention. "It's not for everyone."

"Is it for you?"

"Afraid not. Never been able to see myself like that."

"Like what?" I ask.

"Domesticated."

"Hey, Brad!" Ryan calls from the karaoke booth. "C'mon!"

Brad shakes his head and laughs. There's something different about him. He's having fun, and I've never seen him so relaxed.

"You should go up there. Seeing you sing karaoke would be everything," I say.

He shakes his head but can't beat the smile off his face.

I lay my head on his shoulder and look up at him with puppy dog eyes. "Please."

"You go up there," he says.

"C'mon. Pretty please."

He looks down and shakes his head with a smile from ear to ear.

"Fine." I push the chair back. "I'll have all the fun. I'll have your fun, my fun, and some of their fun while I'm at it. There may not be any left when I'm done."

"By all means, pillage, plunder, and conquer all the fun." He laughs.

I pick the most fitting song I can think of off the top of my head. As the music plays, a smile cuts across Brad's lips, highlighting faint dimples concealed by stubble on his cheeks. Bon Jovi's "You Give Love A Bad Name" plays, and the crowd sings with me, including Ryan, who stands off to the side of the small platform.

Brad watches from the table with a smile, and I notice Grant, Nick, and Bryce clapping and rolling their fists in the air when Ryan jumps on the stage. We perform the song together, playing off each other, and the crowd loves it. Letting go of the fear and insecurity, I'm rewarded with euphoria.

Bryce runs up on stage and plays air guitar, and Grant shows up to play the air drums for our band. Nick joins us and plays the air bass in what I can only describe as overdramatic. Ryan and I belt out the lyrics, but they're personal to me, and every word I sing has emotion embedded in it.

It's liberating. I've never been able to let go like this. Not when I was growing up. Not during my marriage to Wesley. Now, here I am with these four men I've met twice, and I feel more accepted than ever before.

The song ends, and the crowd cheers as we high-five each other. Ryan throws his arms around me and sweeps me up off the floor, spinning me around in a tight hug.

"That's what I'm fucking talking about! You're one of us now!"

Grant twirls his finger in the air like he's rounding us up and points to the bar. "Shots!"

Brad joins us at the bar.

"Sorry, pal." Ryan lays his palm flat against Brad's chest. "Band members only."

"Katie," Brad says to me but eyes Ryan. "Want to know what souvenir Ryan brought back from his Panama City vacation when we were stationed in Georgia?"

Ryan lifts his hand from Brad's chest and passes a shot to him. "I guess you can be an honorary member." He holds a shot out to Nick, but he waves it off.

"I'm the DD, dumbass. You don't offer the DD shots. What the fuck is wrong with you?" He shakes his head. "Besides, if Stacy goes into labor and I show up drunk or can't get to the hospital because I've been drinking, I'll be needing Ryan's services, too."

"Oh, yeah. You'd be the second one of us I rescue from a dismal marriage." A lightbulb goes off in Ryan's head, and he spins on his heels to face Brad. "At least my souvenir didn't cost me two years of alimony."

Ryan gets pulled away by Bryce, and Brad presses his lips together into a thin line, amused but pretending not to be.

"You were married?" I ask.

"It was a long time ago, and I don't like talking about it." He shoots a tense glare toward Ryan, who receives it with a goofy smile and a thumbs up.

"Why do you get to know everything about me, and I don't get to know anything about you?"

"Technically, it's my job to know things, and I've never withheld information from you. You've just never asked the right questions."

"Is that so?"

"It is."

"So, you'll answer any question I ask?"

"I will."

"How long were you married?"

"Two years, but I was deployed for the majority, so it's not fair to say it was that long...and that's all I want to say about it."

"Is that why you don't date?"

"Who says I don't date?"

"I've never known you to have a girlfriend."

He leans into the bar, propping himself up on his elbow, and I do the same so our postures match. He's just taller as he leans closer.

"I can get what I need without a girlfriend." His smile is playful and, dare I say...flirty? "You'd be surprised."

"Please don't tell me you've banged Mia, too. Anybody but her."

He gives me a sheepish smile and eyes me over the rim of his glass as he takes a drink. "No, I have not *banged* Mia."

"Thank God."

"Would it matter if I had? Would we not be friends anymore?"

I shrug. "I expect more from you. You're a gentleman, and gentlemen, don't bang Mia." Brad doesn't seem like the kind of guy who'd sleep with the woman everyone else has. "Are we still being honest?"

"I was under the impression that hasn't changed."

"Beau was convinced you had a crush on me, not to mention everyone else thought we were sleeping together." I sip from my glass, feeling the heat from the whiskey warming my blood as my body relaxes. "People were so busy watching me and you that they didn't notice Beau slip into the picture."

"It'd be easier to list the guys who didn't have a crush on you."

"Did you?"

"You were married."

"That's not what I asked."

He stands upright and gives me a look like he doesn't want to answer my question, but he has to because he won't lie. He curls his bottom lip in and clamps his teeth down on it, shaking his head like he doesn't want to say what he's about to say.

A loud whistle rings from behind Brad, and Ryan waves us over to the other end of the bar.

"You guys ready? DD needs to get home, and we're at his mercy." Ryan turns and waves to Grant, who's chatting up an attractive woman sitting by herself at the bar. "Fuck," he says when Grant flips him the middle finger. "Meet you guys at the truck. Bryce and Nick are already out there." He stalks off, pushing his way through the crowd toward Grant.

As we move through the sea of people, Brad splays his palm over the exposed skin on my lower back and guides me toward the door, but the touch doesn't feel innocent when he hooks his index finger inside one of the belt loops of my jeans to keep me close. Perhaps it doesn't feel innocuous because I've seen him in a different light tonight.

He's been fun and even a little flirtatious at moments. He's laughed more tonight than I've ever known him to, and maybe it's just me. I did have to take a shower recently because of him. It may not have been cold, but a spade is a spade, and a shower is a shower.

The four of us wait inside the Tahoe with the engine running because the temperature dropped while we were in the bar. I pull my denim jacket tight around myself because the vents aren't pushing heat to the third row fast enough.

"Bet you're wishing you would've worn a full shirt now, aren't you?" Brad shifts in the seat next to me. There's no way he can be comfortable back here with those long legs.

"No, because you can't convince me I didn't look super cute tonight."

"I would never do such a thing." He offers a sideways grin as he slips his denim jacket off and lays it over my chest. "You should wear more than half a sweater next time."

I glare at him.

"Just a suggestion." He snakes his arm behind my neck, and I slouch in the seat and nestle under it. Brad is warm and soft but hard and cool, and I close my eyes as I listen to him and the guys talk about Grant's womanizing and why we'll be sitting in this parking lot longer than any of us want to.

The calm is shattered when the backdoor is yanked open by an unknown woman. Drunk off her ass, she practically falls into the Tahoe with the woman Grant was talking to coming in behind her.

They laugh as they move between the seats to the third row. One falls into the seat next to me, and the other tries to make herself fit between me and her friend.

"Seriously?" Brad gives Ryan a 'what-the-fuck' glare as he climbs in the Tahoe.

"He wouldn't leave unless he could take his toys." Ryan pulls the seatbelt across his chest.

The woman next to me wiggles to make room for herself even though there isn't any. Brad shifts toward the window, twisting to free up a bit of space, and taps me on the shoulder before pulling his arm from around my neck.

"C'mon." He slaps the top of his thigh. "We've got to make room."

I don't challenge his request because the look on his face conveys this isn't a scheme to get me on his lap. He's not happy about the situation.

I settle on his lap, and he wraps one arm around my waist and lays the other across my lap, holding me close.

I'll never tell him how nice his hand feels wrapped around me, his skin touching mine. I'll never let him know that, although this isn't where I intended my night to go, I'm glad it went in this direction. And I'll never tell him I think I'm developing a crush on him. My friend. My protector. My ultimate hard no. The place I can't go no matter how tempting it might be.

Grant enters the Tahoe, stretching the seatbelt across his chest and twisting around. His eyes meet Brad's, and he turns his attention to the two women.

"One of you want to sit in my lap?" He displays a cocky grin and long gone is the quiet, reserved guy I thought he was. Make no mistake, Grant is more than meets the eye.

"We were going to get warmed up," one woman says. "But you can watch." She leans forward and kisses the other woman. They make out next to us, and I can't believe my eyes.

Is this really happening?

I'm not a prude—I don't think so anyway—but I thought situations like this only happened in porn movies.

I don't know what to do. Do I watch? It's fucking hot, and I kind of want to, but it's also super awkward because Grant's the only other person watching, which strikes me as strange, considering I'm in a truck full of men. They all seem unphased and uninterested in the performance, including Brad. I expected a physical reaction from him, but as I sit in his lap, I can confirm nothing's stirring underneath me—not even a mouse.

I lean closer to his ear. "Am I having a wet dream because I drank too much and blacked out?"

"Grant's a one is none, two is one kind of guy."

"Oh." I make an 'o' with my lips. "Gotcha." I wink and lean into his ear again. "What about you?" I sit back up to gauge his reaction.

Off limits, Katie.

"What about me?"

I snake my arm around his neck and whisper, "Isn't this every man's fantasy?"

"Two drunk women doing something they'll regret when

they're sober to impress a guy who won't remember their names in the morning?" He presses his lips together and cocks his head. "I'll pass." He shifts me on his lap. "Besides, I'm a picky eater."

"What does that have to do with a fantasy?"

"Being picky about who I eat has everything to do with my fantasy."

"Don't you mean *what* you eat?"

His gaze darkens as his eyes lock with mine, a glimmer in them I've never seen before. "I meant exactly what I said."

And just like that, the mouse stirs.

45

The bedroom is black, apart from a sliver of light bleeding in under the bottom of the door. Sweat soaks my shirt, and the air is thick and humid. Rain pings on the side of the trailer, deafening against the metal.

My arms stretch over my head, and my wrists are tied to the headboard, but my legs are free. Despite the lack of restraints, I can't move them.

My body is numb.

Watching my chest heave up and down is surreal because I'm breathing but can't feel myself taking the breaths.

Footsteps grow closer on the other side of the closed door, and the hasp outside rattles just before he pushes the door open.

I can't see his face, but I smell him.

He doesn't speak as he closes the bedroom door, his enormous frame moving around the cramped room in the dark because he knows the room as well as I do.

Maybe better.

He cuts the rope holding my hands to the bed, and my arms fall to the pillow. I will my body to move because I want to be anywhere but here. Anywhere would be better than in this trailer.

A woman screams from the living room, begging and pleading to be set free. He stands over the bed and stares at me, unresponsive to the woman wailing.

She won't stop, and he's becoming agitated. Why doesn't she just stop? She's making it worse for herself because he's not patient. He leaves the room, and I'm unable to move or scream.

Unable to warn her.

It's not until silence falls over the trailer that I panic because he's coming back.

Feeling creeps back into my arms, and I push into a sitting position. Even though I can't move my legs, I prepare to fight back. And that's what I do as soon as he enters the room. I flail my arms and scream, "Get away from me!"

He grabs me by the arms, shaking me.

I struggle to break free. "I'm sorry! Whatever I did wrong, I'm sorry. Please...I'm sorry!"

He shakes me again. "Katie!"

"Please," I mumble.

"It's me. It's me."

I blink several times, and I'm not in the trailer anymore. Brad grips my arms. "Look at me. It's just a dream."

I'm in my room, in my bed, safe. Brad sees the recognition travel across my face and releases my arms. I bury my face in my hands; embarrassed doesn't even begin to describe what I'm feeling. "I'm sorry."

In just his boxers and nothing else, he sits on the edge of the bed next to me, panic evident on his face. "Don't apologize. You just scared the shit out of me."

"What happened?"

"I woke up to you screaming for someone to get away from you. I grabbed my gun but realized you were dreaming when I got in here."

"Dreams are nice. What that was...it wasn't nice."

"Want to talk about it?"

"Not really." I push my hair away from my face. "I fell asleep without smoking."

"Is that why you smoke?"

I nod. "It keeps the nightmares away."

"Where's your stash?"

"I didn't bring anything with me."

He raises his eyebrows and gives me a look. *The* look.

Memories of what I did before falling asleep flood my mind. It was only about the fantasy. Everyone does it. So I imagined Brad while I masturbated. Big deal. Who hasn't fantasized about someone they know while rubbing one out?

Technically, I've done nothing wrong. Although, I feel like he might know if I stare too long, which is what I'm doing because he's in nothing but boxers.

"Top drawer, the little wooden box behind my unmentionables." I point to the chest of drawers.

He grabs a book from the nightstand and climbs in the bed, sitting crisscross and shirtless as he rolls a joint on a copy of Pride and Prejudice.

"Everything about this is so weird," I say.

"Why's that?" He asks.

"You're a cop rolling a joint in my bed wearing only your underwear." *And I orgasmed a couple of hours ago imagining your face between my legs.*

"Which part of that scenario strikes you as the weird part?"

"Umm...all of it."

He holds the joint up and runs his tongue across the paper. "I should confide in you, then. A confession of sorts." He places the joint between his lips and lights it, pulling a light drag to get it going before passing it to me. "I'm not here for a vacation this week, not entirely, anyway."

"I'm intrigued. Spill."

"Job interviews. I'm resigning once I get something else lined up."

I choke on the smoke as I exhale. "But you love your job."

"That was before Mary Reese started her campaign against me." He sighs. "She's hellbent on getting me thrown out of office. Luckily for me, it's not that easy."

"Is it because of me?"

"I could lie and say it's not, but you don't want me to do that, do you?"

"I'm sorry. I can't stop fucking things up, huh?" I lean back against the headboard and take a long drag from the joint, holding the smoke in my lungs until the burn is too much to stand, and I'm forced to release it. "I'm costing you your job and good luck passing a drug test now."

He takes the joint from me and takes a hit. "Anything involving the government moves slow. My system will be cleaned out well before I get called in for a drug test." He passes it back to me. "As long as I don't smoke past this week." He coughs. "And given how bad this shit is, that won't be a problem. You don't pay for that, do you?"

I roll my eyes and ignore his jab at my habit. "Are you staying in law enforcement?"

"Maybe." He shrugs. "I've got an interview with Homeland, Secret Service, and the FBI this week. This couldn't have happened at a better time. One year later and I'd be too old for all of them. And keep the old jokes to yourself." He smiles. "I want to line something up before I give Mary the resignation she's so bloodthirsty for."

"So, you'll be moving here if you get hired at any of those, huh?"

He nods, pressing his lips together. "I'll sell the house, but you can stay in it until I do or..." He pauses. "Or you could move with me. There are way more opportunities here than in Seymour."

"What you're offering is kind, but it's not your responsibility to take care of me. I'll start looking for somewhere else to live when we get back. I'm a big girl, even if you don't see it." I smile.

"What if I said I like having you around? Would that change your mind?"

"You do?"

"Of course. Life's way more entertaining these days." He passes the joint to me. "Case in point." He laughs. "And I worry about you."

"Why? I'm boring these days. I'm what people in your line of work refer to as low-risk."

"You seem sadder, even compared to when you were with Wesley."

"I am, but it's okay to be sad." I lick the pad of my index finger and thumb, pinching the joint to extinguish it. "And I'm not sadder, I just don't hide it anymore." I place the rest of the joint in the wooden box and put it on the nightstand.

The head change kicks in, and I lie down, tucking my hands under my pillow. "Thank you."

"For what?" He asks.

"Everything."

"You don't have to thank me." He stands from the bed and pulls the blanket up over my shoulder. "Get some sleep."

He turns away, and I grab his wrist. "Just until I fall asleep?"

Without a word, he rounds the end of the bed and climbs in on the other side. He nudges me to flip to my side and pulls me against him, his chest flush with my back as he snakes his arm under my neck and the other over my waist.

His breath is warm against my ear, and his body molds to mine as we lay together. His cock twitches pressed against my ass, and I arch my back, pushing against it.

Don't do it.

The act is subtle, but not so subtle he doesn't notice.

Too late. I did it.

His arm tenses around me, and he splays his palm flat over my stomach, pulling me back into him.

It's not like me to be forward. I wait until guys make the first move for fear of rejection, no matter how clear their signals are. But tonight, with him, I'm not the same Katie.

I place my hand over his and slide it down my stomach, stopping at the edge of my panties. I expect him to be Brad, to tell me why this is a bad idea.

But he doesn't say anything.

He pushes his hand inside my panties, sliding his fingers through my pussy, the wetness coating them as he sinks two inside my channel. He buries his face in my hair, inhaling as he pumps in and out. I clench around them and grind my ass against his cock, his fingers leave me wanting, needing, to be full of him.

But he doesn't give me more.

He circles my clit with his fingertips, applying pressure before dipping into my channel occasionally. It's enough to drive me mad. I wrap my hand around the back of his neck and pull him down because I can't get close enough to him. Even if he were inside me, it wouldn't be close enough.

I pant as my climax builds, but his breathing remains calm as he drives me into oblivion with his fingers. I whimper, the sound so light it could've been imagined, and arch my back into him as I fight to stay in control because we're in a house full of people I don't want to hear me coming.

I clamp my teeth down on my bottom lip as I come apart, waves of pleasure echoing through my body like ripples from my core to my toes, and euphoria settles over me.

Pure fucking bliss.

As I come down from my high, Brad lays his chin on top of my head and says, "Rest."

I close my eyes and try to think of what I should say. But the only thing on my mind is how good this feels.

I'm not sure what'll happen in the morning when I wake up, but tonight, I allow myself to indulge in this fantasy.

46

I woke up this morning with Brad's chest against my back and his arm draped over my stomach. He apologized several times over breakfast for falling asleep in my bed, but I didn't mind.

He doesn't know I laid awake for almost an hour before getting up because I liked the way it felt to lie next to someone.

No, not someone.

Him.

Waking up with him this morning wasn't weird, but him not acknowledging what happened last night was. He didn't speak about it or even behave in a way that indicated it happened. I could take it as a good thing in respect that it won't change things between us if he's pretending it didn't happen.

Another possibility is that it didn't happen, and he's not pretending. It's plausible that I got high and imagined it before drifting to sleep.

Stranger things have happened.

Now, I'm lounging in a chair beside the pool, listening to Ryan go on about his top ten worst clients in a bikini that's way too small but the only one I could find in town. I've relived half a dozen nasty divorces in two hours and standing firm on my decision to never get married again.

"I was shocked when Brad asked if you could tag along this week." He sips from a glass of scotch that probably costs more than I eat in a week. "I thought he was bringing you because you two had a thing going on."

"Me and Brad? No." Although, the idea isn't as out there as it was yesterday morning. But I'd never tell Ryan, or anyone else, why.

"That's what I said when I saw you come out of the house that first night." He sits back in the chair. "Brad's way too uptight to date someone like you."

"Like me?"

"Someone who belts out Bon Jovi in a packed bar on a whim with a backup air band." He rotates the glass of scotch in his hand, transfixed by the golden liquid inside, and raises his eyes to meet mine. "Or someone who smokes weed with a houseful of law enforcement officers downstairs." He grins.

I cringe. "You smelled it, huh?"

"That's all anyone on the ranch smelled. Where did you get that stuff because it's stout?"

"I'm no stitch. Besides, it's medicinal."

"That's what they all say."

"That's what Brad said," I say.

"We're the same in a lot of ways."

"Just not in the uptight ways, right?"

His phone rings and pulls him from the conversation. "I've got to take this. Excuse me." He stands from his lounge chair and goes inside the house.

I look around the pool house and can't believe people live like this. The entire structure is made up of glass walls and ceilings to let in sunlight, and the dark granite floor is heated to precisely sixty-eight degrees, per Ryan's guided tour.

"Having fun?" Brad asks as he lowers himself in the lounge chair beside me.

"It's not bad. Thanks again for bringing me. I didn't realize how much I needed a break." I don't know how to do this. Do I pretend nothing happened last night? Is he waiting to see if I bring it up? What if my theory is correct and nothing happened?

That would explain why he's so nonchalant, talking and hanging out like I didn't come on his fingers last night.

"Is he coming on too strong?" He flicks his eyes toward Ryan pacing in front of the window inside the house.

"What makes you think he's coming on at all?"

"I know him."

"Not too strong. Just strong enough. He said you were uptight. Any truth to that?"

"You tell me."

I swing my legs over the lounge chair toward him and lean forward, resting my elbows on my thighs, aware I'm squishing my breasts together for his benefit. "You have your moments."

"How so?"

"Well, for starters, I thought you'd freak out when you saw my bathing suit because-"

"You're spilling out of it." He raises his eyebrows with the statement.

"Because it's a bit small." I smile.

He grins, showcasing perfect white teeth. "Yes, and every man here has been watching you since you came out in it."

"What about you?" I ask.

"What about me?"

"Have you been watching?"

"You don't need to be spilling out of a bikini to get me to watch you."

I'm playing a dangerous game, and Brad's the one person I don't want to disappoint.

He's too good for me, and I'll find a way to fuck it up, so I'm not willing to destroy what we have.

Beau was a stranger, and when he left my life, he was still a stranger. He broke my heart, but I didn't lose anything when he left.

Brad is different. He's my person. The one I turn to for advice because he won't bullshit me. He's the one I can depend on to be there no matter what. Sick? He's there. Crazy ex-husband on the run and possibly stalking me? He's there.

That settles it.

Off-limits.

"I'm going upstairs. Will you tell Ryan I'll catch up with him tomorrow?" I stand up, and he grabs my wrist, peering up with concern.

"It's still early. You okay?"

"I'm just tired."

I go to my room and do something I shouldn't in a house full of people who could arrest me for doing it. I close myself in my bathroom and pull out the rest of the joint I smoked last night. I crack the window over the toilet, hoist myself up on the bathroom counter, and fire it up.

I did the right thing.

I removed myself from the situation and the temptation. I felt myself going there, and it's a bad idea from any angle I try to see it.

For example, say we throw caution to the wind and fuck like rabbits. How's that going to go once one of us catches feelings? And that's what'll happen.

People go into those arrangements with the agreement they won't let it be more than sex, but that's like saying you're going to chew food and never swallow because you just enjoy the taste and don't care about being full.

"You okay in there?" Brad calls from the other side of the door.

"Yeah." I cough. "It's open."

He steps inside and closes the door behind him. "I thought you didn't do that very often?"

"I don't."

"You just smoked last night."

"It's been a long life. Cut me some slack." I hold the joint out for him to take a hit, but he declines with a subtle hand gesture.

"Thought you might want to know Ryan asked if I minded him asking you out." He leans his shoulder into the door. "He wanted to make sure there wasn't anything between us before he shoots his shot."

The moment of truth.

He won't encourage his friend to ask me out if he wants me for himself.

"What'd you tell him?"

"That it wasn't a good idea because you're a pothead." He grins.

I stick my tongue out and swing my legs back and forth.

"But you're a cute pothead, so he'll still ask you out." He pushes off the wall and ends up in front of me with his hand out. He lifts the joint to his lips, pausing before taking the hit.

"You trust me?" He asks.

"More than anyone."

He positions himself between my legs, taking the longest, deepest drag from the joint I've ever seen anyone take, and presses his lips against my mouth.

I part my lips, and we create a seal for the smoke to travel from him to me. He exhales as I inhale, the smoke leaving his lungs and entering mine. As the smoke passes between us, the exchange is more intimate than just smoking weed.

He pulls his head back but doesn't step away, leaving room for me to expel the rest of the smoke.

"Remind me again, which one of us is the pothead?" I cough.

"The one who has the pot." He looks down at me, and for the first time, I see it.

I see the reason Beau thought he had a thing for me. It's his smile, and I can't believe I never noticed it. He doesn't throw smiles around like some people. No, he's reserved with them. And when he does smile, it's restrained, giving only enough to appease the world.

But not this smile.

This one is big and genuine, reaching his eyes. The kind of smile you smile when you're looking at something that makes you happy. He still hasn't stepped back, so I take the lead.

"So, you never answered my question at the bar."

"You ask a lot of questions, so you'll have to refresh my memory."

"It was the one where I asked if Beau was right about you having a crush on me."

"Oh, yeah. That one." He smiles.

"Yeah, that one."

"Do you think last night would've happened if it wasn't true?"

And there's my answer.

It wasn't a fantasy. It wasn't a drug-induced dream. Brad finger fucked me in my bed last night, and I want him to do it again. I've done nothing but make bad decisions my entire life. Why stop now?

"What's stopping you?" I pull my bottom lip between my teeth, and he tugs it free, running his thumb over it.

"Stopping me from what?" He stares at my lips.

"From kissing me."

He steps back. "It's not a good idea."

My stomach drops with his rejection, but he's right. It isn't a good idea. I don't want to lose him when it goes south, and given my history, it'll only be a matter of time before it nosedives.

"You're right." I slide off the counter and close the window.

"I usually am." He walks out of the bathroom and stops at the foot of the bed, pointing to it. "Want me to sleep on the floor tonight?"

"What's wrong with your room?"

"Ryan didn't tell you?"

I shake my head. "No one has told me anything."

"I'm sure he planned to spring it on you at the last minute and invite you to his room. More people are showing up tonight, and we're doubling up in the rooms. I volunteered us to bunk together since you don't know anyone else."

"Oh..."

"I'm fine with the floor."

I'm not letting this ruin our friendship. Fantasy. Rejection. Whatever. Brad's my person.

"No." I cross the bedroom, pull the blankets back, and sit on the edge of the bed. "Men your age shouldn't sleep on floors. It's not good for your back."

"Hilarious." He rounds the bed and pulls the blankets on his side down. "Just so you know, Ryan's two years older than me."

"Awesome. We can get the senior citizen discount if he takes me out to dinner. Plus, I've heard AAA is where it's at." I curl on my side facing him and tuck my hands under my pillow. "Is he a nice guy?"

Brad pulls his shirt over his head and lays it at the foot of the bed. "He's a good guy." He points to his jeans. "I don't have anything to change into."

"We're adults. We could lay naked next to each other, and it won't be weird unless we make it that way." I clench my eyes closed tight. "I'll keep my eyes closed until you're under the blankets if you're shy."

This is our normal.

Things can get a little weird, but they snap back to normal with him.

He chuckles, and I hear his belt rattle. A few seconds later, the bed dips, and I open my eyes. He's shirtless on his back with the blankets pulled up to his navel. Even in the dark room, his abs are well-defined when he's relaxed.

I tug the blanket up over my shoulder and snuggle against my pillow. "Do you think I should?"

He turns his head to the side and looks at me. "Should what?"

"Go out with Ryan if he asks me."

"If that's what you want."

"That's not what I asked."

"I think you'd have a great time, and I can't think of a reason you shouldn't."

We lay in the bed, the energy growing between us like an invisible web of electricity hanging in the air, and any movement could cause it to spark.

47

I tap my fingers on the linen tablecloth, noting it's smooth and cool, not scratchy like cheap vinyl ones. The table wobbles a little, but it's sturdy, made of something solid. The rich smell of hearty stew wafts from the kitchen as I open the crisp menu.

An older couple sits across from me, laughing over a basket of warm bread and a bottle of wine. He's wearing a white shirt and black slacks. The woman wears a floral print dress and a string of pearls, her hair curled into tight, white ringlets. Her eyes crinkle with delight whenever the man says something the rest of us aren't privy to hear.

They make it look so easy.

I almost didn't come out with Ryan tonight, but I felt like Brad was pushing me to. Maybe it's his way of easing the blow since he doesn't want anything else to happen between us. What better way to be let off the hook than to have another hook in the picture?

My phone vibrates in my purse, and I pull it out, smiling as I open a text from Brad.

How's it going?

Fine. You checking up on me?

Just making sure he's being a gentleman

100%

Good because I warned him

Warned or threatened?

Is there a difference?

What are you doing?

Trying not to fall asleep

It's way past your bedtime

I'm staying up until you get home

Ryan stands in front of the big window overlooking the street, slicing his hand through the air repeatedly.

He's having a work crisis, so I think it'll be sooner rather than later. And you don't have to wait until I get home, dad

The bubbles dance on the screen and go away. They reappear and go away a second time. I stare at the screen, waiting for them to reappear, but they don't. I push the button on the side of the phone, putting it to sleep, and move rice pilaf around on my plate.

I hate when he ghosts me mid-conversation. Ryan's still

pacing outside, and he's taken his jacket off and draped it over his arm.

The phone screen lights up again.

> That mouth is going to get you into trouble one of these days

>> Whatever you say, dad

> Are you going to kiss him?

>> Maybe...unless there's a reason I shouldn't

>> Is there a reason I shouldn't?

Ryan's a nice guy, but there's no spark. Not even a flicker. He's charming, but I'm not attracted to him. Is it wrong that I wish Brad would tell me he doesn't want me to kiss him? But he hasn't said anything, and knowing Brad, he won't.

The bubbles dance on the screen and disappear. After a minute of radio silence, I roll my eyes just as the text notification alerts.

> Yes

>> Is it a good one?

> I don't want you to

>> So, let me get this straight. You don't want to kiss me, but you don't want him to kiss me, either.

>> Is that what you're saying?

> Mostly

>> Mostly?

> The part about me not wanting him to kiss you is right

> And the part about you not wanting to kiss me?

There's another long stretch of silence, and Ryan returns to the table.

"I'm so sorry about that. My client's soon-to-be ex-wife is turning into a pain in *my* ass now. Thank God for prenups. I tell people to never tie the knot without one. Another glass of wine?"

"That'd be great."

I feel guilty because I'm sitting across the table from a nice guy, and all I want to do is check my phone to see if Brad texted back.

I don't understand him.

One minute, he's flirty and forward, but he backs off the moment I engage with him. If I didn't know better, I'd think he was only in it for the chase and not the catch. Maybe he wants to flirt and push limits without crossing the line.

Experience tells me that never works. The lines blur until you can't remember where they were when you started. Next thing you know, you look back, and the line's a hundred yards behind you.

A couple more glasses of wine later, Ryan pays the check, and we start back to the house. It's hard to stay engaged with him because all I can think about is that Brad never texted me back.

When we arrive at the house, Brad's sitting on the front porch drinking a beer and watching one of the barn cats paw at a fallen leaf on the steps.

"You out here to make sure I got her home by curfew?" Ryan asks as we step onto the porch.

"You could say that." Brad brings the beer bottle to his lips. "How was your date?" He eyes me even though he directed the question to Ryan.

Ryan rubs the back of his neck. "Katie's too polite to tell the truth, but it wasn't the best date she's ever been on."

"Is that so?" Brad asks.

I elbow Ryan. "It wasn't *that* bad."

"It wasn't that good, either. Got another one of those?" He points to the beer in Brad's hand.

"In the fridge. Help yourself."

"I'll come with you. It's too cold to stay out here wearing this." I pluck at the hem of the emerald satin dress I bought for tonight.

It falls mid-thigh, has a low-cut front, three-quarter sleeves, and the ability to give Brad anxiety when he saw I was leaving the house in it.

Inside the house, Ryan fetches two beers from the fridge— one for me and one for him. However, my date abandons me after getting his beer, joining Brad in the living room. The two sit on the couch and drink beer while I stand at the French doors, soaking up the beautiful landscape. The moonlight is the only light washing over the cascading grassy hills.

When I reenter the living room, Brad's sitting in the middle of the couch, but Ryan's gone.

"Did you run my date off?" I lean my shoulder into the archway dividing the kitchen and living room.

"He had to take off. Something about an ex-wife and a pain in his ass?" He lays his cell on the cushion next to him. "Said to tell you he had a great time and he'll catch up with you tomorrow."

"Yeah, right. That was the worst date ever, and I'm sure he'd agree."

"What was so bad about it?"

"Well, for starters, I spent most of it alone while he was on the phone for work." I cross my arms over my chest. "And that was forgivable, but then I had a guy texting me, distracting me just enough to make me second guess being on the date but not enough to make me think he was doing anything but cock-blocking my date for his own selfish reasons."

Brad stares down at his lap, smiling to himself at my expense, and that's not okay—not even a little bit.

"Care to explain yourself?" I push off the trim and walk toward him, stopping in front of him.

He has one leg bent and the other stretched out in front of him when I step between them, looking sexy as hell, and I don't like it.

"You're giving me whiplash." As much as I'm trying to be mad at him, it's really hard when he looks up at me with that smile.

"How am I giving you whiplash?"

"Let's see..." I tap my chin. "You were super flirty at the bar, and the texts while I was on a date with your friend telling me you didn't want me to kiss him." There's a flicker in his eyes as I tick off the last of his behavior. "And there's the thing that happened that we aren't mentioning."

"Still doesn't explain why you've got whiplash."

"Oh, that comes into play because you retreat the moment I engage with you. You do a one-eighty and ghost me."

He sucks his bottom lip between his teeth and stares up at me. He wants this. He wants me to come at him this way because it alleviates his part in it if it goes sideways. He doesn't want to feel like he led me astray from this friendship if this doesn't end well.

"So, what's it going to be? Are you going to fuck, fight, or hit the fence?"

"Yeah? You hang out with LEOs a few times, and you're slinging prison references around?" He laughs.

I lean over, placing my hands on his shoulders, aware he

can see down my dress because that's my intent. I settle my knees on either side of his lap so I'm straddling him, and he lays his palms on the outside of my exposed thighs, sliding his hands under the satin material with ease.

"Well? You've got three options. You can see where this goes, keep fighting it, or stop the playful banter because it doesn't feel so playful anymore."

"Those are my only three options?"

I lean closer, my lips hovering over his without touching them because I want him to push back. I want him to be proactive in this decision.

His cock strains behind his jeans under me, and he parts his lips as I move closer to see how close I can get without kissing him first.

"Your move." I shift my hips to feel more of him. It's a dirty tactic, but something's got to give.

"You know, kissing is more intimate than sex." He licks his lips. "Sex fulfills a physical need, but you have to want someone to kiss them."

"Do you want me?"

He squeezes my thighs, his fingers digging into the soft flesh, and pushes me back just to pull me forward again, grinding me over his cock.

"I don't want to lose you as a friend," he says against my lips.

"Then don't."

"This will change everything."

"Only if we let it."

He claims my mouth, passion and desire fueling the kiss as I thread my hands in his hair, and heavy breathing overtakes the silence in the room.

The kiss is intense, far more than I expected, given his reserved nature. I pull back first, and we're both panting, gasping for air we denied ourselves.

But I don't see the look of a man who wants to take a woman to bed. There's something else instead.

Regret.

"Katie, I don't think we sho-"

I press my lips to his and retreat, standing and smoothing my dress down. "You don't have to say it. I understand."

He runs his hands through his hair, blowing a heavy breath out as his head falls back against the couch.

"I shouldn't have let it go that far. I'm sorry. And I'm sorry about tonight. I shouldn't have texted you while you were out with Ryan. I'm sorry about a lot of things."

"Despite what you think, I'm capable of making my own decisions. You didn't let anything happen that I didn't want to happen. Stop giving yourself so much credit and start giving me a little more, sheriff."

"How would it look if the sheriff who connected Wesley to those women happened to be sleeping with his ex-wife? An ex-wife whom the entire town suspected the sheriff was sleeping with before she was the ex-wife, and the ex-wife who shot the suspect."

I pause at the base of the staircase and look over my shoulder. "That scenario would be a defense attorney's wet dream."

"Then you understand why we can't go there."

"I do."

I lay in bed and stare at the ceiling, listening to him climb the stairs. My heart thumps faster as I think about him coming into my room. I close my eyes and imagine him sneaking into my bed, curling up behind me, and holding me tight like he did yesterday morning. It's only when I hear the door of his room open and close that I feel the disappointment he was worried about.

48

Wealth allows for deception.

Right now, I'm lounging in a neon pink bikini by the pool, enjoying the warmth of the bright afternoon sun in a comfortable eighty-five-degree enclosure while the outside world suffers through a windy, fifty-degree day.

Eighties hair metal plays through the sound system because, of course, this place has a built-in sound system. My shades are dark. My hair is piled high on top of my head.

A girl could get used to living like this.

After lunch, the guys went to play golf, and having the place to myself made it feel even more spacious. I watched television on an obnoxiously large television mounted over the fireplace. For lunch, I made grilled cheese in a gourmet kitchen equipped to host a five-star chef. I did a load of laundry in a room the size of a studio apartment. It took ten minutes to figure out the features of a washing machine that may or may not double as a rocket ship.

It's a little much. Overkill. A girl could certainly get used to living like this—just not this girl.

"Hey, you." Brad's voice booms from behind me, and I'm startled.

"You scared me." I slap the side of his leg with the back of my hand as he stops beside my chair. "How long have you been back?" I push up in the lounger.

He's dressed in khaki pants and a baby blue collared shirt that doesn't look right on him. He's more of a T-shirt and jeans kind of guy. He looks like he raided Ryan's wardrobe before leaving the house.

"Not long." His eyes dart around the pool house. "Having fun?"

"Until my heart almost jumped from my chest." I lay my palm over my chest like the act will calm my pounding heart.

"Sorry about that," he says with a smile.

"No, you're not."

"I'm really not." He tilts his head to the side and squints against the sun coming in through the glass walls. "But I can pretend to be if you'd like. Might make you feel better if I feel worse."

"You know what would make me feel better?"

"What's that?"

"An ice cream cone from Dairy Queen."

"Does it have to be Dairy Queen, or will any ice cream cone suffice?"

I push my sunglasses up, nesting them in my hair. "You're the picky one about what you eat, not me. Any ice cream will do."

"*Who* I eat, not what." Walking to the edge of the pool, he gazes down into the calm, clear water. "I was thinking about getting a room downtown tonight because I have an interview first thing in the morning that I don't want to chance being late to. Ryan's having a get-together later, and I don't want to be up all night."

"Will he mind me staying here without you?"

"Why would he care?"

"They're your friends, not mine. I'm kind of your tag-along."

He walks back over to the lounger and looks down at me. His demeanor is different from usual. He's giving off serious nervous energy, and that's not like him because he's the most unbothered person I've ever met.

"You're welcome to stay here if you like, but I was inviting you to come with me. You know, since you're my tag along."

"That'd be fun." I bend my leg at the knee and rock it side to side, noting how his eyes fall to where my thighs meet. Is he thinking about what we did, or is he just being a man standing over a half-naked woman?

It's devious, but I rock my leg farther out because I want to bother him. I want him to remember the way I felt when he touched me in the bed. More importantly, I want him to want to touch me again.

I shouldn't want that because I've convinced myself that getting involved with him is a terrible idea, but I can't stop myself.

His reasons for not doing it are more than valid.

What would people think if he and I were involved? How would that affect the case when Wesley's caught? And he will be caught. Make no mistake about it.

If my marriage to Wesley taught me anything, it's that you can live in the shadows, but light eventually touches everything and forces us to see things we don't want to. My time with him also taught me that life is short, so live it.

Brad's not stupid. He knows what I'm doing. The smile hinting at the corner of his lips as he drags his gaze away lets me know that much for sure.

"Think you can be ready in an hour?"

I lick my lips. "I'm ready now."

He leans over me, placing his hands flat on the lounger

alongside my hips, his mouth inches from mine, and looks me dead in the eyes in such a way I hold my breath.

"You only think you're ready. Trust me, you're not." My mouth falls open, and he stands with an ear-to-ear smile. "An hour." He walks away and leaves me wet without touching the pool.

I SHOWER and lay my clothes out on the bed. I stand in my bra and panties, deciding what to wear, but I can't focus—not after what happened downstairs.

This man's back-and-forth antics will be the death of me. He tells me it's a bad idea to get involved, but then he finger-bangs me. He says we can't go there because it wouldn't look good to the rest of the world, but then he throws that little juicy line out at the pool.

"You only think you're ready."

Damn him because he's making me want him, which would be fine if he intended to do something about it.

He's playing an enticing game, and I know what I want from him. But he's giving me mixed signals that make me question what he wants. Every time I think we're going to take the plunge, he pulls back. He knows which buttons to push and loves pushing them. He's driving me mad, but my heart beats faster when I see him.

As much as I know what I'm doing, so does he. He's enjoying this cat-and-mouse game, and something tells me he's right.

I'm not ready.

TO BE CONTINUED...

Keep reading for a preview of Endless Everythings, Book Two in The Someday Series.

CHAPTER 1

"Are you hungry?" Brad asks.

"Not really, but I could go for a drink." I walk around the room, checking out the amenities.

"There's a restaurant downstairs." He drops the menu on the nightstand between our beds and unzips his bag. "I think there's a dress code, though." He flicks his eyes toward me. "There's also a bar around the corner. I'm sure their dress code is more lax."

I'm dressed in boyfriend jeans, a crop top sweatshirt, and my new pair of hot pink Vans, so I'm sure he's referring to me.

"What? You don't think I can adapt to my surroundings?" I unzip my bag on my bed, pulling out a black dress and matching heels I'm not sure I can walk in. I got them on a whim with the dress to wear to Allison and Elliot's wedding, but I may have overestimated my abilities. "Give me a few minutes." I whisk away into the bathroom.

When I emerge, Brad's standing near the window with his phone, looking handsome as ever in a casual suit.

"Hold on." He holds the phone up. "Let me get a picture of what it looks like when hell freezes over."

"What are you talking about?" I grab my wallet from my messenger bag because it definitely doesn't go with this dress.

"You're wearing clothes appropriate for the situation. No bare midriffs or thin dresses in the freezing cold. I want to mark the occasion in case it never happens again." He crosses the room with ease, thanks to his long stride, and opens the door.

"Bite me." I side-eye him as I walk past him into the hallway.

"Been over that and why it's not a good idea."

THE HOTEL BAR IS PACKED, and the hostess informs us there's a forty-five-minute wait for a table, or we can sit at the bar. That's a no-brainer. We take up at the end of the bar near the wall where it's dark and quieter than the rest of the room.

Brad orders our drinks, and I take in the surroundings. A large group of businessmen occupy the front half of the bar, while the rest of the tables are filled with smaller groups or couples.

"So, tell me about this interview you have in the morning." I take the first sip of my drink.

"Not much to tell. It's with the Secret Service. I'm just under the age cut-off, so I figured I'd start there." He raises his glass to his mouth, the rim barely touching his bottom lip. "You know, since I'm an old man and all."

"You know I'm just joking about that. You're not *that* old."

"Ouch." Wincing, he makes a sour face. "Not *that* old."

"You know what I mean. Yes, you're older than me, but you're not old, old yet."

"Yet." He laughs.

"I wish I was older." I stare into my glass as I swirl the liquid. "Just skip all the bullshit and get to the good stuff."

"Bullshit?"

"Yeah, bullshit. The uncertainty of everything. Stability is where it's at. Do you know how cool it would be to wake up every day and know what your life will be like? To know where you're going to live for the next fifty years or what your job will be? That's the good stuff. All this chaos is the bullshit."

"No matter how stable things are, life can flip on a dime. You should know that better than anyone."

"Doesn't mean I can't appreciate the beauty of predictability."

"Life by its very nature is chaos. Besides, you won't appreciate the good stuff if you don't go through the bullshit." He winks.

"You're one to talk. You never do anything unplanned."

"That's not true." He turns his glass up and empties it.

"Name one thing you've done that wasn't planned. One spur-of-the-moment thing, no thinking-about-it thing." I raise my eyebrows and wait for him to admit he can't come up with anything.

"You."

"Don't turn this around on me. You have to come up with something. We already know I don't plan anything."

Twisting on the stool, his knee brushes against the side of my leg. "You weren't planned. You're my chaos." He leans forward and brushes my hair back over my shoulder. "And my gut tells me this is the calm before the storm."

"What about all that stuff you said before? You know, the reasons this is a bad idea?"

"That's the bullshit."

I take his hand, pulling it into my lap and using the darkness surrounding us as camouflage. My dress is short enough that it takes little effort to slide his hand under it. His eyes never leave mine as his fingertips slide over my panties. No one's the wiser as I lean into him, my lips grazing his earlobe on purpose. "Am I ready yet?"

"You tell me." He presses against the sheer material covering my clit. "You think you are?"

"No."

"Now, we're getting somewhere. The first step to being ready is realizing you're not." His tongue darts out over his bottom lip. "You trust me?"

"More than anyone," I say.

He removes his hand and stands, tossing cash on the bar and turning to me. "Then, let's go."

We don't speak on the way to the room, and I don't know why. We just don't. I'm taken aback because I'm nervous—not because of Brad, but because of Brad.

That doesn't even make sense.

My brain is foggy, but in a good way—almost euphoric with anticipation. The long corridor is empty when we step off the elevator, and I fall behind him as we walk to the room.

I look ahead and can't help but feel like this isn't real. It's Brad. *Brad*. But he's not just Brad anymore. He's handsome and funny. He's sexy and intriguing. I don't know if I'm doing the right thing, but it doesn't feel wrong.

It feels like it was always going to happen, and the time has finally arrived.

Allison's words bounce around in my head as I stand behind him while he slides his keycard through the lock. *"Nothing ever feels bad when it feels good."*

But that's not true.

There were times with Beau when it felt bad, even though it felt good. Maybe I knew he wasn't good for me on some level. This is the first time I've been with a man that I didn't feel something negative running parallel to the positive.

He steps inside and holds the door open. "Nothing has to happen if you don't want it to."

That smile does it for me. I'd be a fool not to see this through. Brad is the kind of man women want. He's the kind of man I want, but I'm not sure he's the kind I can have.

Men like him don't slum it with women like me. He's the war hero sheriff of our little town that everyone looks up to, and I'm the divorced bartender from the trailer park that everyone gossips about.

Our worlds couldn't be more different.

Regardless, I promised myself three months ago that I wasn't letting life pass me by anymore. Even if this is only for tonight and we never speak of it again, I'm okay with that because I won't spend the rest of my life wondering what would've happened.

I'm tired of being afraid to ask for what I want. I'm tired of not speaking up for my desires. I'm tired of waiting to see what's going to happen to me.

"The gentleman thing has been sweet, but I want the guy who finger-banged me without saying a word to me." I play with a button on his shirt. "Fuck, fight, or hit the fence, remember?"

"What am I going to do with that mouth of yours?"

I stare up at him. "Anything you want."

His mouth crashes against mine, his tongue spearing past my lips. We become guilty of needing this as much as we want it as our hands roam over each other. My fingers fumble with the buttons on his shirt as he sheds his jacket, dropping it on the floor.

I pant against his lips as I push his shirt off his shoulders. He squeezes my ass and hauls me up to his waist while I wrap my legs around him and my arms around his neck for support as we fall against the wall.

He presses into me, holding me against the wall as he kisses the side of my neck. I arch my back, feeling his stiff cock pressed against me and wanting so badly to feel it inside me that my channel clenches, aching to be full of him.

"Are we really doing this?" He grinds his hips against me.

"I hope so."

By the time he lowers me to the bed, I'm soaking wet and shedding my clothes as fast as he's shedding his. I stretch out on the bed, my legs falling open as he crawls on top of me. He sits back on his heels, stroking his cock as he gazes down at me.

"Pure chaos." He smiles.

He leans down, sucking my pebbled nipple into his mouth as he slides two fingers inside my drenched channel. Gripping his hair, I hold him to my breast as he pumps his fingers and moves to the other breast, flicking the pink bud with his tongue. He nips it with his teeth and prompts a cry from me before soothing the pain by rolling it between his lips.

He pumps his hand faster, and the tightness in my stomach forms as he increases the pressure until I'm going to explode. I grab his shoulders, trying to pull myself up to ease the release.

"Lay back," he says.

I fall back on the bed, and he slides down, delving into my pussy like a man who's never had a meal. He licks my clit as he fucks me with his fingers, and I buck against his face, desperate to come.

He grips my thigh with his free hand, holding me in place as he groans against my throbbing pussy and slows his hand, focusing on the oral stimulation. He hums against the wetness whenever I try to move, so I give up and take it.

I take everything.

He lifts his face from my pussy, and our eyes meet. "Tell me when you're going to come."

I can't speak, so I nod my understanding.

He pumps his fingers a few times before hooking the middle one upward and hitting my G-spot with precision, directing the pressure to the small area as he jackhammers his tongue on my clit.

I think I may die.

My pussy clenches around his fingers, and I grip the blanket surrounding me, trying to keep my breathing under control. *Inhale. Exhale.* My legs shake, and every breath struggles to get out. I can't anymore. I can't.

"I'm going to come." I gasp.

He hums against my clit and increases the pressure on my G-spot. The room is weird now. Am I seeing fucking stars? I clench my eyes closed and grit my teeth. "I'm coming."

He moans against my clit, the vibration too much as the first wave of my orgasm swells in my core. It happens so fast.

The release begins, and Brad jumps back as fluid gushes from my pussy. My body goes boneless, and Brad leans forward, rubbing my clit with his palm and making more fluid squirt out like he's tapped into it on demand or something. My body jerks each time he does it, and I'm soaked, along with the bed, after the third time.

"Oh, my fucking God!" I cover my face with my hands. "I think my soul dipped out for a minute there."

He moves between my legs and leans over, sucking my nipple into his mouth while kneading the other one. He raises his gaze to mine.

"Are you sure about this?"

"Yes."

He sits back on his heels and grips his enormous cock, dragging the swollen head up and down my soaked slit.

"In case you're wondering, you're ready now." He positions himself at my entrance and pushes forward, opening me to accept him. I'm more than wet enough, but his size makes it difficult. He pushes in and eases out until he stretches me enough to take it all. Finally, I'm able to accept him, and he stills to give my body time to adjust.

"Tell me if I hurt you." He kisses my neck and sits back.

He positions my legs over his shoulders and leans back, watching his cock slide in and out of my pussy. His jaw is clenched, and every muscle in his abdomen flexes as he thrusts in and out.

Gripping my ankles, he picks up speed, and the thrusts become more powerful until his pelvis is smashing into mine. The sound of his balls slapping my ass and the wetness arouses me to the point that another orgasm builds. Not one to wait, I reach down and massage my clit, urging the release along.

He watches me make myself come again, but it's nothing like what he did to me. Nothing has ever come close to that experience.

Almost immediately after I come, he falls over me and pumps several times before letting out a guttural sound that could be interpreted as torturous if happening under different circumstances. He collapses on top of me, his chest and shoulders covered in a sheen of sweat. His cock twitches inside me as it pushes the final bit of semen out, and he rolls onto the bed.

"You made a wet spot." He grins and stretches his arm out, inviting me to his side.

Curling against him, I look up at him like a lost puppy thanks to the endorphins. "*I* made a wet spot?"

He squeezes me and slides his other arm behind his head. "I'll let you share my bed tonight because I'm a gentleman."

I prop up on my elbow so I can see his face. "I don't want to know where or how you learned to do that, but I've got to give credit where credit's due." I hold my hand up, and he slaps it. "That was...wow."

"Told you that you can cram a lot into ten years." He smiles.

"I expected you to last three minutes and call it a night." I wiggle my eyebrows.

In one swift motion, he grabs me, and I'm on top of him. "Three minutes or not, they would've been the best three minutes of your life." He bites his bottom lip, gripping my waist and moving me back and forth over his growing erection.

"Again?" My mouth falls open. "I didn't think men your age could go again this soon."

He reaches up and wraps his hand around the back of my neck, pulling me down and kissing me so hard my lips might bruise. He thrusts his hips upward, his cock sliding inside me without resistance.

"Again with the mouth." He mutters against my lips as I rock back and forth.

Continue reading
Endless Everythings, Book Two in The Someday Series.

If you enjoyed this book, you could help other readers discover it by leaving an honest review on Amazon and Goodreads. Even just a sentence or two can make a huge difference. 🖤

I want to thank you for choosing my book to read out of all the amazing books out there.

CONNECT WITH ME ONLINE!

Join My VIP Newsletter and Receive:

News about upcoming releases

Notifications of sales

Sneak peeks of works in progress

And other exclusive content!

www.daisydelaneybooks.com

ABOUT THE AUTHOR

I'm a Texas-based romance author who writes steamy novels and lives in my own rom-com, just with more responsibilities and fewer shirtless lumberjacks.